Also by Stephen Swartz

THE GRANDDAUGHTER

A Sequel to the FLU SEASON Trilogy

[Book 5]

A Novel

Stephen Swartz

MYRDDIN PUBLISHING GROUP

UNITED STATES ◆ UNITED KINGDOM ◆ AUSTRALIA

ISBN-13: 978-1-68063-034-3

www.myrddinpublishing.com

Cover design by Iris Schaeffer

NOTE

This is a work of imagination created for entertainment purposes and is not intended to convey any medical advice or provide health care information for readers.

What characters may state on the pages is solely a product of their fictional personalities and should not to be construed as the Author's own views on any particular facts and opinions whether accepted or contested.

FLU SEASON

a pandemic trilogy

I.

The Book of Mom

Part 1

Journey

Part 2

Destination

II.

The Way of the Son

Part 1

Exile

Part 2

Vengeance

III.

Dawn of the Daughters

Part 1

Births

Part 2

Deaths

IV.

The Book of Dad

Table of Contents

This will be our reply to violence: to make music more intensely, more beautifully, more devotedly than ever before.

Leonard Bernstein (1918-1990)

THE GRANDDAUGHTER

1

ANOTHER FUNERAL

"AIN'T IT JUST SHORT FER MARGARET?" asks this thin woman in the plain beige dress, not looking at all appropriate for a funeral. She wears a sincere smile, though, like a child, but her long hair is uncombed and she smells like she hasn't bathed in a while.

"I don't really know," I respond, a bit put off by her abruptness. "I've always been called Maggie. Never really thought about it."

The woman simply came up to me, singled me out among all the people gathered at the rear of the church auditorium, as if detecting I might be nice to her, and straightaway asked my name.

"They call me Eve. Please ta meetcha," she says, acting coy like a girl half her apparent age. She might be thirty, I guess, or as young as me, going on twenty-one.

"Nice to meet you, too."

"I's born in th' evening, I reckon."

"Or you were named after that woman in the Bible."

"Bible? What's that?"

"The big book. With all the stories in it."

"Oh." She seems confused. "Well, I never read no Bible like that. Not many other books neither. Aunt Amy says there's nothing in'em worth readin' and no time ta learnin' how."

"I'm sorry," I say, and I am. "We had to learn to read, then I read a lot of books, both old and new. But the old books were falling apart and not approved anyway. New books were on tablets and approved but most of them were boring, just State propaganda."

"Yep, boring's why I don't read no books."

"Well, reading books was considered 'subversive' in the capital. And nobody dared be subversive. That would get you punished."

She stares at me like I'm speaking a foreign language.

"So you're Amy's...niece?" I glance over my shoulder at the crowd standing among the chairs. I don't know anyone else here.

"Well, ain't quite sure what I am. Amy's brother is my pa, so that makes me her niece, we figure. See, Gramma Isla, her first-born was Amy, but she was named June first on account of her being born in June, but they got to calling her Junie then Jaime, then changed to Amy, and then later they added June back so she's Amy June. So Isla's the first-born of Great-granny Hannah, then some others got born, then come a boy she named Raymond. But his pa's Big Joe and Amy's pa was Little Joe, what they called LJ. So when Isla went away and LJ thought she was killt he got him another wife, name of Lori, same woman that was the wife of Big Joe on account of him getting killt in the war. So LJ took up with her an' they got themself a brood of daughters. But then it was Raymond got to pushing down Lori even though she was his step-mama, then she got fat with me. Well, LJ about killt him so he run off with one the daughters, one o' my sister-aunts, see, and then I was born, but LJ didn't know how ta take care of no girls so Amy brought him an' us girls down to the marsh where Gramma Isla lived in her final years. And so I'm here, at her funeral, to send Amy June off to her great reward on account of she deservin' it."

I have to catch my breath although I wasn't the one speaking. This girl sure has a story to tell and I never would've guessed it was so complicated. My dad never explained about our relations down in the southern part of the country. He grew up there after being born in a national park further north. Then he moved north to the capital and had a good life there. Until it wasn't. That's where I was born, along with my two older brothers, Frank and James. I guess we're all related because my dad was Gramma Isla's last child.

"So where you from?" she asks, like I couldn't possibly be from any place more interesting than her home.

"I came from out west," I reply, "a place called Skinner Canyon."

"Skinner Canyon?" She acts surprised. "That's same place as my half-sister an' my pa done run away to. Faith's her name."

"Yes, I know her. We live with her."

"*With Faith?*" She seems about to lose control of herself.

Music starts at the front of the auditorium. They have a machine with a keyboard but no person sits on the bench to play it. It plays on its own. It's an old, simple song that makes me think of sneaking through a graveyard.

We turn at the music and see everyone, about a hundred people, taking their seats so we go, too, sitting awkwardly beside each other – 'awkwardly' because I hoped to escape from her and sit elsewhere.

Oh, well, maybe she needs a friend today, so I give in.

The preacher asks us to pray. I just look forward, studying the fading colors of the pictures on the walls, scenes from that Bible we were talking about. The preacher says "Amen" and everyone looks up. He begins to tell us why we are here today, then launches into a short summary of my Aunt Amy's life.

I never knew much about her. Anecdotes from my dad didn't give me a clear picture. He had mixed feelings about his sisters. He liked even less Amy's aunt by six weeks, Allie, Isla's younger sister, who was often mean to him when he was a little boy. By now Dad's been dead ten years, killed while saving the governor from terrorists. It was in all the streams before we left the capital.

The preacher recounts the whole family and Amy's place in it. As Gramma Isla's first-born she went with her through her harsh and uncomfortable life and witnessed unspeakable things in those years following that ten-year pandemic. When she finally got away from her troubles and they got to the marshes down south – not far from here – they enjoyed a life of peace and deserved rest. Gramma Isla, Amy June, her aunt Allie, another girl, a young daughter, and my dad as a small boy are the ones the preacher refers to.

Allie gets up to speak, leaning on a cane. She looks strange in the outfit she's chosen: a frilly dress more suitable for a dance hall. She carries herself well enough, but lifts a handkerchief to her eyes. Another woman, who I heard is her life-long partner, helps her up the steps to the stage. She tearfully recalls some incidents in the life they shared. I hear sniffling beside me. Eve is upset, so I dig out a handkerchief from my bag and offer it to her.

Allie is overcome with emotion. Her partner – Cathy's her name, I think – helps her off the stage, the cane banging against each step.

The preacher invites anyone else to speak.

Suddenly Eve pops up right beside me, with her hand up like she wants to answer a question. Everyone turns to look at us.

"I gotta say something about my auntie, way she took care of me all them years despite me being what they calls black sheep of the family, but y'all know it weren't my fault, but she still took care of me anyways an' just wanna say how much she meant ta me fer doin' that, see...."

She sneaks a breath and launches into a long list of things Amy did for her. Like she's memorized them. Some of them elicit chuckles from the gathering. Cute stories. Other things give everyone pause.

"On account of my pa an' my big sister run away an' weren't around fer me getting' born, see, an' my mama died pushin' me out, see, so my pa's big brother gotta take care of me but he don't know half o' nothin' so Amy brung us down to these here marshes an' that's how we got to livin' with her an' Cory. An' her daughters, Casey, and them twins, Dixie and Daisy, before they done growed up an' left for their own lives like folks do. So Amy treated me like her own daughter an' I'm mighty grateful to her an' just wanna say it in front of y'all so it's official. I mean, she kept me fed an' she always found good dresses fer me from the rubbage bins, but she wash'em, don't ya worry, taught me everything about letters an' numbers like her mama taught them to her, so I kin read stuff like them bibles an' the news-on-paper. She didn't let me get no child, neither, despite me sure tryin' my best to be some kinda naughty gal, like she complain, no matter what God be sayin', but she weren't havin' none of that, so I'm still pure as driven snow, Amy like to say, but getting older, if any y'all taken a fancy to me, maybe. I just might entertain offers, see."

She finally takes a breath. The audience sits in stunned silence, not used to a speech like hers in this kind of solemn occasion.

"Well, that all I wanna say," Eve starts again. "I ain't no good at talkin' but I gots a good heart an' I loved my aunt so much, I just wanna say it to y'all, never mind what I say is gonna be queer or not, it's truth. Thank you very much."

And she sits down beside me as sharply as she stood up.

The preacher pauses behind the lectern, resetting himself, then solicits other speakers, anyone who has something to say about Amy June. A few men and women get up to speak, saying how much she did for the community or recounting an episode they remember from encounters with her. None of their mentions are as colorful as Eve's. I smile to myself, enjoying how fresh and lively her testimony was.

There wasn't any funeral for my dad after he died. Living in the capital they had rules about the dead. Especially after they had that pandemic a long time ago. His body was quickly disposed of. A small plaque was fixed to a wall in the memorial park near the workers residence where he lived at the time of his death. They didn't even include his name, only his number. That was the custom in the city, the way it was being run then.

I gaze around the auditorium as other people speak. Their words fade in my ears and I find myself lost in a swirl of images covering the walls and ceiling of this ancient place.

In the back row I see a very old woman with short gray hair and dark skin sitting in a chair that has wheels on it, as though she's too old to walk. Beside her is a younger woman with the same dark skin but long, brown hair, likely her grown daughter. Next to her sit two teenage boys who appear bored by the proceedings. People whisper the old woman is Ellie, one of Isla's half-sisters. Everyone's curious about them, muttering gossip, but none goes over to talk to them.

So I do.

"Hello. I'm Isla's granddaughter. My dad is Fritz, her last child."

"My word!" says the older woman.

I offer my hand to shake. Ada accepts, then speaks kindly to me. We exchange stories. Facing forward, Ellie says she remembers a little boy named Fritz back in the National Park. She never went all the way down to the marshes when the others did. She met a young man on the bus and went with him. Ada is their daughter.

"Mama's blind," says Ada. I express my sympathy. "A few years now. Some disease. After my daddy died."

We talk about Amy June for a while. I'm glad to hear more tales. It's interesting to see how wide-spread this family is.

Then I feel Eve take my hand, give it a squeeze, which draws me back to the present.

"Thank ya for sittin' with me," she whispers, leaning over.

We wait through the end of testimonies, then listen to the music machine play a song the preacher says was Amy's favorite, and we sit attentively to the final note. It's a happy tune.

Eve gives me a grin when a humming sound I make slips out.

Afterwards, she follows me as I mill about the crowd. People are sad, yes, but also happy that Amy will be, as they say, in a better place. Maybe she will be able to join her husband, Cory, up there in the clouds. I have to glance at the images on the ceiling and try to imagine that place where people go after they die. My mother says a spirit leaves the body and only the body gets buried or burned or put into a disposal unit while the spirit flies on up to the clouds. Some called it Heaven. My science teachers had other names, said there was no way spirits went to a place like that. They showed pictures of what was actually out there. Even if they could make it to the moon or to another planet the conditions there wouldn't allow them to live there, even as spirits.

"Ya ready ta go?" a voice snaps me from my thoughts.

"Go where?" I ask Eve, seeing that half the people have slipped away. I wonder how long I was daydreaming.

"Well," and she pauses to think, "we kin go back home for a spell, if ya like. It's Amy's house in truth but she done left it for me with a paper she put her name on real official-like an' got stamps on it, so it's truth now. It ain't far."

I look cross-eyed at her, amazed. "She left you her house?"

"Yeah, but it ain't much. I mean, only one room was really mine, but it was borrowed. Used ta be Casey's till she moved out an' moved in with that fella she liked an' they had their kids. She got four or five by now prolly. Ain't seen her fer years."

This woman seems to have gotten hooked on me. However, she being related to me wasn't enough to make us instant friends. I have to excuse myself, which makes her look sad.

I stroll around to the people I think I'm related to, and say hello. Some of them aren't related it turns out. I talk with a few of them a minute or two each, trying to be polite. I especially want to meet Allie, the only full-sister of Gramma Isla.

"Hello," I say to Allie, speaking with two other women. She turns to see who's addressing her, looks down at me like she wants me to go over to someone else. "I'm Frank's daughter."

She looks puzzled. "Frank?"

"Oh – sorry," I say. "I mean I'm the daughter of *Fritz*. He's your nephew. Amy's little brother?"

"Ah! Yes. Right. Easy to forget him, being such a long time ago. Wasn't he the one that saved the vice-president's life?"

"Yes, he was. But she was only a governor at the time. Then she became vice-president. After she married the president – for a while – until he died mysteriously. Then she died, as well."

"Sad times we gotta live through, ain't it?" she says with an air of sympathy in her voice, like she is my own mother.

She stands back, looks me over. I'm dressed appropriately in a black dress, cut for summer heat, my brown hair put up neatly. I wear modest jewelry to fit the occasion. I wear proper shoes, black pumps that hurt my feet; I'm more used to wearing boots in Skinner Canyon.

"Well, look at you!" she cries suddenly. "Little Fritter got him a daughter, like it's required. Good on him."

"He's passed on," I say, which surprises her. Her partner joins us and she tells Cathy who I am and something about my dad.

"I heard he got killed, but never paid attention to details. That was the governor, huh? Really? So he's kinda famous."

"I wouldn't say famous. He just got in the way. They say he took out some of the terrorists and that enabled the governor to escape. It was pure happenstance, actually. But it was ten years ago."

"That's amazing," says Cathy, looking pretty in her blue dress.

They clearly love each other, the way they play off each other as if they were teen girls. But now they're as old as Amy, who has died of old age – or whatever ailments befell her by this age. Like with

Gramma Isla, who passed on her seventy-ninth birthday, Amy June also closed her eyes on her birthday. Her daughters and their kids were around her as she rested on that slumping bed she used. They knew it was time and waited politely. As she expired, they sang her favorite song from her childhood.

"It was something Isla made-up," says Allie, "played on that tuba she had."

"That tuba!" I exclaim. "I remember it."

"That's Great-granny Polly," Allie says. "She brought everybody to that island, thought they be safe there from the blessèd trouble. She passed the time playing that old thing, made-up songs. And Grandma Hannah sang the songs to Isla when she was a babe. Isla sang them to me and Amy June. But I ain't got no kids, so nobody to sing them to. But Amy June, she sang those songs to her kids."

"What songs were they?" I ask, suddenly curious.

"Oh, just her saying out her thoughts, talking out loud," Allie explains, "putting them in a melody. Wonder what happened to that old tuba? Did Fritz take it?"

"Yes, he did. But...."

My father barely mentioned the songs before he died. I was only ten and not very interested in music. He promised I could have that tuba if I wanted it, when I was older. I remember blowing into that thing but never could make a sound. Music was easy to hear in the capital. We had all we could ever want – as long as it was approved – just command the audio system in our residence. No instruments were required.

"Somebody wrote'em down on paper," says Allie, "but who knows where they are now."

"Probably in the Archives," I respond, "if they still exist."

I explain to her, and Cathy who's hanging on her shoulder, how officers took the tuba and put it in a museum, how the notebooks Grampa Sandy wrote ended up in the Archives. Anything on paper went to the Archives, but a lot of it soon left from there in the smoke that blew out from smokestacks where paper materials they didn't want were burned.

"That's a real shame," says Cathy. "I bet there's some interesting old stuff among that pile of trash."

"They determine what's worth saving – not much of it – and get rid of the rest." I have to think. "My dad said I would get that tuba if I asked for it. I don't know about the notebooks."

"So did you ask for it?" asks Allie.

"No, we left the city soon after Dad died. My mother thought it was best to get out when we could and not wait to see if they would change their minds."

"Change their minds? About leaving a city?" asks Cathy.

"It's a strict place," I say.

"That's crazy," says Cathy.

"That Fritter," says Allie, "always gettin' himself in trouble."

"He only wanted to be free," I say, then stop myself. The habits haven't died yet, even after ten years. Have to be careful what I say. Can't be speaking carelessly. But this is a new place, down here on the coast. The government mandates haven't yet spread here.

"He tried to do what he thought was right," I summarize.

"Yeah, he did," says Allie with sudden sadness in her voice. Then she hugs me. "I apologize for everything we did to him when he was just a little fritter. We were terrible to him. It's no wonder he grew up that way, so...what's the word?"

"Paranoid?" Cathy offers. "Schizo...?"

"Well, he made that video of Mama, got her to spill her stories. The bad things she done. Or got done to her. Amy June and me, we saw a lot first-hand. But living here—" She takes Cathy's hand. "—it's easy to forget all that, all them years of hardship."

Allie and I get teary-eyed. She hugs me again.

"Sorry for your loss," she whimpers. "I know he was a good man."

"And yours," I say, parting from the hug. "Wish I'd known her."

"Thanks," says Allie. "And welcome to the family."

We part and I go speak to other people, just to introduce myself since I've come so far to attend the funeral. Mother thought I should go, represent our branch of the family. She wasn't feeling well, some stomach ailment, so she stayed home. My brothers have jobs and couldn't get away. Frank is a lawman. James is a priest.

"There y'are," Eve calls out as I'm exiting the church, stepping onto the stone plaza as the sunshine blinds me.

"Oh, hi." I stop, just to be polite.

She comes up to me and the breeze brings me her sour scent.

"Ya wanna see the house? I make us lunch. Ain't much but it's where Amy an' us all lived. Cory, too, though he died few years back. Went out clamming, got his foot caught in a piece of driftwood, can't get free. Tide come in and he drown right there. Couldn't keep his head up."

2

ANOTHER BIRTH

EVE POINTS TO WHAT REMAINS of the old shack, its weathered front porch, the sand around it. Between the wall boards are gaps. The roof has holes, too. She tells me about Isla, who was already an elderly woman when Eve arrived. Isla sat here or there, laid here or there, and often played her tuba. She had no training but taught herself from instructions written by her granny who was the real tuba player in the family. According to Dad, who got it from Isla, his Great-grandma Polly was a professional musician, played the tuba in the Symphony and was teaching music at a university when the pandemic began. When they eventually fled the growing chaos of the city after six increasingly difficult years, she made sure to take her precious tuba with her – and her teen son, Sandy, who became Isla's father. They picked up Sandy's remaining cousins and one of them was Hannah, also a teen, who became Isla's mother.

"That's th' story we tell," says Eve, with sadness in her voice.

She stares at everything left on this islet like she doesn't want to forget any of it. Yet it's a forlorn place: the old shack surrounded by marsh grass, patches of sand, a few shade trees, and the little foot bridge to the isle barely holding together. I was afraid to cross it but Eve pranced across like a nimble deer.

"Well, this the place, anyways," she says, wiping her eyes. "We come here first, me and Uncle LJ, my sisters. But when Granny Isla died, Amy June took us in. My sisters left when they growed up. But Amy, she kept sayin' I ain't got 'nuff smarts ta be goin' on my own, so I's happy ta stay wit' her, helpin' out as I could. It weren't bad. Sometimes I come out here an' think fer a spell, ya know?"

"It's a nice place to be alone," I say, trying for sympathy.

"Fact is," she says, pointing to the edge of the isle, "right there's where I kissed yer pa. He didn't wanna, but I kinda made him."

"What?" My head jerks. "You kissed my dad?"

"Shore did. Right there." She grins like it's a joke. "But he didn't wanna. But it's all we done. Not one thing more. But I woulda, him being handsome an' sitting buck nekkid on th' sand there."

"Naked?"

"Yup. He come out from swimmin' an' sat down right there doin' his thinkin'. I come up behind him."

"Oh." I give Eve a long look, trying to imagine her with Dad. I know he was separated from Mom then. She'd filed the papers after he was sent for rehabilitation – to save us kids from his reputation. Accused of subversion with his video project. He always insisted he did nothing wrong. He blamed the video he made of his mother, Isla, telling her stories.

Eve wipes her eyes. "But then he left an' went north again, never saw him again."

I can picture Dad wading in, swimming a ways in this marsh. He was back home, where he grew up, feeling everything so vividly. I'd been here before, too, but I was only a baby and didn't remember. I remember being cradled by an old woman. I guess that must've been Grandma Isla.

"He was killed in a raid," I say awkwardly to be sure she knows. "It was an accident that he was even there. He saved the governor but he died in the fighting."

"That's sad." Tears fill her eyes then run down her face. "I never knowed that. He's a nice fella. Never did no wrong ta me."

Yes, he was a nice fellow. But flawed. Had a lot to worry about. Nervous most of his life. Maybe I absorbed some of that. Something that seems to run in our family, he said. When Mom took us out of the city I swore to start fresh. Skinner Canyon isn't a particularly nice place to start over but nobody would find us there.

I stand at the same spot where Dad sat after his swim, where a young Eve leaned over and kissed him. I gaze out over the marsh, tracking a heron launching into the sky, listening to fish popping up from the water to snatch insects flying by. Far out there a boat bobs, people casting lines. I look up at the fluffy clouds drifting overhead and decide this is a peaceful place.

"Right here's where Isla died," says Eve. I turn to look and she's pointing to the front porch of the shack. "She was tellin' stories to them kids. I's here, too. Then she stopped an' bowed her head, an' that was that. Kids called to their mamas. Amy came over to call it."

"Right there, huh?"

"Right there, yep."

Not a sign of anyone ever sitting in that spot. No slump in the wood, no stains. So I go and sit there. I feel how it must've been for my grandmother. Here was where she'd held me in her arms.

"We was grillin' fish over there," Eve says, pointing. "Cuz it was her seventy-ninth birthday."

+   +   +

After Dad died, Mom took the opportunity to get us out of the city, that cold and gray capital, and the only place she thought to go was some place she'd never been before, a town out in the western part of the country she knew only from letters Dad received from one of his cousins, a woman named Faith. The place was Skinner Canyon.

According to the legend, a man named Benjamin Joseph Skinner came out this way seeking his fortune before the pandemic started. He came up to the edge of the canyon and had to stop. He drove a big metal vehicle they called a 'four-by-four' with the label Ram from a company named Dodge, but it was already old so when he shut off the motor it died right there. Wouldn't start again. No store anywhere to get parts to fix it. So he decided it was the place to stop. In fact, you can still see that rusty 4x4 perched on the edge of the canyon, and at sunset it makes a lovely sight.

Skinner set up a camp from supplies he brought with him as he intended to start something new away from people. He had trouble with people all his life and didn't want to be near them. He pitched a tent and started checking around the area for anything valuable. He only found animals – antelopes, coyotes, snakes, wild horses – and minerals. He dug in places, gathered rocks, thought to haul them back to the last town he passed and sell them but he had no need of money out here. He found a spring so he had water. He had a bag of seeds he began planting and in time had a garden growing.

Meantime, other people happened by, many of them escaping the pandemic which was worse in the cities, and later stragglers from the war or families facing hardship and wanting a fresh start like him. By then he'd gotten sad, wanted some company to talk to, but he had few stories to tell. When they asked him what this place was called, he said 'Skinner Canyon', so the name stuck. He figured it used to have a different name but he didn't know what it was so he gave it a new name. In time, settlers formed a town, raised several buildings and got the railway line to come close but only to the next town which was larger. That left a twelve-mile ride by horse-pulled wagon for anyone coming to Skinner Canyon.

When Mom brought us out there, we were amazed to find such a dusty place. We couldn't believe we were supposed to live here. But Cousin Faith greeted us at the depot, welcomed us into her home. It was just a cabin she and Raymond built from logs and other wood they bought, ripped out of the ground, or stole. I grew to like the closeness of us together, especially during storms which came too frequently. We'd get a terrible 'tornado' at least once a year but we survived the swirling, spinning ropes of dark air that usually killed somebody each time.

By then the town was large enough that my brothers found jobs. Frank joined the law force, got the rank of Deputy. James worked in the only bank in town but after it got robbed for the third time, and he got shot in the arm, he left the bank. He went to the little chapel on the bluff and decided to join them. When the old priest died, he took over as priest.

As for Mom, she made do with the small building they used for a school. She taught the kids of Skinner Canyon what they needed to know to get by in this place: basic reading and writing, and a lot of arithmetics. No matter what job they might get they needed to know how to use numbers, she told them. Some days I helped her. I was young so I was only a little ahead of them. I led the exercise sessions and I got them singing. I taught them songs Dad taught me before he went away to learn the correct stories. I had little else to do in Skinner Canyon. That, and fending off male attention daily, making jokes to put them at ease, giving them a cross look to let them know I wasn't interested. Mom scolded them, too. But with the number of men four times the women it was getting to be a situation that was dangerous. Frank always told me to beware.

I remembered Dad telling about some notebooks written by his grandfather – stories about when they lived on an island along the coast and how people there, waiting out the pandemic, made a plan to survive by matching men and women. Isolated on the island, they thought the world had ended so they needed to repopulate it. Dad's Grampa Sandy had a wife already, Grandma Hannah, so they were safe for a while, and then Isla was born.

The same idea cut into my thoughts whenever I saw the men of Skinner Canyon gather to watch girls go by. I almost expected them to grab one off the street and take her back into an alley. But as far as I knew there had only been solo assaults – one man grabbing one woman, usually one or both of them being slathered up with liquor – which still isn't good but less frightening than a gang of men acting together. I dressed in Western style, like a boy – mostly for comfort – and I never let myself look attractive. I advised Mom do the same. She was older so didn't get the attention. Faith dismissed the idea, saying there wasn't any trouble.

Faith told us how Raymond died: shot in a gunfight with another man, both wanting the same woman – not Faith. But Raymond had already gone to jail for a while for shooting a man. That time it was over Faith. After she had Raymond's daughter, who she said was an idiot and left her to die out in the brush, he got mad at her and beat her. She took up with a new fellow, had his child. That's Benjamin, just like the founder of Skinner Canyon. Raymond was jealous so he plotted to kill the man – name of Taylor – and eventually he did.

After Raymond got out of jail, he found that Faith had taken up with a new man named Clem. Raymond called him out one day and they had a gunfight on Main Street. They shot each other. Raymond died there, getting shot in the face. Clem lived for a few days with a belly wound. At the time, Faith was fat with Clem's baby. And that one's named Clemson.

Benjamin and Clemson go to Mom's school.

"Well, that part at th' end sound bad, but not th' first ya said," says Eve, sitting patiently while I try to answer her questions about where I came from.

"I was born in the capital, like my brothers and my mother were. It's a very different place than out west or down south here."

"But y'all settled in just fine, didn't ya?"

"It's an acquired taste," I say, repeating the phrase Mom used to say a lot. "'Try it and you'll like it,' she'd say."

"Well, shore like ta see it," says Eve brightly.

"But you have a house here."

"It just a house," she responds. "It ain't my life."

+   +   +

Laying on that slumping bed Amy slept on isn't good for my back. I toss and turn to find a comfortable position. The small house is too warm due to keeping the windows closed at night for our safety. Eve insists on it, following her aunt's rules. That locks in the mustiness of the house, with a twinge of sour. Eve explains how she sprays vinegar on any black spots of mold when they appear. I tell her it's probably not safe to live here.

Then, somewhere after midnight, I awaken, sensing someone is standing by the bed. My eyes pop open. Eve is looking down at me.

"What is it?" I ask, still sleepy. "What's wrong?"

"Ain't nothing wrong," she says, full voice. "Just wanna say I like ya. I know I'm prolly older but you feel like my big sis."

"All right...."

"You mind if'n I lay here with ya?" she asks, then climbs onto the bed before I can respond. She makes herself comfortable, pushes her body up against me on the narrow bed. "Amy used to like me laying with her to help her go to sleep. Specially if it's chilly out."

"I'm all right," I manage to say and try to return to sleep.

"After Cory passed. Said it brought her some warmth. Prolly the only thing I'm good for. Warmin' folks up."

That awakens me completely. "Aw, you're good at a lot of things, I'm sure. You have many good qualities."

"It's awright, I don't mind," she says softly like it's a secret.

"I understand it's a confusing time for you. Amy took care of you and now she's gone."

Eve nods against my shoulder. "Guess so."

"Everything will be all right," I try to reassure her.

She puts her arm around me. "You mind if I kiss you?"

"I'm not sure if that's the right thing to do."

"Ya don't wanna? I get it. Ain't a problem. Some do, some don't."

She sounds disappointed, ready to cry. Then sniffles in the dark. Her hand slides down my back.

"I'm sorry," I say. "I don't mean to push you away. I'm just not.... I never thought of...that. I mean, with another woman."

She pushes harder against me. "What other way is there?"

"I suppose there's many ways to kiss." I think of them, tell her a few, but she keeps her arm around me. "I suppose it wouldn't be the worst thing."

She presses her lips against mine. A boy in school tried it but his tobacco-tainted lips made it awful. I let another boy try it but I felt nothing even though I really wanted to. This kiss is good.

In the morning I awaken to the smell of eggs cooking. Eve has made breakfast. She knows how to cook, I'm glad to discover. She'll be able to get by. She greets me, wearing that plain dress again. She could be pretty if she would fix herself up a little.

After breakfast, she asks: "You wanna see my baby?"

I'm surprised, not thinking she'd have that experience. She looks thin, no sign of pregnancy in her hips. But the baby she brings to me is just a doll. It's made of cloth, red yarn as hair, lays limp in my lap as she talks to it, telling her 'baby' about me.

"She's Jamie, like Aunt Amy's old name," Eve explains.

This woman is so darling – as if she were a child like I was when we left the city. But she's probably eight years older than me. She's a lot slimmer but buxom and a bit taller.

Right then I decide to take this adult-child with me to Skinner Canyon and take care of her. I don't believe she'll do well on her own with this house. People would take advantage of her.

I hear her singing to her baby. I can't make out the words. Other parts are humming. I eventually ask what song it is.

"I just make it up," she says, "like Amy done. She got the singing thing from her daddy. He had that tuba to play in the woods."

"That's right," I say, my face brightening.

"I know lots of songs," says Eve.

"I remember how much my dad wanted to have more music but in the capital we had strict noise laws. No music allowed except for political purposes. And they took his tuba – put it in a museum."

"That's a sad situation. We always makin' up songs here."

"Like at the funeral. Nobody played that organ. It played itself, like a machine. That isn't right. Like my dad said, it's playing the music that helps us, not just listening."

"Help us what?" asks Eve.

"Helps us get by. Feel some happiness. Helps us think, and do things. Music helps us hold off the end." I think of Dad. "We must hold off the end as long as we can."

She gathers her baby close, starts a new song using the words I just spoke. She smiles at her baby as she sings. Good voice: sweet, clear, like an angel's. I let her finish her song. I want to write down those songs if I can, but I have no paper or pen.

When she finishes, I suggest we go find a store to get paper and pens, and she agrees.

3

ONE MORE FUNERAL

"NOW, WAY OVER THERE'S THE BORDER," says my big brother Frank. He wears pistols on his hips and lays a rifle in the crook of his arm as he directs the horses pulling our wagon. "You can't see it. There's no line in the sand or any fence or wall, but it's guarded fiercely by the tribals." He looks back at us, especially Eve, making sure she's listening. "Pandemic didn't come out here, so the tribals took back their land, won't let any of us cross it."

He points harder as if indicating a place farther away.

"Beyond that border is mountains, then desert, then some more mountains and more deserts until finally you come to a coast. That's where the ocean is. Who knows how far across it is?"

He smiles at us. Eve is staring across the landscape.

"I haven't ever been that way," he says, "but I saw it on some old maps we have. It was part of this country before the pandemic and the war tore it apart. Now we're trying – every group that remains – trying to hold on to what we have against all the others."

Eve seems confused. She holds a hand up to block the hot sun.

"What's a *tribal*?" she asks.

"Those are people that've lived here the longest, they say. Like a thousand years or more. Before any of us arrived. Used to be called Indians. Then Natives. Then Indigenous. They have different names for each group of them. Different tribes. We call all of them together 'tribals'. Mostly around here it's the Comanche and the Kanza. They fight each other, too. Neither of them like us living here. So there are border scrabbles from time to time."

"Do they live like us?" I ask for Eve's benefit.

"They have their settlements, if that's what you mean. It's not like they're playing like it's a hundred years ago, but they keep some customs. Sometimes you can't tell the difference between them and us, the way we dress or horses we ride. Others do look different and you know they're tribals. They have their own ways. But we agree to disagree and keep apart."

We left the marshes a week ago, soon after selling Amy's house. I had to renew my travel voucher in order to stay longer. We cleaned the place as best we could. Then I did the talking when we met with a housing agent. He said the house wasn't worth much, needed lots of repairs. But we didn't have time or money to make repairs before offering it for sale. Whatever we could get would be fine. None of Eve's relations were interested in the house but a few of them came by to take whatever they wanted of the furniture and other items left behind. Eve gathered her possessions into one canvas bag that her step-father, LJ, used when they'd come from the National Park.

Taking an electro-bus from Amy's town to the nearest city, we changed to the new railway system. Fallen into disrepair during the pandemic and the decades following, it needed restoration. But now it was running again between selected destinations so we got tickets and stepped aboard. Eve was amazed at how comfortable the car we rode in was. "This lookin' mighty special," she said over and over as she gazed at the elaborately painted ceiling and the maroon velvet walls. She stretched out, said it felt like a carriage for a princess. Amy had read books to her about princesses; that was the best thing you could be. I began telling her about life in Skinner Canyon and about my brothers, a story that I extended for our entire trip.

The train made several stops as it left the east and entered the vast prairie region, letting people off and picking up more riders. All you could see in some places was grassland to the far horizons. I saw herds of cattle here, of buffalo there. Antelope, too. Sometimes we passed through a forest, or up and down hills, or around a long river valley. Everything was scenic, different from the marshes, and Eve had her eyes fixed to the windows most of the time.

"You like horses?" asks Frank, glancing back over his shoulder.

"Ain't never been with no horses," Eve replies.

"That one's Dixie and the other's Daisy," he says, and I laugh.

"What's funny?" asks Eve.

"He named them after our cousins," I say. "Amy's twin girls. And the black and white pig we have after Casey."

"We're not likely to meet them," says Frank, "not way out here."

"I told him about our cousins a while back," I explain. "He took the names for these horses and the garden pig."

"But that pig finally had to go," says Frank. "Tasted real good as barbeque."

That made me feel sad. I had enjoyed playing with that pig when I was little. She had a lot of personality in her, knew me, and came to me like she wanted to have a serious discussion.

"That's not all," says Frank, his voice turning darker. "You know how Mother likes to visit the tribals, making friendly, teaching them some English, learning some of their words." He turned to glance at Eve. "She wanted to be a bridge to peace ever since we got here." He faces forward. "A couple weeks ago she goes out there again—"

"What happened?" I feel my gut tighten.

"She goes there, to the Mesa tribe. Usual visit, I suppose, but she doesn't return. So I get some boys together and we go get her back. I took Blake, Burns, Baxter, Bane, Brock, and Brown—"

"The B-team," I mutter.

"And Zeke."

"What about James?" I ask.

"He doesn't go on those kind of missions. He's gotta stay pure, he says, stays in that chapel all the time, writing his sermons."

I turn to Eve, remind her of the story I told on the train of how my brother James became a priest. He worked in the bank before he got shot. His arm doesn't work well after pulling the bullet out.

"No, he don't go in for any of the rough stuff," says Frank. "So we show up at their settlement and have to hassle them to get her back. She's not hurt but they had the idea to keep her as some kind of a medicine woman. She had her usual bag of ointments and pills with her. We made a deal, traded a nice shotgun for her."

"That's good," I say, feeling relief.

"Well, now," he continues, then coughs. "We got her back. As we were riding along the canyon the horse she's on spooks at a snake. Off she goes from the horse, tumbles over the side, right off the cliff. A godawful way down. We think she must've died from the fall—"

"What?" I shriek.

"But we made our way down to the bottom anyway. Took about an hour to get to her."

Already I'm in shock, holding my breath. "Was she...dead?"

"No," he says. "She was badly knocked around but she was alive. We start to check her out, see if we can move her, broken bones and the like. She's got some clearly, ain't gonna lie. We tie off the one sticking out. Gonna be tough putting her together again."

"Oh my god!" I exclaim. "Is she all right?"

"Yer ma got hurt?" Eve asks.

"We were figuring how to move her when out from under a rock comes another goddamn snake and bites her right on her arm. I shoot the snake but Mother...well, she gets all twisted up real quick. No time to waste, so we tie her broken bones up and carry her up to the top, get her into town and over to the doc's."

"Is she all right now?"

"We tried the best we could." He fights emotions, not letting me see his face. He slows the horses. "But we were too damn late. Doc did his best. Everything he could do. Probably it was the snake bite that ended her."

"Ended her?" I start bawling. Eve puts her arm around me.

"It's awright," she says. "Everybody's mama gotta go sometime, don'tcha know? They prolly got a big chair with pillows up in heaven waiting for her. That's where dear ones go when they leave us."

"So we buried her in the family plot, right next to Raymond." He looks back at me. "Faith said it was fine."

+   +   +

I stand before Mom's grave as Frank unloads the wagon and takes things inside the cabin. A wooden board stuck in the ground has her name and dates with "Beloved Mother" below. I kneel and pray. It's not a real prayer but me speaking to her, telling her I miss her and that I'll do things to make her proud. I know she was already proud, especially me helping at the school, but I will find more to do.

With Eve behind me at the back porch, I glance at Raymond's grave: just a simple marker of cut tree branches tied cross-wise. No words, not even his name. As I look over to the edge of the property, I see there's enough space for more graves. For our entire family. Someday I'll be resting here.

"Welcome to Skinner Canyon," says Faith, wiping her hands on her apron and going over to give Eve a big hug. "You're welcome like any member of the family, no matter how you came to be. We love you the same. I'm Faith, case you don't remember me. Sorry I wasn't there to greet you when you was born."

I like how she welcomes Eve, her half-sister. We have each other now, like we did in the troubled past, and sure need in an uncertain future. Have to rely on each other. Especially out here in Skinner Canyon.

It's a small cabin, three rooms. I remember Dad telling me of the hut where he was born having just three rooms, dug back into the hillside in that National Park. This cabin was built by Raymond and Faith; now it's all hers.

I show Eve to my room, which I shared with Mom.

Pointing to the bed by the far wall, I tell Eve it's hers. She likes the colorful quilt covering the cot. My bed is by the opposite wall, a brown blanket covering it. She flops down on Mom's bed, bounces to check if it's soft or slumps, but it's firm and she says it might not be comfortable. I let her try out my bed and she likes it, so we switch. I take Mom's bed, with her quilt and sheet and pillow left exactly as she left it that morning a few weeks ago.

I lay face down on the bed and cry.

When I finally get up, Eve is gone. I hear her and Faith outside talking. I hear Faith's boys playing together. Everything seems as it should be. Tomorrow I'll check the school. Fall term will be starting soon. I need to make lesson booklets, clean the boards, caulk up the windows against the winter cold, nail down any errant nails in the floor boards. Eve can be my helper, as I was to my mother.

After a supper of greens and beans, I go out to look at the stars, holding my arms across my chest. The day's heat has faded and a cool breeze blows pleasantly from the north. I try to feel something: this place, this moment in time, my role in it.

What am I supposed to do?

Eve comes up behind me, touches me gingerly, as though she is afraid to startle me. I welcome her with a smile and she moves into a full embrace, staying behind me with her chin on my shoulder.

"Ain't the best place I ever knowed," she says, "but it'll sure do awright if'n yer wit' me. That make all the difference."

I turn within the circle of her arms. "I'm glad you're here. It's a long time since I had anyone to...uh, I don't know, talk to...?"

"I love you, Maggie."

"And I love you, dear cousin."

She kisses my cheek. "I mean more'an sisters."

I break from her arms, afraid of my feelings. "We need to plan a life for you here. You have to do something. In the city everyone had a job, did something for the city. Or they put you in a rehabilitation camp. So...well, there's plenty to do. You can help me at the school."

"I figure I like schooling," she says with a hopeful grin. "But I ain't never gone to none. It were Amy taught me everythin' I know."

"Then we'll refresh your lessons. All right?"

"I specially like you being the teacher."

"Good, then that's what we'll do."

First, I take Eve around town so she will know where places are and meet some of the good people, settler families mostly from the south. I got her bathed and fixed up and in a new dress so she looks pretty. But not too pretty. Don't want any of those cowpokes getting attracted to her. The good people here greet her, welcome her. They recognize me as the teacher now and give me their condolences.

We go over to the jailhouse where Frank is sitting behind a desk reading the latest news-on-paper, snapping the pages straight as he turns them. Not a lot of trouble to deal with today so we chat for a while. He catches me up on the town gossip.

"Shore be right glad ta meet yer missus," says Eve when there's a pause, like she's been waiting to speak.

"She's at the house, I suppose. Vera's from up north like us. The boys, well, who knows where they are, being boys." Frank winks.

"He means his sons," I say. "Jeb, Joe, and Jon."

"Three sons? That's a lucky number," says Eve.

"First two are twins, third came later," Frank explains. "All bad boys, but what're you gonna do? They aim to drive cattle as their life path – so they say."

Then we go to meet my other brother, James. It's a long trek up the slope but the view from the bluff is worth it. You can see forever across the vast landscape, including the black scar cutting the plain that is Skinner Canyon.

"Look!" cries Eve, pointing out at the horizon. "Them buffalos?"

"Sure are. Maybe a thousand of them." But they look like ants at this distance.

"Sure like to ride one o' them someday."

"They don't like anybody riding them," I say, then lead her into the chapel.

It was built by the first group of settlers, who had a priest with them already. The white walls stand out against the red and brown soil. Others painted around the building with red and green flower designs so it would look pretty. You can see the chapel from Faith's cabin, if you know where to look, perched above the canyon on what the old maps call Black Mesa.

"It's good to meet you," says James, coming out of a back room wearing his white robe and a golden sash. He takes Eve's hands in his, looks her straight in the eye. "My condolences for your mother."

"Aunt," I say.

"Apologies. Aunt. Your Aunt."

"Well, she was like my mama," says Eve. "But she got her own kids, too, so she was a mama, so it's all good anyway ya say it."

"I appreciate that," James responds.

He tells her how he became a priest, the same story I told her.

"Those are the facts, Maggie," he says, glaring at me. "But I felt God was sending me a message. I chose to listen and here I am."

He gestures around the sanctuary with his good arm, the other hanging limp and useless.

"We have about fifty souls each Sunday. If you'd like to join us, we welcome you. Don't let the hike dissuade you."

"Well, ain't ne'er been in no church 'fore, 'cept Amy's funeral. But if it's gonna be lotsa singin' then maybe I come." She gives him a big smile. "I like singin', but kinda shy in front o' folks I don't know."

"Everyone is welcome," says James.

He gives her a quick tour; it isn't a large chapel.

Then down the trail we go, watching our steps. I keep an eye out for snakes. There are coyotes, too, and they can be aggressive when they're hungry. And the tribals might be spying us and get a feel for taking us away. I heard of a couple women at different times being captured and made to be wives to warriors. But this day is bright and hot and we get back to town with sweat wetting our clothes.

I take Eve to my favorite café – the other one a little too 'cowboy' for me and Mom. This one, the Cimarron Tea Company, run by a tea merchant who opened up the front of the store with a few tables and chairs for customers to rest and sample teas, is just right. I teach my new sister the etiquette of the tea room and she giggles through the steps. We sip our tea from little cups on little saucers and nibble our finger-size *biscotti*, pretending we're in a modern city where this kind of pleasure is a daily occurrence.

"Shore do like ya takin' me ta this here café," says Eve, grinning.

"My pleasure." I set down my cup. "One gentle act in a dusty cow town. It's small now but we like to believe it will grow into a major population center. It's well-situated to become a transportation hub someday. As far west as you can go before crossing into tribal land. In fact, nobody knows what's happened to people on the west coast. Along the coast Frank was talking about. We lost touch with them way back in the pandemic years. No communication from there. All I know is from some news reports: quakes, volcanos, cities bursting into crime, factions fighting for control of what remains. Maybe it's gossip. You know, to sell more news-papers. If it's true, I'm glad the mountains divide us, keep them over there and us here. Anyway, it's better than the city we left."

She stares at me. "What's wrong with that city y'all done left?"

"Well, first of all...."

I have to think what I'm willing to share. As a school girl my life there was rather regimented. I didn't experience the repression, the constant surveillance, the enforced efficiency, the human machinery or the cost of keeping citizens in line. That was all my father's talk. Mom seldom mentioned it until we were leaving.

"It's a cold, gray place," I say. "We didn't like it. Then my dad died, so we had no reason to stay. In fact, we even got the governor's permission to leave the city."

"You gotta get a governor's permission? To leave a city?" Eve is surprised, and that tells me all I need to know: we should be able to leave anywhere without someone's permission.

"That's right. It's a very strict place," I say. "But not here."

"Shore glad o' that. Cuz I like to come an' go as I please."

I grin at her, seeing crumbs stuck on her lips.

"Then this is the place for you."

We hear a twang from outside, then more. A song plays.

"What's that?" asks Eve, looking around.

"That's our banjo player," I tell her, then explain about the only musician in town: Mr. Ephraim H. Briggs, pushing sixty by anyone's count. Likes to sit outside this café or other places with shade when the sun's bright. He'll strum that old banjo to his heart's delight, no matter if he hits all the notes right. I can't ever recognize any songs he plays.

Eve goes out to see him up close.

"Hey, Mister," she says. "What's that thang?"

"This?" he grumbles, spitting his tobacco juice. "It's my banjo."

He plays a ditty and Eve claps her hands.

"Play more," she laughs.

He does, then Eve is too happy: "Kin I try?"

"Sure, little lady," he says.

Next thing I hear is Eve strumming those strings and making a good sound – no worse than him. Then he's showing her how to play individual notes, having her repeat them, and she does it very well. Her fingers are nimble, I've noticed. She's good at sewing.

That's enough fun for one day. We need to go on to the clothiers to get her a new dress or Western wear and good boots.

They have their music lesson while I enjoy another cup of tea. I like overhearing their conversation. Eve seems happy to be making music, and I'm happy to listen. Makes me think of Dad and what he told me about Grandma Isla's tuba. Now I feel bad: I should've done something to save it, but I was just a child.

"Hey, Cousin, listen ta this here," Eve calls and I go out as she's picking away, making up a song.

Mr. Briggs grins like he's never heard anything like it.

"This gal's a natural," he says. "Few more lessons and she'll be ready for the Cimarron Music Show."

"The Cimarron Music Show? Never heard of it."

"Yeah, over in Cimarron. They come around every year. A bunch of musical folks from back east."

"Hmm," I say, imaging it.

Looking up, the sun carries a big idea in glorious light, striking my face. I have to smile. Eve continues making up her song.

Over supper I share my idea with everyone. Let's see who plays what in this town and get them together to make a musical band. They hoot and hee-haw, of course. All we know for sure is Briggs has a banjo. Faith says she knows another fellow who has a banjo. And maybe somebody's got a bugle; she's heard it. One of the cowpokes has a guitar. It's easy to make a drum, says Benjamin. Clemson starts drumming on the table. Eve can sing, maybe play the banjo, too, if she can get one. I wonder how much it would cost.

"Me? Yer kiddin'. I like singin' but ain't nobody gonna wanna be hearin' me," she says and turns shy.

After supper, Eve comes in from washing at the outdoor shower, wearing a fresh nightgown and carrying her doll. She says nothing, like it's normal for her to keep it tucked in her elbow.

Faith notices. "You still got that?" she asks Eve.

She seems surprised. "It's my baby, is all. She don't eat much."

"I recognize that doll. I was given it when I was a babe. I guess they passed it down to you."

"What?" Eve seems angry at that idea.

"My pa got it from that store down below the mountain. He went down to see what they got, knowing Granny Isla worked there for a spell. When he gave it to me – I was just a li'l girl then – he said Isla picked it for me. I slept with that doll for years, then forgot it."

"Then you run away," says Eve, pouting and hugging her doll.

"Oh, Sis, I never knew how things'd turn out for us. Sometimes ya gotta pick up and go when the moment calls ya. We had to go. I'm sorry I wasn't there for you. But I'm here for you now."

She waves Eve to come get a hug, and they hold each other, the doll between them, for several minutes.

"Like I said before: welcome home, Baby Sis. I ain't never gonna leave you again. Ever. You can count on it."

4

ONE MORE BIRTH

I KEEP THINKING ABOUT MOM, how she didn't think she could make a long trip for Amy's funeral. Complaining about her stomach all the time. And only a couple weeks later she's gone. I never got to say goodbye. I think of my dad, too, how he died. I never got to say goodbye to him. It was so sudden: that attack on the governor, him being in the right place at the right time, taking a shot for her. He was a hero; we have the official certificate as proof. We got a reward and a pass to leave the city anytime we wanted. So we did. Mom said Dad told her to get us out as soon as possible, especially my brothers who were in that awful school.

The wind brings dust to grit my teeth. I raise a handkerchief to clean my teeth. Life in Skinner Canyon, which isn't a true canyon, not formed by a river but a tearing apart of the earth. It's like the opening of a pathway down to Hell, I heard someone say. And my brother's chapel stands over it, watchful of demons coming forth. When I took Eve to the church service on the first Sunday after we arrived, dressed up and looking pretty, she took everything he said to heart and asked strange questions as we rode home. She'd been worrying about demons coming after her.

Demons could still come. Music can hold them off, my dad liked to say. Actually he said that about a lot of things. We couldn't play music in the city. We had music there but it was from machines and didn't sound good. But it was approved by the Department of Audio Engineering. The only music with words was a handful of patriotic songs we sang in school. When I repeated them at home, Mom got angry. One day she shouted at me: "Shut up with that nonsense!" That scared me into silence.

Dad was nicer, let me blow in that tuba even though I wasn't big enough yet to make a sound. Mostly he told stories about how our ancestor brought it from another country and passed it down to the next generation. Now it should be mine. But it wasn't. They took it from Dad, put it in a museum as an oddity, physical manifestation of a quaint age, a delicate age of beauty and elegance soon destroyed by war, then shoved aside by materialism that was disrupted by a ten-year pandemic and more war, then a repressive society trying to start over.

"Gee, I sound like Dad."

"I ain't hear nothin'," says Eve, sitting beside me.

"I was just thinking. My thoughts started to sound like the way my dad talked." A smile unfolds on my face. "I sure do miss him. I've been thinking about that tuba of his. It's supposed to be mine."

"Then why don'tcha go get it?" says Eve. Her thinking is always clear and she's never one to hold back.

"Yes, I should." But the reality of such an adventure overwhelms me. I can't imagine returning to the capital. I can't expect to just be given that instrument. Maybe it doesn't even exist any longer.

+   +   +

The school term starts without problems. Half the time Eve sits in a seat at the rear of the classroom and learns from me, the other half helps me with the younger students. Two students out-grew school since the previous term and we lost one student to illness. Eve is right at home among the children, enjoys learning with them and playing games outside.

I keep thinking of my music plan as we approach winter. Such a scheme! To what end? Just a vanity project? People here have no need of music. But what if there was a band and they liked it? I write some letters on paper, fold them into envelopes, and get the postal boy to take them to his office and from there send them on to three different cities, one north and two east, seeking information.

It takes several weeks before I get any message sent back to me, delivered by the postal boy, Charlie, who has a sweet round face and the minimum whiskers over his upper lip. He gives me the letter and stays to listen to me read it aloud:

> Dear Miss Baumann,
>
> It is with great interest that I have received your inquiry regarding musical instruments for your town's band. Please find under separate cover a catalogue of our products.
>
> I am at your service and shall do my best to fulfill your musical needs. I also wish to make you aware of our large library of musical compositions, especially famous works preserved from before the great pandemic.
>
> Please inform me of whatever you may require and I shall comply forthwith and straightway.
>
> Musically yours,
>
> Hal D. Hill, Ph.D. (Music)

I stare at the signature, trace the big loops with my finger. He has a degree after his name so he must be a top musician. I didn't know you could go to school for that. I always thought you picked up an instrument and figured out how to play it.

"Is he gonna send us some instruments?" asks Charlie.

"Why, I don't exactly know," I respond. "You have a catalogue in your bag?"

"No, ma'am, but it'll be along next few days."

So I wait.

After another week a package does arrive and it is like Ancient Christmas. I flip through the pages gazing at the colorful pictures of musical instruments they show. It is truly amazing! Especially the two pages of tubas. Gold, silver, twisted this way and that, three valves or four, bell pointing up or turned forward. So many different designs to choose from, I don't know where to begin.

Our small town library doesn't have much in it but has a long set of encyclopedia books from the last century. I look through some of them to find information I need. I learn about music bands. What instruments they need, how they sit together, and how each is used in band music. The more excited I get reading about music bands, the more depressed I get, thinking how the cost is impossible. Even a tuba costs as much as a year's credits in the capital. No wonder they don't allow musical instruments there. We don't need to waste money on something like that which will only distract us from our work. I feel sad for my project.

Setting the catalog aside, I resume my daily school lessons. But many evenings I pour over that catalogue, thinking and doing some planning. I think of raising money to buy a basic set of instruments, enough to start a band. We need flute, clarinet, trumpet, trombone, and drums. A tuba would be nice, too. I keep thinking of going back to claim our family tuba, but that trip seems too scary to me.

Then Vera has her baby, a girl she and Frank name Frances. I am an aunt again. Frank teases me about finding a good man and getting hitched. I remind him I'm not a horse. But then I could have my own children, he says, since I like kids so much. I see how happy Frank and his wife are. He and Vera make handsome sons, I have to agree. And now a girl! Our small town's growing. Soon we will have enough people to form a band, I like to muse.

"How much we got?" I ask Frank, like he was Dad.

"Got what?" he asks, setting down the pistol he's cleaning.

"Money," I reply. "The amount of Mom's legacy."

"Money? Who needs money out here? Nothing to buy."

"I'm thinking of the band again."

"The band? Again? Good-golly."

"Yes. Didn't I tell you? I want to get some instruments. We can have our own band right here."

"What a crazy idea, Maggie."

"It's not crazy. It's my dream. You know we left Dad's tuba back in the capital. I want to get it. Then get other instruments. I know what we need and I connected with a salesman already."

He puts his pistol back together, checks it.

"A salesman? Those sneaky fellows? Dumb idea, Maggie."

"It's not a dumb idea. It's an idea – and you can think it's dumb all you like but I'm gonna do it. I just need somebody to go with me to the capital to claim that tuba. If it even exists still. If they haven't destroyed it by now. Anyway, it's mine."

"Crazy idea, Maggie. What's it been? Ten years?"

"Yes, I suppose."

"It's long gone," he says, ready to laugh but doesn't.

"They put it in a museum. It's precious. An antique. Even those people that run the place would want to keep it safe."

"Awrighty then," says my brother. "Go get it. See if it's still there and if they'll let you have it."

"I don't want to go alone. It's a dangerous place. You forgot what it was like when we left. They wanted to turn James into a girl and let him live his life as Jamie."

Frank turns sullen. "I remember that. Don't need to bring it up every damn time. He's found his peace now."

"It's not safe for me to go there alone. Please come with me."

"I got a new babe to look after. I can't leave my family alone. You really gotta go there?"

"It shouldn't take but a week. A few days to get there and a few days to come back. We'll go once the spring term is over. That'll give you a few weeks to bond with your daughter."

"Still a crazy idea, Maggie." He picks up his gun, aiming at the empty jail cell across the room. "You know how to use one of these? In case there's trouble?"

"I can shoot one of those. Maybe I won't kill anybody but I'll sure scare them off. But surely we won't need that."

He laughs. "Scaring them off isn't always good enough."

"Then come with me."

"You know I can't. I'm the deputy. I gotta keep folks here safe."

"But I need you to come with me."

Then a tiny voice from the next room cuts through the silence.

"I kin go witcha," Eve calls out. "I don't mind."

+ + +

As the school term comes to an end and we test our charges on what they've learned, Eve gets better playing that banjo. Mr. Briggs takes a fancy to her, waits eagerly for her to arrive and smiles through her lessons. She's certainly old enough to make her own decisions but I believe she doesn't have a mind for complex things like romance. So I hint to Mr. Briggs that he should keep his heart in check, that Eve is a simple woman. He dips his hat in response.

"Yes, ma'am. I'm too old for those kinda shenanigans."

Meantime, I make lists, calculate costs, arrange tickets for our trip. I also go about town visiting some people who might be able to lend a few credits toward my trip. They laugh at first, as I expected they would. Who in their right mind would want to play a musical instrument? It takes too much time to learn, and there's a lot of ungodly noise until you learn it well enough, they say.

"It would be for the whole town," I explain. "Maybe for the kids at first, but I think it would be wonderful if parents joined in, too."

"What would you play?" asks Mrs. Barker.

"Me? I'd play tuba," I proudly reply.

"Tuba? What's that?"

That opens the door to a lot of stories about Dad and his mother and her grandmother. And that leads to the cold, gray city we left, which doesn't impress Mrs. Barker – nor Mrs. Blaine, Mr. Buttons, Mrs. Booker, Miss Barrington, or other families I visit. They have bad impressions of the capital and happy to be out west where none of those restrictive policies affect us. I tend to agree, although I have little memory of life there.

The Boyle brothers show me a fiddle they've saved but it doesn't have any strings. The bow is long missing, too, and they ask me if I can get another for them. Plus strings. I add it to the list. They give me some credits toward the cost, the rest when I return.

"I'll give you five dollars," says Mrs. Burns. "That's in old money. I still got some in my pa's wallet from before that pandemonium."

"Before the pandemic?" I ask for clarification.

"Whatever they called it, he's long gone now." She digs out from her purse the green bills with some men's faces on them and hands them to me. Not sure they're worth anything but maybe I can trade them at the museum.

"I'll pledge fifteen credits to your cause," says Mr. Boothe. "Used to play a cornet, if you can believe. Got pretty good, if my teacher is to be believed. She was sweet on my big brother and always giving me extra lessons just to see him. You believe it?"

"Would you play the cornet again for us?" I ask.

"Oh, I'm sure I forgot how it goes."

"Would you try?"

He stares hard at me like I'm asking him to dance naked on his wife's grave. "Reckon I could try, but it ain't worth the cost to get another one. Anyways, good luck on your trip."

I thank each of them and go over to the café to take stock. I have a hundred and twenty-two credits given or pledged, plus those old green bills. Enough for one ticket to the capital and a stay in lodging for a few nights, I figure. It's definitely not enough to buy even the cheapest musical instrument.

"Oh, what's the use?" I sputter just as my tea arrives.

"Trouble, ma'am?" asks the boy holding the tray.

I explain my dilemma, then ask him if he is musical.

"My pa gots a guitar and I can play one tune on it he taught me, but that's all."

This boy, Carver, I know from school when I helped Mom there. He's grown out of school, always a shy boy

"That's good," I tell him.

"I can whistle, too." And he bursts into a song that is lively and features many scales and trills. I grin in delight and he is pleased I enjoy his rendition. "Sometimes, when the old man ain't around, I whistle in the shop here." He gives me a wink.

"What's all that racket?" shouts someone from a back room. It's the owner, of course. Mr. Buchanan bulls his way out, stands with hands on his hips, glaring at us. "We'll have none of that noise in here. Not with customers trying to have a rest."

"But I quite enjoyed it," I say.

"You best keep that noise to yerself," he growls. "Save it for after work, boy."

"But you let Mister Briggs play his banjo outside here," I offer.

"Sure, but he's good at it." He thinks a moment. "He's colorful. He lends atmosphere to the place. People stop by cuz of him."

"How would a music band add atmosphere to this town?" I ask.

He frowns, thinking. "Can't imagine it, sorry."

"How about if we have a music festival? Maybe we can advertise and people will come from all over. They'll sit in this café and buy a lot of tea and *biscotti*. The inn will be full. All those people will be spending their credits here. Won't that be good?"

"But they do that over in Cimarron already."

"Yes, so why not have a competition? We can make a band right here and people would come to hear us play a concert!"

"You're a strange woman, Miss Maggie," he says, scratching his balding head. "Mighty strange."

"Would you be willing to contribute to the band fund?"

"What's that?" More head scratching.

"I'm trying to raise funds to purchase musical instruments. We can form a band. It would be great for the kids. And adults can join in, too. We can have a lot of fun and, like I suggested, it would draw good paying visitors. Kind of like tourists. Like they get at Cimarron for their Country Show."

"I don't see it happening. They already have a tradition going on there. People already know where to go for their entertainment."

"They have different music there. Ours would be a band."

"What's being a band got to do with it?"

"It's a different kind of music."

"I see." He rubs his forehead. "But would people wanna listen to that kind? Seems they like the guitar and banjo kinda music whole lot more."

"Maybe they never heard band music before. They might like it."

"Seems an awful lotta trouble to go through to see if anybody's gonna like it."

"We can start small," I say, holding up my tea cup. "Maybe a quartet to start. Or a quintet. A few good songs and people will be enamored."

"Enamored, huh? Well, don't that beat all."

In the end I get Mr. Buchanan to pledge three-hundred credits for the purchase of five instruments, or whatever I can get for that amount. He must sell a lot of tea to be able to pledge that much, but since I'm his best customer I'm likely paying into that pledge. We shake hands on the promise.

Back home after a long day soliciting funds, I'm ready to rest.

I watch Eve helping Faith finish the work in the garden. With spring coming they have a lot to do. Faith showed Eve how to fix the soil, plant seeds, water them. They work together every day, always laughing and chatting over shared memories. I'm happy they're good friends, despite the bad things that happened in the past.

Eve works near the mound of her father with little remorse. On that side of the yard where he is buried only bitter weeds will grow. A thorn bush also took root. On the other side, where Mom is laid to rest, colorful wildflowers bloom.

I go over and kneel by her grave, put my hands together, pray.

"Mom, I'm going to do it. I'm going to start a music band."

Then I stand and gaze off to the dusty horizon, feeling the sunset strike me, thinking of the vast prairie we would have to cross to get home again.

5

TUBA CITY

I HADN'T BEEN IN THE CAPITAL for eleven years, ever since Mom took us away after Dad died. We never looked back. News still comes to us here through the streaming and it's printed out in the communication office and posted on the display board for everyone to read. Not many people living here can read so I read everything twice, once for myself, a second time for anyone who wants to listen to me read aloud. It seems the capital is as bad as ever.

Governor Wornall did become vice-president beside her husband, President William Randolph Wornall. She had no children; when they married she was beyond the age. He had two children from his first marriage: Dina and Oliver. Dina married Bruce Baskin, a Representative of his state of Northland, comprising territory north of the capital. They had a son named William, called Billy, who grew up and also became a Representative. Oliver went into the military, excelled at the Academy and become a General in record time. He leads the campaign against the Quebecois trying to encroach into Northland.

Representative Billy Baskin soon became Senator Baskin, then became the President. Sadly, Vice-President Wornall passed away from food poisoning soon after her husband left office with his terms expired. A ceremony was broadcast on the streams, but we couldn't see it out west. No streaming services at that time. Dad told me a lot about her but clearly not enough. I knew we were related in some way but not sure how. No wonder he saved her from that gang.

49

As the railway cars rolled along, I imagined what I'd find there.

Eve didn't seem afraid. She stayed by me wherever we went, sat with me, held my hand when she wanted to. She kept looking at me with doe-eyes like she was in love. I was her new Aunt Amy, looking out for her. Of course I would do whatever I could for her, us being related. She's my responsibility, taking her away from the marshes to a dusty western town. But she never complains.

Sometimes, when I lay on the bed in the cabin and she's already there she'll roll against the wall. She says "Outside" and climbs over me so she's on the edge toward the open room. She never likes being bunched against the wall. She insists on two kisses before we sleep. She wraps her arms around me until she falls asleep and her arms relax and drop off me.

"My mama died, too," she says one night sleeping in the railway car, bunched up against me, "so I knows how yer feelin'. And my pa, he died, too. Fact is, I never knew none of'em, both them gone before I kin meet'em." A tear falls. "Wish they kin be together again."

I know the story and I'm sure they wouldn't want to be together again, at least not Lori, LJ's wife that Raymond took by force. I have to wonder if Eve knows the whole truth. It wasn't a great love story that brought her into the world – all the more reason I want to be gentle with her. She was a beautiful accident.

By day we sat together, Eve staring out at the landscape passing by – the endless prairie grass, wheat fields, bison herds and people riding horses, small towns, mesas and hills, and occasionally a stand of trees, bridges over narrow streams and wide rivers – while I read one of the magazines the railway provides. I'm learning a lot about trains! We get up and go to the luncheon car to eat then return to our seats. In the afternoons we often nap – one of us leaning against the other.

Occasionally a gentleman will pause at our seat, greet us, asking questions, looking us over. And we will politely dismiss him. I say I am married and Eve is my auntie.

"Is she dumb?" asks one rude man.

"No, she's blessed," I retort.

"Cursed more like it," he snaps, then says a crude remark about her having the kind of body a man could enjoy. Like that matters to us. We have business to conduct.

I'm on the verge of signaling the car monitor but the man leaves.

They aren't rude in the city, I have to believe. Out west we have few laws but people seem nicer. Everyone in Skinner Canyon calls me "ma'am". Perhaps in these passing situations, being on a train, the eager gents choose to take a chance knowing we'll be gone soon. And in the capital? I know they are strict, so this kind of rudeness will be rare. Dad told me how harsh the punishments were for bad behavior.

Finally the train slows and I awaken from my nap to stare out the grimy windows at the cold, gray industrial desert we are passing through. All metal and concrete. Such an ugly scene! Eve gasps at the sight. She complains that it's like a dream of hell she once had.

I ask about her dreams.

"Not so much nowdays, not since I come live with you."

I give her a one-arm hug. "That's good."

"But frightful lot o' them when I's a li'l kid. Monsters comin' at me. Big hairy things with claws grabbin' me. I try to run away but I always trip, like I got no feet, and they catched me and hurt me."

I stop her. "No need to think about that anymore."

Tears fill her eyes. I hug her. She apologizes for making a scene. Other passengers are looking at us.

Thankfully we arrive at the terminal and they get off. We depart last. We're in no hurry. The line is short when we get to the gate. The guard halts us. A monitor smartly dressed in gold coveralls with red epaulets and a red cap holds up a tablet, tapping on its screen as he aims it at us. Likely he scans us for bio data. They did that each day when I entered my school.

"Clean," he says and taps on the tablet.

He asks for our information and I answer for both of us, unsure about my answers. More taps on the tablet.

"What's your number?" he asks me. Eve looks away.

"I don't remember," I say, honestly. "I think it ends with a three. Yes, three. My older brothers are one and two, I guess. I just turned ten and they had a ceremony for us at school, assigning us numbers.

But then we left the city."

I remember my old badge and pull it from my bag. I hold it up to show him but he is focused on the tablet.

"Not residents," he mutters, tapping. "I can arrange a work pass for you to enter."

"Work pass?" I ask, surprised. I put my badge away. "We aren't looking for jobs. We're going to the Museum of Musical Arts – or whatever they call it now. Doing research."

"Where will you stay?" he asks like it's on a checklist.

"You don't have lodging for visitors?"

"All visitors must have a legitimate reason for entering. Then a space can be assigned in temporary housing, up to three nights as a start. Longer can be arranged."

I have a thought. "Would it make a difference if I knew someone inside?"

"Who would that be?"

"My father." I give the monitor Dad's full name.

"No longer listed as resident. Marked deceased." He regards me. "Didn't you know that?"

"I know," I say in a sad voice. "But he's famous, don't you know? He saved Governor Wornall from those assassins."

"Yes, I see it in the record. Lots of links to other information. Yet he is no longer a resident here so you have no place to stay."

"No place to stay? You don't have any lodging?"

"Our governor's Gertrude Smithers now, to get you up-to-date. In charge going on two years." He taps on the tablet screen. "Best I can do is a factory stint, three days of shift work. Comes with three nights in the workers' barracks and two food boxes daily. For each of you."

Then he focuses on Eve. Her ratty blue dress is quite wrinkled from wearing it the whole trip. In front the top buttons are torn off. I know what he is thinking.

"Maybe I could get your sister here a better position," he says, a finger tapping away. "Yes, an opening in Pleasure Services. There's a private room available. It comes with two clients, one hour each, one hour between, and you're done."

"She's not doing that!" I snap at him.

"Doin' what?" asks Eve innocently.

I wave my arm around. "Can't we just stay here, in the station?"

The guard frowns. "Certainly not."

So we give in and accept the factory jobs. A few days of work in exchange for meals and a place to sleep. Not sure how much time we'll have for conducting our business. They don't like idle time.

+   +   +

We stand on the production line, Eve across from me, as paper boxes move along in strict order. Other women, wearing aprons, stand to either side of us. Each of us places an item into the box as it moves past us. Eve's job is to fold down the top of the box after I place the final item in: a cracker in a clear wrapper. But the lid has wings which always catch on the side walls and crumple the box. She was trained for an hour before put on the line but she gets admonished countless times by supervisors wielding slapsticks. I offer to trade tasks with her but our supervisors say they can't allow it based on our papers. So we have to endure it.

After helping put together food boxes for ten hours – plus the hour of training, and an hour of signing out which includes checking for any items we might've stolen – we're free to do as we like in the factory cubicles. But we're too tired to do anything but sit, catch our breaths, and wonder how life would be if we actually were residents here instead of only visitors who want entry.

"It won't be too bad," I mumble to Eve.

"Well, ain't never done day o' work in my life 'til this one an' ain't no way I'm gonna wanna do this all my life no more, lemme tell ya. Rather be starvin' in the marsh but in the marsh I kin catch fish for to eat an' that ain't much work but sittin' down an' holdin' a pole."

I have to smile at her. "I think you're right."

We share bunks with other workers. That is, we take the bunks for sleeping while they get up for their shift. I don't think the bunks are clean. I put down fresh sheets. They cost 1 credit each but worth it. Sleeping in a large room with the other workers, lying on bunks fixed to walls or free-standing cots in the middle is awkward. Some people stay awake talking while others snore or groan through their sleep. A couple of the workers get flirty on a bunk.

Coming off the line, we're given food boxes like the ones we had been putting together, but with different items. By the date stamped on the bottom, I see mine is two days old and Eve's one day. Tastes like paper no matter which item we bite into.

"This is what we get for our hard work?" I ask a supervisor.

"It's Class C ration, suitable for line workers."

We eat, feeling hungry after, then get a shower, being sore and sweaty. The shower room is full of naked women who are used to it. Eve is shy but I take her hand, lead her in. We use the same spigot and a tiny cake of soap given to us when we arrived. A few women give us looks. An older, thick-set woman says we look cute together. It isn't worth explaining to them that Eve's my cousin.

After a fitful sleep, we're roused by bright lights and a loud horn. It's time for work. Another day on the line, doing the same task but with different items to put into each box. Eve is better at reaching over the line as it moves along and folding down the tops of the boxes. She gets a kind word from a supervisor, and the suggestion that a long-term job can be found for her if she wants to stay.

What would be the use in staying? Not if every day is like this: you get up and work, then you're too tired to do anything after work. The work earns you a place to sleep and two food boxes a day. And it never stops. I heard they ended the custom of Sundays being free of work. In fact, they renamed the day Seventhday, made it another work day. There are no days off – until you die.

Finally we fulfill our requirements to enter the city proper and go about our business. However, we no longer have any place to go sleep. That doesn't matter; we're glad to get out of that factory. I thank Mom again for getting us out of this city when she did, before it went so crazy.

Fixing ourselves as pretty as we can, saving our best dresses for conducting our business – a nice dress is proper attire in the city, a way to show we're more than basic workers, at the risk of drawing attention. 'She must be one of those élites' someone might call after us in derisive tone, but we go on our way. I put Eve's mousy brown hair into a lovely ponytail and clip pearl rings on her ears that Mom wore before she shaved off her hair to be in fashion.

I usher Eve along the dirty streets.

The Museum of Musical Arts is a stately building, designed as a museum long before the pandemic came, then abandoned during the years that followed. As society rebuilt, it was renovated and devoted solely to music. I recall it from Mom or Dad taking me there to see everything. The most important thing was the great silver tuba that Dad saved, the one that Grandma Isla played. It was in a display of brass instruments with a plaque explaining how they were used, the kind of music they produced, and why they fell into disfavor. Too loud, was the main objection, I recall.

Now the building appears as a mausoleum, left to decay, its tall concrete columns chipping away.

"Still lookin' better'n that food box place," Eve comments.

It's open, so we step inside and are quickly confronted by a guard who demands we show our passes. After all, not everyone is allowed to view the precious things they keep here! That makes sense: with everyone working constantly, there's no time to visit any museum. Only mothers – what they were calling 'breeders' before we left (but you had to be officially approved; Mom was on a list to be matched with a well-suited partner after she separated from Dad, but we left before her number came up). Only they have the time to usher their children to such places of education.

"I need to speak to the director," I boldly state, holding up our visitor passes. "We came from outside the city on this matter."

The grizzled man isn't immediately impressed, but when I show my identification badge he knows I'm serious. The badge has my ten-year-old image and official number. Also the gold embossed seal, a special designation we were awarded because of Dad's heroism. That didn't helped us entering the city but it helps now. He dawdles off to inform the director of our annoying presence while we wait by the information desk.

"They shore got lotsa stuff in here," says Eve, craning her head around to see everything. "Real shame they end up a place like this.

Don't folks wanna use'em no more?"

"Times change," I say, keeping my eyes on the corridor where he disappeared. "People lose interest in things, get interested in other things. Nothing wrong with that. But we should keep things around for the people who want them."

"Ya makin' lotsa sense," she says, nodding.

I tell her about trying to blow notes into that tuba when I was a little girl but not able to make any sound, no matter how much Dad instructed me. It's a fond memory for me.

Eventually, the old guard returns. He gives a bow, waves us to follow him. We go down the corridor, then up to a higher floor in the clanging elevator box. Here's the office, he says, then waits outside as we enter. I look back and he pouts, then turns to leave.

Inside, a dowdy woman with her head shaved sits behind a desk, busy at her work. What work could that be for such a forlorn place as this? Nobody visits. It's a warehouse of unused things, the things nobody wants any longer, a collection of curiosities suitable only for the curious who haven't yet accepted the way this new society has become. I frown at my thoughts.

We wait longer, standing before the desk.

"State your business," the woman intones, keeping focused on a stack of paper records. It appears she is entering the information on the papers into a tablet.

"I wish to speak to the director," I say with confidence.

"About?"

"An item that used to be on display here. But I don't see it where it used to be. It was a donation from my father. About eleven years ago. I'd like to claim it."

"Citizen, you can have it all," the woman sneers, not looking up. "Less for me to hafta keep track of." She looks up, almost smiles. "But it's a job, anyway. That's what's important. Got a place to be."

"Yes," I say, wondering what she means. "So...if I could speak to the director...?"

"I'm it," she says, amusement in her tone.

"You?" I'm surprised. She doesn't seem like a museum director.

"Closest you're going to find. Fifty-one is no longer with us. He was taken away weeks ago. Insisted we call him Mister Hobbs. Gee willikers, guess it's been about a year now. Already! Hmm. He liked blowing into the instruments. Or scratching a bow across a fiddle. Made too much noise."

"Noise? That's all it took for him to be arrested?"

"We have strict laws here."

"I see. We'll be as quiet as we can be, I promise."

"You're fine. Gold seal, right? You can do as you like."

"We can?" I collect my confidence. "Yes, of course we can."

She pauses, chin resting on her clasped hands.

"Now then, you're wanting something?"

"Yes," I say. "There's a silver tuba which my father donated long ago. It's likely dull gray now. It was when I last saw it. It's very old. Handed down for generations. And it's—"

Her face pleasantly contorts. "I remember. In the center of that big display in the front." She frowns, then fumbles with the stack of papers on the desk. "Not sure what happened to it. They changed the display one day and put everything in the back rooms. It had a bunch of music on paper that somebody wrote by hand. They had it on the stands so anyone could see it, but nobody could read it, rough as it was written. Strange art they had back then. All I recall is a name at the top. Large letters. Something like *Polly*, and something with a B."

"Polly Baumann?" I exclaim, excited. "That's the name?"

"Not sure. The music paper was found inside a pocket of the case of that tuba you want."

"Yes, that's it! It's my great-great-grandmother."

"You can have that, too. All of it. Gotta get rid of it. Planning to shut this place down. No more saving old things, they say. No space for it. New order coming down. New governor, Gertrude Smithers. She's worse than the previous one was."

"*Gertrude?*" Eve laughs. "That's a funny name."

"How can they get rid of these old things? They're precious."

"And *Smithers*, that's even more funnier."

"Maybe precious to you, but not to them – those higher-ups. No, nothing that came before them is considered valuable. Every year is a fresh start, they like to say. Always more new things, more factory production, more jobs. It's an endless cycle."

"I see."

The woman stands and I notice how short she is but with a thick body, reminds me of our butcher in Skinner Canyon.

"Follow me," says the woman. She doesn't wear any badge so I have no idea about her name or her number.

"Thank you for your help," I say, "Miss...uh?"

"Not a miss," she says, glancing back as we go down the corridor. "Ninety-six is my number, if that's what you're asking. I'm not any of the above now. She pats her crotch. "All gone and good riddance."

"Oh." I'm not sure what to say. "I'm glad for your help."

"I'm glad to get rid of this stuff."

Eve trails behind us, distracted, pausing to look at things sitting along the corridor. Some items we can't identify. She asks what each item is but neither Ninety-six nor I can give an answer. Some look like musical instruments, others aren't. It's a mess.

"This it?" asks Ninety-six, opening the double doors to a closet in a rather small room packed full of items, half of them in boxes or crates, others out in the open. We have to squeeze through the items stacked there. She forces one door further open, pushing back a pair of crates.

Inside I see a black case in the shape of a tuba. I reach for it, run my fingers along it, feeling the rough, leathery surface. I push my fingers into it, feel something hard inside. My heart leaps with joy!

"I think so."

We dig it out and set it gently on the floor in the limited space. The lighting isn't the best but I can't believe my eyes. Is it the same tuba Grandma Isla played? I examine the plaque on the bell: the name of the manufacturer and the date is clear but tarnished. I get a cloth from my bag and wipe it. It won't polish to a shine any longer but I can read the ornate letters, elegantly scrolled as they are.

"This is it," I say with a relieved sigh.

"Shore do look like what Miss Isla playin' on," Eve confirms.

I tug at the broken zipper, get it down half-way, enough to look inside. One side of the bell has been bent down. A few small dents mark the sides of the bell, the largest and most easily damaged part. A few scratches in the once-silver finish. A little rust in a few places where the finish has been disturbed. Yet it warms my heart to see it, to finally hold it.

"I'll clean it up and it will be good as new."

"Take anything you like," says Ninety-six. "It's all gotta go some day, I've been ordered. And you have a gold stamp."

"Gold stamp?" I question. "You mean the special gold seal on my identification badge?"

"That's the one. It's like you're a special citizen here. You can do what you want, go where you like. Don't have to work but still get regular credits. Best you can be without being in the government. But everyone works for the government – or works for someone who works for the government. It's a perfect system."

Nodding, my focus is on the tuba.

The gray metal seems to shine back at me. It calls me. I jerk the zipper down more, getting it open. Then I lift out the coils of metal and the light in the packed room throws shadows on the walls, and I see Grandma Isla holding the beast in her lap, making it call to the horizon. I fill with joy!

I gather it in my arms and put my mouth to the small end, then realize the mouthpiece is missing. I check the pocket of the case and there it is. I find music paper there, too. In fact, it's a notebook with a metal coil binding. I give the notebook to Eve, ask her to hold it up for me to see it. I insert the mouthpiece and put my lips to it. I take a huge breath, like I did as a child, and send the air into that metal monster, allowing my lips to quiver as Dad taught me.

A note sounds! Eve cheers.

"Don't that beat all?" says Ninety-six.

I remember the basics from Dad's lessons, staring at the lines written across the page, sprinkled with dots. I recall how to push the valves down in different combinations to make different notes. But they are sticky; one won't move. They need some oil.

"This is it," I sing. "My grandma's tuba. *Her* grandmother played it in an orchestra a long time ago. Before the pandemic. She was an artist. She could make this thing sound like God calling down from the heavens."

Eve giggles. "What happen to her?"

I wipe my hand over the mouthpiece. "Died, of course."

It wasn't a happy story, I knew from Dad's retelling. He read his grandfather's notebooks. Grandma Isla's grandmother was killed by an angry man. Nothing to do with playing this tuba. In uncertain times some people isolated themselves on an island, trying to form a community to survive the end of the world. But tensions can arise in that kind of situation.

"You know, the pandemic...?" I say instead.

"Just another one yer sad stories," says Eve.

"My granny died back then," says Ninety-six. "At least you got a tuba from way back. Better make sure it's clean. I mean free of the virus. I wouldn't be putting my mouth to that thing just yet."

She has a point. "It was clean enough, I suppose, when my dad brought it to this city."

I pack it up and put the music papers in the pocket of the case. We push our way out of the room. It is great to take a big breath in the open corridor, free of the stale air we found in that small room. I pull the tuba onto my shoulders, the straps of the case worn but holding firm. I feel the weight of generations.

"Ya look like a bear," says Eve.

I look back at Ninety-six, call out my thanks.

No hassles after all, thanks to my gold seal, thanks to my dad's heroic acts.

6

COLD GRAY CITY

"NO, THAT'S TOO LARGE," the tram monitor declares as we try to board. "You need to call a taxi-cart for that thing."

Maybe we should've gone to the Archives first. I wouldn't need to carry the tuba on my back the whole way along the streets. I have to stop and adjust it a few times before I find the right position to be somewhat comfortable. I can't imagine how my dad's Grampa Sandy carried this tuba from that island north to the National Park while his Grandma Hannah carried Baby Isla. We're civilized again, far from that savage era. Now the world is polite – polite or else.

A hurrying walker bumps into Eve as he passes. I shout at him.

"Ain't fond o' this here place," says Eve with a frown. "Full of dirt an' icky things an' mean folk. I wanna go home."

"I know." I explain what tasks are left for us to do. "We can leave tomorrow. Maybe."

"Well, awrighty, but ain't gonna hold ma breath."

Right then an ear-piercing alarm sounds.

People on the street stop, pull out masks, place them over nose and mouth. We don't have masks. A monitor rushes to us, shouting for us to cover our faces. Eve turns to me, puts her face into my chest as I hold a hand over my face.

A black discharge from somewhere billows out. The cloud of icky material covers the street like spots of oil that street cleaners were working to remove before the alarm.

We duck under the eaves of the nearest building, wait for an all-clear call. Sometimes a dust storm blows over our town and we have to wait inside for it to pass, then sweep the dust that's collected. But I prefer the dust to this grimy industrial discharge.

A monitor passes us without a mask on, so we think it must be clear now. When we step out to the street, he waves us back to our hiding spot. Eve is crying; rather, her irritated eyes water. My eyes feel the sting, too. The air is nasty.

Finally, another alarm sounds. I look out at the street: the air is clear again. People resume their walking. The monitor waves us out, like it's a normal day.

We continue on our way, finding the right path to the Archives. The quicker I find what I'm looking for the sooner we can get out of this horrible place.

The building was standing long before the pandemic, too huge to move, too costly to tear down: a concrete fortress meant to endure a barrage of bombs. They stuffed it full of everything they wanted to protect from the end of the world. And left it there. They added to it every day, according to Dad. That was where his precious notebooks went after he was arrested.

We trudge up the many steps to the entrance. Being at the top of that mountain of steps, the doors are three levels up from the street. Maybe the steps are meant to discourage visitors, or else to impress a conquering army. But Eve and I mount them, take it slow, shifting the tuba on my back. How could my dad's Grampa Sandy do it? I'm out of breath at the top. We take deep breaths, then enter.

"Listen, lady," says the grumpy woman sitting behind the guard station, red hair falling down in front of her eyes while the rest of her head has hair that's cut short. "We got everything, sure. But it isn't organized. Not at all. And I'm not about to use my whole shift looking for things like that. I got better to do."

All I asked was where I could find the notebooks. I already knew it would be an effort to locate such things in this huge building. I was willing to do the work of locating it; I just asked for directions.

"We got this building," the woman explains, "and we got twenty more locations around the capital. They're warehouses, not libraries. Things are stacked up, shoved in boxes – boxes on boxes, crates on top of crates. You're going to go through all that?"

I wasn't sure.

"Maybe they got'em last place ya look," says Eve thoughtfully.

She's always thinking differently – clearly.

"The last place would probably be some sort of 'in-take' station, I would think." I regard the woman. "But where's that? Where does everything go first when they arrive?"

"They bring everything in through the big doors downstairs, out back. Loading dock. First sort is just inside those big doors. Ask for Thirty-two."

I smile and thank her.

We follow the route through the building, noting the arrows on the walls directing people to different destinations: red, green, blue, white, black lines to take us to various sections. It is confusing.

"This like a finding game, ain't it?" says Eve. "I like findin' my way like this. To a big ol' treasure."

"Yes, a treasure hunt," I respond, shifting the tuba on my back.

It takes a while but we come upon stairs.

At the bottom more arrows and lines on the walls send us in the right direction. More stairs going down. More signs. Eventually we arrive at the bottom level and see the large doors, now closed, where vehicles bring their loads. Mostly documents or other artifacts they wanted to preserve from the annihilation of wars they anticipated in days past. Those kind of 'end-all' wars never came; too many people falling sick and dying from the pandemic, nobody left to fight.

Nothing was on display now, not like they had been when I was a child and came here on school trips. Mom brought me here after Dad died, too, showed me those notebooks he obsessed over, set in a glass case, pages open as though they were important: something to show how desperate people were back then during the pandemic, how they made up stories to entertain themselves as they sat cold and hungry around a small campfire. Mom made sure I knew those notebooks were our family's legacy.

"What do you want?" Thirty-two responds gruffly when I call out his number from a narrow aisle, surrounded by boxes and crates stacked up to the ceiling, like canyon walls to block us in. We can't see anyone, have to assume someone is nearby.

The man bulls his way out from an aisle between stacked crates. His eyes brighten when he sees two women.

"How may I help you?" he says, flipping his demeanor, cobbling together a smile. His old coveralls used to be red, badly faded now, with a few rips and stains. He fills out the garment, like he's able to lift the larger boxes.

I explain what we're looking for and he just laughs.

"Help yourself," says Thirty-two. "If it isn't here you can try one of the other buildings it might be in. Or maybe nobody thought it worth saving and tossed it in the furnace. We did that back then."

I lose my breath. "Oh, dear."

Eve helps me lower the tuba off my shoulders, set it on the floor.

"Well, ya gotcher tuba anyways," she says. "Better'n nothin'."

"I want to get those notebooks," I insist. "We came all this way."

"Listen, lady, not a good chance of finding something like that in here. You say it's been ten years? How much stuff has been added to the pile these past ten years?"

"So everything is added by year? Chronologically?"

"Chrono-what?"

"The oldest is at the bottom and newer things put on top."

"Yep. That's the way it's done. But how deep you wanna dig?"

"If something was put on display at the front, so that the public could see it, but then was put away...where would they have put it? Being important enough to display it, I'd think they'd put it in some place special, not just toss it into the pile here."

"That sound like a good idea," says Eve.

"You're right," Thirty-two agrees. "I wasn't here then but it'd be my guess they took it to the gallery. Then wait to decide what to do with it."

"And where is this gallery?"

"Come on. I'll show you."

Eve helps me put the tuba on my back and we traipse through the aisles of boxes to an elevator which Eve is still nervous to go in. She fears it might stop and we can't get out. But we go up to what is the main floor, the box rattling and making noise the whole way, and we step out.

"That wasn't so bad," says Thirty-two to Eve.

"It's scary," she responds.

Before us are double doors, opened wide to a large room, a grand hall at one time, like a place to display art or other items a museum would have. But the room is packed with things now: a few statues rise above the stacks of boxes. Shelving along the walls are stuffed with old books. I see a long-dead horse rearing up, a headless soldier plunked on its saddle.

"General Collins," says Thirty-two at my stare. "Battle of North Venture. We won that one, at least. He had a head originally, but it got knocked off when they were moving it here."

"I need to read more history," I say.

"It's all here," he says, grinning. He waves his arm around at the vast collection. "You can take your time going through it, but that'd be your whole life by the time you finished. Then what're you gonna do with what you learn? Teach it to others? What good's doing that when they keep changing it?"

We follow him as he worms his way through the stacks, pausing to move a large bone out of our way. Eve is frightened of the bone, thinking of the monster it must've come from.

"T-Rex," he calls it, lifting it in both arms and dropping it on top of another box. "Damn thing rolls off sometimes."

"They don't live no more, right?" Eve checks with him.

"Not for a long time," he replies.

I get my bearings from the ornate ceiling. The painting up there shows scenes from famous stories, I recognize. And angels, or how I imagine they would look. I think it's the story of Mr. Noah with his ship of animals searching for a new home after getting lost at sea. Mom showed it to me in a book called *Bible* she got from her mother. I couldn't believe he got all the animals onto one ship.

I crash into a stack of boxes, my attention focused above.

"Careful," says Thirty-two.

He lifts more boxes out of our way, sends us out through an aisle to the far side of the round room. We emerge in front of the endless shelving curling along the wall, overflowing with books, magazines, and other paper items, all in disarray.

"Here's what they got," says Thirty-two.

"Ain't never seen so many these book things," says Eve, her eyes wide. "Can we get some them? I done learned readin'."

"Take what you want," says Thirty-two with a laugh. "Nobody's gonna miss them, believe me."

There is just enough space in front of the shelving to put down the tuba. I begin scanning the shelves even as I lower the tuba.

I step slowly along the shelves, scanning titles. Some are old but familiar to me. Others are unknown. All are in poor shape – worse than the books we have in the tiny library in Skinner Canyon. I look for metal coils which is the binding method of those notebooks.

The shelves extend half-way around the curve of the hall. It will take days to look over just this portion of the collection.

"Here's where they took things that used to be on display," says our burly guide. "The first place they would be put, I'm guessing, if it's been that long. Maybe they're here. If not here then I wouldn't know where to even guess."

I thank him, expecting him to leave, but he waits as I peruse the shelves. I have no plan, no organized search direction. I pull out a few books as I stand before the shelves, just to have a closer look. I set aside three books to take with me. I ask Eve to start at the other end and come toward me, looking for those metal coils. We make it a game. Who will find them first?

There must be a thousand books here, plus magazines and other small items stuffed among the books. Pamphlets, brochures, plastic-wrapped cards of information, children's school work, handwritten letters with famous signatures, paper photographs. If I had time, I would love to organize the collection, make it impressive, show the world of the past. That seems to be my calling; my teachers always admired my way of organizing things.

"Okey-dokey now," says Thirty-two. "I'll come back after lunch to check on you. If you find what you're looking for before then, just go back the way you came. Or, if you got a tablet, hit my number and I'll come get you."

"Tablet?" asks Eve, pausing from her search. "What's that?"

With a grin, he explains about a tablet and she giggles. He starts flirting, talking about how his daughter acts the same way, but she's grown up now. Eve acts coy. I watch them, pretending to search for the notebooks.

I pull out a few items I think are the notebooks I'm looking for but they're someone else's notebooks. One is full of sketches: winter trees and snowball men. Others I find are little more than school assignments. Another one's full of mathematical equations, charts, and formulas. I set it aside to take back to my school.

Eve resumes her searching as Thirty-two exits.

"He's a nice fella," she offers, "but he gots a daughter same age as you, so ain't never gonna work out." She laughs sadly.

We resume our search. Hours go by. The light outside changes, a shift coming through the high windows down into the room. There is no artificial light turned on in this huge hall. I feel nervous at what may lurk among the boxes. The headless horseman seems to watch. The old monster bone gets up and stalks us. The strange noises of an old building shifting and settling, creaking and cracking, pipes gurgling somewhere, otherwise silence as the room grows dark.

"Maybe we should be gettin' on home," says Eve, coming to me.

I gaze around the room: almost too dark to read the spines of the books. "Yes, I suppose we should be leaving. We'll return tomorrow. Still more than half of this shelving to search."

"It's really so important?" she asks.

"It is to me." I give her a reassuring smile. "Besides, we came all this way. Yes, for the tuba, and thank goodness we found it. But the notebooks are important, too. They're our history. Dad's history and your history, too. Lots in there about LJ and his dad, Big Joe. You should know about them."

"I know all I need to," she says, tight-lipped, as she helps put the tuba on my back again.

We start to make our way out, squeezing through the stacks of boxes. The light in the room is almost gone.

Noise stops us. Then Thirty-two is calling to us from outside the great hall. We follow his voice and exit the piles of boxes.

"Sorry I didn't come back after lunch," he says. "Got other work needed doing."

"That's all right," I say.

He asks if we found what we're looking for and I have to confirm we did not and need to return tomorrow. But first, we need to find a place to stay overnight.

"Or you can settle down right here," he suggests. "I'll bring you a couple food boxes, whatever they got in the break room. I'll get you a lantern, too."

"And blankies?" asks Eve.

"Not sure we got any blankets, but I think we got some of those padded covers for wrapping around art and stuff."

He goes to get them and returns after several minutes.

"Goodnight, ladies," he says with a smile that puts be on alert.

There's no lighting in the hall, not even back-up safety lights I recall from my childhood. It seems the entire building has been shut down for the night. The tiny sounds are creepy.

Eve scoots against me as we lie on the floor.

"You afraid?" I ask her.

"Not if I'm with you," she says, and kisses my cheek.

I tell her stories of my childhood in this city as we get sleepy.

+   +   +

We awaken in the morning by a sharp crack of sunlight hitting the windows coated in industrial grime, illuminating the great hall.

I get up and stretch, straighten my clothes. I let Eve sleep, as I yawn and plan the day's search.

"Good morning," calls Thirty-two, working his way through the stacks, zigzagging among the boxes. He breaks through to our camp.

Eve awakens, pulls the wrap around herself.

"Good morning," I greet him. He holds up a thick book.

"You find what you're looking for?" he asks, standing before us. He seems giddy, holding that book in his hands.

"No, it got dark. But I'll continue today, if that's allowed."

"Whatever you want," he says, "you got the gold seal."

"Thanks." I point to the book in his hand. "What's that?"

"A book about music. That's what you want, isn't it? Anything about music?"

He holds the book so I can see the front cover. In big letters it reads *The World of Music*, with *Music* in giant letters.

"That sure is a big book," I say, impressed.

"See? Says 'Music' right there. And..." He starts to open the book, letting the pages flip, "got lots of words and pictures in it so you can learn all there is to know about music. Got stories of famous music people, too. I didn't read much but when I saw it, I knew you would want it, so here it is. Take it. Nobody's gonna miss it."

He offers the book and I accept it into my two hands, the sudden weight almost making me drop it.

"Careful," he says. "It's got everything."

"I gotta go potty," says Eve softly to me, standing with the wrap around herself.

"Would you excuse us? Where is the toilet?" I ask Thirty-two.

"Oh, there ain't really one now. We have a room where there's a collection bin. You see, they take it out and make it into fertilizer or some other products. Nothing is wasted."

"Can you show us to that room?"

"Sure, happy to." He grins at Eve.

It's an odd moment for us, but we take turns in the little room, squatting over the metal deposit bin, careful not to touch anything, then a quick wash of our hands with sanitizer gel.

When Eve and I have finished our morning ritual – the factory's toilet area was much nicer – Thirty-two presses a button on the wall outside the room and a red light flashes inside, leaking through the door gaps, a way to sterilize the room, I guess. We hear machinery moving inside it.

"It's being dumped into the larger box outside," he explains, "it's through a pipe."

"Back to Skinner Canyon we got us a long drop out the cabin in back," says Eve and Thirty-two chuckles.

"This is indoor tube disposal," he counters.

I'm not impressed but thankful we can feel better now.

We return to the great hall, squeeze our way through the boxes to where we last searched the shelving. I instruct Eve what to look for again and she starts scanning the spines of books, alert for any metal coil binding stuffed between the books.

Thirty-two picks up the thick music book, holding it like I hadn't properly thanked him for finding it.

"It's got pages with music on them. Those dots on the lines. And pictures of music instruments. There's a picture of a orchestra, with everybody sitting on stage to play music, and this white-haired man standing in front of them, waving his arms like none of them are playing it right."

I lean over to look.

The lavish picture spreads across the two pages, with a caption reading: *Leonard Bernstein conducts the New York Philharmonic in a performance of Mahler's 5th Symphony at Lincoln Center, 1960.* My eyes linger on the picture. I'm astonished. A century and a half past already. It's an amazing image. So this is how life used to be! How grand it must have been! People dressing elegantly, going to this impressive music hall and enjoying a grand performance, not having a care in the world for the time it took for the concert to begin and end.

"So long ago," I say with a sigh, wishing I could experience it.

"See? I knew you would like it. It's about real music. Long time ago. Not like now, when it's all made on machines. And all for their propaganda. No, this stuff...this is the *real* music."

I straighten, smiling at him. "I agree. That's why I'm here. Why I returned to the city of my birth. To claim my heritage."

"Your heritage, huh?"

He's about to say more but Eve comes over to see what I'm so amazed by. She stares at the picture of the orchestra in the big book that Thirty-two holds.

"They shore do look purdy in them black suits," she says.

"I found some disks, too," he says. "They play on a machine – if it still works – and you can see the music and hear it as they play it. I guess you gotta find a power plug on the walls here. Machines don't work unless you plug them in."

"Oh, you're so kind," I tell him, feeling uncomfortable. Why is he helping us? The boys in Skinner Canyon, I've learned, act nice then expect you to flirt with them. "Thank you for finding this book and the machine and.... Do you have a name?"

He grins, like I ask something intimate. "Name? Why...not sure. I remember my mother calling me Billy for a while. That a name?"

"Sure is." I smile at him. "Same as the president, isn't it? Billy Baskins? And we have three Billys back where I come from."

He asks where that is so I tell him about Skinner Canyon and we sit down on the hard floor to talk. I forget my search. He holds that music book in his lap, his trousers dirty, and now I don't want to touch the book. I tell him I must continue my search.

He suggests looking in these boxes. Could be in one of them.

"That's an impossible task," I say with a breathy sigh, as I scan the stacks of boxes, many higher than my head.

"I would help you but I got a list of things to do today," he says, "but I'll check on you later. Got some food boxes for you. And I'll get that disk machine for you, too."

I thank him once more and, leaving the heavy book on the floor, he disappears among the boxes. I wait as still as possible, with Eve at the shelving rattling books. I listen toward the doors for sounds that will indicate he is gone. Silence, at last.

7

MOONLIGHT

"WHAT'S THIS ONE?" asks Eve regarding a picture of an orchestra with sixty musicians sitting in a semi-circle before the white-haired conductor waving his arms.

"That one is a flute, obviously."

"Oh, yeah, I 'member Cory making somethin' like it out of a reed he pull from the marsh."

"Yes, I've heard of people doing that."

"What's that black thing they got there?"

"I think that's an *oboe*. No—a clarinet. Remember the oboe has a sharp sound and a clarinet has a round, woody sound."

"Then what's them tall, brown things?"

"I think those are called *bassoons*. Great-grampa Sandy's mother warned him about them. But I don't know why."

Eve studies the picture. "Shore do got lots of fiddles. And got big ones, too. I kin count twelve here on this side, and twelve more over th' other side. Six big ones, too! Got three sizes so everybody kin get a chance to play."

"And there's the tuba in the back," I say, pointing.

"Really wonderful they kin play together an' nobody makes no bad notes an' they finish same time."

"It's called practice. They rehearse a lot before they ever play for an audience."

"Shore do wish we could be audience."

I have to smile at my cousin's excitement. "We will. Someday we will be an audience. I promise you."

We flip through several pages in the big book of music, pausing at whatever catches Eve's eye. She asks questions and I try to give answers, but I hardly know more than her. All I know is from my dad, and all he knew came from his mother, who wasn't trained on that tuba, just figured it out from written instructions left by her grandmother. So long ago, so many lives involved with this music thing. I have to learn it. I must continue their legacy.

"Why ya tearing up?" asks Eve.

"I'm sad." A moment to wipe my eyes. "And I'm happy."

"That's crazy," she responds, then refocuses her attention on the book. "What's all this here?"

"That's a page of music, how it looks when it's written out. The caption says it's the handwritten *score* of a famous music writer, a *composer*. I can hardly make out the notes as rough as it's written."

"Tell me about music." She's like a child in a candy shop. "What's these dots and lines mean? How you know what notes to play? And how you make instruments play'em?"

I shake my head, overwhelmed. "We have a lot to learn."

Hours later, after Billy brings us food boxes, we haven't returned to our search of the shelves. Instead, we're studying the music book. I read parts of it and we discuss the lesson. We look at pictures and examine diagrams. Here's the circle of fifths. Here's the range of the instruments. Here's a diagram of *sonata* format. This picture shows an excerpt of a sonata written for a piano, printed clearly instead of handwritten. We look at the picture of a piano and Eve is amazed by all the 'levers' to push to play the notes. I've only seen the well-worn piano at the back of the classroom in Skinner Canyon but it's seldom played.

We pause to figure out how to work the machine Billy's brought for us. He's happy to give us another gift and I keep wondering why he's giving us things we don't ask for. He set the boxy thing on the floor and dropped a stack of disks beside it, each about the size of my hand. Explaining how he took it from a room of old gadgets, he ran a cord from the machine over to the wall, pulled out books from the shelves to get to the hole in the wall where he inserted the end of the cord. The machine lit up and the lid on top opened on its own. He described how it worked. The disks are meant to accompany the big book of music, so we look at the list at the back of the book and find the disk with the piano sonata we see printed on that page. We put the disk into the chamber, close the lid, push the play button. The disk spins quickly – but it isn't a piano we hear. We check the list again, then push the buttons until the right number shows.

There it is: the piano song. It plays such dark yet delicate music. A mysterious mood envelopes us like we never could've imagined. Eve sits enraptured through the whole song. I feel tears fill my eyes. So few notes, yet just the right notes. My whole body is touched, my soul unfolding into paradise and my mind open to the universe. Eve takes my hand.

The song finishes and the next starts, something lively, but I stop it. We have to take a moment to rest from the emotional strain of the song we've just heard. Eve gets up on her knees and hugs me, pushing my face against her. I feel a tear hit my ear.

"It's so beautiful," she moans. "Kin we hear it again?"

She releases me and we both have tears on our faces.

"Yes, of course." And I push the buttons to repeat the song.

"Sounds like moonlight shining across the marsh," she says. "It takes me back home."

"Reminds me of foggy nights in the city," I offer, "and the tired workers rushing home before industrial discharges pollute the air."

We listen to it again, forgetting our search for the notebooks.

"Hello," calls Billy, finding his way through the boxes once more. I startle at his voice. He carries a few more books in his two hands. "Found these for you. Back in deep storage."

I'm delighted to see more books. These are the *scores* the leader of the orchestra uses to conduct from, showing all the parts at once. Another book is piano music, two staves at a time across the pages. He presents them to us like they're pieces of gold.

"Thank you," I say, getting up to receive them. "Why are you so nice? You don't need to help us. I'm sure you have other work to do."

"I *was* doing other work," he says, his voice sounding upset, "but I found these and thought you might want them."

"Yes, they're nice. Thanks. But why are you helping us?"

"I don't know, guess I like you. Nobody else ever comes in here. I'm happy to help. Breaks up my usual routine."

I feel bad, thinking the worst. Too much time in Skinner Canyon where a man doesn't say anything or give you attention without him wanting something from you. I expect worse in this city.

"Sorry," I say. I try to explain my concerns but it goes nowhere.

"That's awright," he replies. "It's been a long time since I last did any sweet talk. Forgot how. Believe me, I wasn't ever any good at it back when I was young so I'm sure not good at it now. Forgive me if I come across as too...weird? I don't get to meet anyone in this job."

"I apologize. I didn't mean to accuse you of anything."

He waves his hand to dismiss my apology. "I mean, your sister's kinda cute, but I'm much too old for her. And I suppose you're even younger. See, I have a daughter over in Kanza City – with my wife who died a while back – grown up and married. Dorothy's her name. I forget her number. Haven't seen her for a while. See, I can't leave the capital. I'm an essential worker, they say, so they won't give me a pass. Gotta keep working."

"Oh, that's terrible."

Dad couldn't get an exit pass either. But after he died, Mom got an exit pass and whisked us out of the city as fast as she could. Just another cog in the machinery – *geez, I sound like Dad!*

"You have a gold seal," says Billy, pointing to my badge hanging on a ribbon around my neck. "That gets you through any checkpoint, come and go as you like."

The piano music is still playing, Eve pressing the repeat button every time it comes to an end.

"She sure does like it," says Billy. "Anyway, I'll let you get on to your searching. I'll keep my eyes open for anything else you might be looking for."

I thank him again and he saunters away, banging through the stacks of boxes. He was being kind, I know, but I'm not used to it, so I didn't give him the benefit of my doubt. Oh, well, he's gone now, so back to work.

I get Eve up and we resume searching the shelves as the music continues to play. The 'moonlight' song finishes and the next song starts. We let the entire disk play until it comes to an end, an hour of different kinds of music. We hum along to some of it.

We don't find any metal coil bindings to signal notebooks stuffed among the things on these shelves. I turn to the nearest box. It isn't sealed with tape, so I open the flaps and look inside: more books and paper items. I can flip through the stack inside and see there are no metal coils. I go to the next box, the same. It's beginning to appear hopeless. Do I really need those notebooks? They may have already disposed of them, tossed them into a fire and my efforts are in vain.

I call over to Eve that we should take a break.

As we meet at the spot where we slept on the floor, Billy arrives bearing two food boxes. His grin seems sincere.

"All we got, but you're welcome to them," he says, handing them to us. "I already ate mine."

We sit on the floor and eat the food from the boxes. I think of my school days. No boxes, just a line of children holding out a plate and old women slapping spoonfuls of mush on the plate. It was different mush each day. I recall one time when the spoon slapped my plate too hard and I dropped it. My teacher put me in the corner and I had no lunch that day.

"You awright, Cousin?" asks Eve at my sudden trance.

"Sure. Fine. Just a memory," I say.

Billy tells us about his life growing up near the capital following the pandemic. Everything was thrown back to older times having no electricity or communication lines, no motor vehicles just a horse or two, and food was hard to get. His parents died and he and his sister were on their own. He didn't have any plan, didn't know what to do, so they walked all the way to the capital. He found a job and worked hard to pay for food. His wages went toward food. Eventually, as the capital was rebuilt, everything became more stable – too stable, in fact. Now he was forced to stay and work. He was needed. No time off, no chance for a vacation.

"You want to go away for your own enjoyment? That's what they say. You don't want to stay and help us build an ideal society? Try to make us feel bad for stopping our work."

Eve and I laugh at his drama. I recall the announcements at my school, always chiding us to work hard and think of Big Sister. We knew she cared for us.

"It's just my luck this job is easy," he says, "just move this here, move that there. And, of course, help anyone that comes in here for something. That's a good day, believe me. I like helping you ladies."

"What would you do if you could leave the city?" I ask, packing up the empty food box.

"Oh, maybe I'll go see my daughter. She's got a girl of her own now so I want to see her. Maybe she'll remember me."

"Aw, that sounds wonderful." A thought weaves its way through my head. "It's like me returning here searching for my past, or what Dad left for me. I'm lucky. Dad was a hero so we got the gold seal. What do you need to be able to leave here?"

He regards me a moment, then looks down. "If I were married, I could get a pass. They think if people are married, what they call domestic partners, it would be a reason to return. I would have to come back but, honestly, I would just stay away. Don't tell nobody. That's what I would do, believe me."

"Marriage would do that? Allow you to leave?"

"Well...marriage to somebody who has a pass, that is."

Suddenly I understand his interest in us. I look squarely at him. "So if you were married you could leave?"

"That's what I said," and his eyes soften, a grin playing on his face. He fidgets, fumbles with his fingers.

"You could marry anybody?"

"It has to be someone with a gold seal," he says, looking up from under his brow.

"Like me."

"Like you, yes."

"I see."

A moment of silence for the details to settle in my mind. He does seem like a decent fellow. And I pity him.

"We wouldn't have to, you know, be together for real," he says. "Not like in bed. It would just be in the registration. A notice in the system. That's all. Then I could leave with you when you go, but I'll go my own way and you can go yours. Just like that. Then you can file for dissolution later, I don't mind."

I tried to hold back a grin. "Just like that, huh?"

"Just like that, yes, ma'am."

"No 'citizen'?" I teased with a smug face.

"Well, you're a higher rank than a citizen, in my humble opinion, believe me."

+   +   +

The next day the three of us go into the Department of Registration and get a number. We wait three hours before we are called to the official desk. We have to act out a 'love story' even with our health records in the system already.

"Compatible," the clerk announces. "You may proceed."

And we wait another couple of hours for the next desk.

"This all there is for to get wedded? Just wait a spell?" asks Eve, holding my hand again.

"It's supposed to be worth the wait," I say to her and smile at my new husband.

When we are called, we go up to the desk.

"You and her?" asks the woman in official uniform there, seeing Eve holding my hand.

I blush. "No, it's me and him." I let go of Eve's hand, take Billy's arm. "This one."

He grins happily, standing in his work coveralls like a good cog.

"Numbers?" the woman asks.

He gives his full number, then adds: "William B. Kirk."

"What's the *B* for?" I ask under my breath.

"Bernard." He pats my hand on his arm. "You can call me Billy."

"I will."

I have to read my number off my badge. I make sure the woman sees my gold seal. "Maggie Baumann," I add.

"No middle name?" asks my husband-to-be.

"No." Then I clear my throat. "It's *I*."

"*I* for what?" he asks.

"*I* for Isla. After my grandmother." But I only now invent it. My parents never gave me a middle name. Didn't seem worth the effort, Mom said, not with everyone starting to use identification numbers.

"Raise your right thumbs," says the clerk, presenting a tablet to us. "Place your thumbs on the marks on the screen."

We do.

"I pronounce you Joint Partners In Common Domicile as coupled citizens by mutual decree from this day forward. Congratulations. You may signal acceptance in a traditional or Ideal Society method. Couple housing is limited but you're on the list. You will be notified. Probably take a month."

"Thank you," I say automatically.

Billy thanks the woman, then thanks me. It's an awkward pause deciding what to do next. Should we kiss? In front of everyone? The couple ahead of us did. Might as well. That's the traditional method. The Ideal Society method is a firm handshake.

I stretch up and my lips meet Billy's. He's ready, maybe expects it. Just a peck, but enough to please everyone waiting in this office. About like when I kissed Ricky Johnson, a boy in my school. Or that Lee Unger, who pushed me into a corner after school when I agreed to kiss him, then put his creepy hands everywhere—

"Ma'am?" calls Billy.

"You should call me Maggie," I say, breaking from my memories.

Smiling, he takes my hand and leads us out of the office.

Once on the street, he stops us, gazes up at the pale sun fighting through the industrial haze. He seems relieved.

"Now you can go see your daughter," I tell him.

"That's mighty kind of you," he says in a more serious voice.

"You've been kind to us, so we're kind to you," I say cheerfully.

"Let's go to my unit. I get the rest of the day off because of the occasion. I have something for you. You'll like it. A gift."

"You get a day off just for getting married?" I laugh at the irony, holding his arm. "You should get married every week then."

He smiles at me a moment then it fades, like he feels regret.

"Yes, I should," he says, looking down as if checking his shoes. "It's been a long time. A real long time since.... Well, never mind."

We go to his building, a ten-floor tower which is for single male workers, like where my dad lived after Mom separated from him. It was about saving us from his bad reputation after he returned from rehabilitation. I think she still loved him, though.

"Here," Billy says, and puts his hand to the pad by a door.

The door slides open. He waves me forward. I start to take a step inside when I feel a hard shove from behind. I fall to my knees, Billy standing behind me. Clumsy me! I start to get up as the door closes behind him, leaving Eve outside in the corridor.

He pulls me up by my arm and tosses me roughly on the narrow bunk attached to the wall. I hit my head on the wall.

"What're you doing?" I cry out, my hand going to my head.

"We just married," he reminds me. "Now is the best part."

"What? But you said no bed stuff."

"Did I?"

Then he's grabbing at my clothing, tearing my blouse open to get it off. I push him back so he won't ruin my clothing.

"This isn't what we agreed," I cry.

He grabs at my blouse again and I beat his hand away. I pretend to give in, say I'll take off the clothes, just don't rip them.

He waits impatiently as I unbutton my blouse and slip it off. He grunts at my appearance. I hold my arm across my chest. I've never felt so unattractive. My slacks off, too, he demands. I protest and he slaps my face.

"I don't want this," I say, wanting to growl but I've about lost my voice. "I've never done this before."

He raises his fist to me, so I tearfully slide the slacks down over my hips as he unzips his coveralls, showing that he is ready.

"I really wanted your idiot sister, but you'll have to do."

"Please don't do this," I beg, holding my hands up.

"We're married now! You belong to me!"

Breathing hard, I say: "I think you rather belong to me. I'm the one with the gold seal." I hope my act moves him to be kinder, but he presses against me with his hot, hairy body.

"We're married now," he grunts. "We're in the system. Besides, I gave you things. Lots of things you wanted. You owe me."

"There is no owing!"

"There is!"

Eve is beating on the door, calling for me. She sounds frantic and I cry out for her to get help, telling her to get a monitor.

Billy drops on top of me as I squirm wildly, my fists pounding his shoulders. He forces his mouth on mine, his hands probing, groping.

I push him away, scream: "No!"

The door slides open with a comforting *swoosh* and two monitors in blue uniforms fill the doorway, Eve behind them.

"Off," commands one monitor, both of them with batons in their hands, the kind with stinger tips.

He's slow to get off me so he gets a stinger in his butt that makes him howl in pain.

I throw the sheet around me as they pull him off the bed, leave him writhing on the floor. They ask me questions but I can't answer. If it's true what Billy said, then I have no excuse. I don't know what will happen now. He is, actually, my husband.

"You can go to Emergency Services," a monitor instructs. "They will assess your situation, act accordingly. If necessary, marriages can be dissolved."

They drag Billy out of the unit, his body shaking in spasms and his coveralls encircling his ankles.

Eve rushes in, hugs me, asking if I'm hurt.

"I'm fine," I say to calm her. "More embarrassed than hurt. He went crazy. I shouldn't have been so damn naïve. I really thought he was, I don't know...*nice?*"

"He was nice for a spell, anyways," she says.

I get up, put my clothes on, though my blouse is torn. I sit on the bed trying to breathe deeply. Remaining in his unit, which is rather messy, I wonder what to do. Should I go to a medical office if I'm not actually hurt? I look around the disgusting unit, clearly the space of a bachelor. I don't want to touch anything.

Yet there, on the shelf above the propaganda screen, is a stack of metal-coil notebooks.

I get up to look at them closer. On top lays a leather-bound book with a strap and a broken lock. I gather it in my hands, dare to open it and gaze down upon the blue squiggles of handwritten words.

Eve notices. "What's that?"

I gasp when I see German words on the first page. Then I grab the other notebooks, open them and I'm in shock.

"Them's what yer lookin' fer?" asks Eve.

"Yes," I say with no breath to expel.

"How'd he get hold of them?"

What was that man thinking? Was this meant to be a reward for giving in to him? But he attacked me. No pause to get romantic, just lust. Was he planning to give me these notebooks – my notebooks! – as a gift? Doesn't make any sense. But here they are.

He must've found them after I described them. Then he held on to them for his scheme. Or he already had them, taking them from the Archives, and was only tricking us. He acted like he was helping us but it was all a scheme.

"I'm so stupid." I threw my hands to my face and cried.

"Don'tcha cry now," Eve responds, hugging me. "You ain't stupid. Least not as much as me. Plenty more woulda done same as you."

+ + +

Eve and I return to the Archives and gather what we left there, our mission complete. We take the music machine and the box of disks, too, as well as the thick book about music. Maybe meeting Billy was worth getting these precious items. I have a lot to learn, but it's a long trip back to Skinner Canyon, where the boys say "Ma'am" and wait for you to smile back at them. But if you don't they'll call out a crude remark.

Before we go, Eve wants to hear more music. Says it will calm us from the dramatic day we've had. I have to agree.

She flips through the pages of the heavy book, finds a picture of a bearded man. I read the name and find his music on the right disk and start it playing in the machine. We sit back to listen.

"Shore looks wise," says Eve about the man named Tchaikovsky, which I couldn't guess how to say. The song is called *1812 Overture* which starts quiet but gets loud. Something happened in that year, I guess. There is even the noise of guns at the end. Very scary!

A guard appears and complains about the noise. The new man is a little older than Thirty-two, that creepy Billy, and I'm glad to find he's been replaced. I can relax.

"Look at this fella," says Eve, her fingers tracing a picture in the book. "He's clean-shaved, kinda handsome."

I look at the picture, read the name: Shostakovich.

"They all got long names," she says. "Longer the name the better their music, s'pose."

"Seems that way, doesn't it?"

"Here's one seems a girl: Fanny Mendelsohn. Says here she's the sister of this Felix Mendelsohn. Reckon ya gotta have a big brother to get in a book like this, huh?"

"I'm sure there are other women in music," I tell her.

We finish the song, what the list says is a *symphony*, a long one in four parts, and then we pack up everything. I heft the tuba onto my shoulders and Eve gathers up the music machine and the disks in a cardboard box. We work our way through the stacks, out to the corridor, then to the stairs and down.

"Find what you were looking for?" calls the red-haired woman at the front desk.

"More than," I call back.

On the way out of the city, we pass through the neighborhood of my former home. I point to the gray building, the last place we lived before Mom took us west. I no longer feel sadness. I'm satisfied and happy to be leaving, promising never to return.

As I lay my head back, riding the railway westward, I remember a pair of workers having lunch in the terminal, complaining openly about the city. I had to smile at that.

"...worse than before," said the first man. "Wornall had the right idea, making the society better. This Baskins is only about himself, enriching him and his friends."

"This is how tyranny begins," the second man responded. "With little steps, little rules, little punishments. Then larger and larger ones until everyone is afraid to do anything at all for fear they aren't doing it right and someone will notice and get them arrested."

"Even our thoughts have to be correct, no wavering."

"There is only one opinion," the man said with a dry laugh.

"You blink wrong and away you go."

"Have a pandemic and they think they can start everything over again their own way, like we forgot what we had before."

"But what we had before, was it so good?" asked the first man.

"Better than now, I'd say."

And they both laughed.

Eve nudges me. "Whatcha smilin' about?"

"Just thinking of those men talking back in the terminal."

8

THE MUSIC LADY

REALLY, I MARRIED HIM. Still can't believe it. Not what I wanted for my life. Yet I'm a married woman now. It feels strange. A tear hangs in my eye, then another. I'm safe now, but what obligations do I have? What will happen to my 'husband'? Will he be freed and come after me? We didn't stay in the city long enough to do anything official to fix the situation. When we return to Skinner Canyon I'll apply to dissolve the marriage, petition the appropriate department.

I shake my head, knowing how foolish I've been.

"Don't be sad," says Eve sitting beside me in the ladies' car of the express, for which we pay extra to be away from 'kindly gentlemen'. "He just one them bad men. Plenty o' them, no matter where ya go. Ya didn't do nothin' wrong. Least he didn't hurt ya."

"I regret the whole matter," I say. "Please don't tell anyone."

"I shore wouldn't never tell on ya."

Eve tries to improve my mood by asking me about music, getting me to teach her something. We heft the big book of music out of the bag and turn to the chapter about writing music.

First, there was no written style, only people making the sounds on their own, from a flute made of a reed, beating on an animal skin, or simply singing. They didn't write down what they did. Later, they wanted to remember it, so they invented a system for writing the sounds so other people could play the same songs. Different writing systems in different parts of the world. In Europe....

I read a few paragraphs to Eve.

"How kin they tell what notes ta play?" She points to a picture of an old manuscript with handwritten notes on it.

"That's what all the dots and lines are for."

My mood changes. I tell her about the five lines being a *staff* and the notes are put on the lines or in the spaces between the lines. The musicians read the notes and know what to play. Other marks can change the notes by raising or lowering the *pitch*. The way a note is written, open or colored in, with stems and flags, tells you how long to play it. Like the big fat notes without stems are *whole* notes, and you play them for the whole *measure*, which is a portion of the song separated by horizontal lines on the staff. Every few *beats*, in fact, so it's a regular pattern. Other marks tell when not to play.

"Those are called *rests*," I say.

"Well, they gotta take some breaths, s'pose."

I explain about the *clefs* marking certain staves so the musicians know how the notes line up on the staff. Such a complex system. I don't know how anyone can learn it. I recall Dad showing me music his great-grandmother wrote for tuba. Her handwriting was neat, easy to read. Some of her songs were funny, like "Sandy's Bride" or "A Sand Flea in a Butt" – but they were meant for tuba. Now I want to learn to play it just so I can hear how her songs sound.

+   +   +

Frank and his eldest son Jeb meet us when we get off the railway and go through the depot. Jeb tips his hat just like his dad does.

"Welcome home," says Frank glumly, then gives me a quick hug.

I guess I'm home; this is my home, as it has been since I was just eleven. Frank takes the tuba from my shoulders, hangs it from one of his as I shriek at him to be careful with it.

"This what you went all the way there for?"

"What is it?" asks Jeb.

"It's your aunt's goldarn tuba," Frank answers.

They greet Eve, never being too comfortable with her. She's from the bad side of the family.

Jeb, growing into a fine young man, takes the large bag with the music machine and disks in it. Eve imitates me calling for him to be careful and Jeb laughs.

"You sure did come back with a whole lot more'an you left with," says Frank as he leads us to the wagon.

I pat the horses' noses then climb aboard. Jeb raises the canvas awning over us to protect us from the harsh sun.

Frank calls the horses to giddy-up and we start the twelve-mile trip to Skinner Canyon. He tells about some of the troubles they've had since we left. The local tribes are getting more aggressive along the border. Couple cattle herders were attacked but got away. They lost a steer. Then a platoon of Mexican soldiers appeared, unaware how far north they had wandered.

"A couple weeks' ride, I'd say. Almost had a fight."

They were chasing bandits, so he agreed to work with them. In a couple days they cornered the bandits in a well-known cave at Black Mesa and killed some of them. The Mexican soldiers took the others away, returning south.

"Shows how lawless this land's become," I respond. "Where's the border? Nobody respects borders."

"That's what you get living at the junction of five territories," he says with a weary chuckle.

"Still don't add up to what all Maggie done," says Eve, bless her sweet heart. I try to shush her. "We met this fella in them *Archives* an' he was real nice to us so she married him. But then he weren't."

"You *what?*" cries Frank, turning to glare at me. "Should at least bring the fellow out here so we can get a look at him. And he can see if this is where he wants to be."

"She don't even wear purdy dresses or put those cosmetics on her face," Eve laughs. "But they fallin' fer her anyways."

"That true?" asks Jeb.

"I regret it." And I give Eve a harsh look. "I'll straighten it out. It was a bad decision. The main thing is we got the tuba back and all Grampa Sandy's notebooks."

"An' she got one them *German* books, too," Eve adds. She turns to me. "What's a German anyways?"

"She means the journal of Old Fritz. Our dad's namesake."

"Amazing!" Frank cheers. "You sure do get whatever you put yer mind to, that's fer sure. Mom was right about you."

"Well, she gonna start up a music band, she is!" sings Eve.

"A music band?" asks Jeb, turning to look at us.

"Yes, a band," I answer.

"With an old banjo and a native drum?" asks Frank. "That's all what we got around here."

"No," I say, feeling how impossible this project is going to be. "I already contacted a music company to get what we need. I'll teach people to play the instruments. I can do it."

+   +   +

In the following weeks I study that book of music as Eve returns to helping Faith with the gardening. They have 24 rows of vegetables and an acre of wheat and corn. The boys will harvest the grains with their machine but the gals pick the vegetables by hand. They get mighty moist under the western sun and one day I see Eve pull off her shabby dress and continue in undergarments, getting herself quite dirty with dust sticking to her sweaty skin. We have to wash her off with a bucket of well water.

Eve is always nice and fresh when she comes to bed and we have a lesson about music before blowing out the candles. I'm learning a lot and so is she. She takes a fancy to the 'fiddles' – actually *violin* – but I don't think she's be able to learn to play one of those. And a banjo isn't part of a band. I suggest a brass instrument for her and she chooses the *cornet*, a smaller kind of trumpet.

I return to the school after summer comes to an end and add music lessons for the kids: thirty-seven children ages 6 to 13, with the grades mixed but divided into three levels. We can only sing, having no instruments, but we manage to learn music, especially how to read it. Most children enjoy our lessons. A few of the older boys think it's just for little kids – yet they still whistle trail tunes while pretending to herd cattle like their brothers, fathers, and uncles do. They wait impatiently until they turn fourteen and can quit school.

Walking through town, I put up posters everywhere announcing that I want to form a band and ask who wants to join. I put posters in the café, the bank, the sheriff's office, the communications office, general store, greengrocer, and at the two hotels, five saloons, and the livery. I put one at the school house and when parents come to get their kids they see it. They ask too many questions about instruments, how to get them and how to pay for them. They like my enthusiasm but doubt I can get a band together. That makes me more determined to prove them wrong. They start calling me "the music lady" like I'm crazy. But I'm only bothersome, not crazy. I persevere; it's my project.

I return to the catalog and see the company is located in Kanza City, a long ride on the express. I laugh, thinking how our express went through Kanza City. We stopped for about thirty minutes. Eve and I stepped off long enough to get a snack.

Perusing the pages, I linger over pictures of the instruments. The brass instruments are so beautiful with gold or silver shine. I don't think the string instruments will be good out here in this hot and dry climate, but a wind band is possible. In the back of the catalog are lists of the many songs that can be purchased, a score and set of individual parts for each. I don't know the songs by their titles. Maybe it doesn't matter, seeing the prices. We might need to have a music festival just to raise funds.

Then strange things begin to happen. Out back of the cabin, I notice a new *billy* goat bullying the nanny goats. I ask Faith and she tells me how the billy was given to her in exchange for a basket of vegetables. It's how we do things in Skinner Canyon. Hopefully, she said, some of her nannies will get some kids soon.

Then, as I'm passing through town another odd moment.

"Good morning, Missus Kirk," a boy calls to me. He pauses just long enough to say his greeting before running to catch up with his friends. That same day other kids are addressing me by that same name and I shudder each time.

I have to wonder why they call me by that name. I check in the town office. Yes, the national information system has me listed as a married woman with my husband's name. I hate to start the hassle of undoing that mistake, but there it is. I wonder if Billy Kirk has gotten out of whatever detention he's endured. How will he think of me? Will he come looking for me? That thought sends a shiver through me. He'd be quite angry. I start carrying a knife.

Three boys in the school are named Billy, and every time I hear other kids call them, I shake. And so I start mentioning, to anyone who might ask, that my 'husband' died back in the capital. It was a weird accident, happening right after our registration. Yet it isn't much better being referred to as Widow Kirk.

To distract myself, I write to Dr. Hill in Kanza City to ask about purchases. He writes back promptly, explaining in lovely language how it works. Being an official representation of the company, he can bring some instruments with him and help me start the band. It is an amazing offer.

I write to him, explaining my idea. He writes back to answer my questions. We develop a conversation over the winter months. I find myself waiting eagerly for his messages, coming by the express. I suppose it's becoming a curious fantasy. Having such an intimate chat with someone I've never met is an odd thing, how we delve easily into some non-music topics. I ask him to please switch from 'Dear Mrs. Kirk' – the registration had fully circulated around the country – to 'Dear Maggie'. Even so, he makes sure to congratulate me on my marriage!

Despite that jolt to my self-esteem, I feel confident I'm doing the right thing for our town. That's what matters. Dr. Hill agrees. A town band is the best thing to improve morale in an 'ungodly' place like Skinner Canyon. I've described my town to him. God often takes a look, I want to tell him, then moves quickly on to more pressing matters. Besides, Dr. Hill writes, helping the kids learn music will give them a whole host of useful skills. It's a noble goal.

Again I seek funding from our local businesses, all of whom are happy to help, eager to find something for the kids to do outside of school, but they can't offer much. I'm becoming discouraged. The kids are excited at the possibility of a band so I keep a smile on my face for them.

Dear Maggie,

I feel blessed by your latest letter and your continuing interest. I am happy to know you are well and remain quite excited for our new venture.

It would be my great pleasure to visit your environs and deliver to you and yours a suitable assortment of our finest musical instruments in order to populate your new ensemble. I shall partake of such a journey into the wilder region upon a full deposit of the agreed upon portion toward the total cost of the items you have selected.

Please use the secure transfer system directly from your credit hosting institution to 'Kanza City Musical Instrument Company' (address in letterhead) and I shall acknowledge payment as soon as received. Please kindly note myself as your representative.

I look forward to our meeting and I shall greatly enjoy our first rehearsal with all of the fine instruments manufactured by our company.

Musically yours,

Hal D. Hill, Ph.D. (Music)

"What do you think?" I ask Eve after reading out the message. We finished the next chapter in the big book of music and I was reminded of the letter. I jumped out of bed to fetch it, then rejoined her as I unfolded the paper.

"S'pose it's good idea him comin' all th' way out here."

"And he'll bring some instruments. Enough to get us started."

"But how ya gonna pay fer all them things?"

"Yes, that is the problem." I regard her, thinking. "Who has a lot of credits around here?"

"Prolly gonna be them ranchers. Ones got big spreads, hundreds cows, big fancy house on the hill. One them folks."

I smile. "I think you're right. Their kids attend school, so they will want to see them perform in a band. Not all the boys have to act tough and turn their backs to music."

"Like y'always sayin', they got tunes already in'em but cain't sit still long 'nough to play a song, gotta keep movin'."

I light up. "They could march!"

We flip through the book to find a picture of a marching band, see the tubas with large bells towering over everyone's heads. The man in a fancy uniform marching in front of the group has the name of John Philip Sousa. He waves his scepter in the air to mark the beat.

"Like this?" I ask my cousin.

"Yep." She grins at me. "You could do that."

+   +   +

Dr. Hill indicates what we will need and I find it confirmed by the information in the music book. I write out a list of the instruments. What do I need to start a band? A band that can perform most songs should have the following instruments:

> 3 flutes (1 can also play piccolo)
> 1 oboe
> 3 clarinets
> 1 bass clarinet
> 2 alto saxophones
> 2 tenor saxophones
> 1 baritone saxophone
> 1 bassoon
> 3 trumpets (or cornets)
> 2 French horns
> 3 trombones
> 1 tuba
> percussion instruments played by 2 or 3 players: snare drum, field drum, bass drum, pair of cymbals, xylophone, and if performing on a stage could add a set of 3 timpani drums

"Shore do seem lots o' music there," Eve comments when I read her the list and check it twice.

"At least we have the tuba already," I say with a laugh.

Since we returned to Skinner Canyon, I've been working on that tuba. I thoroughly cleaned it, noting places where there's damage. Then I took it to the blacksmith's to get help repairing it. When he was finished, mostly tapping out dents, I oiled the valves and gave it a big blow. I made a sound – what I couldn't do when I was a child and Dad tried to teach me. The goats in back of the house didn't like the noise, but that didn't stop me from trying each note. I played them in order, going up and then down. I tried to blow for as long as I could on each note, until I got dizzy.

Faith wasn't impressed, saying they should've left it buried with those kids that died in the National Park a long time ago. Grandma Isla dug it out of there when Faith was only a toddler. It was what once had been their underground home during the pandemic. Then marauders put the little kids inside and sealed it up. That was years before Faith was born. When Isla left, she took the tuba with her, and my dad and his sisters, down to the marshes where she played it until she died. Dad took it to the capital where I was introduced to it. And before all that happened, Isla's dad played it, or tried to, and before him Isla's grandmother Polly – all the way back to Old Fritz who brought it from 'an old country' after the war that was fought long before we ever had a pandemic. Dad was named after him but he preferred going by his father's name, Frank – then had to use his number instead.

I tried to imagine how terrible those times must've been, and I gave the tuba an extra long look, thinking of all the hands that had held it. And now it was my turn. Dad had never really played it, was saving it for me, as his mother wanted. I'm Isla's granddaughter, after all. I have to learn to play this huge coil of metal, do my best to make it sound good, for all those who played it before me. I have a notebook containing instructions written by Polly for her son and songs written on paper by her, too.

First, I learn which combination of valves to push down to get each note. I know from Dad's lessons how to put my lips together and make them buzz. Eve laughs when I show her. Then, with my mouth against the mouthpiece, I make notes.

Soon I can play a simple song. Eve sits patiently, claps when I finish and says it sounds better and better. I try a few of Polly's songs and think I've got them right. Over and over I play until a squad of Comanche come to the edge of the canyon to see what's making all the noise! I wave, then return to practicing. They stay a while, then ride off, satisfied I'm not a threat, just annoying.

"You wait until we have a whole band playing," I call to the wind as their horses leave a cloud of dust behind.

In that spirit of celebration, I visit the richest rancher in this area, Magnus Lilly, who has two daughters in school. I catch him finishing his late lunch on a Sunday but he's kind, knowing me as the teacher and a widow. We chat about my plan for a band. It will mostly be for children but any community member can join. We need about twenty musicians to start but hope to have thirty-six in total eventually. I ask him if he's ever played an instrument and he calls his housekeeper to bring his guitar. Just as I suspect: guitars are the only music here in this dusty corner of the country.

"No guitars in a band, sir," I explain. "But any instrument can be learned with a few lessons."

"That all sounds mighty fine," says Mr. Lilly. "And I do think my Beverly and Magnolia would enjoy it."

So he offers to fund the purchase of some of the instruments. I thank him and practically dance out of his large house.

Another day I visit Jim Brewster, a rancher living a ways out. His kids have graduated from school so he has no interest in paying for other people's kids to play around. But I have to correct him: not playing around, playing *music*. But he refuses to help.

Karen Kyle, the wealthiest woman rancher here, also a widow, is happy to help but doesn't offer much. Her five children will benefit from the music lessons, she agrees, as long as it won't interfere with their chores around the ranch. We will make the concerts part of a season of music so the children will be free to help during the rest of the year. Lessons will be part of the school day.

I visit other ranchers: Simon Brunt, Horace Grimm, Emma Lee, George Funk, Emery J. Burr, Elias Gray, and Dan Crusher – with mixed results.

Next I ask Mr. Oliver Penny, owner of Pennywise, our general store, if he might pledge to fund our music project. He's happy to be a part of the musical revival of the town. He tells me about a band that once played here, just five people, playing what they call *jazz* but other folks ran them out of town because of certain non-musical activities which caused a scandal.

"Now, over in Cimarron, their music festival is gonna draw a lot of folks, and they would be mighty jealous if you got a band started here," Mr. Penny cautions.

"Do you think they'd come here to cause trouble?" I ask.

"Don't know about that. Probably if it's just the kids, they ain't gonna worry if you'll be taking away from their festival."

"Well, first we need to get the kids interested."

"That shouldn't be too hard," he says, "the way they like making a whole lotta noise."

I go to each of the businesses in town, asking for pledges. If I have pledges, and they come through with their credits, then I can give Dr. Hill permission to bring sample instruments. I'll still need to provide the credits to cover ten percent of the total. I haven't even calculated the total. I know I have enough to get started, thanks to what Mom left for us.

"Y'all gotta start small, not have too many them instruments," Eve suggests. "You kin start with what they call *quartet.*"

I tell her about the jazz band Mr. Penny mentioned. They had a trumpet, saxophone, trombone, stringed bass, and someone playing drums. That's a good start. We have enough kids to join in.

"You kin ask them Comanches for drums," says Eve with a grin. "Bet they got'em real cheap."

Mayor Taylor agrees to hold a fundraiser for the band but it's up to me to arrange everything. He'll say a few words. Frank says I'm too bull-headed when I get an idea. Well, I am stubborn.

Mayor Taylor grins at me like I'm rude for asking him.

"That's about the stupidest idea I ever did hear of," he says with a dry laugh. "Why, I would've thought it was your idiot sister who thought that one up."

"It's my idea," I say. "And she's neither my sister nor an idiot.

She's my cousin, and she's got special talents people can't see."

"Anyways, it'll serve us both," he says, thinking it over. "I'll look good being nice to the kids, and you...well, whatever. You can pitch your idea to the folks gathered there."

"That sounds fine."

I calm myself because I need his help. He agrees to have the fundraiser event but there's a catch. It has to be for his re-election, too. We will split the funds received, fifty-fifty. I stop myself from expressing my derision at that idea. It's that or nothing, he says, so I have to agree. Yet I consider right then to vote for his estranged daughter-in-law, Beatrice, for mayor.

9

THE MUSIC MAN

"FRIDAY EVENING AGAIN," I say to myself and any spirits in the room. "Everything is unremarkably the same. I look out the window beside me, see the stars coming out, hear the wind stir the brush, goats baying, and..." I smile up at Eve, who's come over and leans down for a kiss. "And my dear cousin is close by to help me, Mom. I know you never got to meet her yet she's become my best friend and more. She's a special person, I want you to know. It's already more than a couple years gone by since she came to live with us. And you know what, Mom? We have big plans. Yes, Mom, plans for a band. The Band Plan. Thanks to you, we can afford a few instruments. Enough to get started. I only wish you were here to see it and hear it, and enjoy what Dad wanted me to do."

"What he wantcha ta do?" asks Eve. She takes my hand in hers, swings herself cheerfully down onto my lap. I squirm; she remains thin but I'm not so large myself.

"Everything," I answer as I wrap my arms around her. "He was a nervous man, Mom said, always afraid. No doubt that came from the way he grew up. Then living in the capital. That would make it worse. He was always getting into trouble."

"But we come out here an' got lots o' freedom an' no nerves."

"Yes, Eve. No stress at all." I have to chuckle. "Mexican soldiers, tribal squads, town ruffians, mean cowpokes, drunken seducers, and the coyotes and snakes."

"Them's lotta trouble." Her hands settle on my shoulders.

"It's good we have each other," I say softly, gazing up at her.

I wouldn't have the strength to do what I have to do without Eve always by my side. People in town tease her but I protect her. Boys flirt with her, thinking she's easy, but I keep her out of trouble. She works hard with Faith, and they get along. The garden is growing so they hired two more women to help out.

"You'd be happy, Mom," I whisper, gazing out the window. "You didn't get to know that side of the family, but you'd want them to be safe and happy, I'm sure."

"We's all happy an' safe," Eve calls out, giggling. She gets up and my lap can relax. "Ya ready for coming to bed? Or still mopin' about them music instruments?"

"No," I tell her, getting up and letting her lead me by the hand to our bed. "I mope no more. What Mom left for us will help pay for the band. Our dream will come true at last."

She lifts the covers, checking for spiders, snaps the sheet then turns to me. "Mighty fine dream we got, ain't it?"

I sit on the edge and she sits beside me. "It is."

Before we can blow out the candles, Eve starts humming a tune she must've heard me humming earlier. Smiling, I take her hand. We get up and I twirl her around. She laughs. We spin and dance, silly as kids. Pausing for a breath, she pulls her nightgown straight up and throws it off over her head. Laughing, I do the same, and we continue dancing together.

"Shore don't mind dancing with a married gal," Eve says.

Married gal? That reference irritates but I try to smile anyway.

"I would prefer being married to you."

Alarmed at the noise, Faith enters and halts at the sight of us.

"What're you doing?" she shrieks.

"Just a little dance," I say as we grab our nightgowns.

"Well, we got 'pressionable boys in this house, so if you two don't mind not getting them all excited."

"We won't," I say, laughing too hard to pull my nightgown down over myself. When my head finally pops out, I see Benjamin and Clemson peering into the room from behind Faith, their eyes wide.

"Besides, don't y'all got an early start? You wanna get over to the depot on time," she says, sternly. "Got that music man coming in."

"Yes, ma'am," says Eve and I give a nod as the boys duck away.

Faith grins at us, the fun over. "Goodnight, ladies."

+ + +

I go with Frank to pick up Dr. Hill at the railway depot, eager to meet him, to see how he can help us form a band. There aren't many folks getting off so it's easy to pick him out. He stands in a brown and tan checkered suit with a red bow tie, a black bowler hat atop his head, looking every bit the salesman.

I call to him. He turns to me, waves as I approach.

"Doctor Hill, I presume?"

I have to press my skirt down against the breeze, brush my hair back from my face. This land isn't good for pretty dresses and neat hairstyles but I rarely present myself in such a femininely style.

"Greetings and salutations!" Dr. Hill cries with a tip of his hat.

The man appears about forty, tall but not too tall, taller than me anyway, broad-shouldered but not as much as cowboys. He is well-dressed, has a waxed mustache curling in the sunshine, his hound's-tooth suit rumbled from the long trip. His face is pale but his cheeks are rosy. His eyes are small but his smile even and firm.

"Harold Hill, Doctor of Music, at your service."

Frank greets him coolly. "They got doctors for music, huh?"

They shake hands. Dr. Hill seems alarmed seeing the pistols on Frank's hips. My brother explains about being a lawman.

"I would surely imagine that to be a good thing to have in these desperate times," says Dr. Hill. "Although in Kanza City we like to believe 'music soothes the savage beast' and have no need of guns."

Frank chuckles, lists the three biggest dangers we face here: the tribals, snakes, and drunken cowpokes.

"My! My! Such a truly savage *environs*," says Dr. Hill, adding an accent on the final word. "I am absolutely *thrilled* to be here. I can feel the danger already."

He excuses himself to direct the unloading of his trunks.

Frank watches four trunks being manhandled from the railcar.

"He thinks those'll fit on the wagon?"

"Those must be the musical instruments," I say. "He promised to bring a few samples, enough to start a band."

"Good he didn't have to bring a tuba," says Frank with a snort.

Dr. Hill escorts two trunks over to us, says the other two will be put in storage at the depot. We all go to the wagon where the horses wait patiently for us, lapping up water from buckets.

Pausing to look around, Dr. Hill remarks on each Western thing he sees; it's ordinary to us. "And actual horses! My! My!"

"You're not afraid of horses, are you?" I ask with a laugh.

"We've few in Kanza City, I assure you. To get around we merely hop aboard an electro-bus, which is convenient. Having a sensible street plan, it's easy to go where you wish, whether it's down Grand Avenue or along Forty-seventh Street through the Plaza district."

"We hope one day to have the same here," I respond. "Meantime, we must use horses and wagons to get around."

"You can walk, if you like," Frank offers and I give him a jab.

Dr. Hill looks down at his shoes, now dirty from walking through the railyard. "I'm afraid these puppies are done with. Barely suited me while sitting for such a long travel. Twelve hours! I can't wait to settle into a comfy room at your finest inn and pull them off, let the pups get some air." He regards me fearfully. "Mmm, you do have an inn here, do you not?"

Frank laughs. He's trying to be polite for me, I know, so I take his arm. He always looks out for me.

"We have three," I reply. "One is more of a brothel, however."

"My! My!"

The depot men load the two trunks on the rear of the wagon and we climb aboard. No room on the bench for Dr. Hill so he must ride in back on top of the trunks. It's unsteady. On the way to Skinner Canyon, he falls off twice. The first time no harm done. The second, he hurts his wrist, holds it tight the rest of the way.

"Now don't you worry, Mister Doctor," says Frank with a glance back over his shoulder, "cuz our Maggie here, she's a smart cookie. She can do anything she puts her mind to. Knows a lot, too. In fact, she's read every book in our town library."

I give Frank a poke in the ribs as thanks for saying that.

"She's a quick study, too," he says, winking at me. "Don't you think she looks real pretty in that dress with herself all fixed up? And she's got her mama's rosy cheeks—"

"Oh, stop it!" I laugh. He knows I don't like cosmetics.

Frank keeps talking, building me up, like a good big brother, but finally we arrive in town and not a moment too soon. Dr. Hill is none the worse for wear, but he's mighty nervous. Like my dad was.

"Don't go poking 'round no dark places," says Frank. "Could be snakes in there."

"It is indeed a rough life out here," Dr. Hill concedes.

We check him into the Skinner Lodge, our best hotel, and put the trunks up in his room. The owner's sons aren't happy to heft the trunks up the stairs. In the room, Dr. Hill moans like he's just been through the worst day of his life. He straightaway collapses on the bed, pulling his hat over his face.

"Forgive me," he says, "for I am a city man, and not used to these vicious detriments to my character."

"You need time to rest," I say, but he doesn't respond. "I'll visit you later. At supper time. Is that all right?"

"That shall be fine," he mumbles from under his hat, sounding a little upset. "Pardons for my uncharacteristic bout with fatigue. We are not usually engaged in such a struggle."

"That's quite all right, Doctor Hill. It's your first time coming out west. I had the same reaction when I arrived here twelve years ago. You get used to it. Now I wouldn't want to live any other place."

He was snoring by then, big honks followed by slow squeals, like a pig in labor. Cute. I have to grin.

I step out of the room and go down to the front desk.

"Please see to anything he may need," I instruct Mrs. Beale, who runs the inn with her husband.

"He seems a delicate sorta fella," she says.

"Well, he's got a degree. That's probably it. Works with his mind, not his body."

Mrs. Beale gives me a smirk. "Won't last a week here."

When the afternoon reaches evening I return to fetch Dr. Hill for a supper meeting. He's rested, wearing fresh clothes similar to what he wore when he arrived. He greets me with a big smile, opening the door immediately at my knock.

"You look fresh as a daisy," he says, looking me over.

"Thank you," I say, a bit shy. "I don't always dress like this."

I always try to make myself appear nice and clean – presentable, as Mom would say. I mean ready for commonsense activities, not for drawing one into a romance, but I fear he thinks I'm interested in him that way. As a child I wore boy clothes, playing cowgirl. I like the way those clothes feel, but I'm on business so I wear the pretty dress and fix my hair neatly.

"That is truly a shame. You look mighty fine in that outfit."

He continues saying flirty things like it's required as he dawdles in the room. I notice the open trunks, see instruments fixed inside, held securely in velvet crutches to prevent them from shaking as the trunk is moved. I step over to have a closer look. I bend down to admire the shiny brass cornet, the dark wooden clarinet, the silvery flute. I put my hands together as if in prayer.

Suddenly I straighten up, a rush of alarm shooting through me. I don't know the reason for it. I entered his room, left the door open. But what if he'd closed the door behind me? Perhaps I fear this man coming at me. Dammit! That incident in the capital is almost a year past, yet I still feel it, that awful ten minutes.

I turn to face Dr. Hill, find him beside the door, ready to leave.

"Like what you see?" he asks from way over there.

"Yes," I respond, glancing back at the instruments. "They're all I've dreamed of for the past year."

We go downstairs to the dining room. I pay for my supper; his is included in the room fare.

As we wait to be served, and as we eat the common fare of our humble town – noodles and beef chunks, greens, bread and lots of fresh butter – we talk about music. He is amazingly knowledgeable, almost as though he's read the entire big book of music ahead of me. I tell him about my tuba and he sits enraptured by my family's long history – the history of our tuba. Most people get bored when I tell of older generations' adventures. Almost seems like I'm inventing a story yet it's all true, I swear. Yet he's attentive.

"Do you play?" I ask. It's a silly question. Of course he must have an instrument he calls his own, or else he wouldn't be in the music business. Looking him over, it must be something elegant.

"Why, yes I do. I know all of them to a degree. It was the policy of the Conservatory for us to learn all the instruments. Thus, I had lessons on each of the woodwinds, the brass, and the strings, plus the percussion assortment, although I avoided the harp. Percussion instruments I have no talent for. Lots and lots of piano lessons, too. Do you have a piano in this town?"

I told him about the only pianos I know of: one in the Slippery Gulch Saloon, but nobody plays it. Several keys are missing, and the others sound bad. There's also a piano that's in worse condition at the back of the classroom in the school house.

"That is indeed a pity. However, it is the French horn which I call my home. In fact, I was at one time a member of the Kanza City Philharmonia, a professional orchestra. That was a couple years."

"Only a couple?" I think I batted my eyes at him, not sure.

"It was poorly funded." He acts demure. "It only lasted six years before disbanding. Hah! *Disband.* Curious word! Indeed, I was there for only the final two seasons. Long enough to get to play the famous *andante cantabile* solo in Tchaikovsky's Fifth Symphony."

"So then you switched to selling musical instruments."

"Not at first. I continued to play, or tried to play, where I could, such as at parties and other gatherings, most often for free or for old coins. It was a miserable life."

"Then you started the company."

"No, I'm afraid. That was started by Mister Jeremiah Berkowitz, a man who made his reputation in the metallurgy, oddly enough. He had need of other uses for his spare metals. Someone suggested he put aside a portion for shaping into musical instruments."

"And that's the start of your business."

"Not quite." He gives me a big smile like he's about to tell a lie. "I found the company and offered to help him get people to buy those instruments. I showed him schematics for making brass horns and after many tries we made one that sounded suitable."

"So then you joined the company."

"I played the horn for him. I used my best technique. I played it and he was amazed. He agreed to make more instruments, with me as his salesman. I marched up and down the streets whilst playing that horn made in his factory and people would be amazed and ask where I got it. I would inform them of the wonderful possibilities for them and their children in the world of music."

"Because we need music to hold off the end."

"Hold off the end?" he asks.

"It's what my dad liked to say. He got it from his mother, who got it from her father who got it from his mother. And she was a real tuba player, playing professionally in a real orchestra. Also a music teacher. Like I told you before."

He smiles at me, thinking back to our messages no doubt.

"So you were the only salesman?" I ask to hide my blush.

"Oh no. Instruments were literally flying off the shelves."

"Literally?" I asked with a tilt of my head.

"They didn't grow wings, that's true, but enthusiastic customers could not help but buy them, often for the whole family at once. It was a phase we went through: the family band. We partnered with a woodshop to make the woodwind instruments. We do not have any string instruments, I'm sorry to say. That is for another company. However, I didn't know where those bands were forming yet we had to hire more salesmen to handle the load. Now we have plenty. Let's see: there's Jones, Wang, Rhee – the grandson of the pandemic pops singer, Jewel Rhee, you've heard of her? – and Greyson, Minken, Allegretti, Landau, McCoy, and—"

"That's so wonderful!"

"However, I am in charge of the western region so here I am, at your service. Out in the Wild West."

"I really do appreciate it. It's not so bad once you get used to it."

We've hardly touched our food, we realize, lost in conversation, so we rush to eat our fill as the serving girl waits patiently to deliver our dessert: a slice of cream pie.

Then we say goodnight. He lingers in the doorway to his room but doesn't invite me in. I like that. He is such a darling man.

+ + +

The next day I take Dr. Hill around town and introduce him to each business that pledged funding for the band. It is going to be real, I know by their welcoming behavior, happy to see him. Dr. Hill does much to impress them, citing musical facts, singing a song or two, getting into discussions about the manufacture of brass instruments with Mr. Block, the blacksmith, who boasts he can make a horn.

"But you—" He refers to Dr. Hill. "—probably couldn't lift it."

"Like my tuba?" I ask.

"Bigger," he says with a hearty guffaw. He waves at the sheets of metal hanging on the wall. "Gotcher big horn right there."

Then, walking down Main Street, a school boy runs past us and calls out a greeting: "Morning, Widow Kirk!"

Dr. Hill stops me. "Why does he call you Widow Kirk?"

"It's a long story, a frightful story...."

"My, my, dear Maggie – if I may address you in such an intimate manner. Please, do tell."

"Maggie is fine, Doctor Hill."

"Please, call me Hal. It's short for Harold, of course, but nobody ever calls me Hal D. Hill. Sounds too much like 'howdy' and that's not very professional."

That makes me laugh. I take his arm in mine. He's so charming.

"What's the D for?"

He frowns. "The D is for Daedalus."

"Daedalus? What's that?"

"An ancient story of a man who built a labyrinth for his king but later had to escape. He built huge wings out of wax, and he and his son flew away from the island. However, his son tried to fly too high and his wax wings melted and he fell into the sea."

"Oh! That's awful!"

"I'm sure Daedalus thought so, as well."

I think of the story, seeing Dad and me in it.

My grip on his arm tightens. He notices, puts his hand over my wrist. "Widow Kirk?"

We stop in the street, my eyes blinking as he waits.

"If you must know…. I thought I was doing a good deed. Helping a poor, sad man get his freedom. So I married him. That way, he could leave the city and go be with his daughter. An act of kindness only. I was married for just an hour."

"I'm sorry. You are a kind woman. Yet you remain married?"

"Then a terrible accident took him away," I say, trying to appear truthful. I quickly invent an excuse: "A large stack of boxes in the Archives fell on him."

"My, my! How dreadful."

"Yes, dreadful," and I have to look away to hide my lie.

He pauses to calculate a moment. "Therefore, you are, sadly, a widow. My condolences."

"Yes, sadly." Now I regret telling the lie. "I don't think of myself as being married."

"It's unfortunate what happened. My sympathies, Missus Kirk."

"Call me Maggie, I said. I don't want to be known as a widow."

+   +   +

I arrive home by carriage long after dusk and find Eve sitting cross-legged atop her father's grave, speaking in an angry voice. It seems a serious moment so I dare not interrupt her.

After taking care of Pepper, our horse, I watch Eve continue to rant. She grows rather animated as she speaks; I can't hear clearly what she's saying. She gets up on her feet, into a squat, lets loose a stream from between her legs. When she stands and turns to the cabin, she sees me.

"Ain't none yer bidness. Him an' me talkin' out ev'erthin'."

"That's fine," I respond. "Just was wondering where you were, so I looked out back."

"Me an' him's got words, is all. Lotta words we never said before, mostly me. Gotta let'im know how I feel 'bout him hurtin' Mama. Ya know he killt her by what he did. Hurt her before that even. I's just a babe but folks tell me what he done soon as I kin unnerstand. An' folks bin raggin' me e'er since, like it's all my fault."

"There's nothing wrong with you, Eve."

"There is!" She narrows her eyes at me. "Like you. Goin' off with that purdy boy, making moon eyes at him. I see it. What about me?"

I have to laugh. "He's a salesman. He acts that way. Hopes to get a customer to like him. I want a good bargain, so I play along."

"I mean...." She sucks in air, expels it. "Me bein' what they call dumb. Like I'm just idiot girl only good for bedding. What they say in town."

"Did someone hurt you?" I ask with concern.

"That banjo fella, he grab me in unnatural way, if ya know what I mean. Right unnatural. Few boys saw us an' it weren't purdy, no sir. Right nasty, lemme tell ya."

I go to her, hold her in my arms and feel her tears on my neck.

"I'm so sorry," is all I can say.

"My pa, he done it to my ma, made her bend over in them woods, they tell me. Made her give in or he was gonna go after my sisters. Then Ma got fat with me an' bleed out when she push me from her."

"I'm sorry, Eve. That was a long time ago, and things happen we can't control. We have to keep going, do the best we can."

She sobs against my shoulder. There's nothing I can say that can help. So I turn us to the cabin, lead her to our room. Her sobbing is louder inside.

Faith comes to see what Eve's crying about. I wave her out and she makes a cross face but leaves.

"There, there," I coo into Eve's ear. "You're a wonderful woman. Nothing you need to do. Forget what anyone says. I love you and that's plenty, isn't it?"

"I hate him!" she cries with her face against my chest.

I hold her away so I can wipe her tears. "I know it hurts but life goes on. Like what happened in the capital. I'm getting over it. I'm pretending he died in an accident and that's that. He's dead to me. I'll go see Frank about Mister Briggs. If anybody hurts you, you should tell someone you trust. Or a lawman."

She continues weeping into the evening and only in brief words do I understand what happened. Mr. Briggs, giving a banjo lesson, had her sit on his lap. Sitting there she felt a poke. He laughed and put his hand there, patted her leg. When she told him to take his hand away, he tugged on her skirt and some school boys passing by saw her bare skin. Briggs complimented her body then and the boys laughed. She tore away from him despite him holding her and she ran home. Yet she blamed her father for the terrible things in her life. It all began with him, with what he did.

"Kin we move him outta there?" she asks, meaning her father. "I hate seein' him out there ev'ry day, remind me how dumb I am. Like I never did ask ta be born, never did wanna be here. Ain't no dang toy fer no fellas. Never want that kinda life."

"Nor should you." I hold her tight again. I remind her how she's in charge of the two workers they hired to help with the garden. She knows what to do, has a lot of experience, and can tell them what to do and how to do it. That's being a boss, I remind her.

"Thanks, Cousin."

"I'll speak to Frank in the morning, see if anything can be done. Mister Briggs is an old man. I warned him to leave you alone, not bother you, but he's likely an old fool and forgot, let animal instinct get the better of him."

"I don't like them animal stinks. Ain't nothin' good about'em."

10

TROUBLE IN TOWN

I KNOW WHAT DR. HILL MEANS when he points out the trouble brewing in our town. It's so obvious. Boys leering at women walking by. Older boys sitting and puffing rolled tobacco or chewing it and spitting on the ground. Boisterous men crowing in our five saloons, often fighting, going out and drunkenly harassing anyone they cross paths with. And the billiard hall is a frequent destination for young men hiding from school or who don't want to work. They spend all day in there, which is such a waste of time.

"There's trouble in town! Trouble, I say. I see it all around. You have all the classic signs of delinquency," says Dr. Hill in a cautious tone. "You have indeed called me just in time, thankfully. It is not too late. We can fix these problems."

"Do you think it will work? Starting a band?" I ask. "Would they want to join? Learn to play an instrument?"

"There is no telling what might attract their attention, but I can tell you, being one of the male persuasion, that a music teacher such as yourself, so beautiful and feminine, would be quite attractive to a young man, no matter which instrument he wishes to play."

"Well, I'm not going to be on stage for them to ogle," I say in as cheerful a tone as I can. "I doubt I'm 'beautiful and feminine' as you say. I usually wear boy clothes. It's better for this dusty place. I try to look proper today because you've come all this way on business, but a dress like this one isn't my usual garb."

"Pardon me, Maggie. Please forgive my words, for I didn't intend to cause you any discomfort. You see, in Kanza City, ladies like to be complimented on their appearance."

"Oh," I say, realizing customs may be different there.

"Indeed, you look beautiful and feminine *to me* – if I am honest. I have little experience with the fair sex. I hope my assessment will nevertheless count in your ledger. I cannot imagine you arraying yourself in the tawdry garb of a cowboy. I should like to see that but only a glimpse, for curiosity's sake, then have you return quickly to your delightful lady wardrobe."

I blush. I'm not appreciative of his disagreement regarding how I may choose to dress myself. It's always been my choice. Yet seldom do I hear a compliment about my appearance from anyone but Eve.

"Then I should say 'thank you'."

He grins, possibly likewise embarrassed.

"However, what I meant was, realistically speaking, young men would be more willing to be part of a group if there were attractive young women in the group, too. You or any other female musicians, that is. It's simple nature. Are there any in this town? Or only you?"

"I tried to ask around," I say, thinking back through the previous weeks. "I'm afraid there aren't many. The girls who have any music skills are guitar players, piano players, or singers. Saloon gals."

"Anyone who can play one instrument can learn to play another. The skills transfer rather well. And even if they don't, having them present will boost the boys' morale."

"So it's all about the boys...."

A pair of boys tumble out of the storefront before us, fighting and throwing up a cloud of dust. I wave the dust away. I call to the boys to stop their fighting, now wrestling in the dirt of the street. A beefy man comes out of the store, grabs the boys, holding them apart, and starts scolding them. He sees me, smiles shamefully.

"Real sorry, ma'am," says Mr. Lucas, the hardware store owner. One boy is his son, Lincoln. The other, he announces, was stealing. His son called the boy out. He's 'Dirty' Damon, the son of a surly vagrant who sneaks about the town.

"This is exactly the sort of trouble I'm referring to," says Dr. Hill. "Trouble in your town, yes, ma'am. It's starting. I see the signs all around us. Imagine how this situation will be next year. Or the year after. A mess, indeed. You must start the band immediately – today, if possible. Right away! Before it is too late and you have lost them. There is a small window to catch their interest and escort them into the wonderful world of music. If that window is missed, I fear you will forever lose them."

Mr. Lucas asks what my musical companion is blabbering about. I introduce them. They shake hands. I tell Dr. Hill that Mr. Lucas provided some accessories for helping me take care of my tuba.

"I'm all for some kind of band, if that's what you call it," says Mr. Lucas. "Anything to keep these boys outta trouble."

"There's trouble is this town, for certain. It's brewing now," says Dr. Hill. "It could boil over any day now."

Mr. Lucas calls his son over. "Son, you ever think of getting into one of them bands?"

"Band? What's that, Pa?"

The other boy stands nearby. "He means a music band."

"That's correct," I say, feeling encouraged.

Dr. Hill speaks: "Missus Kirk here has the idea—"

"Please, let's go with Miss Baumann."

"Very well then. *Miss Baumann* has a marvelous plan to start a band for the youth of this town. A fun and practical engagement of these youths' effusive energy – keeping them out of trouble, for one benefit. Music skills transfer well to other aspects of life. However, there is a need for musical instruments and the printed music, too. She will supervise and instruct. She—"

"We can create something to rival the Cimarron Music Festival," I cut in. "But, as he says, the benefit is mostly for our youth, for our town here. Something to instill pride."

"And keepin'em outta trouble," adds Mr. Lucas. He turns to his son. "That sound inner'stin' to you?"

"What I hafta do, Pa?"

"How would you like to play a cornet?" I ask, smiling.

"Cornet? What's that?"

I can see it in my mind. "It's like...."

"It is similar to a trumpet," says Dr. Hill. "Which is like a bugle."

"A bugle?" asks the little thief, coming up to us.

"What the soldiers toot on," says Mr. Lucas' son.

"That's right," I say, then describe other instruments they might like. The boys are curious. I study Damon, dirty as usual, and know his father can't afford to pay for an instrument. Perhaps a wealthy patron could help us. Or I will contribute funds.

Mr. Lucas is with us. He suggests a town meeting be held to see what people think of my idea. Dr. Hill can speak to them, too, using his great powers of persuasion. He is a born salesman.

"Wonderful!" I cry out, clapping my hands.

Then I excuse myself, leaving them to discuss various details, as I stop in at the jailhouse to talk with Frank.

+ + +

"Why, I've seen boys pulling wings off butterflies," cries one mother at the town meeting after Dr. Hill gets them all riled up sharing his observations of our town.

"I saw boys putting ants in a jar with a scorpion," says another alarmed mother, "just to watch the ants kill it. Downright cruel."

"Yep, I seen'em put red ants in a big jar and black ants, too, then shake up the jar and watch'em fight each other! To the death!"

"Which ones won?" calls a man from the side of the courthouse room where we have our town meetings.

"Black ones," she answers.

"Well, I witnessed boys capturing snakes, even poisonous ones," another woman testifies, "then they was cutting off their heads and watchin'em wriggle in death throes."

"Snakes deserve to die," cries someone at the back.

"Boys always gettin' into fights," another parent speaks up.

"Damn right!" an older man shouts.

"Bruises, scrapes, cuts," says the mother. "It's downright terrible fixing up my boy's wounds."

Dr. Hill raises his hands to calm the crowd. "These are serious signs of youth on the verge of delinquency, I tell you. However, good people of Skinner Canyon, it is not too late. We have intercepted bad behavior at just the right time, I assure you. Worry not, for we have good, wholesome activities for your youth to put their energies into. No more smoking of tobacco or sneaking sips of moonshine. No more getting into fights. No more skipping school or church. No stealing sundry items from shops, or grabbing food off other people's tables. Let not your heart be troubled, for it ends today."

The crowd erupts in joy, half jumping up and most applauding. I stand beside Dr. Hill, clapping. He smiles like a good salesman. He's dressed in his finest tweed suit, hair combed neatly and parted in the middle, slicked back. His mustache is freshly oiled and curled. He brings a cornet with him to show to the gathered parents of our undisciplined youth. Boys carried in a trunk of musical instruments and sat it on the raised floor.

Frank's sons, twins Jeb and Joe, and younger son Jon come to hear the Good Word, with wife Vera sitting half-way back holding Baby Frances. The boys seem excited to hear what Dr. Hill has to say. I gave the boys a good talking before the meeting, making them curious. Faith's boys, Benjamin and Clemson, are here, too. And Eve is posed at the back of the room, almost hiding, afraid of any man looking in her direction, but she wants to join the band. She has her eye on that shiny gold cornet. Even my brother, James, comes down from the hillside chapel to see what the commotion is about.

I am pleased how packed the room is.

"This wish we all have to see our youth go in a new and positive direction," Dr. Hill calls above the dying applause, "is our goal. It is school teacher Maggie Kirk's idea to start a town band. It is a music band of which she speaks, a band which will absorb our fidgeting youth's youthful energies and provide them youthful aspirations. An activity of note, pun accepted, and provide them a wealth of pride in themselves and the community, imparting a plethora of useful skills – skills such as arithmetics, attention to details, a trained ear, a sharp eye, and a God-given sense of beauty about the world, the joy of camaraderie and learning to work together for a common good – all skills which transfer wholesomely to any endeavor in which they shall engage as they reach adulthood and continuing throughout the years to come."

I thank Dr. Hill for his speech and prepare to speak my own, but he has described everything I planned to say.

"I defer to Doctor Hill's recommendations," I say. "My idea began with a focus on music for its own sake, as my father wished for me. Yet Doctor Hill easily observed the trouble we have in our town. We managed to put two things together and here we are: a solution to multiple problems in one wonderful opportunity. A town band. The Skinner Canyon Youth Band!"

I explain how I envision this new activity as mainly for children, being part of their education, but the band can include adults. After we get started, it should be for anyone who wishes to enjoy playing music together.

"I will be the band's teacher and supervisor—"

"The conductor!" exclaims Dr. Hill.

"Oh, I'm not ready for that role. I simply want to play music. We play music for our own enjoyment, right? And to offer enjoyment to others, true? It's a simple yet effective solution to the savage heart that beats in our breast." A few ladies gasp at me saying the word. "It's a quotation, ladies. I do not intend to be vulgar. Now, as I was about to say, the band should begin with basic instrumentation."

Dr. Hill lists the instruments we need to begin, in total twelve, plus an assortment of percussion instruments. He announces he will offer them at discount because we are beginners and he is impressed with our enthusiasm. I add my thanks. We have pledges from many in the crowd; Dr. Hill only needs deposits to provide instruments, including what he's brought with him, with the remaining payments made later. We will continue to get discounts for the coming year as we build our band.

"The music and musical instruction manuals, however," Dr. Hill continues, "printed on high-quality paper, we cannot offer discounts. Reason being we must pay royalties on the use of those songs, which is only fair to those who composed the music for us to perform. The instruments themselves, I can discount, especially when purchased in bulk. That is to say, if you order five trumpets, I can discount one of them. You get a trumpet for free essentially. However, due to the high cost, I cannot do the same for a tuba." He frowns at me.

"But I already have a tuba," I happily announce.

"She sure does," Mr. Lucas declares, raising his hand. "We got it back in good shape and she sounds rather good blowing it now."

I thank Mr. Lucas in front of everyone and launch into a brief history of that tuba, how it survived the great pandemic and how it was carried from here to there for many years, how it brought joy to my grandmother and my dad, how I promised to continue playing it but had to go all the way to the capital to retrieve it, and how our distant ancestor brought it over from his old country and became a professional tuba player. Everyone waits patiently as I talk.

"Sorry to go on so long," I say to them, seeing their faces growing tense, no doubt wondering how long I will talk. "I'm happy to have that instrument in the family again."

"And I, as well," Dr. Hill jumps in, "do welcome your heavy bass prodding as the firm foundation of the band. Good people of Skinner Canyon may not need to purchase any tuba for your band if Missus Kirk plays hers. But I offer the other fine instruments, as I've been saying. All I need is for you to place a deposit on the instrument of your child's choice. Half the full price – discounted price, remember. Plus instruction manual. Do not hesitate in making your selection."

Then Dr. Hill plays his French horn, a lively song called 'Rondo' which has the audience enraptured. He announces the song is from *Horn Concerto* number 3 by Mr. Mozart. Next he picks up a clarinet and plays again, a different Mozart song. Then a flute, also Mozart. Then tenor saxophone, which sounds like a banjo song. I'm amazed how the instruments sound so different. He plays a new song on the xylophone using two sticks grasped in each hand.

"Who's this Mozart fella got so many songs?" cries one mother.

"My Tommy's gonna want one o' them wood stick thingy," shouts another parent.

"That shiny bugle is for my gal, Sal," cheers a woman.

Parents press to the front, hands full of the old paper vouchers, calling out their choices. I try to write down the names and items as Dr. Hill accepts their money and tells me which instrument for each child. One instrument per child plus instruction manual. Those who pledged funding have already placed their orders. One rancher, rich enough to buy all the instruments, insists his son play 'first chair trumpet' if he agrees to fund the band. I respond by saying it will depend on how talented his son is.

Everyone is excited and hopeful of a new direction for our town. But it also falls upon me to get it started and keep it going. For that I feel a great weigh bearing down on me. Honestly, I only want to play music for myself and maybe with other musicians. I want to hear music! The fun part of it. I'm not excited about teaching them how to play the instruments; that will be hard work and require a lot of patience. Even now, I'm not so good at playing the tuba. Yet I will do it for the sake of our town and my soul. I have to. I told Mom I would and I know Grandma Isla is watching me.

Almost everyone in the courtroom is on board, of course, but a few dissenters resist. One man points out we should put our band money toward renovating the school house, which is fifty years old and showing its age, and could be dangerous. "It could fall over any day now!" But everyone thinks having a band is a lot more fun that repairing the school.

One mother objects when Dr. Hill demonstrates the instruments he brought. He talks about each one, shows the valves and explains how they operate. But when he picks up the trombone and plays it for us, the woman cries out that she isn't about to pay full credit for an instrument with no valves. He has to take time to explain that the sliding tube changes the notes so there is no need for valves. She argues why other instruments have valves instead of sliding tubes. Dr. Hill remains calm, smiling through her display. In the end she's satisfied. She chooses a French horn for her daughter, which most certainly has valves. She likes that it has a large bell, too. "That's extra fancy," she brags.

As the crowd slowly disperses, I spy Eve in the corner of my eye, like a statue by the back wall. Her eyes are bright but her mouth is taut. She folds her arms over her chest, wearing a yellow cardigan and a long brown skirt, looking nicer than I've seen her in a while. I spoke to Frank before the meeting regarding the incident with Mr. Briggs and he promised to speak to the man.

Meantime, we have enough interest in our town and enough kids for a band. The difficulty is finding children who will play different instruments so all the parts are played. It won't do for everyone to play cornets, for example. We have enough to go around, thankfully – twenty-four kids! – and in the end, as Dr. Hill and I compare the list we made to the needs of a real band, we are pleased. Satisfied with the meeting, we celebrate with a fine dinner.

We talk more about music. He tells his experiences playing in an orchestra, and he lets me go on again about my tuba. After a rich dessert of custard pie, he gives me a firm handshake and bids me good night. I almost expect a kiss to my cheek. I move awkwardly to accept it but it doesn't arrive and I feel foolish.

+   +   +

He shuffles along like his legs are sore, wiping his sweaty brow with the back of his gnarly hand, swinging his old ratty hat off and on his balding head as he steps onto the property, banjo in hand. I go out to greet him, unsure why he would come to visit. I'm afraid Eve will see Mr. Briggs and get mad.

"Howdy-do, ma'am," he calls, making sure to keep at a distance.

"Good morning," I say plainly. It's Saturday and the kids are out of school or else I wouldn't be home to protect Eve from this man.

"Thinkin' ta come out here, see if I kin make amends," he says, standing in the dust and dirt of our front yard. A tumble bush blows between us. "Ain't plannin' no bad acts, ma'am. Not like yer brother talk about."

"What did my brother say to you?" I ask from the porch.

"Oh, he come at me like he's arrestin' me, saying I broke laws. I knowed what he talkin' about, said I'm sorry."

"And are you sorry?"

"Yes'am, right sorry. That's why I'm here. To make amends."

I wave him closer, then hold up my hand when he's ten steps away. He sets the banjo atop the toe of his boot, leaning it against his hip.

"Reason being, I wanna give this here banjo to yer sister."

"Cousin."

"She's making frightful progress on it and should really have it to play on full time. It were my idea. Honest. Well, after talkin' with your brother. But it make sense."

"Why does it make sense?"

"She playin' it better'n me now. Plus I owe her for...for that bad bidness th' other day. Listen, Miss Maggie, I just wanna apologize to her. She around?"

I know Eve is inside the cabin but by now she might've heard us talking and started watching us from a window. I look around to see if she's witnessing the conversation.

Then Eve peeks out the front door behind me.

"Morning, ma'am," he calls out, tipping his hat. "I brung you the banjo. It's yours, if you want it."

Eve steps from the shadow of the doorway, comes out to the top porch step, barefoot, wearing her 'at-home dress' which is full of rips and stains. She raises her hand to block the sun from her eyes.

"Ya sayin' truth?" she asks.

"Right true, now," he replies. "I'm givin' this here banjo to you, on account of me being sorry for th' other day and because you're a lot better'n me now. I wanna apologize, too. Like Deputy Baumann says, I gotta follow laws, and they say I cain't touch nobody in those places without getting permission, no matter how I feel or if I wanna touch and cain't help myself. It weren't right. I'm sorry it happened. Please, Miss Eve, I'll be mighty grateful if ya forgive me. I swear it won't happen ever again. I swear."

Eve steps down to the yard, her head tilted, glaring at him.

"Ya mean it?" she calls gruffly to him.

Then he drops down, struggles to lower himself on aching knees. He pulls his hat off, clenches it in his hands, bows his head.

"Yes, ma'am." He lifts his face, regards her. "I solemnly apologize for what I done. Never happen again. I swear it. I was bein' a fool. A dang fool. And them boys happenin' by is just bad timing, is all. I'm purdy sure they'll forget what they saw."

Then Eve rushes up to him, anger turning to steam, and swings her fist as hard as I've ever seen her and strikes his jaw hard. He is bowled over, tries to get up. He rubs his jaw, shakes his head.

"I deserve it, I know. Dang, you could be a boxer, ya know?"

"Ain't no boxer!" she shouts at him. "I'm a woman. An' ya better not ever forget!"

"Gonna treat ya right," he says, rising to a knee. He picks up the banjo, starts brushing off the dust from its fall, a motion that makes the strings twang. "Let this here banjo be a peace offering. I'm right sorry and you go on and enjoy it, Miss Eve."

But she doesn't take the banjo. Instead she stands over him, her arms folded across her chest.

"Don't need no banjo," she says in brighter tone. "I'm gonna play in my cousin's band. Gonna play a *coronet*."

Cornet, she means, but I'm happy at her declaration.

"*Coronet?* What's that?" he asks from where he fell.

"It's what I play music on nowdays," Eve growls.

Mr. Briggs gets up, steadies himself. He brushes off his shirt and jeans, then places his hat on his head, adjusts the brim against the sunshine. He grabs the banjo and tucks it under his arm.

"That's awright with me, ma'am. I wish you – and *you*," he turns to me, then back to Eve, "a mighty fine day."

11

WRONG NOTES

THERE'S A LOT OF WORK TO DO, much to prepare, so I dive into the big book of music every night to learn as much as I can. I study the charts for each instrument, seeing which keys or valves to push to get different notes. I read about reeds, their care and trimming. It seems impossible. I concentrate on the cornet fingerings, thinking at least I can get one instrument to sound right. I practice moving my fingers in the air, pretending I hold a flute or in front of me like I'm playing a clarinet. I memorize the charts and they float around in my head all night. When I awake each morning Eve tells me I made sounds in my sleep and we laugh together.

Finally the day comes for our music group to meet in the school. I arrange a practice area in the classroom, setting the chairs in a semi-circle. We will make a lot of noise to begin, but we are away from businesses. Children and youth arrive with their instruments: seventeen of us, with a good distribution of the parts. The other two trunks of instruments were delivered from the depot once Dr. Hill collected credits from parents. A few children have no instruments yet. Mentioning payment, Dr. Hill assures us that more instruments will arrive in a few weeks.

Dr. Hill joins in to help me, but it's clear that this is my project, so I have to be in charge. I study the pages in the music book that explain how the conductor should wave the arms. It's a pattern. A downward stroke starts the measure, then to the right, to the left, and up before down again – the basic 4x4 measure. Four beats for each measure, that is, and a quarter note gets one beat. I practice all evening, until my arm can't move. Seems a strange custom for a conductor to hold a stick; maybe to threaten musicians if they play wrong notes – I guess.

Dr. Hill helps hand out instruments. He gives instruction on how to care for them. Lots of practical advice. I add my concerns about keeping them clean in the dusty *environs* we have here. Then we try making any sound at all, then making a good sound that's smooth and round, as Dr. Hill says. The young musicians just blow a long note, then another long note. It's a terrible cacophony!

"You don't need the paper music," he tells us, "you can play notes from what is in your head. The paper music is only to remember the song, so everybody plays it together. You just think of the music and you play it. I heard it called the 'think system': you hear the music enough times and you can straightaway play it for yourselves."

I hold up a few pages of our first song to show them what I use: all the parts written on one page, what's called a *score*.

"You see this?" I say to the young musicians. "I can see what all of you are supposed to play. So no getting away with wrong notes."

A few of the kids laugh and I smile at them.

It will be a test for us, and for me: to determine if I'm crazy or not. The first days of basic instruction are hectic and confusing, as I expected, but we have all come together for a purpose. Gradually we sound...*umm*...well, not as bad as we did at the start. At least I can recognize the song.

"Let's try it again," I urge them.

Some get tired, grow impatient, but I keep encouraging them. It takes practice, I remind them, like learning spelling or equations. You have to work at it, but it will give you pride and joy when it's done right. We press on until it's getting dark. I have to let them go home while they can see the way. I'm exhausted but happy.

Then, after days of instruction, it's time for us to rehearse one particular song, just to get us started and to have something to show parents that their investment is a good one.

Dr. Hill recommends a song by a man named Mr. Beethoven. I read his name as *Bee* like the insect and *th* like 'thought', but Dr.

Hill corrects me: *Bay-toe-vin*. The picture in the big book shows an angry man with long tussled hair. It says he couldn't hear anything by the end of his career. That's mighty impressive, that he couldn't hear the music he was writing, but I guess he could hear it just fine in his head. Like the songs I hear, too.

The song Dr. Hill chooses for us is called "Minuet in G". That's because it's a *minuet*, a kind of dance, and it's in the key of G. I'm learning so much. I remember how Dr. Hill played the song on the xylophone at the meeting, using two sticks in each hand. Eve was so delighted she almost wanted to switch to that instrument.

"You give that new cornet a good run first," I say whenever she starts tapping away on those wooden keys. "Then you can switch if you still want to."

+ + +

I play the tuba day and night and the goats are not too happy. They bleat at me, trying to sing along or complain that I should be quiet, even as I get better playing Polly's songs or something from the big book of music. Lots of them in that book. I can match the page in the book with the disk and put the music machine on the porch to hook it to the only electric terminal we have. That way I can play the song on the machine – or any song on any disk, but the electricity is going to be expensive so I limit it to only a few songs each day.

The goats continue to complain. Faith will come out to tell me to stop when it's time for the boys to sleep.

To my tuba practicing, Eve plays her cornet. The first lesson is making our lips buzz. We practice that by kissing, buzzing our lips against the other's lips, but we burst into giggling. She gets the idea and makes a good sound. We work on holding notes even and steady with enough air to keep the tone true. I teach her all the valve combinations and she starts playing different notes. That makes her happy. I caution her to keep the tone even and strong, but she tends to let them fall out of tune.

We play together, me on tuba and Eve on cornet, holding a note or playing a scale. In that way we both improve. Then we find some songs in the music book which I adapted so we have different parts but they sound good played together.

Faith again has something to say about the noise. She fears the goats will stop producing milk. I swear we're not noise. In the book I find a song called "Billy the Kid" by a man named Mr. Copland. The disk only has one song from the whole musical piece, a ballet. *Ballet*, the book says, is another kind of dance. So the music is for folks to dance to. I take Eve's hand and we twirl around as the disk plays, making up our own dance.

Then Faith shouts from inside the cabin: "Y'all sure using up my garden wages with that electric power!"

The only problem is this song is about a gunman named Billy. I think of that Billy back in the capital. I hate that I'm married to him in the official register. It means I can't marry any other person, but I keep my eyes on Eve and feel better. Then there's Dr. Hill, but he's too neat and proper to ever be interested in a country girl like me. We are only business partners.

I keep worrying about what happened to that Billy Kirk after he was arrested. Maybe they released him once they heard his side of the story. Maybe he was sent to jail. Either way, I worry he will find me, somehow figure out the way west and show up one night to get his revenge. I keep Dad's pistol by the bed just in case. It's actually Grandma Isla's pistol but she got it from her dad, who got it from Polly. Frank got some new bullets for it. I've shot at cans with it. I have Eve to protect me, but I doubt the two of us could fight him.

"Ya comin' to bed?" Eve calls, taking me out of my thoughts.

We spend time holding each other before we close our eyes so a long hard day will melt nicely into a soft night of sweet dreams.

"You two gettin' mighty frisky," Faith chides us in the morning, but we don't care, just laugh at her. Her boys will tease us, ask us if we are married and which of us is the husband, which is the wife. I threaten to chase them and they stop teasing us.

Faith shoos them out, sends them off to school. Boys being boys, they take their strapped books and run to town, about a mile along the dirt road, often pausing to chase a rabbit or kill a snake. They're in their seats when I arrive behind them, taking the carriage. They stay after school for a music lesson or band rehearsal, then ride back with me as the sky grows dark. Faith has dinner ready by the time we get home, with Eve serving it to the table for us.

Such fine days we have! Common days with our steady routine. From that I can ignore troubles behind me and anything that might be coming.

I still get spooked easily. Frank laughs at my stories, how I react to every noise in the night or shadow in daylight. He says I'm like our dad. James is always sympathetic but pleads with me to relax and not worry. He says God watches over me. I know Mom does. Eve simply hugs me, tells me she will protect me.

Music improves my mood the best, listening to different songs. Another song by Mr. Copland is "Appalachian Spring" but I don't know what 'Appalachian' is. Frank explains it's a part of the country where the national park is where our dad was born, the place where our great-grandparents hid during the long pandemic. I'm glad to know they have a nice spring there.

"Appalachian Spring" only needs thirteen instruments. Dr. Hill and I agree it will be the center piece of our first concert. He orders the paper music, individual parts and the score. I find it among the disks in the collection, so I put it in the machine. Eve and I listen, shoulder to shoulder on the porch, and I put my arm around her as it ends. We love it! We listen to the song a few times, spinning the disk in the machine until I have it stuck in my head and can play it from what I see in my head. Eve claps at my performance, then joins me as best she can with her cornet. We sound good together!

The tuba part for most songs isn't hard. I can play them without any bad notes. But I long to play melodies. I have songs in my head and try to play them then I scribble the notes on the paper to save them. That proves a hard task and I become amazed even more at those musical people thinking up songs and writing them down in this code for us to play those same songs a hundred years or more later. I have Polly's songs to play, and they are as old as Grandma Isla's birth – a hundred years now. There's a song Polly wrote called "New Baby" that I like to play before going to bed. It's a lullaby.

Slowly I see improvement in our band. The kids like coming to practice and having their lessons with me. I take a lot of joy from their enthusiasm. Parents come by the school from time to time and compliment me. The boys are better behaved having music on their minds, everyone agrees. We ask a seamstress in town to make fancy vests for the boys to wear so everyone knows they are with the band. A few boys march down Main Street, look like a squadron of soldiers on patrol, but they carry musical instruments instead of guns.

Some days when I hold rehearsals after school, I see tribals on their horses posed along the ridge watching us, listening. That has to frighten them, not knowing what the music might mean for them. Are we getting ourselves worked up for an attack? I want to explain to them that our music is completely benign. It's to soothe our sour mood and uplift our spirits. They're welcome to join us or at least come closer to listen. We appreciate having an audience. But Frank doesn't think it's a good idea to include them, never quite sure what they may try to do.

Even so, life goes on, and our musical life expands. The town is full of music: everyone talking about the band, kids going to music lessons and rehearsals, people eagerly awaiting our first concert.

+ + +

Dr. Hill and I have been exchanging messages over the weeks since he left Skinner Canyon, strictly professional until this one arrives:

> *My Dear Maggie,*
>
> *First of all, do allow me to apologize for being so familiar in addressing you; I pray you take no offense. I shall not continue so if it displeases you. However, I do believe that in our time together we have developed a familiar connection to which we both would agree. If I am mistaken, please inform me to the contrary and I shall return to the state of our initial meeting and think no ill will toward you.*
>
> *Secondly, allow me to wish you continuing success with your band endeavor! It is with great feelings of elation that I stand*

ready to assist with any needs you may have, whether they be instruments or accessories, printed music, or uniforms suitable for band members to wear for performance, whether it be in a concert hall setting or in a parade formation. I am always at your service.

I should be especially welcoming of a fresh call to visit you once more, to do what I can to assure your success, and – if I am not too bold – to have the pleasure of another lovely dinner with you. I would dare to risk the wild environs of Kanza country for that stupendous luxury.

Please inform me of whatever you may require and I shall comply forthwith and straightway, as always.

Musically yours,

Hal D. Hill, Ph.D. (Music)

Naturally, I want to send a message back to him right away but Faith cautions me not to send it too soon. He needs to worry a little bit if I will write back, she says. I guess I've been too obvious about my interest. I try to write using pretty words and in the curly style he uses. Perhaps he might think I'm mocking him, so I rewrite the whole message in my own style.

Dear Hal,

There is not any offense taken, I assure you! I agree the time we were together was a pleasure and I may be willing to have subsequent pleasure, if you are so inclined to be the one inviting. I apologize if this remark seems untoward.

Your help has been impossible to forget, although some of the children's parents remind me every day about the costs and the availability of what you have promised for us. Many items have yet to arrive and I receive their complaints. I am not complaining about you and your efforts on our behalf. I merely share with you what the reaction has been – for business information, which I am sure will aid in fine-tuning your company's procedures.

As always, I look forward to your messages, and for your
music wares coming our way soon, as well as – if you should be
so thoughtful – another visit to Skinner Canyon. Dinner shall be
my treat this time, so long as you fluff the pillows

I have to stop myself, wondering if I dare mention that. It seems much too flirty. Do I intend to flirt? Surely he will know I refer to the time we spent in his hotel room before he left. It wasn't anything that we planned. Only a simple suggestion to check information in the catalogue of supplies and fill out an order form – up in his room. Perfectly innocent. It took a couple hours.

When I came down the stairs, Mrs. Beale was there grinning at me. She added an odd wink as I arrived at the front desk.

"Do I need to keep a secret?" she asked, lowering her voice.

She held out her hand, palm open. I didn't know what she meant at first, then I did. So I pulled out a fifty-credit note from my purse and handed it over.

"There is nothing to keep secret," I said as an afterthought, "but I know how it may appear. Best to be discreet in either case."

"And I'll expect my Bonnie to be first chair from her next lesson," she added as I turned to exit. Her daughter wasn't the best of flute players, but I would give her the extra assistance needed to help her improve and achieve first chair.

Going home that night I felt a jumble of feelings as the carriage rolled along. The music, the band, the children. And Dr. Hill, who is such a kind gentleman and subtly handsome in his clean dandy suit. Perhaps that is the reason I feel comfortable with him: just another woman by his gentle mannerisms and personality – not at all like my brother Frank who can be brusque at the drop of a hat and often acting manly to a fault. Yet Hal reacted, responded as I imagine any man would given the circumstance.

I had time to think as Pepper followed the well-trod path home.

Did I do anything wrong? Yes, I decided. Then I wondered why it was wrong. Because of Billy? Because I'm faithful to Eve? Was it so spontaneous there wasn't a moment to raise an objection? Was he so persuasive – hardly a word was spoken, to be honest – or was it me who'd wished to give it a try, see what the fuss was about? Well, Frank said I should find a nice man to marry. And Hal is the nicest man I've ever met. But I didn't know what to do, how to win his heart. So I tripped clumsily through a vain proposal.

"My, my! Dare we?" he practically gasped.

To me it was only to be a test, like picking up a new instrument and giving it a toot to see if it's the one I prefer then setting it back in the case if it's not for me. Or perhaps it could be the instrument I'm meant to play.

I start writing a new message, copying out my text from the first one but I change the end:

> Dinner shall be my treat this time. No further obligations shall
> be necessary.

After a few anxious days, I go to the communications office and send it. I'm not sure if I should but I can't *not* reply. Certainly not after we shared such an intimate episode.

We stood together, leaning over the bed to peruse the catalog we had spread open there. I sensed his hand hovering by my hip, ready to steady me should I lose my balance in that awkward position. As a gentleman. My brothers did that, too, although I'm fit and can balance myself well. Hal and I were discussing the printed music as I bent over to scan the list.

When I straightened up, my backside brushed against his front. It seemed as if a metal tube from a trumpet might be lodged there. As I turned around, his body forced upon me, he blushed innocently. In that quicksilver instant I noticed a change in the topography of his trousers, demonstrating a curious rise of emotion.

"Pardon me," he said, taking a step back.

"Nothing to pardon," I said, claiming that step.

We stood together, gazing eye to eye, my breath quickening, my heart beating faster. His smile remained wary, as if knowing what I wanted yet afraid to offer it. His hands went to my waist, as if called to duty, resting gently upon me.

My eyes closed, inviting him, but no kiss followed.

I opened my eyes, disappointed and feeling foolish.

"A lady's imagination is very rapid," I said, recalling lines from a book I'd found in our library. "It jumps from admiration to love, then from love to matrimony in a mere moment. Or else to sex."

No telling which of us reddened more. Yet we stood tight in the same space, never moved an inch.

"Do let me apologize if I seem too...what's the word? Improper?" I tried to be serious. "Is that it? I only wished.... I don't know how to say it exactly...." I felt panic filling me. "This is new to me, honestly. Perhaps you know.... I only thought that—"

"I confess little experience in this area, too," he stammered. "The pandemic.... Indeed, people hesitate to be intimate for fear of...."

"Forgive me," I said, hardly more than a whisper.

"It isn't that you've no attractive qualities...."

We didn't move, our front sides pressing, our chests breathing as one, that trumpet threatening a fanfare.

"However, I do understand," he said, his voice without breath, as though he feared being heard. "It is indeed a miracle many a couple find themselves facing: the test of true love, as it were. Possibilities. And actions. A scheme of ambition. Ideas swirling about one's head with no place to land."

"We must help them to land," I said, trying to put breath behind my words. "Like a baby bird must eventually leave its nest. A first moment for everything...."

"And everything has its first iteration," he finished.

"It *is* a first time," I said, not knowing how to express my desire. "The first stretching of baby wings, let's say. And the sky is so wide, so high. What shall we do? How do we fly? Do you know, sir?"

He blushed as I felt his firmness against me.

"I must say, to be completely forthright – due to my great respect for you – I do not have a fair degree of expertise in this area. I have, in the alternative, seen a fine collection of pictures in a book or two. I believe those books were intended for...as you call them: cowpokes. Nasty fodder, I'm afraid, for their, umm, self abuse, as it well may be defined. For their secret entertainment. I confess I was forced by dastardly peers to view the unsavory images. Perhaps I retain some knowledge from them."

Wondering if those pictures gave any useful information, I could not refuse. The decision had arrived between two heartbeats, now that the door was open. His foot slid perhaps deliberately between mine yet in that innocuous gesture I recognized the significance of the awful experience I previously endured and how precious this one might be.

"Is it so unsavory?" I dared ask.

"I do believe I might be able to guide you through the steps," he offered, "if you will allow."

"Yes, yes." I tried to catch my breath. "What do we do first? How do we begin? Is there a set of steps, like playing a song?"

"Yes, like playing a song. We put the instrument to our lips."

He leaned forward until our lips met, a sweet kiss, then parted.

"But we do not blow into...do we?" I laughed a little.

"I would not think so, no."

Pondering what to do next, I grabbed his hand and placed it over my breast, feeling its weigh there. He must like that. Cowpokes try to grab women's breasts, after all. Or the rear end. I took his other hand, escorted it to the curve of my posterior. He seemed to know what to do by then, my move prodding his memory. His hand slid over the curve as we remained eye to eye.

"Is that all right?" I asked. "You don't find it *untoward*?"

"Not untoward at all," he mumbled, and we kissed again, longer.

His hands slowly departed from where I'd placed them and his fingers engaged a new task: releasing the buttons of my blouse. I breathed deeply as he carefully, gingerly slid my moist blouse off my shoulders, letting it fall blithely to the floor. A kiss. I unclasped my brassiere to reveal my naked chest. Yet he didn't display the delight I expected. I wondered if he'd ever seen a female bosom before.

"I...I think I'm supposed to kiss them," he muttered nervously.

"That's the next step?" I could barely get the words out.

Then he was like a baby searching for milk, his tongue slopping over the nozzle and making everything wet.

"Please do what you think is best," I told him. "Whatever may be the next step. We were never taught such things in my school in the capital. Being productive was the lesson. Sex was a science lesson:

white rabbits and black rabbits."

"That is a serious regret," he mumbled from against my chest.

His hands hesitated, light upon my breasts, his eyes widening at the sight of them: like a hungry man before a buffet.

"We must play by ear," I said, drowned by my heartbeats.

"I think we know instinctively what to do," he said, raising his head from my nipple. "I am sure our hearts will guide us."

We worked through each step, seemed to presume the next ones: falling upon the squeaky bed, crushing the catalogue, my skirt off, his trousers ringing his ankles, then rushing to the sacred touches which managed to feel proper, racing to the strange yet satisfying meeting of body and soul in an inner fire I'd never felt before: brief moment of agony that unlocked the gate, erupting into outrageous glory that let me glimpse heaven.

We lay together under the sheet, breathing hard.

"I apologize if I was too heavy atop you," I thought to say after a long silence.

"No, no – not at all. I rather enjoyed it that way," he whispered, gasping for breath. "That's how the picture was."

"We both must be about the same weight," I said stupidly.

"Yes, yes, the same." More raspy breaths. "I liked what you did."

"It was good." I grinned. "I understand why it's called the cowgirl stance. And the saddle is...*you*."

His hair had become messy, mustache limp, his city man's body now slick with unsightly moisture.

"Sorry," was the only word I could think to say.

Slipping out from under the sheet, I dressed quickly as he gazed at me. Only then, with me fully dressed and he still naked under the sheet, did it feel awkward, now that we'd finished the forbidden act. It felt like I was the cowpoke ready to run and he the poor saloon gal mourning the end of the episode.

"I know the sound of a bed being shook," Mrs. Beale had said as I headed for the doors.

The next morning my nephews Jeb and Joe took Dr. Hill out to the depot for the train back to Kanza City.

Nobody asked me about Dr. Hill or what might've happened that evening. Eve could've noticed something different about me, like the way I acted *so tired*, not needing our usual close time but wanting to go straight off to sleep. She kissed my cheek anyway, said I smelled funny. I hadn't noticed his cologne sticking to me.

Later, on random days, I would go out to the edge of the canyon, check around for snakes, then sit and stare at the sunset, watching as reds and oranges, pinks and blues, smudged across the horizon like paint. I'd think of music to fit the scene. I'd hum a few tunes I knew from the disks. I made up a song or two. I put my lips together and whistled like Dad taught me when I was little. A lot of thinking: about Dad, Mom, my cousin Eve, all the people who went before me, and that awful Billy Kirk.

I thought of Dr. Hill, considering whether I might be of a mind to marry such as him. If he made a baby in me then I probably would. Mom taught me to count the days, which seemed an easy thing at first. In our poor western town there isn't a lot of other methods to put off what came naturally. Yet nothing Mom warned me to watch for occurred, so I supposed I was free from any lingering effects of that evening's dalliance.

However, the sting of my betrayal crawled through me, like sand rubbing in a wound, never letting me forget.

It's good that Time goes on like it does – like it always does, never concerned with us folks down here on this dusty earth, feeling the dry wind in our faces, or the hot sun beating down, or lightning crackling through the dark skies, or tornadoes twisting, or blizzards during the winters. For a few days this is a lovely place to be.

I gaze out from the rocky rim of Skinner Canyon once more, but can't ever see far enough across the landscape or far enough into the future, for that matter, to know my fate. What's a grown woman to do? I'm going on twenty-five and only have the steady life of a school teacher to sustain me. What else is there for me? The band? Is that a start to something bigger or only a band?

The future hides behind thunderheads that darken the plains at the far limit of my eyes, coming for me.

12

OLD BETTY, JACKRABBIT, AND A BAD DAY

I THROW MYSELF INTO THE BAND every day, studying the big book and the music scores, teaching myself everything, staying two chapters and three lessons ahead of the kids. I have to make this thing real or my efforts will be for nothing. It is becoming a religion, with earnest prayers spoken daily, rituals repeated faithfully: *Please let everything go well today.* Even my brother, Father James, notices how devout I've become, obsessed with my goal, and he cautions me to give myself a break sometimes. I tell him I'll rest when our first concert is done.

To relax at the end of the day, I take Dad's tuba in my lap and blow out some songs, half just made up to vent my frustration. Eve likes to sit on the porch with me and listen patiently. Or sometimes she will take out her cornet and try to play along. That sure makes a strange noise!

Despite my continued improvement, Faith hollers when I play that tuba out behind the cabin, saying I'm killing her garden and frightening the goats. I didn't think a tuba could have that kind of effect. The goats know who I am and shouldn't be afraid. But Faith insists I go off a ways to do my practicing.

I put the tuba in the carriage and hitch up our old plow horse, Betty, short for 'betcha can't pull a carriage', a stubborn creature if ever there was one, and off we ride down a dirt road leading to who knows where but not any place I've ever been before. The road ends eventually, pitters out to nothing, only scrub. I'm lost well enough that I feel safe to play my tuba.

I release Betty from the staves but keep her on a loose tether so she can wander a bit and enjoy the day, munching on whatever she finds and fancies.

Sitting on the end of the carriage's bench, I set the tuba in my lap. I run through basic exercises first. I play some of Granny Polly's songs. I especially like one called "Sandy's Bride" but I'm not sure if the last note of each phrase is correct; sounds like a wrong note, but I guess she meant them to be that way if she's describing in music form how my dad's grandparents got along being newly married.

Betty doesn't give a hoot what I do, never looks cross at me like Faith does. So I play more and let the notes sail through the dusty air, blowing them far and wide, and whoever hears them might feel the same joy I feel by playing them. A tuba's thunderous tone seems perfectly suited for this wild chaparral country, a voice thicker than the wind, rolling hard over the sage and cactus, like God is giving a lecture on how to make our garden grow then apologizing for giving us this scrubland.

It's a wonderful thing, music, the way hearing a bunch of sounds in some kind of purposeful arrangement can lift your spirits, make you want to dance, make you want to move or, equally, make you sit still for a while and just think thoughts you never could find in the silences. I like both kinds of music. Eve does, too. She's happy to sit with me whenever I practice. She only practices her cornet when I'm away, afraid I'll complain about her playing wrong notes. I'm glad she takes an interest in the band. We walk down Main Street with heads held high and everyone knows us as the 'music ladies'. We often declare "We're with the band" to part a crowd or enter a shop.

Maybe townsfolk are amused by us, happy to let us pretend to be musicians. Easier than complaining and causing a ruckus. Most of them are polite, well-behaved, generally kind people. I take Eve's arm or we hold hands, safe together. We get comments, but we don't mind. We are 'more than sisters', Eve says, although we're actually cousins. Most of all we're musicians.

Eve is a great help with after-school practice sessions. She gets students in order for their lessons with me. She runs them through drills. She helps with the music notation quizzes. She polishes the brass instruments and wipes down the woodwinds. She likes to play the percussion instruments because she can make a sound without blowing air through a tube. She goes straight over to the xylophone when we arrive at school each day and hammers out a song on the wooden bars. I praise each new song she invents and that makes her smile. I suggest she give the songs titles. "This here song's called 'A Woodpecker's Gotta Peck'." She laughs, hitting the wooden keys in rapid succession. I can't imagine a day without Eve in my life.

Sitting on the carriage, I finish working on a difficult song that Polly wrote. The title at the top of the page is: *Concerto for Tuba.* There is supposed to be an orchestra playing, too, but I look out at the waving grasses and wonder where they are. It's only me here. I don't have the orchestra pages anyway, but she must've written them. I like the tune she composed: a lively dance right from the start, music we can move to, then the blank parts when the tuba rests and the orchestra plays. Then more of the tuba playing. At that point, it's too difficult for me to play, even if I go slow. But Polly was a professional tuba player and excellent according to Grandma Isla, the last to hear her play, back when Isla was just a baby.

The date Polly wrote on that first page is the date of the first lockdown in their city when the pandemic arrived. They taught us the date in school, said we should forever remember it, then later told us to forget it. Polly had time to write this long piece of music: three movements. Things got worse, not better, and after six years, she took her teenage son, Sandy, and left the city. They got to an island where they thought they would be safe, but she was killed there, murdered. She never got to hear this music performed. And everything got much worse after that.

Now I have the same tuba she took with her, passed down from Sandy to Isla, to my dad, and now me.

The sun has shifted and I've lost my will to play more. I decide to pack up and return to the cabin. I'm far out in sagebrush country. Dust has coated the tuba, so I take my time carefully wiping it off, being gentle so the grains won't scratch the gray metal. When it was new it was a shiny silver.

As I sit on the carriage, I see a pair of people walking toward me. I look harder, identify them as tribals. But there's no time to hitch the horse to the carriage and ride away.

"Howdy!" I call as they arrive. I don't want to be unfriendly; we all have to share this land.

A girl about fourteen and an old man, probably her grandfather, who looks a hundred years old but still walks, halt before me. The grandfather wears a sleeveless red/white/blue plaid shirt and rough, ragged dungarees, looking like a cowpoke. His long hair is in two braids with a colorful band around his head. He sits down right there in the last of the road, crossing his legs with the ease of a child. The girl tries to help him down but he waves her off, speaks a few words to her.

The girl is dressed similarly: clothes like the cowpokes wear, not girl clothes, not tribal clothes. But she has soft leather shoes on her feet. Her braided hair has feathers tied to the ends. She remains standing, then she makes a gesture of greeting.

"Hi, how are you?" I say.

The grandfather points to the carriage, to where the tuba leans, and speaks some words. Of course, I don't understand him. The girl listens, then turns to me.

"He wanna know what's that thing," she says in English, adding a smile. "He thinks it's big gun."

I laugh, then explain what it is and why we made it, how it is used in an orchestra, and a lot about music they probably don't care to know. She says the old man heard it on the wind and worried. He had to see if it was dangerous.

"It's not any kind of weapon," I say, "although my cousin thinks it damages the plants in her garden."

The girl translates to her grandfather, and he grins.

"He says it's not problem," says the girl, "as long as it isn't the Great Spirit giving a warning about something."

"No, it's definitely not God, not the Great Spirit, just something a man thought to make a long time ago. Now it's here. It's been in my family for more than a hundred years."

"He is hundred years in my family, too," she says, gesturing at her grandfather. "He is less noise." She laughs and her grandfather snaps at her.

I tell her about starting a band in town. I go on and on, venting my frustration, listing the problems I've faced. Then I catch myself and apologize for rambling.

Every sentence or two she turns to translate my words. She is a clever girl. I ask where she learned English and she says from the Wizard Woman. I know she means my mother who often visited the villages offering medical help and teaching them English. She tried to learn their language, too.

Since the pandemic, tribes returned to their original languages and the elders forbid learning the settlers' language. We could keep apart or else try to share this land. Someone has to learn the other's language if we are to communicate, get along, or do any trading.

"She's my mother," I tell the girl, who says it to the old man. He claps in delight. "I'm Maggie, her daughter. What's your name?"

"Jackrabbit," she replies. "*Mashcí"ge.*"

That makes me chuckle. "What a funny name."

"What Maggie mean?" she comes back. "It's funny name, too."

"Yes, I suppose it is," I say, believing it now that I think of it. "I don't know what it means, actually. Yours is clear. So I will call you Jackrabbit, if you like."

She laughs like I said something funny. "Call me Jackie."

"That's fine." I recall someone in my family being named Jackie but who it was escapes me at that moment.

"His name is Tall Bear," she says.

"Not so many bears out in these parts," I say in amused tone.

"He come from mountains," she responds, pointing west. "Many bears there. He kill five bears when he is young."

I give the old man a sincere greeting, showing my respect for his age and wisdom. I imagine my dad's father, Frank senior, being the same age if he had lived.

We talk more about the band. Jackie seems interested. She asks lots of questions on her own, some from her grandfather. Back and forth we talk, with her pausing to say some of it to Tall Bear. He waves her to continue.

I tell her about Kanza City, what I learned from Dr. Hill.

"We know the place. Big village. We never visit there, too far by horse," says Jackie, looking a bit sad.

"I went through it on a train. Do you know trains?"

"We know trains. We not dumb. Iron horse, hah hah."

"I'm sorry, Jackie."

"It's no worry. It's *ooo-kay*." She smiles at me like I'm a child.

She explains how the people of her tribe run Kanza City, taking the leadership roles. It started with gaming houses, Mom told me, until they finally owned everything. They allow people who aren't Kanza or other tribes to continue business free of any interference. However, there is a fee paid to the tribe for credits earned. Tribal tax, they call it. Someday, Jackie says, she will visit Kanza City and see if it's a good place to start a family. Many hungry men there.

And the sun drops lower, the wind picking up.

Finally Jackie asks and gets approval from Tall Bear to try the band. She makes him believe she will be a spy for them, seeing what evil the settlers are up to. She will learn the magical music spells.

I don't know the Kanza language. Jackie tries to teach me some of the words. Pointing to Old Betty, she says "*shóⁿge*" and then says "horse". She rubs her belly, says "*ilózhu*". I get it.

She pulls a bracelet off her arm, gives it to me. "This is *áxebe*," she says. "Gift for you, Maggie."

I don't have anything to give in return. So I unclasp my favorite belt, slip it from the loops, and hand it to her. "Please."

"Thanks – *Wíblaha*," she says with a big grin. "*Waché áyusta*."

"That means 'belt', I'm guessing."

"Yes – *Oⁿhá*."

"It is *shábe* – brown."

"Ong-hay," I say and she laughs at my pronunciation.

She's so darling I want to hug her, but I hold back, unsure of the customs. She is welcome to come to band practice, I tell her, so we can talk more then.

Her grandfather says Jackie can bring a drum, although only the men are allowed to bang on the drum in the village. In the town she will be a different girl, can pretend to be a settler.

"He say I am extra girl, so no loss if bad comes to me," she says. Tall Bear speaks again and Jackie translates: "Also, he want you to guard me from dirty settlers."

I readily agree.

"We are always happy to welcome new musicians," I say, adding a gesture of welcome for the sake of her grandfather. Jackie tells me I don't need to do the funny gestures.

Agreeing on everything, I begin to put the tuba in its case. But the grandfather has to touch it. He slides his fingers up and down the big tube and around the bell, like he hopes to absorb its magic. Jackie says they have listened to me for a long time before daring to approach me.

"It is an honor to have an audience," I say.

I watch them depart as the late afternoon sunshine hits my face. Jackie pauses three times on the path to turn and wave back as they go. I wave to them.

My long skirt slips low on my hips without the belt. I hitch it up but it settles down again. I pull the bracelet Jackie gave me onto my wrist and admire it.

Then, as I pull Betty back to hitch her to the staves, she gets a spook from a snake and jumps backwards, knocking me down.

The horse's rump is in the air over me, rear legs scrambling for a place to put hooves down. One hoof lands on the point of my hip as I twist away – but not in time and the pain of bone breaking erupts through me. Betty finds steady ground but the injury is done.

I lay in pain, my arm outstretched – just as that snake wriggles toward me, its rattles sounding. Betty, not seeing the snake, sets a hoof down on it and cuts the snake in two.

My shrieking in pain sails on the wind, all the way to Jackie and her grandfather a half-mile down the road. They hurry back to me, see the injury and help steady me. I can't move. It's more pain than I've ever felt before. The grandfather instructs Jackie to go get help, and she follows her name, racing down the road as fast as she can.

The grandfather stays with me, speaking a prayer over me.

He gets up, goes into the brush and gathers particular plants. Beating them against a rock, he gets their juice out, rubs it between his hands. He pulls back the top of my skirt, places his wet hands there. It eases the pain, but it won't mend broken bone. I fear then I will never have a child – the first time I've ever worried about that.

I learn later how Jackie ran for help. She got to the cabin, and she and Faith drove the wagon to me. Frank arrived later, fetched by Faith's sons. They wrapped me tight so the break wouldn't move, and lifted me carefully onto the back of the wagon. Frank drove us into town, going slow to ease the pain, while Faith brought the carriage back to the cabin. I was in too much pain to thank Jackie and her grandfather. Then I passed out.

+   +   +

Faith likes to tell the story, even as she sees me frowning again. She seems to enjoy tormenting me. But she does care for me, I know, and lets us live in her cabin without us paying. We're all family, she is quick to remind us.

I don't remember much because I was unconscious. The old town doctor was having his daily nap but snapped awake at Frank's loud call from out front. They moved me into the examination room and the doc just shook his head, poking at the badly bruised corner of my hip. He feared my whole pelvis was broken, that my insides were in a bad way. Further examination let him give a sigh of relief. Not as bad as he first thought. I had to stay in bed there for a week with his wife, Bertha, and daughter, Becky, tending to me. Their little boy, Bobby, would look in at me from time to time.

"Sure enough, Miss Maggie," said Dr. Baker. "As you suspected, we can't do much about that break but let it mend on its own time. You're gonna be on your back a while, any case. No walking for you. Not now, not for a spell, and – heck, sorry to say it – maybe never again. We got to see how it mends."

I wept until Eve arrived and held my hand. She spoke soft words to me. I didn't listen, didn't bother to comprehend, just the sound of her voice soothing me as she caressed my hand, brushed my hair.

Jackie visited me at the doctor's office. Then she accompanied us back to the cabin when it was time. She stayed with us like a new boarder. Faith liked her the same as she enjoyed seeing a new kid pop out of her best nanny goat and prance around.

"That Jackrabbit," Faith would say to me, "she sure did show off her name. Never saw a girl run so fast. Faster'n any boy I seen. If'n she was any slower maybe you woulda died out there."

I had to agree, not recalling the details. I sat in discomfort in the chair they made for me, fixed with extra cushions and wheels to roll me around. I couldn't do much more than sit and listen to Faith as she rattled on, half the time words of encouragement and the other half complaints about needing to care for a cripple when she had lots of work that needed doing.

She liked Jackie, though, and thought of hiring her to help with gardening. Eve noticed.

"Cousin Eve," said Faith, "you can keep on helping in the garden and we'll let Jackrabbit look after our Maggie. She's mighty good at fetching things quick, ain't she?"

I saw Eve give Jackie a hard stare. Maybe it would be better for a new person to do things for me. There was no date for me to look forward to when I would be healed. It could be forever. I've been ordered to stay in the wheel-chair or lay on the bed for six months. No pressure on my leg, Dr. Baker insisted, and stay away from horses.

13

A COLD PRAIRIE WINTER

SITTING IN THIS CHAIR set on wheels, I try to keep up my study of the big book of music. I consider whether I can continue teaching the kids. Classes were cancelled for two weeks, then parents stepped up to teach what they knew. Yet nobody knew music, not like me. Kids became discouraged without their regular lessons. I sent out instructions for them to practice what they'd learned and be ready to play it for me soon.

The arrival of the first winter storm, though still in autumn out here, put a halt to the planning and practicing. Parents complained again about the cost of their children's interest in this famous band I promised. Instruments arrived – some of them. Not all. I wrote to Dr. Hill to ask about them. I was too ashamed to dare mention my accident, certain he had designs on our relationship. He wrote back assuring me he would check on the issue.

Then, as winter came on full, boys needed to help with rounding up cattle and tending to them. Girls helped at home. I grew more anxious, feeling that the band was a hopeless endeavor. If it was going to be a reality, it was up to me. Me alone. Now the only music I heard was Eve playing her cornet occasionally or putting a disk in the machine. We chose calm music to help me relax. I thought to play the tuba, yet it hurt to have the big thing on my lap. Besides, it reminded me of that bad day. When Eve held it for me while I tried to play, the vibration from playing made my whole body rattle with pain and I had to give it up.

I spent countless hours sitting in my chair as terrible thoughts marched through my head. My cousins tended to the garden and the animals, fighting the cold wind and blowing snow while I sat near the fireplace, a blanket over my legs, feeling useless. Sometimes I would roll myself to the porch to use the electric terminal despite the cold, and play a disk in the machine until Faith complained.

"You're gonna make a big electric bill," she'd say in a calm voice which cut deeper than when she got angry.

"I can pay for it," I told her.

"Where you get that kinda credit?" she challenged.

"From my mother's legacy. And from my father's."

"You got that kind of credit? Then why you ain't been payin' me these past years?"

"Why? I thought we were related. Like sisters almost, so...."

"I ain't too proud to accept credits."

"Then I'll pay you." I took a moment, calculating. "And I'll pay for Jackie's help, too. Will that satisfy you?"

"That would surely help a lot."

Jackie comes a few days each week to help me, other days she has to mind her grandfather. "To keep him away from trouble," she says. Tall Bear tends to take everything too seriously, still caught up in the new-found freedom of the pandemic when settlers stayed indoors and the prairie was open again. No more 'iron sheep' rolling along the stone roads, he was happy to discover.

She still wants to join the band but, as I explain to her, not much is happening with me stuck in a chair.

"I fear the kids have stopped practicing," I say in mournful tone. "They'll lose interest, forget to take out their instruments even to give them a toot just for fun. Then we'll either have to start again from scratch or it will never start again and everything will be lost."

Jackie starts patting my shoulders when I voice my concerns. I like having her here. Not much she has to do for me, grab this or that, put a lunch together for us. Mostly we talk. I learn more of her language and village history which fascinates me. Makes me think of my mother's visits there and how much she enjoyed them. But I know I'm not going anywhere.

I think of riding into town on the carriage, but Frank has seen to that plow horse, putting Old Betty down and giving her over to the butcher. Dr. Baker said I might've been put down, too, if I'd been a horse instead of a woman.

I try to get word to Myra and Tess, the mothers who cover my classes, that Jackie wouldn't mind helping, if they want her. I offer to pay her wage. They decline, and not politely either. They aren't keen on the idea or Jackie herself. Who could hate a teenage girl? I feel disappointment in my fellow townsfolk, acting that harsh way, thinking in that limited manner. Jackie is a good girl, I explain. Her contributing a drum to the band doesn't sway them.

I apologize to Jackie for those women.

"Grandfather say people of different ways better not live in same place," says Jackie. "If push together they argue and fight. Not good. He say if they agree to share ways then each people lose their way and they not those people any longer."

I have to nod in agreement. She is a smart girl.

"That's likely why your people and mine keep apart so willingly," I tell her, wondering whether it is the best way to live. I know what Mom would say. "Well, I like you, and I like having you here."

"I like be here, too."

That is a comforting moment that gives me some hope.

Seeing how everything is going south further disappoints me. It can only be me if we are to get the band back together. Nobody has the knowledge or skill, or the motivation to make it happen.

I write to Dr. Hill, asking for ideas – and some encouragement. He writes back saying it's common for young musicians to give up once the novelty of the experience wears off and they have to put more effort to progress. I know that from making myself practice the tuba. It is hard but I force myself to play it more, until my lips are numb and my back aches – and now I dare not hold it in my lap for fear of pain. My skills will fade.

I must at least get to the school house, to lead the kids once more in rehearsal, see how much they've lost by sitting idle. But wintry roads don't make it easy to roll a chair like mine. Wouldn't be any easier transferring me and my chair to a wagon, either. Frank's had enough of that idea after three attempts. He was willing to keep on trying for me, but I saw how miserable he looked helping me, so I let him go with my thanks. When the winter ends, I should be mended enough to go to the school house.

James comes down from the chapel to see how I am mending. Attendance at Sunday services drops off during the winter but he makes the long trek through the snow to visit me.

"Perhaps it's a blessing in a strange, roundabout way," he says after we've talked a while. "As though God is telling you to take a rest from your stress. You're allowed a good rest. You have the same disposition as Dad. Worrying about everything, like the world is reliant on you alone."

"I don't think it's a blessing," I respond. "But I guess I do have some of Dad's ways."

He says a lovely prayer over me and whether it works we will have to wait and see.

And so I sit, day by day, watching snow fall and the wind blow, some days full of sun that makes you feel warm and plenty of cloudy days that look colder than they are. I see tribals riding by on their horses once in a while, taking long looks at the music lady's home, knowing one of their girls works here. Sometimes, when Jackie is outside, she waves at them and they raise a hand in reply.

At night, Eve eases me onto the bed and hopes I don't wince in pain. She returns to her bed across the room so she won't jostle me as we slept. I lie awake much of the night, worrying that as soon as I fall asleep, I'll turn over and that will bring pain. Staying in one position is hard. When I do fall asleep and move too much and burst awake at the pain, Eve comes over, kneels beside my bed, speaks soft words to me and pats my hand.

I'm supposed to take care of her. That's the agreement we made without words being spoken. Although she's older, I know she has a young mind and needs my help and my protection. Now I can't do much of either. I need her help now but she's always ready to assist me and never complains.

Having little medical knowledge, I take what Dr. Baker said to heart: maybe I won't walk again. He comes out to check on me a few times over the winter weeks. He throws back my gown and puts his fingers to my hip, poking and pinching. I feel pain but try to remain calm. He thinks the bone is setting right and he doesn't know why there should be so much pain.

"I do detect some fragments," he says seemingly to himself, "that aren't fusing. That could be a source of pain. May need to cut them out. But missing those chips shouldn't affect your ability to stand up or walk a step or two."

I'm grateful for an explanation.

So Frank gets me and my chair up on the wagon with the aid of Faith, Eve, Jeb, and Jackie. My maturing nephew has eyes for my young helper, who appeared about fourteen at first but was actually sixteen. Jackie rides with us into town. They help unload me from the wagon, Frank lifting me in his strong arms, and carrying me as gently as he can into the doctor's office. James arrives soon after and I fear he's come to give a final prayer if things go wrong.

A surgery room is prepared and the doctor's wife assists. They give me some funny air to relax me and push a needle into my hip to numb the area, then proceed to cut into my hip, digging out the fragments that loosely impale my flesh whenever I move. Twelve of them, the smallest no more than a needle sliver and the largest like a tooth. He stitches me again and I stay there until the effects of the medicine fade.

"That should do it," says Dr. Baker. "Might not look pretty."

Frank gets me ready for the trip home.

"But first," I insist groggily, "take me by the school house. It's still school hours and I want to see the kids."

So Frank takes me there and the kids come out despite the cold and surround the wagon to greet me. The sun breaks through the clouds. I must look a fright, but they are kind, speak kind words. Many ask when I will return. A few ask me if we are still going to have a band.

My heart bursts with joy, so glad for their enthusiasm. I clasp hands with many kids, tell them to keep practicing, especially the "Minuet in G". That will be our first song.

"I'll see you soon," I tell them. "We'll have a good rehearsal."

I can stand, maybe with crutches, and wave the baton in front of them. I can brace myself against the lectern. It will be good to have them play something, anything, no matter how poorly. Parents want to hear something, to see their investment pay off.

Once home, I start to compose a new message to Dr. Hill, and I explain in detail about my accident and how it affects the band's progress. I don't know why but I ask whether he will be visiting this way soon – to check our band's development, of course, in a strictly professional capacity. I don't think it seems too forward.

His reply is endlessly delayed; I wait and wait until I give up hope of receiving a reply. Perhaps he has no further interest in me because of my accident. I'm injured and might never recover. Of course I understand, but I feel good that I've been honest with him. Maybe he won't ever visit again.

I'm thankful I have Eve.

One night, she takes her cornet and tries to play a song or two to make me happy. The way she puts the mouthpiece to her lips is off-center, sounds lazy, makes the notes fall away rather than staying true. I correct her *embouchure*, the position of the mouth on the mouthpiece, but she slips back into her lazy style after a while. However, the more I listen, the more her song matches how I feel. I recall hearing a song like hers on one of the disks – it started next after the song I was listening to ended – and it's in the same style: 'lazy music'. A little sad, too. The book lists the song as an example of 'blues' and gives a description of the style and its history.

"You're playing *blues*," I say to her. "Skinner Canyon blues."

"What blues ya talkin' 'bout?"

"The blues I've got," I reply, teasing her. "Oh, yes, I've got those Skinner Canyon blues."

"What blues ya meanin'?"

"*Stuck in my chair, like a sleepy ol' bear*," I sing. "*Can't dance with Eve, can't kiss my Steve.*"

"Who's Steve?"

"*Just sitting in my chair all alone every day, I've got the Skinner Canyon blues. Oh, yeah. Those Skinner Canyon blues.*"

"You're silly, Mags!" Eve laughs, then puts the cornet to her lips and plays whatever she likes that fits with my singing.

"*Oh, yeah, I've got those Skinner Canyon Blues....*"

We laugh and try a new song, me thinking up the words and she playing notes to go with them. We keep on with our musical game until Faith comes to remind us her boys are trying to sleep and it's a school night.

+   +   +

The cross-country railway has been blocked for weeks with the snow covering the tracks but, eventually, as a brief thaw arrives, the train comes, delivering various goods and messages from far away. One result is more of the instruments Dr. Hill promised were sent. Also, a message for me.

> *Dear Maggie,*
>
> *It is with much sorrow that I regret to inform you of my long illness which has forced me to the infirmary these many weeks. However, worry not for the affliction has ended and was never the Great Virus of the past. I am, however, left in a weakened state, and my physician suggests I may never fully recover my youth and vigor. It is with great shame that I must excuse myself from any and all travel in the near-term.*
>
> *In addition, I regret that your musical purchases have not yet arrived as scheduled. I fear such delay may have disrupted your plans and preparation. Let not your heart be troubled for good music is always worth the wait. I am assured the items were sent in a timely manner from our manufacturing facility and should be on the way. They may yet arrive prior to this message.*
>
> *Lastly, as our relations appear to have met an untimely impasse, despite a pleasant evening once upon a time (if I dare to remind you), I recommend that we continue on strictly as*

professional actors acting for the benefit of our special missions. I remain at your service musically, as always, and sincerely wish you the best in your career. I shall forever applaud your determination and talent. You are an inspiration to all!

Musically yours,

Hal D. Hill, Ph.D. (Music)

Honestly, I wasn't expecting much from him, given the long wait for a reply. The winter weather might be a fair excuse, yet he wrote his message, according to the date on it, soon after mine must've arrived, before the first blizzard. I do feel bad that he suffered an illness, but in my belly I feel he's presenting me false information. It isn't a big disappointment; it was expected.

I focus on the new instruments and other items that arrived. My nephews Jeb and Joe help deliver them around town. Everyone is happy. That makes my heart soar although getting out in the cold causes my hip to ache fiercely. I push myself to make it to the school house. The wheel-chair doesn't move smoothly over packed snow but it rolls better than over loose dirt. It slid a bit more than necessary, yet I managed not to tip over or get stuck along the path that my nephews shoveled.

Mrs. Booker, volunteer teacher, is surprised to see me approach. She calls the kids and they rush out to greet me and help me inside. They are happy to see me again. That raises my spirits. They roll me to the fireplace as I catch my breath. Am I back for good? When can we rehearse? Will I really marry that music salesman?

I hold my hands up to end their questions.

"Life is hard," I say to them, then have to take a breath. "Rolling my chair over the path isn't easy. But I want to come back. I want to get started again. I haven't forgotten you. Yes, we must get the band back together. We have a concert to prepare."

The kids cheer. Some kids try to give me hugs but Mrs. Booker cautions them not to touch me for fear of causing me pain. I haven't taken medicine today so my mind is clear, but so is my discomfort.

But I smile to let them know they haven't hurt me.

"I will be right soon enough," I say. "I've been studying music all this time and I'm ready to continue lessons. We can have our first rehearsal very soon."

Then I notice someone standing at the rear of the room: my dear helper, Jackie. I didn't know she was attending school. I thought she returned to her village to care for her grandfather. When she sees me looking at her, she frowns like she's been caught in some bad behavior. I wave her forward.

"That's Bunny," says Karen, a teenage student.

"We call her that," says Karen's friend, Helena, "because she's as fast as a bunny."

"Her real name's Jackrabbit," says Fanny, as if I didn't know.

"She never says nothing," David tells me in a complaining voice. "Not even her 'injun' talk."

"Please be kind," I speak out. "Jackie is my friend."

They get quiet as I roll myself down the aisle to her.

Jackie is tearful as I arrive in front of her. I ask why she cries.

"Grandfather died," she tells me.

"Oh, no. I'm so sorry," I say. We try to hug, despite the awkward position with me in the chair. "He was very old, wasn't he? And this winter has been particularly harsh. But why are you here? In this school house?"

"Grandfather," she begins, then wipes her tears, "his last words. Go to school. Learn all you can. Return and teach us. Lead us into a better life." She cries more and I squeeze her hand.

I turn to the group of kids. "You treat her kindly. She's like us. We are like her. I'm sure she knows a lot more than any of you, and can do more, too."

"She can run fast," Benjamin offers.

"Sometimes we chase her away," says Nate, lowering his head.

"But nobody can catch her," says Jimmy.

"We have to share," I say, still holding her hand. "Now apologize and let's be friends."

The kids mumble their apologies.

"I like her," says little Gregory from behind the others. "She gave me buffalo jerky that time."

"It's not about what you get from someone," I say, "it's what you can do for someone. And why's that? Why would you want to help someone?" It's a good moment for an important lesson.

"Because it's a nice thing to do...?" Sarah offers.

"Not *nice* – the *right* thing to do," I answer.

"But how do you know?" asks Kyle.

"If you can help, you should help," I say. "That's easy enough to remember, isn't it?"

"It's fabulous to have you back," says Mrs. Booker. "Sure does sound like you're back."

The kids give a cheer.

Jackie steps forward, pushes my wheel-chair to the front of the room, turns me to face the kids. She adjusts the blanket over my legs and I thank her.

"Now what were you learning before I interrupted?"

"It was History," Mrs. Booker announces. "I was telling them what happened over the ocean in Europe while we was having that pandemic. The rise of an empire that took over most of the continent before war started. Invasion from the east ended that blood-thirsty cult. Thankfully, that vile emperor disappeared. Lots of different things happened over there than what we experienced here. Folks called *vampires* took over. But not to worry, I'm not telling anything outside of the textbook."

"That's fine," I tell her, uncertain about European history.

I'd only read some reports in the news-paper about Europe, how they dealt with the pandemic and their own disruption of society. A cult arose in the southeastern region that took over the whole land. People were forced to pledge allegiance to Emperor Stefan of House Székely, the chief vampire. Likely their affliction was the hideous effect of the virus; they could only sustain themselves by consuming blood. Maybe it was only a nasty rumor. Being far away from that, it seems like only a horror tale to frighten children.

"Leave all of that talk about Europe to the politicians."

"But we can finish tomorrow," says Mrs. Booker. "You can teach whatever you like, Missus Kirk. Feel free."

My whole body twitches at that name. Everyone in town knows the story by now: our dear lady went to the capital and married a man who died the next day in an accident. How sad! Poor Maggie! All she has to keep her going is her crazy idea to start a band in this dusty town.

I shake it off and begin quizzing the kids on music terms first. I tell them about me and Eve coming up with a few songs to play at the Cimarron Music Festival in summer. Maybe we can win a prize. I explain about 'blues' but I can only show them. I sing "Skinner Canyon Blues" for them and they clap in appreciation. For the next song, Jackie adds a steady drum beat. The kids cheer her on. I see Hank, Mrs. Booker's teenage son, giving attention to Jackie from the side of the room. I recognize that look on his face: the pining of infatuation.

I never had that when I was young. But I didn't mind. I believed the government would match me with a suitable partner, just as we were taught. At thirteen I would've been tested for fertility and if I passed, I would've been directed into the breeding program. Long before my age of registration, however, Mom brought us out west where there were only cowpokes to look at me, me dressed the same as them. I didn't care how I looked, didn't want them. Then Hal D. Hill comes into my life: a handsome dandy with all his fancy words. He was like a fresh breath of air to blow away the dirt and dust. And that curly mustache!

Eve teased him about it once: "Like yer lip hair, it's like a extra smile." He didn't take offense, said it was the fashion in Kanza City.

I rather like it too. A tickle with the kiss.

Regarding Mrs. Booker, I know I'm like her in one way: an adult with responsibilities. And unlike her, too. I don't have any children to look after – nobody to look after me when I'm old, either. A tear pops from my eye, rolls obviously down my cheek. One girl standing near me asks what it's for, as though there must be a one-to-one correspondence between a tear and a thought.

"Just a speck of dust that got in my eye," I say.

14

CONCERT SEASON

"WHEN WE GONNA GET TO HEAR this fantastic band you been growing?" asks Mrs. Butler, the mother of our lead clarinet player, Felix. "Lotsa lessons and nothing to show for it."

I came into town on business, pleased to enjoy a chance to be out on a fine spring morning with a warm sun and cool breeze. Wrapped in a shawl that Faith's mother Lorelei, also called Lori, had woven, I manage to stand using sturdy crutches Mr. Barlow made for me out of the strongest wood he could find around in this mostly grassland area. It was his thanks to me for being the school teacher and music teacher for his boy, Braden, a saxophone player.

Everyone is kind to me, opening doors, giving me a hand, one time picking me up to get me over the broken steps in front of the bank. No longer called the 'music lady' but the 'cripple lady' – which I hate. I'll prove them wrong in time. I will walk on my own again. Even if it hurts me down to my soul.

"We are rehearsing for our first concert," I tell Mrs. Butler.

"That's good to hear," she responds with a snooty air. "Not gonna throw good money after bad, Missus Kirk."

She stalks off on another errand as I enter the Communications Office. I want to check on the status of some correspondence. There should be another credit voucher from the capital, the final payment from my mother's account. That will pay for the final delivery of the instruments and accessories Dr. Hill is sending.

"No voucher, Missus Kirk," says Mr. Bell. "Maybe tomorrow."

159

I can't keep making the long trip into town every day, I tell him. The school house is tough enough, being half the distance. With Eve pushing me it isn't too bad. Jackie doesn't have the strength to get me and the chair over the ruts in the road or through the mud when it rains. I remember when it was a pleasant walk and I could look forward to going to the school house each day.

"There's a marker on your account," says Mr. Bell, "if you want to access it."

I go into the private booth and push the buttons for my account, seeing the numbers flash on the small screen before me. I can sit on the tiny stool in the booth and rest my back. The screen presents a message: an update to my registration status. I'm still Mrs. Kirk, wife of William. Apparently, I have a daughter. That's news to me. I realize she's actually Billy's daughter with his first wife – being my step-daughter, I don't feel responsible for her.

But, dammit, we are officially married by the national registry! I hate being reminded of that man, so I curse and Mr. Bell calls out to ask if I need any help.

This woman, unrelated to me by nature, has filed a claim on my account, wanting to have my credits transferred to her account. She thinks she's entitled by being my step-daughter. More curses! That's likely the reason my credits haven't been sent to me. Well, I don't want to return to the capital just to straightened it out.

I ask Mr. Bell what I can do from here. He gets me the form to fill out, a counterclaim, and prepares to send it through our limited communications connection. I confess I was stupid when I went to get my dad's tuba, thought I was doing a good deed for a sad man, but now I'm trapped.

"Happens to a lot of good folks," he says, nodding in sympathy. "I see it all the time. You good folks are easily tricked. Gotta be gnarly sometimes, you know? Not so quick to trust others. It's like a game, and if you're not skilled at it, then you're going to lose every time."

I purse my lips. "I'm far from an expert."

Everyone learns lessons as they grow up. You get hurt and it's a lesson. The people who care about you just hope it isn't too much so the hurt is only a lesson and not a wound that stays with you the rest of your life. Dad told me that when I was little. I've been hurt many times and I always rise again. I'm stupid in that way: always getting up when I could've stayed down and wept, gotten people's sympathy and lots of charity. My dad sure never backed down and he got hurt a lot more than me.

So I refuse to let whatever hurts me keep me down.

"I'll fight it," I say to Mr. Bell. "Make her come out here to get it if she wants my credits so badly."

"There's the fighter!" he exclaims, flexing his arm muscles, thick from his days as a wrestler back east. "I can add that to the form as a condition, if you wish. Probably she wouldn't want to go to all the trouble to make the trip way out here."

+ + +

To my shock, Dr. Hill arrives in town, fresh from the depot, catching a ride with a freight wagon, which messes up his nice suit. We have to laugh at the way he shrinks from the equine scent covering him. With his French horn case in hand, he begs to have time for a bath and switch to a new suit but it is already time for rehearsal.

I manage to get myself to the school house most days and teach a couple classes. Two parents continue to assist with the other classes. I stand at the lectern, desperately holding on to it while I teach the kids. Sometimes, I prop myself on the crutches. If my back gets too tired and starts to ache, I sit in the wheel-chair. Students like to take turns pushing me around, back and forth as needed, wherever I want to go. They take it as an honor to be chosen and I'm grateful.

After the classes we set up the room for our rehearsal, everyone sitting in a semi-circle before the lectern. I stand again; with a baton in one hand, it's hard to keep myself upright for long without my hip causing me pain. I often stop in the middle of a song because I have to sit again. The kids are disappointed, thinking we are done. But I rise with a smile so the kids feel I can lead them. The concert's been scheduled for a month already, with Mr. Bell making posters and boys pasting them up about town. So we must carry on.

News must've traveled far and wide, I'm embarrassed to think.

Dr. Hill got word of our concert before my message could've arrived. He appears sooner than if he'd waited to depart until after receiving my message. I considered it a professional courtesy to inform him of our concert yet I never expected he would come all the way out here for it. Now that he's here, looking dapper but smudged with country soil, I feel a strange warmth in my chest. I'm sure my eyes must be twinkling.

He sits at the rear of the room, one leg over the opposite knee, hands clasped in his lap, his curly mustache balanced on his upper lip like a proper gentleman. Being a bit roughed up from his bumpy ride to town, he looks even more handsome. Delicate and beautiful. A doll you can't wait to hold. I smile at him, a stare I can't put away, until a student comes to ask me a question.

We set a rehearsal schedule after I started coming to the school house again, and the kids look forward to it. It is hard making the instruments sound just right but I give them encouragement. They don't mind trying again. And again. And once more. I usually stay late to help individual kids. I remind them about the 'think method' that Dr. Hill told them. It has some benefit, I realize after many lessons: you have to think the note – to hear it in your head – before you can play it. The kids seem to agree and we start to sound better. We can hear the difference.

Jackie returned one day bearing a big drum, saying it was a gift from her village. The drum was so large she had to roll it along the path to the school. She's happy to beat it to the music. She grinned when she hit it the first time and looked for my reaction. The boys act like she's interrupting the music, but she's on the beat, unlike many of them.

As Dr. Hill patiently observes, we play through four songs – one has three parts – then return to a few places where we need to try again. I sing out the melody for them, clap out the rhythms, remind them of the correct valves or keys to push, and how to place their mouths on the mouthpieces. I check the beat and *tempo*, swinging the baton to mark the beats so it's clear to them. And we go again, from the top, even as my back and hip are aching and I can barely endure another play-through.

Then we are finally done. I can take a breath, ready to collapse from the pain in my hip. Actually, the pain comes from my poor back and pelvic muscles, asked to hold me up in place, a strain they do not enjoy.

I thank the kids for their devotion, giving their attention. I pay compliments and urge them to practice more, then bid them a good night. As they pack up and reset the room for morning classes, I drag myself over to the wheel-chair and catch my breath. I answer a few questions the kids come to ask me, then focus on Dr. Hill and Eve sitting at the rear of the room, chatting like old friends.

After a moment watching them, I roll myself down the aisle.

"So my pa was Joe," Eve explains, holding her cornet in her lap. "But ever'body call him Little Joe on account of him being son of Big Joe, an' he's right big, lemme tell ya. Now Maggie's pa, he was Fritz but he go by Frank on account of his pa was called Frank. But Fritz, his ma was Isla, same as Raymond's. So they was brothers, or half-brothers. So then Raymond, he took Joe's wife, her name's Lorelei. He treat her rough, like she gotta fight him off but she couldn't, so I got made inside her, like them stories go. Raymond's my real pa but I's raised by Little Joe. 'Til he died. Then it was Amy raised me. She's Isla's oldest. 'Til she died. It's Maggie raisin' me now even tho' I'm older'an her. But she mighty kind to me an' I love her, love her fine, yessir. Anyways, my ma, Lorelei, she died pushin' me outta her so I never knowed her. Raymond, he run away with my sister, one named Faith. So turns out Maggie brung me out here an' now we live with Faith an' her boys, but she treat me good, gotta say. Well, most times, she do. We got Raymond out back under dirt, cuz he got shot in a gunfight. But don'tcha worry, not a week go by I don't go out there an' let out some pee over his grave jus' ta let'im know I'm thinkin' o' him."

I have to step in. "All right, Eve, that's quite enough."

Eve remains firm. "Well, he need ta know what he's gettin' if'n yous two fixin' to marry. He gotta know 'bout me on account o' I come with you as part of the package, see."

"Yes, that's quite true," Dr. Hill confirms, giving me an awkward grin. "However, Miss Eve, we've no intention of marriage. Thus, you needn't be concerned. However, we do—"

"You ain't got no hankerin' fer my cousin?" Eve presses and my face goes red. "Thought you sweet on her? That's what she says. You come all the way out here ta see her."

"Eve, please. We can discuss it later. After the concert."

"But he need ta know," Eve insists, and won't stop. "So Raymond is a Baumann on account of Granny Hannah, she's Baumann, too, gettin' with Big Joe, that's when Grampa Sandy was away at the war an' she think he never comin' back, but Big Joe an' her, they never did get married, see. Big Joe was a Grady, so Little Joe was a Grady, but Little Joe, he did get married to Isla, but he took up with Lorelei on account of him thinking Isla got taken away an' died, but she weren't dead, just sold to a farmer to get some kids for him on account of his wife cain't have no kids after lots of jabs. But Isla, she got free after some years an' come home to that mountain. Then Isla met up with Frank again an' they made Fritz. That's Maggie's pa. But he likes be called Frank after his pa, but he died up in the capital, see. He's a hero for savin' the governor from some bad men. It was on the streams. Anyways, yew kin see how we all related. So I cain't ever know for official what I am, a Baumann or a Grady, see. Could be Baumann on account of my pa was, or could be Grady on account of my ma's husband was. So now ya know what yer gettin' if you go an' marry Maggie."

Dr. Hill lets out his breath, a weary sigh. "I see." He turns to me. "That's an interesting tale, I must say."

"It's not as though we are a rag-tag bunch of country folk," I say, half in jest.

"Well, I shore is," says Eve to break the spell. She points to me. "She was born in the capital, so she got lots of learnin' an' you be mighty proud ta have her as yer missus. All I'm sayin'."

+ + +

For the concert the next evening, I wear my best dress, white with frills down the front. Eve and Faith make sure my hair is fixed up neat on top of my head the way high-class ladies wear it. I choose a dress with billowing sleeves so I can move my arms freely as I wave the baton. The wide belt cinches tight around my waist to help keep my hips in proper alignment. I tend to slump and lean whenever the muscles grow tired and start to ache.

We go together on the good wagon over to the school house. A lot of parents are already gathered outside. The kids are inside getting ready, unwrapping their instruments and tooting to warm them up, as I've instructed. A few parents clap when they see us arrive. They help me down from the wagon, bring my wheel-chair around so I can sit in it, then roll me into the school house. The kids who see me first raise a cheer and the others quickly joining in. A few of them compliment my appearance.

More townsfolk arrive and the room is packed, many standing at the rear of the room and along the sides. I grow nervous. I am full of confidence standing before the kids, but with so many adults in the audience, I worry about not fulfilling everything I've promised. They are excited to finally get to hear their sons and daughters play the instruments they've paid for. A lot depends on our first song.

I find Dr. Hill sitting in the last row of chairs, his eyes on me. Seeing me noticing him, he smiles back. I sigh, then take a breath and go to the lectern using my crutches. My music is already placed there, thanks to my lovely musicians. First is *Minuet in G* by Mr. Beethoven, an easy song to provide a confident start.

I raise my hands. Kids sit up, at attention, their instruments up, ready to play. The room falls silent. All eyes on me.

Downbeat.

My hand shakes but the kids start to play. It doesn't sound good, off-key and off the beat. But we can't start over. I press on, marking the beat with my baton. I'm embarrassed how we sound, not as good as our last rehearsal. Perhaps the kids are nervous like me. Yet they press on. Then I hear a parent cheer for her kid – inappropriate at a concert. Another parent calls out a compliment, boasting about his son, a trumpet player. Other parents take up the same attitude and cheer for their kids playing this awful song. All the notes are off, but it is a musical sound by anyone's definition. And we come to the end at last, thankfully. I hold my hands up to bring the kids together for the final note. And close.

The audience bursts into extravagant applause, like I really did something great. The kids smile like I've never seen them smile, all pleased by the delighted reactions to our first song. Having watched an old concert on streams, I know we should remain serious. But I decide to let the kids stand and take a bow with me.

I gesture for everyone to sit and we play our next song. It's a trio of pieces that sound like a peaceful countryside. Titled *English Folk Suite*, I know the townsfolk will like folk songs. As the music plays, it's as if woodland creatures prance around in time to us. The final part is a march and the trombone boys get to shine. If only we had more of them, I think, wouldn't that be grand? Twenty of them! No, fifty! Maybe seventy! We could have a big parade through the town. Info-recorders would write about this special event and send their reports to the streams. I can see the title now: *Western Youth Band Thrills In Town Parade!*

My ears are numb with the applause we receive. I beam with joy. I see the radiance in my kids' faces, proud of themselves and happy to be here making this music for everyone's enjoyment.

I have to calm myself to get on to the next song. It's something soft and sad yet inspiring. It's a version of the 'moonlight' song we listened to back in the Archives, but written for a band. I took notes off the piano score and changed them for band instruments. It does sound good. But I sense the audience doesn't understand it, can't see the images that flow from the music. I want to explain it to them.

Our final song is a lively dance which one parent thought was too bawdy for kids to play. I assured her that we would play only the notes, not sing the lyrics. We performed a rendition of a song called "A Whole Lot Of Love" by a band called the Led Zeppelin. When I found it in the catalog Dr. Hill showed me, I presumed they worked as balloon pilots, a way to transport people in older days, but no one can say for certain. The song really needs a tuba but I'm conducting instead. We get by with Jason, the farrier's eldest son, playing the baritone horn. And Jackie really gets to beat her drum in this song, difficult rhythms, much to everyone's chagrin. We make them want to dance!

The audience of parents, curious townsfolk, and a few members of Jackie's village watching through the open windows, cheer again. I have the kids stand and take a bow like we've practiced. I bow, too, and when I straighten up again, my hip tweaks and I cringe in pain. I'm sure everyone saw that on my face. It is time to sit again.

"Thank you all so much for coming to our first concert," I say in a strong voice after taking myself to the wheel-chair. "I hope we will have many more and continue to educate our students about the joy of music and everything that music teaches them, the way they can apply what they've learned from music to their other endeavors, and how we escape the rigors of our daily lives with a good song played over and over...."

Yes, I know I go too long with my speech. The audience prepares to leave, the kids putting their instruments away. The noise covers my message, so I let my words fall into silence and just smile.

+   +   +

After the applause, I feel a vague sadness, as though there won't be any more joy. I know we will have another concert, but that is far off. We will need to begin again with new music. Perhaps it won't be as hard the next time because the kids will continue to improve. But our music will be harder, too.

We arrive at the inn where Dr. Hill is staying, same as before. It fits his travel budget and I know Mrs. Beale will keep silent about anything that happens. But what could possibly happen there now? I'm a cripple.

Dr. Hill helps me stand, his hands around my waist. I'm talking about what we should play for the next concert when he smiles in a romantic way.

"*Trés excellent,*" he says. "*Et vous est trés jolie.*"

"What's that? Cherokee?"

"It means 'very good' in French. And 'you're very pretty' tonight."

I blush, which doesn't go unnoticed by the front desk clerk.

"You best not be speaking that Quebecker talk," I caution.

"Do you wish to go up?" asks the good doctor. "I have catalogues of music you can look at."

"That would be lovely," I say, knowing what the problem is. "But I shouldn't. I can't actually."

"Can't?" He frowns. "Should I carry you?"

"Can you?" I doubt he can. "I'm five-four and one-hundred-twelve pounds. Maybe more since I've been sitting a spell."

"Why, that's nearly my weight," he exclaims, feigning surprise. He sizes me up, takes a good look from my head to my shoes. "Well, a hundred-forty or thereabouts for me, I suppose."

He puts his arm around my back, forms a seat with his other arm and bids me to fit into this cradle. The movement causes pain. I have to refuse. He looks so disappointed.

"In Kanza City all the finer buildings have electric lifts," he says, throwing a glance at the front desk clerk.

"This's a cow town, sir. Most us get up them stairs just fine," the woman at the front desk says. Then she whistles loudly.

In stumbles a grainy young man wearing cowpoke clothes, like he's been drinking in the saloon next door.

"Duke," says the woman, "can you carry Miss Maggie upstairs? I hear she got some bidness with this gentleman tonight."

I don't like the way she phrases her request. Dr. Hill could bring the catalogues down to the lobby, of course.

"You want I should carry you up there?" he checks with me.

I agree, and the cowpoke sweeps me up into his strong arms and starts up the staircase, bearing my weight like I'm nothing more than a saddle, with Dr. Hill following sheepishly. Poor man!

I thank the young man and he returns downstairs.

Dr. Hill is clearly embarrassed and fumbles with his room key as a distraction. He pushes the door open, acts like he's weak as a joke. Pretends he strains his arm pushing the door. I laugh, but in a nice way, lady-like. I think he appreciates that.

"Well, now," he says calmly as he lights the lamps on both end tables. "That was an adventure! I'm not as fit as I once was, I dare say." His mouth tightens. "Hope you're not too disappointed."

"I know you're not some musclebound strongman, Hal. You're a musician. A man of the arts. That's what I like."

"Do you?" He still acts embarrassed. "I appreciate that."

"You have catalogues?" I remind him, but I know it's only a ruse to get me in his room, no matter how difficult it was. And I'm happy to be here, too. We always have such wonderful conversations about music. Music and life. Everything.

"Yes...the catalogues." He looks around for them. He checks or pretends to check his luggage, shaking his head. "I seem to have left them in Kanza City." He regards me with a devious grin. He knows I know he's lying, but I don't care.

"Oh," I sigh, acting disappointed.

"I apologize again, this time for my inadvertent failings." He lets go a loud breath, shrugging. "Oh, well." He glances about the room, eyes settling finally on the neatly tucked bed, its taut white cover. "Since you've gone to so much trouble coming upstairs...."

He gazes at me, his eyes soft yet steamy. He steps toward me as I balance myself, holding on to the bed post. Up come his hands.

"May I...?"

"What?" I say but I know exactly what he means.

His hands go to my waist, and then our lips are meeting and I don't want to pull away. Yet I must.

"I can't," I say, and turn away. "My accident. Doctor Baker said if I'd been a horse they would've shot me. But they let me go on. Doc set the break as best he could, but it always hurts. You don't break your ilium and go on as normal."

"I see. Yes, that's awful. I apologize."

"It's not you, Hal, it's me." I look into his eyes. "I want to, but...."

"I understand." He looks down at his shoes.

"Furthermore, you should know I can't risk a pregnancy. Besides it causing me a lot of pain, pregnancy could put too much pressure on that repaired bone. Therefore, no children for me, I'm afraid." His eyes hesitate, looking at my chin, then my eyes. "It makes me glad we dared have that special moment together last year. My one and only time. A memory I shall always cherish."

"It was wonderful for me, too." He can barely get the words out, choked up as he is.

"So...would you still want to be with me?"

"Oh, my dear Maggie, it has always been your bright, sparkling soul calling to me, that shines through the night storm. I recognized it the first time I ever put my eyes on you. How you radiate joy! How you bear all the goodness of the world within your heart. Any man would be pleased to be with you. Even in a sexless household."

I take a step from the bed post to embrace him, and we hold each other for I-don't-know-how-long, with me putting my weight against him to ease my pain.

+   +   +

Eve continues teasing me, not satisfied with my account of a simple dinner at the lodge and some digestion time after.

"He only rubbed my shoulders. Quite innocently – like you do," I tell her. "I had tense muscles after conducting the concert."

"Ever'body wanna rub ya," she says with a childish pout.

Vince Bloom, the oldest boy still attending school, a flute player, and his gruff father drove me home on their wagon, tying me in my chair on the flatbed. Arriving, they untied me and helped me down. I felt like a load of cargo. Faith had her sons bring my chair from the wagon, carrying it up the steps to the porch. I hobbled into the cabin using my crutches.

"That's all he did," I tell Eve when we go out back. "Always a gentleman. He's no cowpoke, that's for certain. In fact, I...."

Stopping myself, I watch Eve go unassumingly about her routine in preparation for bed. I'm about to say I adore him, but decide that kind of declaration might hurt Eve.

"Well, I knowed he right sweet on ya. Ever'body kin see it," she says with a laugh, "so I expect a whole lot more."

Eve raises the bucket and pours the water over herself, shivers a moment, then applies the bar of soap, uses the washcloth. I rest in my wheel-chair. I could use a wash, too, after waving my arms all evening. That inn had a lovely basin in a side room. I imagine using it, filled with soap bubbles – then Hal rises from the water to hold me in his naked arms. I have to shake away the thought.

"So you two's getting hitched?" she calls over to me.

170

"Honestly, we didn't talk about that. We discussed what music to play for the next concert. He can order the printed sheets."

"Maybe he order some bed sheets, too."

"No, it can't happen. I told him. Me being a cripple, it wouldn't be fair to him. I wouldn't want to burden him."

Eve wraps the towel around herself and steps nibbling to me.

"But it's fair fer me?" she asks.

I regard her, trying to smile. "You and I are already related."

It's not fair to anyone to have to take care of me. I am a burden. I've become useless. I will always need someone to help me. And the only thing I have to offer in return are my music skills.

In our room, we lie together and I feel tears building in my eyes. One runs down my cheek, falls on Eve's hand. She licks it off and then kisses me.

15

BILLY THE CURSE

WE CONTINUE PRACTICING as a group. I give individual music lessons to the kids who need them – most of them. Parents give me credits in appreciation, saying my 'sparkling attitude' is what makes the kids enjoy learning music. I shouldn't have a sparkling attitude, but I can't help it when I'm working with the kids and we're playing songs. I guess this is what I'm meant to do.

I feel the need to write down songs that come into my head. I've taught myself the basics about notes and harmony. I've studied the scores of the songs we play, see how they put the notes together, and I try my best to imitate them. My notation is neat on the staff paper Mr. Bell printed for me, a whole sheaf of them.

Eve says I should write more blues songs. I agree, though I must focus on what makes me sad to do that. Living here isn't too bad if you can stand the dust, the smell of cattle, the threat of bandits, or snakes. I write a song called "Snakebite Blues" and another I call "Mama's Gone". Eve plays along on cornet. Her lazy style of playing fits. She makes it more blues style by emphasizing the falling tones. "Banjo Blues" is a song Eve came up with based on her trouble with Briggs: "*He gots a banjo, but that ain't the hardest thing....*" Faith says I should make a song called "Too Loud Blues".

It becomes our evening routine, playing blues songs together or making up new songs. Sometimes I hear Eve playing her cornet like she's practicing a song or two, repeating phrases until she gets them right. I'm so proud of her.

At the start of summer we go to the Cimarron Music Festival in the town of Cimarron. It's thirty miles from Skinner Canyon. Jeb and Joe, my nephews, nearly grown men, drive the wagon bearing me and Eve, and our pretend daughter Jackie. We arrive and find lodgings full. We must make do with a canvas over the wagon: us women sleeping on the flatbed, the boys on the ground. Having the nephews with us is awkward. We find a 'women only' washhouse set up for the festival.

The town is larger than Skinner Canyon, with a lot of buildings along its many streets. The main streets are paved with concrete. I see those unique stands where people would pump some liquid fuel into their vehicles long ago, but nothing flows from them now. A few electric vehicles go by us but mostly it's the horse carriages in the streets. I imagine what it would be like to live here. Mom took us to Skinner Canyon because that was where Faith was, but Cimarron is a nicer town. A lot of food stalls have been set up as well as kiosks selling items from tribes. A good number of tribal folks are visiting. It seems a happy place, everyone getting along just fine. I feel bad for not visiting the previous festivals. It always seemed too far and a bit dangerous crossing the chaparral country.

We go from music event to music event. Besides bands of three to a dozen people, there are people telling jokes, people dancing to music, and even a magician who makes a horse disappear from the stage – before someone shouts he sees the horse behind the stage in back of a curtain. Some shout they want their ticket money back.

Getting food, we go sit at one of the tables they've set up. They say it's 'turkey leg' but I don't know what a turkey is, and can't eat much of it anyway. Jeb finishes it for me. Eve chomps away on a sandwich of chopped veggies and eggs. Jackie chews on dried beef sticks, refusing anything else that's offered.

A man is stirring up iced cream further on. We get some scooped into crunchy bread-cones that break apart as we lick the iced cream. Tastes like chocolate – which reminds me of Hal's gift of chocolate delights laid in a fancy red box with a gold ribbon. He said it was "sweets for my sweetie" and smiled like he expected I'd swoon over it. I did swoon but over him, setting the box aside. A late Valentine gift, he said, then had to explain about the custom. I felt so stupid; we never learned about that in the capital.

Eve nudges me, breaking me from my memory.

"Is that the fella we met in the city?" she asks, directing her eyes at a bedraggled man in tan coveralls. He stands out because nobody wears coveralls out west here. Over the coveralls he wears a black leather vest with silver studs, something you can purchase easily in this town. It doesn't match the coveralls. On his head is set a black, wide-brimmed cowboy hat, pulled down in front enough to block the sun or hide from people like us wondering who he is.

It's difficult to tell, the way the hat hides his face. I ask her why she thinks so.

"Got the same figure, got the same walk."

"You're very observant," I say, not taking her seriously.

"What is about man?" asks Jackie, cautiously holding my arm.

"Oh, he's—"

"The bad man from the city we got away from," Eve cuts in.

"She means that Mister Kirk," I explain. "The man I married in the capital." An awkward laugh. "For one day. But then he died." I eye Eve. "Or so we thought."

"I have knife," says Jackie, showing me the handle, sliding down her sleeve.

"We won't need that, I'm sure. It's festival time. No troubles."

Yet the idea of Billy Kirk being here, no matter how ridiculous it might be, continues to annoy me as we try to enjoy ourselves with the musical entertainment. He's like a curse that follows me.

We try to go on, to enjoy the festival. I collect ideas for our own festival in Skinner Canyon. Maybe next summer. We have the town parade coming up first, then an autumn concert.

At one point, Eve excuses herself to visit the lavatory. She says we should go ahead and go on to the next stage. She's sure I'll like the music there. So, unsuspecting, Jackie and I go on. The nephews have found their own amusements, the cowboy events, and agree to meet us at the wagon later.

The venue has several seats arranged before the stage. Mostly people stand for the show. With me in a wheel-chair, we get the spot in front. Jackie crouches beside me. People give me strange looks, like I'm a rich old widow able to hire a care-taker.

The announcer, a fat man in a white suit, comes on stage with a big paper cone to shout through, telling us what's coming up:

"And now for your entertainment today, a new band, actually a duo, calling themselves Banjo Blues. Let's give a big hand to them!"

To my complete surprise, out comes Mr. Briggs in his usual dirty dungarees and button shirt, carrying his banjo. But even more of a shock is Eve stepping on stage in a short white dress, showing her legs from her knees down to her bare feet. She holds her cornet. The way the sun strikes her, I can almost see through that dress.

I can't speak, being in such disbelief!

But they play! They play duets of banjo and cornet. Mr. Briggs sings some words, blues words. When they finish he says the song is called "I'm Sorry" and waves at Eve to take a bow. She does. "That's on account of we fixed our troubles."

Straightening up, Eve gives him a nod and grins.

"Our next song is called 'Evening', yeah," he says. "It's about this here little lady. Her name's Eve, see. *Eve*-ning. Y'all get it?"

He strums on the banjo as Eve beams. When he starts picking she puts the cornet to her mouth and plays out her bluesy tones. It sounds wonderful the way they're playing together, like they've been practicing for a while. I smile, glad they've resolved the bad feelings and have become friends.

They play two more songs, apparently made up by them and not memorized from printed sheets. "Only You" is my favorite, but "Dust Dance" is good, too. Eve kicks her feet a bit for that one, swirling around like a tornado. The men in the crowd hoot and holler.

I clap my hands hard as they exit the stage.

"It's great day for you," Jackie cheers Eve when she rejoins us a half-hour later, wearing her previous long dress.

We hug and I praise Eve for her performance, for working with Briggs, and for having the courage to get up before an audience that way. And she played that cornet good, too.

"There's that fella again," Eve says in a lowered voice.

I turn to look, then duck behind a canvas wall separating venues and try to see in my mind what my glimpse captured. From that image, I see him clearly. Could it really be him? Did he see us at the venue where Eve played? Is he following us?

"Come on," I say. "Let's get away from here."

I take Jackie's hand. Eve pushes me in my chair. But my Kanza girl keeps looking back at the man in question.

She pulls her hand away suddenly, stalks toward him. I want to call after her but I don't want to draw attention to us. She goes right up to him, talks to him, making him halt. He hands her something, then acts mean. She says more and he waves her away, turns to go in the opposite direction.

Jackie comes back. "He say his name is Thirty-two."

My face blanches.

"It is number, not name?" she asks.

"That's him." Eve puts her hand on my shoulder.

"What did you say to him?" I ask Jackie.

"I am poor child, ask for coin. He curse but I ask again and he give me coin to go away. I say: 'Thank you, Mister...uh?' And he says number. It's strange to have number?"

"They go by account numbers in the capital," I explain.

"Any fool out here goin' by numbers gotta be bad," Eve adds.

"You did good," I tell Jackie, and now we know.

My so-called husband has found us. I think back to our visit to the capital and our encounter with him there. What did I tell him? What information could I have shared that would let him know where to find us? I'm sure I mentioned Skinner Canyon a few times. But it's been nearly three years.

Then I realize: Mr. Bell put that note on the message about my account being claimed by his daughter. That must be it. I told her to come get it if she wants it. Maybe it wasn't her but *him* who located us. It was a trick to get our location. Now he's here.

Did he see me sitting in a wheel-chair? Did he recognize me? I'm sure he must have vengeance in his heart to come all this way. And I'm in no condition to fight him. I fear for my companions.

"We better tell Frank," I say and Eve agrees.

Remeeting my nephews, we leave the festival earlier than we'd planned, heading home well before dusk. The sun begins to set on us. Paint smears the horizon as we roll along, the bumps and slips in the road tweaking my hip to ache. I can barely endure being lifted off the wagon when we arrive home.

+   +   +

"Nothing we can do," says my brother. "I may be deputy sheriff but we got a civil'zation here. Can't be arresting a man for thinking his thoughts, even they're evil ones."

"I know, Frank," and in my heart I know he's right.

"Maybe he just wants to see you again. You *are* his wife. And he ain't dead like you said he was. That's gotta hurt. I don't know why you felt you had to lie to us." He lets out a sigh, places his hand on my shoulder. "You can be alone out here with a husband in the city. Maybe that's where his job is. Not strange at all. But if my wife ran away, I'd sure go looking for her."

Frank knows the whole story. I was only doing a kind gesture. It wasn't supposed to be a real marriage. Billy knew it, too. There's no reason for him to look for me but revenge. I can't imagine what may have happened to him after the monitors dragged him out of the unit but it couldn't have been good. He would hate me for that and want to get back at me.

Frank goes to the cabinet against the wall, opens the door and selects a pistol for me to carry – or keep in my lap since I'm stuck in a wheel-chair. He gathers enough bullets to load the chambers.

"You know what to do, right?" He narrows his eyes at me.

When we came to Skinner Canyon, we all took turns shooting at cans and bottles. I was better than my brothers expected me to be. I had a steady hand and a sharp eye. I beat them in one round of our shooting. But that was years ago. I haven't pulled a trigger in a very long time.

"I kin take it," says Eve, reaching for the pistol. "I knows how ta plug'em just fine. Use ta pop muskrats in the marsh."

"Please be careful," says Frank, studying Eve. "We don't want no accidents. Or a murder. If you have to, strictly for defense, aim for a leg. If you're damn sure he's fixing to kill you, you aim for the chest. That's your best target. Then there won't be any questions. But only if he's got a gun pointed at you."

"I knows what to do," says Eve in a defiant tone.

Frank wipes his brow. "We ain't had a shooting in years around here and I don't want any shootout on my watch."

We promise to be careful, and we keep the pistol close by at all times. At the cabin, we caution Faith's boys to not play with it. Not a toy, we remind them daily. Clemson is always curious, sneaking in to touch it, mostly to see if he can get away with it before we scold him. Benjamin is hesitant, as though the pistol is a snake that will bite him if he gets too close. Faith complains to us about the pistol, not to her sons, though she's got a shotgun leaning in the corner of the front room for when coyotes or tribals come too near.

Life must go on. Days go by and no sign of Billy. We return to our routine.

In the summer, when school is out, the kids are free to play or, more likely, help at their family's farm or ranch. I still have music lessons for those who want to learn more and keep up their skills. I go to the school house on the same schedule as for classes. We have a lesson in the small side room, what's supposed to be the teacher's office. I can fit in two or three kids at once. I try to finish in time to roll myself back home before dark. The road is rough and already two wheels have needed to be replaced.

I can stand. I can do everything a normal person would want to do, but with pain. At best it breaks me from whatever I want to do, reminds me of the injury. At its worst, I freeze with pain and dare not move. Actually sitting in the wheel-chair isn't the best position. Flat on my belly is the most comfortable. Next best is standing up straight – without leaning forward as when I hold on to the lectern – like when using crutches. I've noticed myself leaning to the opposite side from my injury when I sit, trying to keep any pressure off that part of me. That makes my back muscles seize up after a while, and that causes pain. There's no position that's good for too long before I must shift to another.

And walking? On a level surface I can take several steps without aid but with some pain. I've graduated to a cane for short distances but continue to use the wheel-chair for longer travel. The crutches are of little use unless I wish to stand for a while, but that awkward situation looks ridiculous. In bed, I rest on my good side, with Eve propping me up that way, pressing up against me most of the night. When we slip and I roll on my back or belly I awaken in pain and we must try again to sleep. Not even the brace Mr. Barlow made for me of leather and steel ribs works well enough for me to ever forget this terrible disruption happened.

Yet we must go on.

We have rehearsals coming for the big parade. Long ago – as we learned in the books they had us read in my school – what was once a nation of thirteen states declared its independence from the large country that ruled over them. They fought a war to make sure that independence was accepted. They called it 'Independence Day' and celebrated it on July 4 – or Fourth of Seven, as they called it in the capital, forgetting how it began.

We haven't forgotten it out here in Skinner Canyon. Even before we ever started the band people put up flags of red and white stripes with white stars in the blue corner – not the somber red and gray of official flags. I remember Mom holding my hand, still a young girl, keeping me safe from horses prancing down Main Street.

After the parade, she explained the history, then gave a sigh of regret for how so much had changed after the pandemic destroyed everything, how the country was so cruelly rebuilt. She was sorry it destroyed my dad. She was glad we came out to this dusty western town and see remnants of the old ways.

+   +   +

In a strange way it's beautiful how the kids hold the note as long as I keep my hand up, baton poised, and keep holding it until they run out of breath. There isn't actually a *fermata*, the symbol for holding a note. But the kids follow my lead so well now.

When kids run out of breath, they look behind, in the direction I'm staring, to see what it is that's frozen me in place.

A large, scruffy man, coated in fresh-blown dust, with a scraggily beard, has entered the school house and stands at the rear. His dark eyebrows hide his angry eyes as he clasps his wide-brimmed hat in his hands. At first glance I thought he was a parent come to pick up his kid early or just listen, as I've welcomed them to do. Then I see who it is, wearing the same tan coverall and black vest. I freeze and the kids play on, then fall silent.

I brace myself against the lectern while conducting the band, one hand holding the edge while my other hand lifts up the baton that Mr. Birch crafted for me. As I lower the baton, I keep my eyes on the man, worrying about those kids sitting between him and me.

What should I do?

Eve is to the side of the room with her cornet, at the end of the row. A couple of older boys playing trombones are closer to him. Thankfully, the younger kids happen to be on the other side, away from him.

"Good day," I call to him for the sake of the kids. "Come to hear a rehearsal?"

Some kids think it's genuine and they smile, pleased to play for a guest. They have gained confidence, even though they are far from sounding good. "Better and better," I always tell them.

Eve looks back, recognizes the man and lets out a gasp. She sets down her cornet on the floor and picks up her bag, sets it in her lap. I see her hand go into the bag.

"I didn't mean to hurt you," the man growls, then coughs. "But you didn't need to get me arrested."

So it's to be this? An argument three years old.

"We had an agreement," I say. "But you broke our agreement. I know it and you know it. I'm not to blame for what happened to you after what you tried to do."

The kids are awestruck, sensing danger growing in the room. I see them fidget, asking with their eyes what they should do.

Eve stands up, her hand still in her bag, held by her other hand.

"Kids, y'all best be movin' on outside now, just fer a spell," she says calmly. Some of the kids get up to obey while others look to me for confirmation.

I nod to them. "Yes, go ahead and take your instruments outside. We'll continue our rehearsal there. After all, we'll be marching in a parade, won't we?"

The kids move in an orderly fashion up to the front of the room and out the door behind me, rather than the main doors where that man is standing.

That man!

William B. Kirk, also known as Thirty-two, formerly of the City Archives. My husband. Three years since he was hauled out of his unit by monitors responding to Eve's alert, saving me from assault. Plenty of time for his hatred to compound. Time enough to find me.

"How are you?" I ask half in earnest, half to calm him.

"I've been better," he mutters, not moving from his spot.

My back tenses, standing so long, and I must sit. I drag myself to the wheel-chair and lower myself into it. His eyes follow me, widen at the sight of the chair.

"What's that for?" he asks, pointing at the chair.

Once I settle myself in the chair, watching Eve take her position along the side wall, hand still in her bag, I answer him.

"Accident. A horse tripped over me. I'm not in good shape now," I say, watching his face turn a notch toward sympathy.

"You're wounded?" he asks from the rear of the room, then takes a couple steps up the aisle.

"Yes." Reality surrounds me, closing in on me again. "I'm afraid it's a permanent disability. My movement is limited. I'm in constant discomfort, often pain. However, this is the part of my life I never expected. Same as meeting you. Same as the deal we made."

"Deal, huh?" His tone returns to anger.

"I only agreed to marry you so you could get a pass to leave the city. You said you wanted to see your daughter. So I felt pity for you. Then you try to...well, what you did. Not what I wanted."

"The normal thing for married people to do," he responds.

"Except you promised we wouldn't do any of that sexual activity. It's the only reason I agreed."

"And that would've been so bad?" he seems to be teasing.

"Not with you," I retort, which seems to anger him.

He doesn't have an answer, just shuffles another step closer.

"Looks like it don't matter now, the way you are."

"You came here to be with me again? Because I'm your wife?"

"No...." Now he's acting humble.

"Did you see your daughter? At least that part was true?"

"Saw her. From afar. She didn't wanna see me close though. As usual. I'm not a bad man. She won't believe me or accept me. Same as you. I'm just a man. A normal man. I want what any man wants."

I straighten myself in the chair. "And what's that?"

"Treated right. Respected. Loved." He seems to get emotional.

"I think you have to earn those. That's what my mom said. My dad thought he earned them. Actually I don't know anymore."

He clears his throat and takes another step forward, his hat still clenched in his hands.

"Time's are tough. Tough for everybody."

He seems humble, not so dangerous now as I feared. Not much I can do from my wheel-chair. Talking is fine. Let's sort this out.

"So why are you here?" I ask him.

"Came to find you."

"But why?"

He clears his throat again. "Because you're my wife."

I almost laugh but try to hold back so I don't upset him.

"Your wife? That was a long time ago, and only a couple hours."

"Well, I did like being married for a little while," he says.

"So you had some interest in me?" That surprises me. Maybe it's his trick to gain sympathy. "I don't believe you. As you said, it was purely a deal."

"Well, marriage is a sorta deal, isn't it?"

"Yes, an agreement. Then you broke the terms."

He nods, looking at the floor. "If you say."

I don't know what to think. Was he in love with me back then? Did he come up with that exit pass idea to persuade me into that arrangement – something I never would've agreed to if he acted like an actual suitor. We hadn't known each other very long and had no other connections. Just him bringing us things at the Archives and me thanking him.

"What happened to you?" I gesture for him to sit down on one of the chairs. "Take a seat. It may be a while."

"You want me to get the kids lined up?" Eve calls over to me.

"Could you wait a little longer?" I respond.

"Shore thang." She shifts the cloth bag, keeping one hand inside. I know then she has the pistol Frank gave us.

I focus on Billy, feeling less worried how he will act.

"What happened?"

"Your sister called the officers," he says, taking a seat. "I was put in a van and taken to some office, thrown in a cell for a while, and I never got any food. Then they pulled me out of there, started asking strange questions and I answered as honestly as I could. You *are* my wife and we were having the wedding night. But you weren't around to confirm it, so they didn't believe me."

"But the registration would show it, wouldn't it?" I ask, unsure why I'm taking his side now.

"Took a few days. Maybe they never checked."

"Then they released you?"

"Took a few days – a few more days. Lost track of me, you could say. It was some time before they figured it out and came to get me. By then I was sick, starving, so they put me in a hospital until I was better. Then I was released. That was three months later."

"Oh, my! That's awful."

"They released me to a rehabilitation facility," he continues, "and said I needed to learn how to act right, get 'rehabilitation', whatever that was supposed to be. More like being in prison. Guards beating any will to live outta you. Don't know what they were feeding us."

"That's awful," I say, then catch myself, wonder if he is making it up. "But you got out. They released you back into the city."

"A year and two months later." He wipes a smirk off his face. "I had to stay longer because I didn't obey them."

"What a pity." I narrow my eyes at him. "I only wanted you to stop hurting me, to get away from me. I never expected you to have your life disrupted for a year and a half. That was the government's doing, not me."

"I got out. But no more unit. My things gone. No more job. They assigned me a job but it was just sweeping the streets."

"Like my dad did," I mutter, seeing Eve perk up. Then I speak to Billy: "You had my dad's notebooks there in your unit. Why? How'd you get them?"

He lowers his gaze, shaking his head. "I saw them in the display. I took a look, read some of it. Decided to keep them when they were taken off display. You know, finish reading them. Nobody'd care."

"Really? You're a fan of pandemic literature?"

"It was a good story. I wanted to know what happened next."

"My grampa's adventures?" Maybe he was telling a lie again.

"Sure." He mugs for me. "And then you showed up to claim them. I didn't know what to do. But, heck, I liked seeing you. You and your sister. Best week of working in the Archives ever. I liked you being there. I wanted to help you."

"So you brought us music things instead. We searched for those notebooks for days. Nothing. You could've told us you had them and that would've saved us a lot of time and trouble."

"But I...I liked you. I wanted you to stay."

Tamara, one of our section leaders, pops her head in, asks when I will join them. I explain it may be a while so go ahead and practice the marching. I give them the song to play while marching, a simple version of a Sousa song I rewrote to make it easier to play.

I notice Billy's gotten up and moved forward. Me reacting with alarm at his sudden movement sets him off.

"I wanted you – or your sister. She's better looking," he says in a rough voice. "But you two caused me lots of trouble and I swore to find you. It isn't an easy thing to do, lemme tell you. Way out here in this dirty town. Why anybody ever come here is—"

"This is our home. Mom brought us here when we finally got to leave the capital."

He comes closer down the center aisle, kicking chairs to the side to make his path wider.

"Stop right there," I speak firmly.

"Hey, mister," Eve barks at him.

He doesn't stop but continues toward me.

"I saw on the register we're still husband and wife. I'm not being foolish. I'm giving you another chance. Ready to take you back."

"Not a chance, Billy. I'm sorry." I glance around for something to fight with. Not a baton. The pointer on the blackboard tray?

"Why not?" He sets his hat down on a chair, punches his fists to his hips, ready for action.

I have to face him: "I was going to file for dissolution but then I had my accident. I never thought I'd see you out here anyway."

"But here I am." His face turns into a mask of evil intent.

Eve kicks a chair away from in front of her, making a noise that distracts him. He glares at her.

"That ain't what she want," says Eve, letting the bag drop off her hand to the floor. Her hand holds the pistol, raising it at him.

"Whoa!" He puts his hands up half-way. "Be careful with that."

"In these here parts ya never go nowhere without a gun."

He fakes a laugh, shaking his head.

"You're not gonna shoot me," he says. "You're a woman."

"I shoot all the time. Fact, I can hit cans at fifty feet." Eve looks back at me, says: "Really it's thirty, but he don't know."

As she glances back at me, I see past her to Billy starting to rush at me. My eyes reflect his threat and Eve sees my expression.

She snaps her head forward, finger tight on the trigger. The gun fires. I'm too startled to do anything but cringe against the noise.

When I dare to look, I see Billy on his knees, hands to his head. Blood runs down his face. I see where the bullet hit the wall behind him, cracking the wooden frame around Mr. Beethoven that we put up there to inspire the kids.

Eve takes a polishing cloth from a chair and tosses it to Billy. As he wipes blood from his head, we see how the shot grazed him, cut a line across his scalp.

The kids outside shout at us, asking if we are all right. One boy says he sent another kid to get Deputy Baumann.

"That was *not* necessary," Billy howls, blood running down.

"*Was* necessary," Eve counters, keeping the pistol on him, "cuz ya gots bad intentions for my cousin an' I ain't gonna let ya hurt her no more."

16

J & J

I KNEW THAT LOOK: same as every young man has when he sees his young lady, whoever the girl is who catches his eye. The sight of her goes straight into his heart and he can't think clearly. His eyes lock on her and it's not a stare but a gaze of awe, of devout worship. At that stage it's not about wanting sex or even a simple gesture of affection; it's the innocent desire to simply be within the circle of her presence, to breathe in her perfume, perhaps brush his hand against hers, to know she is real, or take her hand in his and beautifully exist as one in time and space. He is too young to hope for more. He doesn't yet desire anything else. It's almost as though he's found his mother again: the safe and comforting feminine aura.

My nephew Jeb has that look when I arrive at the jailhouse with Jackie. Of course, his gaze is completely for her, not me. I'm amused by it nevertheless. I never had a boy look at me the way Jeb looks at Jackie. She hangs back as I go into my brother's office.

Frank's out on official business, says Buck, one of the jailers, but he welcomes me to wait. I don't like sitting for any length of time or my hip will ache, but for Jackie's sake, and maybe my nephew's, I'll wait a while. They can have some time to talk.

I sit by the door, lowering myself into the wooden chair, letting my cane lean against my knee like an old woman. I feel foolish, but the wheel-chair won't go up the steps to the landing.

Sitting by the open door, I hear the shy mumblings of two teens in love – in love from afar. They haven't had time to be together.

"You been doing awright?" Jeb asks.

"I'm *ooo-kay*," Jackie replies.

"It's a fine day today."

"It's fine."

"That's a pretty shirt."

"Thanks."

"You order it from Kanza City?"

"No, it's from General Store."

"Oh."

"Miss Maggie give to me."

"That's nice."

"It's *ooo-kay*."

And deeper conversation about the state of the cattle around our town, then a detour to tribal issues, returning by way of the band.

"I sure like yer drum playing," says Jeb, letting his nervousness show in the shaking of his voice.

"Thanks." After a moment: "You play horn good, too."

"Thanks." A long pause. "I practice much as I can."

"That's good."

"I know."

"Maybe you can practice...with me?" Her voice falls off, unsure.

"With you?"

"I mean we practice same time."

"Oh," says Jeb. "I get it."

"If Miss Maggie say *ooo-kay*."

"She never says 'okay'. It's always 'all right' for her."

They giggle at the joke and I feel happy for them.

"She play tuba," says Jackie, and I think she must be making a strange face, cheeks ballooning out, for Jeb because he laughs.

"Yeah, she likes it," he says. "It's real old, like a hundred years, I heard her say. Her grandmother used to play it."

"She tell me."

"Yep, it's old," he says. "Real old."

I sit, pleased by their first inkling of young love.

And then it happens: my sandy-haired nephew – sandy but a bit on the red side like his mother – finally gets his gumption gathered and works up some words and makes his proposal.

"Excuse me," he says in a stronger voice. "Miss Jackie, would you like to go down to the General Store and get a soda? It's my treat. I got a few coins from my pa."

Two breaths later Jackie pokes her head into the office and asks me if she can go for a soda with Jeb. Smiling at her, I approve.

I hear the clap of Jeb's boots and the swish of Jackie's moccasins across the wooden floor, their steps getting louder as they exit, free from the aunt's prying ears.

That leaves me free, as well – to consider William B. Kirk, who sits in the jail cell nearby.

He saw me enter the office, called to me, but I didn't answer.

After Jeb and Jackie leave, he calls out my name again. Me not replying, he makes a crude remark. Buck shouts at him to be quiet.

When Frank rushed to the school, he and his men took Billy straight over to Dr. Baker for stitching his scalp. He lost a good strip of hair on top of his head. Doc said it would likely never grow back. It gave him a skunk look. Overall not too bad of a wounding. Now he sits awaiting his trial.

Eve actually got it worse. Being the shooter, she had to give up her gun and submit to fixing her hands in the steel cuffs for the ride to the jail. She complained all the way. Frank had to do it, standard procedure. He couldn't show favorites to anyone, his cousin most of all. I begged him to go easy on her. Everyone knows Eve is 'feeble-minded', 'crazy', or 'dumb' – whichever words they use, all insulting.

At her session before Judge Taylor, a few witnesses testified to her being 'slow-witted' and so she didn't know what she was doing. I wanted to object to their offensive terms, but I saw the strategy: she being 'not-so-smart' she couldn't be held to a harsh punishment.

"I ain't slow-witted, *yer* slow-witted," she shouted at the judge at one point when he described her that way. That was after a witness described an odd incident a year before when Eve seemed confused about something common in Skinner Canyon.

I answered questions put to me about what happened, and I took the blame for Mr. Kirk coming here, looking for me, and causing this whole kerfuffle. No telling what he was prepared to do.

"I's protectin' my kin," Eve cut into the proceedings, "and you'da done the same."

Even Mr. Briggs got up to speak about Eve, saying she had rare talent on both banjo and cornet, like she was struck by the hand of God, a blessèd child.

"So it be right fair," said Mr. Briggs, "and He'll look favorably on this here Court, and by townsfolk, too, if Yer Honor went just a little easy on her."

Eve was ordered by the judge to spend 48 hours in a jail cell: one day for being careless with a gun, and one day for disrespecting the bench.

"I ain't dis'pectin' no bench," Eve growled. "You be sittin' behind a desk, all it is."

"The 'bench' is what we call the judgeship, ma'am," said Judge Taylor. "It is a custom we observe. Like saying 'Your Honor' instead of Judge."

"Well, if'n you wanna be called 'Junior', then I reckon I will."

"It's 'Your Honor'," I quickly corrected her, "not 'Junior'."

The judge tried to hide a grin, then waved her out.

It was almost comical, the way she sat in the cell demanding this and that of the jailers. They brought her food and they brought her drinks. She had a great feast by the end. And she demanded use of the lavatory and they had to close their eyes while she squatted over the tin bucket out back. She could've run away but everybody knew where she'd go: to our cabin.

She insisted I bring her cornet and she played it in her cell all through the night. Buck said she sounded good so he didn't mind it. Blues, huh? They fit here just fine. She told him about the band, got him to come to the next concert.

The concert would be later in the year, after the parade, which wasn't delayed by the drama of Billy coming for me.

The platoon of kids and a few grown-ups wore their official red vests and caps, held their instruments like real troopers, proud and excited to march down Main Street while playing our three songs. I did my best to lead them, sitting on the wagon Jeb and Joe drove ahead of the band. I sat backwards, facing the kids, as we marched down Main Street, with me waving my arms to mark the time. They sounded good, but marching while blowing into an instrument was a challenge. Remembering the notes was another; we had no sheets to carry and look at so they had to memorize the music. They did a fine job, in my opinion, and we received constant applause.

+ + +

Beauty and horror often happen in the same moment, I've learned, found in the same act yet separated by mere degrees. In the end you take the balance of them, draw your lot from the average, and claim what you can of life's joys and sorrows in mixed measure. I could see that as time marched on.

Jeb keeps wandering out to the cabin, making up excuses, saying he's looking for a lost steer, or he wants to check on our garden, see if it's still growing, or he wants to ask something but always forgets it when he gets here. I know exactly what he's doing: trying to meet Jackie. Boys can be that way: love sick. Strange thing is she wants to meet my quirky nephew, too.

"You sure you want to be bothering her?" I ask when I catch him loitering at our homestead. "Shouldn't you let her go be with a nice Kanza boy?"

"But she's fancy on me," he says, acting hurt by my remark.

"It's only fair she be with her own kind," I counter, half teasing him. "Isn't it?"

Standing on the porch, I lean against my cane, feeling old, like my own daughter is courting now and I'll have to get on without her someday. Jeb is a polite young man, I'll grant, a fine specimen of cowboy handsomeness, with a good measure of ambition thrown in. I approve of him coming to see Jackie, as long as she is for it. Soon I catch them kissing on the porch and feel a little jealous.

I think of Dr. Hill, wondering what he is doing in Kanza City, now that he knows there's no hope with me, no chance of us getting married or having children. When I went to the Justice of the Peace to file the forms to dissolve my marriage to a stranger named Billy Kirk, I filed another form to change my name back to Baumann. I didn't want anything to remind me of that error. Baumann was the name I know best – all my kinfolk going back a long, long time.

One night, Eve is stretched out on the bed reading one of those notebooks Great-grandfather Sandy wrote in during their pandemic days. I watch her lips move to sound out the words. She finishes the page and turns to the next, then closes the cover.

"Think I got it," she says, looking up. "So Fritz, that first fella, he was gonna be a tuba player in that old country but then come a war an' he had ta fight but he got caught an' put in a prison camp. Then he got out an' he married woman name of Beryl, an' they got kids named Paulina an' Ludwig, an' that girl she got the tuba after Fritz died. So she's the first girl ta play it."

"That's right," I call across the room. "But she didn't like it and gave it to her brother."

"So Paulina didn't become a tuba player? She marry a fella name of Carl, got three boys: Hans, Jacob, and Werner. Lemme see now. That Ludwig – Uncle Louie – he got married to Elisabeth an' they got three kids: Lloyd, then Rose an' Lily. So they got the tuba after she died, ain't that right?"

"Louie gave the tuba to Lloyd's daughters but it was only Polly who took an interest in it."

"Then who's Grace? Not my sister but the older lady."

"She's the wife of Lloyd," I explain, getting up and going to sit on the edge of the bed. "He married Grace. But she's...well, she is also a relative of ours, you see. Old Fritz, when he was a professor, he had an affair with one of his students, according to my dad. He said his sister told him. That was the reason his wife hit him with the car."

Eve sits up, her mouth agape. "What...?"

"So Lloyd and Grace...they were half-siblings."

"I get it. Them's the Laura, Jackie, an' Polly I read in that other notebook."

"That's right. Polly is Sandy's mother. See, Lloyd had an affair with a girl on that island years before – that's Polly's mother – but Grace agreed to raise her as their own. That's a family secret. Polly's the real tuba player in the family, the best that ever played it. But she died during the pandemic – killed by a man on that island, not because of the virus. That's what Sandy wrote."

"That's real sad." Eve puts a finger to her eye.

"Now you know about us. And you're one of us, too."

"Maybe off way to the side. Where it's more safer."

"No, a direct line," I insist. "Polly's son is Sandy. He and his half-cousin Hannah had a daughter: Isla. She's the grandmother of both of us. Isla had a son named Raymond: your father. Then she had a son named Fritz: my father. It's a direct line from both of us back to Old Fritz. You're here. I'm here. We're the same family even though we moved out west."

"Shore do sound whole lot queer if ya list ever'body like here in this notebook. Course, he don't know 'bout you an' me an' how we get by without no kids." She laughs. "That makes a chart easy."

"Things happen." I take a breath. "Frank has four kids, so that's where our family continues, I suppose. Jeb and Jackie, too – maybe. Who knows what's next? Joe will meet somebody. Then Jon. Then little Miss Frances. I think the tuba will go to her, if she wants it. She's Isla's granddaughter, after all. I'll teach her."

+ + +

The Fourth of Seven parade is a success. Best of all is Billy having to listen to it from his jail cell.

The trial was quick, the judge determining Billy hadn't actually done anything, although it came to light he was thinking of doing something. Eve halted his plan. He had to get up and apologize in front of everyone in the courtroom, curiosity drawing folks in. I had to tell the truth before everyone. The judge granted us a dissolution, declaring it hadn't been a real marriage and everything should go back to the way it was before we met.

Everything came out. Their sweet Maggie was telling stories. I was branded a liar. My husband wasn't killed in an accident the day after we signed the form. Here he was, angry and looking for her. A runaway bride! If I had any integrity, I should've stayed in the city with my husband. How I disappointed these townfolk!

Billy rode the railway out to the nearest depot. He started to ask around if anybody knew a school teacher named Maggie Kirk. A few folks told him I was in Skinner Canyon. He asked which way it was. Someone offered him a ride on a delivery wagon. He arrived, asked around for Maggie Kirk, said he was her husband from the capital. Oh? Why wasn't he dead, like Maggie told everyone? Because she's a liar and a tramp, he replied.

They sent him to the school house because that was where she'd be, rehearsing with kids for the Fourth of Seven parade. He planned to only talk, see how I was doing, not knowing about my accident, and thinking maybe we'd get back together like the married couple we'd briefly been. He'd be happy to have a wife.

But Billy never got the chance to talk to me, showing up hot and bothered, looking like a madman with evil intent in his eyes. Given what he'd done on our wedding day, it seemed reasonable to expect he would act the same. So Eve stepped in.

The judge didn't see it that way, said Billy was unjustly shot and deserved another chance. So he stood up in the Court and spoke his peace to me and I had to stand and listen to him, with everyone else hearing it all:

"It wasn't any kind of trick, Maggie. It was me tripping over a couple chances. First, like I told you back then, just to get an exit pass, to see my daughter who never wanted to see me. And then the second was because I really did like you – love you, even – from all I read in those notebooks. I kinda got to know your family, the way your great-grampa wrote about what they did back then. When you showed up with your sister, it was like a miracle. And I—"

"My cousin," I had to speak up. "Other side of the family."

"So I'm looking at you and thinking you could be a fine wife, and not just to get a pass to leave the city. You like music so much and I helped you with that, and.... Well, yeah, I know I did wrong to you. Couldn't wait. That was foolish. But you did it to me. Made me love you. Got me excited. At least I waited for signing the form. I waited that long. Could've gotten you in the Archives, nobody'd hear us, but I didn't. Anyways.... That's all I got to say."

Judge Taylor asked him if he wanted to say any apology and he bowed his head.

"Yessir, Your Honor, I do." He kept his head bowed, not meeting my eyes. The judge told him to look at me, so he raised his eyes and spoke: "I'm real sorry. For everything. I hope you can forgive me. I wish you the best for the rest of your life. I won't be bothering you no more. Sorry for everything."

"Thank you," I responded solemnly.

Judge Taylor asked if I had anything to say to Billy.

"No, Your Honor. He knows how I feel. And I'm in no condition nowdays to do much more than be here today. That's enough for any kind of apology. I'll be happy to see him go away and stay away."

The judge agreed, pounded the gavel on the desk, called the trial done. People clapped their hands.

By then, my nephew Jeb was happy to hold Jackie's hand sitting on the back row of seats in the Court. But when they got up to leave, they quickly let go so nobody would tease them. That was the only good thing about being in the Court: seeing these two together, what I took to be a sign of better days to come.

Then, on the same day a group of us, including Frank, stand at the edge of town to watch Billy depart on the courier wagon headed to the depot, ordered never to return to Skinner Canyon or face 30 days of jail time, the courier hands me a message from Dr. Hill.

> *Dearest Maggie,*
>
> *I pray for your improved health and well-being with every breath of every day, and I wish you continuing success with your illustrious town band, a true miracle blooming in the desert!*
>
> *I write to you this day by way of presenting an invitation to a grand enterprise of which I am privy. In our fair city, the music culture has blossomed. It is another miracle. I suspect as more of our citizenry become more comfortable in our changing world, they welcome music into their lives again. This confirms what I have always maintained: that music is central to the culturing of our souls and the curing of all manner of maladies.*
>
> *However, not to delay the latest news I offer for your serious*

consideration, there is an opportunity now present which I do believe would be a wonderful turn in your career, should you wish to partake of it. What is it of which I refer? How about I tease you? I offer you a position leading an orchestra – not a mere band of wind instruments and drums but a full orchestra with the ideal compliment of stringed instruments staffed by competent musicians, all familiar with and ready to perform the standard works in the repertoire.

What say you? Does the idea strike you warmly? It should be an honor for me to introduce you to those who are in charge of the orchestra. I have spoken with them previously, advising them on a particularly interesting choice: a young woman, though crippled, who has taught herself about music, gained proficiency on a tuba, and led a band of youths in both concert and parade to great acclaim. They are fascinated at the prospect of such a person leading their orchestra, and I wholeheartedly agree.

Please inform me of your decision and I shall forthwith make the necessary arrangements to bring you here (& whomever shall be assisting you). The orchestra committee authorizes tickets aboard the express, in a private chamber where you will have a maximum of comfort and safety. To be thoroughly honest, I cannot wait long to see you again.

Musically yours,

Hal D. Hill, Ph.D. (Music)

His offer brightens an ugly day and I don't notice the ride home. My heart warms. He wants to see me! The bulk of his message fades to the background, something about an orchestra.

Evening comes and I have to take stock of my situation. It isn't going to be possible for me to travel such a great distance, even with assistants (I imagine it would be Eve). How will I get around a city that size? They have a grid of paved streets unlike Skinner Canyon. Buildings ten floors high! And an orchestra? Stringed instruments?

I don't know much about those instruments, only about the music for them, the famous ones I've listened to from the disks.

Filled with dread, I have disturbing dreams and usually awaken covered in sweat. Eve cleans me, helps me change to a fresh gown.

"Ya best stop havin' them kinda dreams," she cautions, like it's my choice to welcome them into my sleep.

"I'm trying not to think of all that," I say in a weary tone.

"Well, I think ya should go. Me and Jackrabbit's gonna be right by your side to keep you safe, an' we's gonna play music with you."

"Is that right?" I try to smile for her but the candlelight puts me in shadow. "I should go? But what about—"

"You wanna see him again, don'tcha?"

I realize I might be stopping myself from taking this opportunity because of Hal. He can only be a friend now, I suppose. He believes in me, nevertheless. What do I have to fear? I can lead an orchestra of musicians who know more than me, but him? Dr. Hill? Hal? What do I have to fear from him? Maybe I'm still influenced by the trial of Billy Kirk. I don't trust myself. But Hal is not Billy. And I'm not the woman I was yesterday or last year or in the capital.

"You should go," Eve says, then blows out the candle.

+ + +

I thought the matter was finished, but Billy Kirk's visit to Skinner Canyon has lasting effects.

First was him arriving, which provided proof that he wasn't dead and therefore I wasn't a poor widow.

Next was everybody knowing my business and happy to gossip more. I was a 'lovely lady' as school teacher. Everyone respected me. They were comfortable having me be with kids all day and talking with them. I never talked politics or discussed any sensitive subjects with kids. They liked what I accomplished in starting a band, and took great pride in their kids' triumphs.

But then that man appeared and everything was thrown upside-down. Maggie was a liar: he didn't die. So why did she marry him? Why did she run away from him? Is she still a good person? Should she continue teaching our kids? A lot of gossip going around town. Maggie came from the capital, and we know what those folks are like. Maybe she's been playing us for fools. And what about that music salesman?

"I know for fact," Mrs. Beale stood to say at the parents meeting, "she went up to his room and stayed for over two hours. I'd say most ordinary business chat would've taken only fifteen minutes. But she was there for over two hours. And...."

She paused to look around the room, making sure all eyes were on her. You could hear a needle drop. As the silence deepened, more eyes shifted to me, like needles stabbing.

"And it was plain as thunderheads banging overhead how that bed upstairs went a-squeaking. I couldn't hardly do the books at the front desk with that racket going on."

The crowd gasped, all eyes shooting to me again.

I held myself strong, refusing to look at them, staring at the wall at the back of the room.

"So if she really was married to that criminal," asks Mrs. Barker like the town gossip she is, "then she was being adulterous with that sales fellow. Ain't it true?"

More gasps as they figure it out.

In my heart I never believed I married Billy, so I was still free to be with whomever I wanted. Maybe a court wouldn't see things my way but I didn't feel I was wrong. Whatever problems I've caused, given all we've been through these past fifty years – no, a hundred years now – they don't amount to a hill of beans.

Then came suggestions that I was an amoral woman, no better than saloon gals. That I wore cowboy clothes most days didn't add to my impression; it was a disguise to cover my floosy ways.

"And she lives with that other woman, the dumb one, them two holding hands in town, I seen'em."

"All three of them women out there, living without a man."

"That older one's Raymond's widow, and he's buried out there."

"The whole lot of them's strange, gotta be sharp on them."

"And Miss Maggie, if that's her real name, she took in that injun girl. What's that about?"

"Her mother kept going out there, flirting with them injuns, too."

"We can't trust her no more!"

Then Mrs. Booker, who was covering classes during my recovery, stands and announces that she's willing to continue on as the school teacher. "If you want to keep her from our kids," she says. "Until we can hire someone new."

"Can't have a loose woman near our kids. What'll they pick up from her?"

"She's a liar, that's fer shore."

"Prancing about in her cowboy clothes like she's a man!"

"I'll send out an advertisement tomorrow, send it to the nearby towns, even over to Kanza City and Wichita."

"Seems she got what she deserve, that horse stomping on her for her misdeeds. God knows how to pay it back."

Mr. Boothe waves the boisterous crowd to silence before they can say worse things about me. He stands a moment, and everyone gives him their attention, he being the elected head of the school council. He turns to me and I don't want to meet his eyes.

"It seems pretty clear, Maggie, how folks feel." A few start to add their remarks but Mr. Boothe waves them quiet again. "I like you. Many of us here also like you. We wish you well in your life as you continue to recover from your injury. And a whole lot of us thank you for putting a band together. It's real nice, and our kids sure love playing music. So we thank you for all you've done for us and for Skinner Canyon. But it seems we agree it's time to move on, get us a new school teacher. You understand. It's gotta be for the kids."

I do understand. I see how it looks. Nothing I can say that would change their minds. Nothing I can promise to do or not do, so I give a solemn nod and finally let the tears fall.

"Then it's decided," says Mr. Boothe, hand up like a preacher. "If there's any counter opinions, raise your hand now." He gazes around the room.

One hand goes up. I turn to see Jackie standing firm at the back of the room. Half the crowd also turns to see who dares raise a hand.

"Yes, Miss, what is it?" asks Mr. Boothe.

"She ain't got no right to talk," shouts a woman up front.

"Can't even speak no English," a man says, laughing.

"I speak English," Jackie says, voice light yet full of confidence. "Miss Sandra taught me. I go to the school because of Miss Maggie. I learn a lot from her. She is nicest person of the town. She is number one kind woman here. She is best teacher. Please let her stay."

I tear up at Jackie's words, but I know they won't be of any use.

"That's fine," says Mr. Boothe, dismissing a few objections. "We appreciate your opinion, but you're not old enough to vote. And not a town citizen, neither."

"I'm eighteen from last week," she speaks up. I never knew when her birthday was and feel bad for that. "I live in this town more than one year, so I am citizen. It is law. I read the law list."

"That's all good and well, darling, but we have decided." He looks over the crowd, checking that nobody else has objections. None. "So it's agreed: Maggie Baumann shall cease being our school teacher immediately."

"What about the band? We put so much money into it already."

"I want my money's worth!"

"Yeah, what about the band?"

"Who else knows music?"

"Well, she is the most music-minded of anyone here."

"But she better stay away from that swanky salesman."

"Maybe they in league together."

The crowd's debate rises until Mr. Boothe waves them quiet.

I take a deep breath. Maybe there is some hope after all.

"Well, maybe she could still continue leading the band," says Mr. Boothe, then scans the crowd for other voices. "With supervision. No more working with kids without some other adult being there. That all right with you?"

"Parents have always been welcome at any of our rehearsals and at the kids' individual lessons," I respond. "I will continue with the band, if you will let me."

"And no more injuns in the school house!" someone cries out at the side of the room, cheered by a few others.

"Very well," Mr. Boothe says, ignoring the remark. "Miss Maggie will continue with the band, but with another adult, someone not of her family, always being present. Agreed?"

The crowd applauds, the decision final.

"Thank you for what you said," I tell Jackie as she rolls me down the street after the meeting ends. "That was brave of you."

"Not brave," she says. "Truth."

"That may be so, but you see there's some variety to truth. Each person sees things differently. It's amazing anyone can ever agree on anything. But at least I can still lead the band."

"You are good band leader," she says and pats my shoulder.

She rolls me to where Jeb's left the wagon. The two young folks help me up, put my wheel-chair on the flatbed, and take me home with his horse tethered to the wagon.

They help me inside, but I can see them smooching on the porch for several minutes before Jeb reluctantly bids Jackie farewell and mounts his horse for home.

17

SKINNER CANYON BLUES

THE REST OF THE SUMMER I occupy myself writing new blues songs. I have a lot of inspiration, you might say. Feeling blue most days, singing the blues, not caring much about anything other than my misery. Sometimes Eve gets her cornet out to play along. She feels blue, too. A few songs and our spirits seem a little better.

When I return to the school house for classes, I have to face the kids – with Mrs. Booker present to monitor me. I give them a good smile and a little speech about treating each other kindly. I say we need to follow rules, too. Then I confess to breaking some rules their parents think I should've followed, even though anything I did or might've done had nothing to do with what I taught the kids or anything I said to them or did with them. The accusations were only about my behavior away from school. I promise to be a good citizen and a good teacher. I explain how I'm only allowed to teach music. The townsfolk want to keep the band going, and I'm the only person with the knowledge to teach music. For now.

Most kids take the news well but a few get upset. I assure them I'll be coming to the school on the same schedule. But Mrs. Booker will do most of the teaching from now on.

"They plan to hire a new teacher," I add, trying to be honest with them. "Maybe the new teacher will also know about music and can lead the band. Who knows?"

They have awkward questions, some about the new teacher they have yet to hire. I don't know, I say. Mom willingly took over the job when we came to Skinner Canyon, then it passed to me. I've enjoyed it so much, and thought I'd found my purpose. But things happened I never could've anticipated, I tell them.

"But d-did you...uh, M-Miss Maggie, uh...is it t-true?" asks Jane, a shy girl who is growing out of it day by day. "What they s-said?"

"Well, some of it is true, yes," I respond. "Other things, I think they misinterpreted. And others are plain wrong. But what can I do? They decided and I can't go against what they decided."

"So are you really married?" asks David with a sly grin.

"Not any longer. It was a big mistake. Now it's corrected."

"What do we call you now?" asks Georgia. "Are you Missus Kirk or Miss Baumann?"

"Miss Maggie will be fine," I reply.

"But what about Doctor Hill? Is he gonna be your new husband?" asks little Liza. "He's very pretty."

"Pretty's for girls," snaps Luke. "It's 'handsome' for boys."

"I have no plans to marry anyone right now, kids. I'm focused on our music endeavors. We have a concert to prepare for."

And we do. I spend my days at the school house, using the side room to study the music we will play. While the kids learn history, arithmetics, reading and writing, I scribble down a few songs I have in my head. I can hear tunes between my ears and I know notation well enough to mark the paper without having to pick the keys of the old piano at the back of the classroom to see if I got them right. Even so, while the kids play outside, I play my songs on the piano. Then I scurry back to the side room before the kids come inside again. I'm not allowed to be in the same room with them unless Mrs. Booker or another parent is present.

All of that disappointment, even angst, goes into my songs. Not all of them have words but they all have feelings. Strong feelings, so I use the minor keys. Back home I play them out through my tuba, forgetting the discomfort of setting the hunk of metal on my delicate lap or the tremendous vibrations that rumble through my body as I play. Again Eve comes out to join me with her cornet or leaves me to myself if she recognizes I want to be alone. A few evenings, a coyote will bark or howl along with my tuba playing.

"Them's wolfs," Eve says, then howls back into the darkness.

Meantime, the townsfolk are not so kind, not like before when I tried to get myself around on a wheel-chair or using crutches. They would help me, open doors, even carry me up stairs. Not now; they move aside for me, just keep going, like I'm not there. Some will be rude, say a nasty remark or a vile comment about what I do at night or offer a good chuckle about my condition like it's well-deserved. If I have to choose, I prefer the ones who shun me, who keep quiet as I pass. Yet I'm left heartbroken every time I have business in town.

I write to Dr. Hill again, telling him of this awful arrangement, and wait for his reply. He mentions again when I finally receive his message that the offer stands. He will welcome me to Kanza City as a famous conductor, or at least a curiosity. A young woman from out west, crippled and conducting from a wheel-chair, will bring lots of folks out to concerts, he assures me. The problem, as I write back, is that I don't want to be that woman – not that kind of woman, nor an orchestra conductor. I'm much better being a tuba player. What do I know about stringed instruments?

Dr. Hill continues to encourage me in his further messages, each inviting me to Kanza City. I must consider the situation. I love these kids. I enjoy teaching them music and getting the band started, but what more is there for me in Skinner Canyon? I have to think about my future, what there is of it, what paths are available as a disabled woman who refuses help.

I visit Simon Bailey at his usual saloon, The Five Whores, and have him show me how to play his fiddle. I don't think his technique is quite the same as what a violinist would use in an orchestra, but it's good to get the basic knowledge of a stringed instrument in my head. I give it a try and Simon corrects me several times. Finally I make fairly good sounds drawing the bow across the strings. I press down on the strings here and there, changing the notes. I repeat a phrase I've invented and after a few tries it sounds acceptable. He tells me the notes of a song he knows and I follow his instructions.

"That ain't half bad fer cripple woman just startin' out," he says with a toothless grin.

I buy him a beer for the lesson, which gets people talking.

During school days and evenings I read more in the big book of music, trying not to think of who gave me the book. I memorize the fingering charts for each stringed instrument, as I did for woodwind and brass instruments. I listen to a few more disks on the machine while Faith and Eve are out back in the garden. I follow, looking at the score, my finger on the melody line as it moves across the pages. I hold up my baton, mark the time along with the music. Of course, I know I'm reacting to the music when the way it's supposed to be is for the musicians to react to my directions as the conductor. I grow bolder as I regain my ability to stand longer without discomfort.

"That's lookin' real good," calls Eve one afternoon, catching me conducting to the music coming out of the machine.

"I must rehearse," I reply with a smile.

Eve stays to watch a while, then has to return to her work in the garden. She has a job; I have only dreams.

I get through the complete symphony of someone named Mahler and after five movements cannot lift my arms.

Another message arrives from Hal, urging me to come to Kanza City. A position's been created: assistant to the assistant conductor. I can't believe it. Is it the April's Fool day? Why would anyone hire me without meeting me? We did get a mention in the news-paper, I know from a clipping Hal sent with his last message, but a kids' band in a small town led by a woman in a wheel-chair isn't anything special to city folks. Yet he insists I must visit.

> *You know more than you think you know. I see your talent. I see your dedication. You will go far, and nothing would make me happier than seeing you reach your full potential.*

Potential? I laugh. I reached my full potential the day Old Betty stomped on me. That is the truth.

"So why don'tcha just go an' see what he's yappin' about?" says Eve as we talk it over in bed. "Just a railway ticket an' he's offerin' ta pay it fer ya."

"I suppose you're right," I say. "But I hate to leave the kids."

"Them kids'll unnerstand. Heck, don't hardly teach'em now."

"I suppose you're right."

"After the fall concert, you kin take off a bit. You kin come back later if'n ya like." Eve smiles sadly in the candlelight. "Or if'n ya like it there, just stay. We'll be awright here. Y'ain't doin' much no-ways, Faith says. Just takin' up our veg'table 'lotment, is all."

"Well, since you put it that way," I say, half amused, "I might as well go and see what the fuss is about."

+   +   +

The fall concert includes works written by John Bach, Wolf Mozart, Ralph Vaughan Williams, John Philip Sousa (Eve likes long names, says they write the best songs), and a little tune composed by me, *M. Baumann*, that I call "Kids Band Blues". Jackie likes the drum part, written especially for her.

Despite my lower status in town, everyone appreciates the kids' performance and applauds loudly. I step aside and let the kids enjoy the praise. Then I sneak out on my crutches, find my wheel-chair by our wagon, and wait for the ride home.

A week later, I get Jeb to take me and Jackie out to the railway depot. He's happy to help me just to get to see her, but he's sad that she's going away with me to Kanza City for a while.

"Go on, now," I tell them at the depot. "Get your good-bye kissing done." And I look away.

Eve stays behind to continue helping Faith with the harvest. She can't leave or the business will suffer. I promise to be quick, only a month at the most, and Jackie is old enough now to not be in school. She's practically like a daughter to us.

We get the tickets Hal sent by communication stream, waiting for us in the railway office. We board the Women Only carriage, find our seats, and make ourselves comfortable for the long trip.

"Iron horse," Jackie says and giggles.

It's her first time aboard one of these, although she's seen them passing her village many times.

"We sit in belly of horse," she laughs.

Only a half-hour into our trip the man in railway uniform comes to check our tickets. He questions Jackie's presence. We show our tickets, printed at the railway office.

"You see, ma'am, this is a high-class car," the man says, "so we don't allow her kind in here. Other riders will object."

"Other riders?" I respond. "It's none of their business."

"But she's...she's one of those tribals."

"She's with me. Understand? She's my daughter."

"Daughter, hmm? Don't look much like you."

"She's adopted, obviously. But a daughter is a daughter. And, as my grandma liked to say: 'daughters is good to have' – am I right?"

Jackie gives a nod, grins at the man.

"Fine," he says in a huff. "But you keep an eye on her. Don't want any thieving going on. Somebody loses something, they'll be blaming her first. And I don't want any trouble on my train."

I have to laugh. "She doesn't want anything they have."

The rest of the trip is mostly watching the grass grow in quick-motion, with a few burly buffalo gazing back at us, wondering where we're going. We pass through small towns that appear worse than Skinner Canyon and pretty meadows where I'd stop for a picnic.

We eventually pull into Kanza City, like when Eve and I were going to the capital. But the terminal is too busy for me to handle, especially in a wheel-chair. Hal is there on the platform to greet us and escorts us to a waiting hire-carriage. He rolls me in the wheel-chair despite my insistence I can walk a short distance.

"It's better that you stay in the chair," he says, leaning down to speak into my ear against the station noise. "It looks more pitiful this way. People want to see a poor woman take the stage."

"But I'm not poor," I say, but he's already straightened up and can't hear me through the din.

We exit the station, get settled in the carriage, and soon arrive at a grand hotel rising several floors, reminding me of the buildings in the capital.

"Your new home, my dear," Hal beams.

Entering the magnificent doorway into the opulent lobby, I find a small crowd of people turning to welcome me to their city. They seem to be connected to the orchestra or the news-paper, all pleased to have me visit. I am overwhelmed. I play my part by staying in my wheel-chair, letting hotel staff push me around, including into a lift box like what they have in the capital. Jackie is shy at first, but I assure her it's safe, then hope it is. It clangs but moves up steadily and stops at the top floor. We are assigned the Executive Suite.

"How about this!" Hal says. "The best we have."

"A children's band in a small western town isn't much worthy of a feature in a big city news-paper," I say. "Or this suite."

"It is," says Hal – only Dr. Hill in public, professional situations. "This is the center of the music world now. There is great respect for the Musical Arts here in Kanza City. A resurgence, you might say. We recognize the value of music in our lives, and rely on it to lift our spirits and inspire us. You have come to the best place to continue your music career. The Society of Musical Arts welcomes you."

"Oh, my," I say, shuddering. "I'm not sure I can be at their level. All I know is what I've taught myself."

"That is what makes you so special. You are self-taught! That's a miracle, a fascination for people here. They are delighted with your story. You're the talk of the town. And I've been leading a publicity campaign ahead of your arrival. Now you must prove me correct."

"So that's why they gathered downstairs to welcome me."

"Did you like that? Were you impressed?"

"I—I was frightened, to be honest."

"Indeed! You impressed them, I'm certain." He turns to Jackie, standing to the side of the room, still holding her bag. "Am I right?"

"Yes," she mumbles. "Miss Maggie is good people."

"She is at that," says Hal, gazing down at me in my chair. "Just remember to always use this chair."

"What about the stage? I can't roll everywhere."

"We shall find the best way to get you on the stage, over to the podium, and help you rise to conduct the orchestra."

"Conduct the orchestra?" I practically shriek.

"That is the reason you've come here, isn't it?" he teases. "That is what everyone expects. You are more than a curiosity. They want to see the woman in the wheel-chair conduct the orchestra. Then, I do believe, you will be a star."

"But what is the song?" I have to ask.

"Maestro Guillaume shall conduct the majority of the program. I believe the opening piece, too. Then you will be introduced. You will come on the stage and take your place. You conduct your piece, and you exit. Maestro Guillaume will conclude the program."

"I know how to take my place," I say with irony.

"So you will fit in quite nicely," says Hal, with a soft pat to my shoulder. "You are meant to be here. Enjoy this experience."

"Thank you, Hal." My heart is fluttering. "You've done so much for me. I can't ever thank you enough."

"I'm fine, Maggie – if I may call you by your first name."

"Always."

"It is one of the many reasons I adore you."

I'm blushing, so I turn to regard Jackie who is biting her lips to keep from laughing.

"Now what is the song I must conduct?" I ask Hal.

"I'll have the score sent to you. I believe Maestro Guillaume has selected the Mahler *Adagietto* for you. It's fairly easy to conduct, he says. Rehearsals begin tomorrow, after your interview."

Terror begins to sweep through me but I try my best to not let it show. Then Jackie comes and takes my hand and I feel stronger.

"That sounds fine," I manage to reply.

We have a lovely dinner in the hotel's restaurant, a room that is so beyond my expectations I must gaze around it throughout the five courses. Hal becomes a bit annoyed, as though I'm not listening to him, but I pat his hand to let him know I am. He's put off having Jackie with us, but she has to eat, too. She likes the bison steaks we are served. Potatoes cut into cubes and covered in a spicy red sauce called 'catsup'. A hank of two different greens mixed with yellow and red peppers. Fresh hard bread and whipped white butter. The finest dinner I've had in my life! I thank Hal for ordering for us. Jackie smiles her enjoyment, using the knife and fork correctly as we have practiced. Dessert is a slice of cream pie with blueberries on top.

"My pleasure," says Hal, an air of disappointment in his voice.

I see the look in his eyes, how he wants to say more but not with Jackie with us. He might wish to do more than talk, perhaps if we were in a private setting. He offers to get a separate room for Jackie, but I insist I need her to help me so it's best if she stays in the same room with me. It's a suite, after all. Plenty of space. I'm here for a music event, aren't I? This isn't what the youngsters call 'dating': picking a date on the calendar to meet your favorite person for some affectionate activity or something more intimate.

"I'm sorry, Hal," I say, taking his hand. "You know all about my injury. I'm not able to do the things I may wish to do."

Returning to our room, I let Jackie go in ahead of me as I remain in the corridor with Hal. He presses forward and I know he wants to kiss, so I don't lean away but welcome his lips upon mine. Such a delight after so much absence! His mustache tickles pleasantly. His hands cradle my waist, try to draw me to him but it is awkward for me, standing on shaky legs. I remind him I can walk but with some discomfort. Standing is nearly as bad, so he has me rest against the wall as he kisses me again – and we go at it rather like two lovesick kids for a while.

Until Jackie pokes her head out to ask if I'm coming in the room soon. She wishes to wash up and change into sleeping clothes. She's become so 'proper' now after living with us a while.

"Give us a minute, please," I say.

I have to refresh myself, sweep strands of loose hair aside.

She can guess what we're doing in the corridor. Thank goodness no guests stroll by to witness our debauchery! My face feels flush, and in that instant Hal bids me a good night.

He gives a glance at Jackie, then offers me a simple peck on the cheek, like a gentleman, and departs.

"I hope you don't think poorly of me," I say to Jackie inside our grand room. "We haven't seen each other for a long time."

She grins like she has a secret she can use against me.

"Very happy for you. Yeah, it's *ooo-kay*." She likes that word, I've noticed. Probably she picked it up from cowpokes.

"I'm sorry if it makes you feel awkward," I say as she helps me get out of the elegant dinner dress. Even without my injury I'd need help with this complicated garment. This is the reason I prefer the cowboy clothes, a simple shirt and trousers.

"It's no problem," she says solemnly. I've only seen her laugh in the presence of Jeb. "You have Doctor Hill. I have Jeb Baumann. It's good for you and good for me. We are happy now."

"Thank you for understanding."

"I like to do with Jeb. You like to do same with Doctor."

I smile to myself. "Yes, I suppose that's true."

She helps me to the bathing room, a ceramic palace larger than our whole cabin in Skinner Canyon. There's a basin large enough for a person to lie down flat in, so I fill it with hot water directly from a gold faucet and plan to enjoy it before bedtime. No having to heat the water on a brazier then pour it from a bucket like we do back home. On a long shelf are bottles of bathing liquids and shampoos to choose from, each different scents. Jackie chooses one and pours it into the bath water for me. Maybe she pours too much, I think, as the bubbles rise higher and higher.

Meantime, I slip off the fluffy lounging gown which the hotel has provided. Just as I step over the rim of the basin, my foot grazes the tepid water full of a mountain of foam. At that very instant, I catch a strange image in the mirror.

I'm no longer a little girl, no longer a young woman, either. I see myself clearly: the scars from the stitches, the dry, pale skin that appears sickly, my ribs announcing themselves, and meager breasts trying to hide. And untrimmed hair everywhere, too difficult to tend to in my condition. Wearing my daily garments, I have no need to care for myself in such detail. I realize I must present myself better, not only for Hal, if our fates should align, but for my own soul. For the audience, too. I am better than I've let myself become.

I slip into the hot water, cover myself with the foam, hiding from the world.

Jackie starts to slather the fluffy ball full of soap foam over my body. It's like a massage. The warmth of the water soothes my body, helps relax my muscles. I feel no pain. My mind goes soft. I forget where I am, and that Jackie's with me here.

Until a splash awakens me.

Opening my eyes, I find her sitting at the other end of this large basin, her knees tucked up out of the water, making space in the foam. She regards me with a child-like grin. Her smooth, brown skin is lovely. She looks as thin as me without her usual bulky clothing. I want to give her more space to enjoy this luxurious place, so I pull my legs up as best I can and scoot myself back against the end of the curved basin. My feet rest flat on the bottom. Her feet are already in place. We jostle them, laughing, letting our toes wriggle in mock fight. Then we settle back, relaxing until the bathing water grows cool and the foam dissolves.

We rise together, shivering, and reach for the enormous towels, gather ourselves within their comfortable wrappings and giggle all the way to the bed. I feel like a little girl for a few minutes, and can recall how Mom received me in her warm arms after a quick wash under our strict water usage rules in the capital.

I think of Eve, miss her. I tell Jackie how much I miss Eve and she does, too. We talk about Eve, laugh at some anecdotes. Eve is like the funny dad in our family.

We turn down the lamps, these on electric instead of oil. I pull back the covers of the large, well-padded bed, enough for three or four of us, and I slide in, like meat into a sandwich, let the coverings fall back over me. Their weight reminds me of Eve laying beside me, holding me, the way we were before my injury. I feel a hand on my shoulder.

"Goodnight, Mama," I hear whispered in the darkness, and think it's in my head. But it's Jackie laying beside me.

"I mean good night, Miss Maggie," she corrects herself.

"Mama is *ooo-kay*," I say.

18

FAME & FORTUNE

LILA ROSE BENTON, a news-reporter for *The Daily Informant* and well-known gossip according to Dr. Hill, arranges to meet me at the Music Hall for an in-depth interview that Hal's arranged as part of the publicity campaign for the Kanza City Symphonia. He warns me that she will likely ask a few scandalous questions for her inquiring readers who wish to know everything.

I discover they have a wardrobe budget for me. I take Jackie with me to several shops in the central business district, selecting an appropriate garment for each of my social engagements. A few outfits for Jackie, too; she's never looked so pretty as wearing the ribbon skirt and shawl, the style trend in Kanza City. I choose four dresses as well as a skirt and three blouses. I select a formal black gown, a bit low in front but sleeveless to aid in conducting – and I've already shaved under my arms, a tiresome task. A pair of black not-too-high heeled shoes completes my costume. I plan to stand tall at the podium to conduct. I can't help but be concerned how the reverse side will appear to the audience when I face the musicians.

We hit the limit and I try to pay the extra from my account back in Skinner Canyon but the shop clerk questions my account. What unmarried woman has her own account? It must be full of ill-gotten gains, he snickers, acting as though he's hiding a secret for me. No, I explain in a stern voice, it is my own business, me and my cousins: the Grady Vegetorium, an agriculture enterprise. More checking on his tablet, snooty air thickening, and he must acknowledge that it's a legitimate business. My payment is accepted.

I get a full tour of the Music Hall. The auditorium is huge, can hold nearly a thousand people in rows of fixed seats covered in rich red velvet that fold up so guests can move through the rows. In the school house back in Skinner Canyon we could barely fit in twenty-five musicians and twenty-five parents as an audience. Jackie keeps her head swiveling at everything she sees, amazed by the facility.

I'm shown the backstage area, dressing rooms, rehearsal rooms, offices, and other places I never could've imagined existing here. My dressing room has my name on the door. Can I be so famous already or is it merely further enticement to be impressive? In the room is everything a famous performer could ask for. Jackie is impressed, takes a turn sitting in the cosmetics chair and spins it around a few times watching herself in the wide mirror. She pokes at the tray of cosmetics on the counter, asks what they are for. My escort answers her, then asks if Jackie is my daughter and I confirm she is.

Seeing myself in that wide mirror, my stomach begins to rattle, acid building, and my heart beats faster. I understand how my dad felt most of his life being a nervous type. I take long, deep breaths. It feels like I'm heading out a dirt path that will end with a horse stomping on me. This time there will be hundreds of people to see it happen. Jackie sees my nervousness, gives me a hug.

"You can do it," she intones. "Everything gonna be *ooo-kay*."

I know this event is just a ruse to get the orchestra noticed, to promote ticket sales, and draw attention to the city's music scene. Everyone wants to see the crippled girl from out west make a fool of herself in front of a professional orchestra and sophisticated concert-goers. At least my back will be towards most of them.

"So how do you feel being in the big city for the first time?" asks the snooty Miss Benton, dolled up like a brothel madam – like what I've seen in pictures from days past.

I wear one of my new outfits: a pink blouse with a short-waisted peach blazer, white pleated knee-length skirt and baby-blue hosiery, daring to expose my calves and ankles to a stranger's gaze, with tan-and-white shoes that are unusually comfortable. Miss Benton says, with bemused eyebrow rising, that I appear more like a school girl than an orchestra conductor. I remind her that I used to be a school teacher. Until I took up conducting, I add for Hal's sake. I started a kid's band, I tell Miss Benton. Jackie says my colorful outfit reminds her of the spring meadows around her village.

"I was born in the capital actually," I say. "Then we went west."

Miss Benton presses for more details, so I give her the shortened version: how Mother was born in the capital, Dad down south, how they met, a few highlights of my family's time there, then how my dad died while saving the governor from a terrorist plot. That makes her perk up, scribbling wildly on a paper pad with ornate ink pen, quite old-fashion. She uses the fancy, curly style of writing.

"Mother took us out of the capital as soon as she could. Too many bad things happening there. I was eleven. We went out to Skinner Canyon because my cousin lives there. We've been there ever since, although my mother was killed in an unfortunate accident."

"Same as your incident?" asks this noodling nincompoop.

"Oh, no. Hers was years before mine."

"It does seem misfortune mocks you," she says in a cutesy voice.

"Misfortune? Perhaps. But I don't believe Fate with a capital F is following us. I'm here, aren't I? That's good fortune, isn't it? But Life happens. I've heard people say: 'Life comes at you fast; if you're not smelling roses, then you might miss it.' Or something like that. It's a Southern expression."

I give a little laugh that endears me to her.

She gets to the scandal questions. Yes, I was briefly married but that's been resolved, corrected. No children. Obviously we weren't married long enough for that. And Dr. Hill? Oh, he's just a friend, an admirer, a promoter of music like me. Very helpful in starting the kid's band. I'm sure he has his infatuations, and perhaps I let him go on a bit too much in my distracted moments, but isn't that the Life we're supposed to notice? The roses that can look like just about anyone.

Our conversation goes for two hours, a staff member bringing us bottled water that fizzes, setting a new bottle on the table whenever we finish a previous bottle. Mine has the tart flavor of lemons. Miss Benton's drink is purple. We cover everything on her list. Most of all are the reasons I turned to music. I give her the quick answer: our family history, the tuba handed down generation to generation, and so on. I tell her about my great-grandmother Polly, the professional tuba player and music professor who died during the long pandemic. In fact, she was composing a concerto for tuba and orchestra when the pandemic struck. I told about our ancestor, the original Fritz my dad was named after, who brought the tuba to our country, played it in an orchestra and also taught music at a college, up to the day he tragically died, hit by a motorcar while crossing the street.

"Seems you do have a strong musical background," Miss Benton suggests with a wink. "Something ingrained in your family lineage."

I agree with her to make it easy. Then I go off on a long-winded journey through the history of music. It seems to fascinate her how much I know, garnered from reading that big book of music Billy gave me. Because of that awful man, I can talk about movements, list composers' names, musical styles, trends, and criticism. I offer a few examples of famous tunes, which I either sing or hum for her.

"Will we be able to hear you play the tuba during your visit?" she asks, sounding like she's setting a trap.

"My tuba, we left it at home," I reply.

"I'm sure the Symphonia's tubist wouldn't mind you giving us a tiny demonstration."

"I wouldn't want a stranger playing my instrument, so I'm sure she wouldn't either."

She corrects me: the tuba player here is a man.

"I'm sure he can handle the position," I say, not at all smug.

"I can introduce you, if you like," she offers.

"I would be happy to perform a recital, given the necessary time to prepare and certainly playing my own instrument. Perhaps on my next visit."

"Yes, yes, of course," she says, adding a dismissive laugh like the whole idea was only a joke.

Miss Benton offers to show me the article she will write about me before it goes to the pressing or on the streams. I thank her for the opportunity to review it. She unleashes her puppy laugh again, like she doesn't really mean it. What awful things could she write about me? I said nothing that is particularly scandalous. She asked nothing odd or embarrassing, nothing I haven't addressed already.

Later, when I report on the interview with Hal, he's proud of me for standing up to Miss Benton, who can be a bully.

"Have to know how to handle cowpokes, then you get some skills dealing with bullies," I tell him. Jackie laughs behind us.

"Yes, indeed," says Hal. "She does have many of the features of a 'cowpoke', as you so eloquently insinuate."

After the interview, my designated escort, a statuesque woman about my age named Marie who is one of the orchestra's librarians, takes us to the dressing room so we can rest a few minutes before meeting the orchestra.

Meeting the orchestra! My heart trips into a faster speed as my skin releases a new layer of moisture underneath my clothes. Jackie calms me, taking a cloth from the lavatory and dabbing it on my neck. She massages my tight shoulders.

"It's same as kids band," says Jackie. "They look at you and you count for them."

I pat her hand, laid on my shoulder. "Thanks. It's a little more than that, I think."

Marie returns, says it's time to go. She leads us through winding corridors to the auditorium. Jackie pushes me in the wheel-chair.

We halt at the stage door, looking out at the many chairs, at the empty auditorium.

I roll myself through the doorway onto the stage. I see all of the musicians in place, some still warming up, others adjusting chairs, music stands, the music pages on the stands. They dress in simple, everyday clothes, not concert garments. That helps relax me. I still feel wet, my blouse sticking to me.

"Our next guest conductor, everyone," calls Maestro Guillaume, excitedly, looking in my direction. He starts the applause.

The whole orchestra claps and many of them stand while I wheel myself down an aisle they've made between the violin sections, right up to the podium where the real conductor waits for me.

Maestro is an older man, with flowing gray hair and a well-lined face as though he's been in many battles on and off the stage. He is taller than me. Wider, too; his belly strains against his buttons. He steps down from the podium, offering his hand to shake.

I take it, smiling up at him.

He tries to help me get up from the chair but I wave him off with a delicate flip of my fingers. I take my cane from across my lap and place the tip firmly on the floor of the stage. Then I rise, like the wounded woman I am, feeling a wave of discomfort ripple through me. I ignore it for the sake of my smile and this golden opportunity.

Actually, I don't need this. In a flash I run through a checklist of reasons *not* to be here. But it adds up to nothing. I can turn and roll myself back. I can return to Skinner Canyon and just be the music teacher for the kids. I can write blues songs in the evening with Eve. And my life will go on with no more difficulties.

Maestro Guillaume takes my hand to steady me, urging me onto the podium. He hands me the baton from the music stand. I take it, holding on to my cane with my other hand. Thinking what to do with it, I set the cane against the music stand, grasp the metal fixture. It isn't strong enough to hold me, everyone can see, not like the lectern in the school.

Maestro sees the problem and calls over to a staff person at the side of the stage. In short order two men bring out a full lectern, a large wooden piece of furniture, and set it where the music stand is, replacing the music score for me.

Again, Maestro introduces me, gesturing to the musicians of the Kanza City Symphonia: "Miss Maggie Baumann, everyone."

They probably know my background from the notes posted in the section rooms. I'm director of the Skinner Canyon children's band. Quite impressive! I want to laugh at this joke I'm participating in.

He steps off the podium and I suddenly feel so alone, with sixty musicians staring at me, expecting something amazing to happen. But I'm just a school teacher. All I know is from what I've read. I practice a lot, sure, but I've never had this kind of stress.

Scanning the musicians' faces, I locate the instrument sections. I see mostly men but a few women appear: violins, flutes, clarinet and oboe. The orchestra is reduced for this particular piece: only string instruments. The other musicians sit quietly. Hal, one of the horn players, has gone to the audience seats to watch me.

I look down at the music score laid open on the lectern before me: Gustav Mahler, Symphony #5, Movement #4, designated *Sehr Langsam* – 'very slowly' in German. In some odd way, I feel like I've come home, like if certain events hadn't happened I'd be right here now anyway. Just as Old Fritz's own grandfather, the conductor.

I take a long breath. I've never seen this music before, but I've heard some of this man's music on the disks on the music machine so I know his style, his moods, his way of creating feelings. It's the notes which almost get in the way.

I study the first page of the score, find the melody. I turn to the next page, following the notes. Then the next page and a quick look at the next one. I sense the musicians getting restless so I return to the first page and look up at them. Forcing a confident smile, I try to meet their eyes. I *can't* meet their eyes – except for a few who smile back to me, giving me confidence.

"Well," I say, and take a breath, "you're certainly not children."

A few of them laugh. I nod to acknowledge them.

"I better apologize first," I say, "before I act like a fool."

Some of them fidget, maybe feel embarrassed for me, or they're no longer willing to endure my amateurish mockery of these great institutions of music. They are losing patience with me.

"This is our first play-through," I tell them like they are my kids back home, "so just do your best. We'll fix things later."

I sneak another look at the first page, second page. Don't forget to slow a bit for all those *appoggiatura*, I remind myself – checking the glossary from the back of the music book that's now stuck in my head: an ornamental note played *on the beat* rather than ahead of the main note that falls on the beat.

And it's *adagietto*, not *adagio*.

"All right then," I say. "Let's see how it sounds."

I raise my hands, baton in my right, and mark the tempo, then give the downbeat and they play.

They play! Violins sigh their first note, hold it.

Cue the harp. *Harp? We have a harp?*

The heavenly notes unfold, rising and falling in accordance with my directions. They know this piece better than me, I believe, so just keep the beat steady, I tell myself. But as I follow the notes on the page, and occasionally look up at them, give a cue here and there, I feel the music coming into me. It fills me like too much wine, like an infusion of fresh blood. My arms do not tire but gain strength. My gut settles into a firm foundation as my heart not only beats in hot fever but feeds me more. The notes are sad, grim even, yet hopeful: every line is filled with equal measure of sorrow and joy. That is Mr. Mahler's special gift, as the book described. Intimate yet expansive. I can feel it. I know now what my dad meant.

I let the sounds fill me, lift me, and I'm soaring, forgetting the score. The musicians are following my directions: pulling from deep within their souls to match this melody, these harmonies, the whole crackling storm of emotion! Passion! Love! Death! Together! Let us create a dream together! Let us be human once more! It is Heaven shining down on us, welcoming us!

We hold the final note and I cannot let my hands drop when it's time for the note to end. I am too stricken with ethereal joy.

I hear applause and open my eyes. The musicians are smiling at me. Some of them wipe away tears. I feel my own cheeks wet from tears. I smile back as I wipe my eyes, then humbly bow my head.

Maestro Guillaume returns to the podium, clapping.

"Bravo! Bravo!" he cries, taking my baton hand in his two hands, shaking it. "And you never saw this before? It's true?"

"I heard this man's music, another piece, but not this one."

"Yet you feel it within you. Marvelous!"

"It is easy to conduct," I say, not really believing it.

More applause from orchestra members and I make my way into my wheel-chair and roll myself up the aisle to the doorway. Jackie is there waiting to roll me further, back to the dressing room.

Once inside, with the door shut, I can finally let go. My entire body crashes at the horror of what I've just done. My mind's on fire. I break out in a flood of wetness, my clothes soaked. Jackie tries to clean me up but it's no use. I send her back to the hotel, four blocks away, to fetch me a new outfit. I want to be presentable when Hal arrives once the rehearsal ends.

"I was so moved!" he cries out, coming to the room later, ecstatic over my first rehearsal, bearing his French horn under his arm.

"It's only a rehearsal," I say humbly. "We'll get better."

"I know how you conducted the children's band but this – *this!* It was tremendous! I've never seen you conduct so dramatically, quite unlike anything I ever imagined."

"It's easy when you feel the music."

"But you only saw it today."

Actually, the score was delivered the previous evening but I only gave it a glance, too afraid to look at it more. They could forgive me for not seeing it before a rehearsal, but if I had time to study it they would expect more from me.

"You were practically dancing along with the music," he goes on.

"I can't dance. Have you forgotten?"

Trying to accept his praise, I somehow feel like a fool, a trained pony to show off. Hal continues being effusive, going on and on with his compliments, becoming unrealistic.

"But why, Hal?" I have to ask, holding up a hand. "Why me? I'm only an amateur. From a small western town. I only lead a band for kids. For kids!"

His mouth tightens. "I have confidence in you. I put your name in for the position. I trust you'll forgive me."

"You could've set me up for a truly embarrassing disaster."

"I have faith in you, Maggie. And, to be frank, there are not so many available who are as qualified as you these days, even in this large city. We lost a whole generation of music-trained individuals during and since the pandemic. Music is new to us – its return to us in recent years is a gift. There hasn't been enough time for many to be trained. So I thought of you."

"Me? The only one?"

"Plus I'm a Symphonia board member. And I'm in the musicians guild, too. So I put in your name for consideration. I apologize if I've put you in an awkward position. That was not at all my intention. However, I believe you can do it."

"Do what? Be the savior of your music?"

"Not quite that. Anyway, I want to help you."

"Help me? How? Move to the big city? Try something I've never done before? Suffer the stress of worrying whether I will look like a fool in front of everyone? *That?*"

"Indeed." He pulls on a sour face, realizing what he's done. "As I said: I believe in you, Maggie. I knew you could do it. And I was correct. Look at you! What you did out there only a little while ago. You impressed everyone."

"Look at me?" I feel the wetness of my shirt. "Look at me: this is all because of what you set me up for."

"You move so elegantly," he fumbles. "Perspiration is expected."

I cross my arms over my chest, uncross them, re-cross them.

"Believe me, you impressed them," he says.

"To what end, though?"

I want to cry, my frustration cutting through whatever joy I felt at conducting that heart-wrenching piece.

Hal holds out his arms. "I'm so sorry, Maggie."

"Am I supposed to live here now? Be a rehearsal conductor now? Go on to conduct bigger and better works? Become famous? Is that your grand scheme?"

He gazes at me like a lovesick school boy. "Well, yes."

"Yes...." I glare at him, like he's spilled a bottle of lemon soda.

"Yes," he confirms, letting a grin spread across his face.

He extends his arms for a hug.

"No, I'm too wet. Jackie's gone for another outfit."

"I don't mind your wetness." He comes against me and places his hands on my waist. My hip twitches. "I welcome it, all of it, all that is you, no matter how messy you might be, no matter how moist – along with the rest of you, the wonder of you, in every moment we are together, dear Maggie."

"Oh, stop it with your fancy words, Hal." I step back. "I feel like it's all a game to you."

"No, Maggie, I'm serious." He turns then, as though hiding tears. "You are special to me. No matter what's occurred between us in our long relation. I don't count that tryst we had. It was so lovely but I know there's a lot more to you. The music things. I get such joy from your success. I only want more of that for you."

"Hal," I call in rough tone, "I'm not your trained rodeo pony!"

"I know you're not. I'm not trying to train you. I want you to run free. I only wish to accompany you."

"I have to step forward on my own. I appreciate your help. How can I not be thankful? And yet, it must be me who takes each step."

"But you're injured, my dear." He pauses for effect. "I'm trying to help you. That's all. I'll let you take the lead...as you always have, my dear. As I have always welcomed you to do."

"What do you get from this? What do you expect will be the final outcome? What do you desire, Hal?"

He looks down. "You, Maggie. I desire you."

"Me? Really?" I feel it's his standard utterance. He cannot truly be serious. He's a salesman above all.

"That music. The *Adagietto*. The way you let it infuse you with its full complement of emotion. The way you turned it around and sent it out. The glory of that act! I...I fell in love with you all over again. It's true. You are a monstrous love. I fear you. I fear losing you. I fear—"

The knock on the door stops our argument.

Hal stands straight, hands stuffed into his trouser pockets so that everything looks proper as I open the door.

It's Maestro Guillaume come to give his praise. He doesn't seem surprised to find Hal in my room. He gives Hal a nod.

"We have four other candidates," says the maestro with false solemnity. "Each of you will have one movement to conduct. The audience will help us decide. It was I who 'drew the straws', as it were. You got the *Adagietto* movement. And you were magnificent with it. As of now, though I cannot officially make such a statement, I feel very comfortable giving the baton to you. And I very much look forward to the concert."

+   +   +

So that's the game I've entered: a contest against more skilled and better prepared opponents. I remain angry with Hal for setting this up. Yet I'm here, and what is the worst that can happen? I lose and go home? I'm resolved to that conclusion. I'm not meant to be here, never meant to be a conductor. It's a foolish idea.

I cannot stay with Hal, not after this deception. I don't like how he tricked me into coming for this dubious event.

What's worse is the official reception for the candidates, where I must be a good girl and smile for everyone. From my wheel-chair. Yes, I could stand and walk around the room if I wanted to, but Hal insists I remain in the chair so I'll appear more pitiful. After several people greet me, passing me off from one dignitary to another, one section leader to the next, somehow I end up in the corner, staring out the windows at the evening, watching the city's flashing lights. Plenty of electric power here, it seems.

I don't mind being pushed into the corner. I think through the music, wishing Jackie was allowed to attend or else I could be back in our hotel room enjoying a stream with her. Indigenous history is all the rage now and she enjoys the streaming.

She must be amazed at the new things she's found in the city, like the distractions she found that kept her from returning straight to the dressing room with a fresh dress. I had to talk with Maestro Guillaume in my sweat-soaked clothes. Thankfully, he seemed not to mind. I had lots of cologne in the room. Jackie found many things that caught her eye while she was out. She caught the eye of various vagabonds, too, she reported. A few citizens detoured her into sordid trinket shops and a gaming center. Some shops made her leave, ordered her out unless she could show she had credits to spend. I laughed as she told me the story.

Being a formal reception, I'm given a modest slice of cake on a delicate plate, then the staff person forgets a fork. I try my best with my fingers. A different staff person brings me a napkin.

I meet the other candidates, but we only play at being friendly to each other. Gino Allegretti, a stout fellow, worked for Hal's musical instrument company, and paid his way through music school so he can compete against me. Burton Resnick stands tall and has grown out his hair to create a dramatic appearance on the stage. Friedrich ("Freddy") Klemperer pretends to be German, even affecting a false accent, but people know he grew up in the next city down the river, a rebuilt city called Louis. He lost the beat late in his movement and couldn't finish; had the orchestra stop and start again from the last rehearsal mark. I hid my grin. Chandra Park is the other woman in this competition, stately and exotic, but Hal assures me she won't be selected despite her dashing good looks and perfect performance.

And me? I have a slim chance. It depends on the concert.

However, I have this quaint wheel-chair, always a vote-getter. It doesn't seem to draw much sympathy, after all. People are afraid to talk to me, afraid to acknowledge my inability to dance. I don't want to dance anyway. Only with my cousins, maybe. I balance the small plate of cake on my lap, take a bite every few minutes, waiting until I can politely leave.

The Symphonia's tuba player, a chunky fellow by the name Bart Tuttle, comes over and introduces himself, saying he heard that I'm also a tuba player. I confess to my poor skills and we compare notes – a pun, to be sure. He's a friendly young man, but his toothy smile, pudgy cheeks, and that alarming red hair cut very short puts him in another category. I'm not so bold to be judging people. Who am I? A plain woman who can barely wave a baton, much less get herself up on a podium or around town on her own.

I glance at Hal across the room, schmoozing with the big-wigs. He knows what to do, what he wants. Bart, on the other hand, finds himself awkwardly in the presence of a wheel-chair girl. He chooses the option of ignoring my wheel-chair, which is nice. Better to avoid that discussion. Instead, we just enjoy talking about our tubas. We should get together to play duets, he offers and I accept, but I don't expect it will ever happen. It's good to have someone to talk with here, so the others won't think I'm such a bore.

I mention my great-great-grandmother Polly and Bart's heard of her, played a book of *bel canto* etudes she wrote. He played them in lessons during his school days. He's pleased we're related. I tell him about her unfinished tuba concerto which she started during the first lockdown long ago.

"Why unfinished?" he naturally asks.

"Pandemic," I say.

"Yes," he says, sounding sad, "times were tough back then."

He expresses regret for the music being unavailable. I tell him I have the tuba part – her actual handwritten pages, the solo part. I don't have the orchestra score, though. I know she wrote it – part of it, anyway. It was lost somewhere during their journey.

"What a pity," he says. "Sure wish I could see that."

I offer to send him a copy of the solo pages. Maybe he can extract the themes and help to write the orchestra parts.

"That sounds like a fun project."

Perhaps he is humoring me now. It would be impossible to create an orchestra score to match the solo. I've taken a hard look at trying it. He admits to not being much of a composer. I admit to inventing some blues songs. He laughs like he thinks I'm joking. I recite some of my songs and he smiles like he's thinking of other ways to spend the evening. What a weird lady!

We fall silent, exhausting our list of suitable topics.

Fortunately for Bart, someone calls him over.

He excuses himself for more interesting guests, and I'm alone again, wishing I was back in Skinner Canyon with Eve, who always knows what to say and do to cheer me. Half mother and half sister. I miss her, although Jackie's been a great help on this trip.

Everyone here lacks confidence in addressing my situation. How much hassle will it be to have this woman coming on stage? Indeed, how much discomfort for the audience, waiting to see if she will fall off the podium? If she will falter in her conducting? Will she misstep and trip, crash into the cellos? Then the audience can enjoy a good amusement as she picks herself up. A pair of horn players will carry her away. What a scandal! I'm sure it isn't likely they would choose me for the exalted position with the Kanza City Symphonia.

"Hello," speaks a voice behind me. "I just wanted to say...."

I turn my head and see the woman who addresses me: older and white-haired, several strings of beads around her neck, her dress cut unusually low for her age but covered in sequins like a queen might wear. She hunches a bit to get to my level.

"...how delighted I was by your performance. I must say, I had no idea you had *limitation*. I thought you handled the entire situation quite admirably, nevertheless."

"Thank you," I say, feeling better at her compliment, which does sound genuine. "I did my best for the first play-through. We will get better. We have two more rehearsals before the concert."

"I'm Eleanor Hill," she says. "You seem to know my son, Harold. He speaks highly of you."

"Hal? Oh, dear." My tone is obvious. "Yes, he's been wonderful."

"Has he?" She gives me the pinched-lip expression of motherly concern. "I was rather worried. He's turned glum, you see. However, I cannot get a word out of him. The secrets a grown son must keep from his mother! So I thought, seeing you here at this reception, I might seek answers at the source, such as it were."

I blush. "What's the trouble?"

"I am sure I do not know." She offers a painfully taut smile.

"We had words, yes. I'm grateful to him for this opportunity, of course. And for how he helped me start the children's band in my town. I'm afraid, though, he may have ideas about our relationship which I don't share. Perhaps he's reflecting on that."

"I see," and she gives me that look of disapproval, straightens up while complaining about her aching back, like I have no idea what pain is. "Then I shan't be expecting wedding bells any time soon." A tiny laugh.

"Not any time soon, I'm sure." I give her a sincere smile. "I'm not able to have children, also, if that is a worry of yours."

Then she blanches. "Oh, not at all. And I'm sorry."

We go through fake pleasantries of parting and I'm happy to see her go. I hear the name in my head; no, Hal never mentioned her. I heard Eleanor *Cahill* among the Society of Musical Arts benefactors, but not Eleanor *K. Hill*. I grab one the SOMA pamphlets spread out on a little table nearby. I scan the names. Yes, here she is: Mrs. Eleanor K. Hill, head of the Arts Council and a ranking member of SOMA. My breath immediately leaves me. Why am I even here? She will certainly vote against me. I should go on back to the hotel and start packing tonight.

Through the din of conversation and the clink of metal utensils, Mom's voice calls to me, stopping me as I pause near the exit. I've carefully rolled myself through the gathering without bumping into anyone. Mom tells me not to give up, no matter what I think about it. She worked hard to build a friendly bridge between the town and neighboring tribals, after all. "You don't have to try everything," I recall her saying many times over the years, "but if you give it a go, you go all the way." She's right, I realize.

So I won't quit. I have another week in this city, anyway. Might shop for more souvenirs. Clothiers are better here than in Skinner Canyon. Maybe buy some music staff paper, too.

The next evening, I sit at dinner with Hal – his invitation, which I'm happy to accept. We're still friends. He confirms that I met his mother, then begins apologizing for her, hoping I didn't get a poor impression. She's a character, he admits.

He looks as dashing as ever, maybe more than usual, trying to show off how handsome he can be. On the other hand, I wear my comfortable clothing: a plain shirt and trousers, showing him how casual I can dress. Some people might mistake me for being a man. Together we are a sight.

We order dinner in the hotel's restaurant. As we wait, I open the score I've brought and start reading through the music.

"Must you?" he says, his voice lowered. He's aware of the other diners watching us. Must be because of my wheel-chair.

"Yes," I say, regarding him. "Will you help me?"

"Help you?" He seems surprised. "With the score?"

"Can you talk me through these key changes? I'm confused."

"Certainly, my dear."

"Not a dear, Hal, but thank you for your assistance."

"Of course, Maggie."

Our dinner arrives and we continue our score study, laying out the pages between us, taking bites between key changes. He's good at explaining how the tonal center shifts while still maintaining the illusion of continuation of the previous key. Those sustained notes in the strings creates the effect while the harp *arpeggios* introduce the new key. It is magical how Mr. Mahler composed this effect.

"That's the ambiguity of whichever key we're in," he says, and I finally understand. "It's meant to be two things at once."

"What should I do to show that? How should I introduce it?"

"You don't. Not actually. The point is to slip effortlessly from one to the next. You don't want to be signaling the shift too obviously. That would ruin it. It should be rather like the vague images in a dream, coming and going without calling attention to themselves."

We discuss the piece through dessert which we hardly touch, full from the dinner we hardly touched.

"But it's so slow," I say, a bit amused, "Slow enough I have time to think what to do next before the following beat comes."

Hal sits back, satisfied, staring at his slice of pie. "Then it is a good selection for you. Fits your passion. Luck of the draw. You're a passionate woman. You should win this."

I glance at him, and my glance grows into a hard stare, my eyes narrowing. He shifts nervously.

"I'm certain I would do better with a Sousa march," I come back. "*The Stars and Stripes Forever* should elate them. Hah! Before the great pandemic and the civil war, back when there was a flag with stars and stripes on it. Not like the sad gray banner we have now, with the blood-red stripe."

"Perhaps," says Hal with a gentle humor to his voice. "However, Maggie, where will that lead you? Not many marching bands around these days. Nobody having parades. Nothing to celebrate. The only real music now – not counting that noise constructed by machines – is what's produced by full-fledged orchestras. It's a revival of the old culture: nostalgia, let us say. For those who remember it."

"A counter-movement to modern vices. Is that it?"

"Perhaps. We're far enough from the capital that we can do most anything we wish. We shall play our music and the capital's music monitors be damned."

"I like that someone's fighting back."

"Fighting back?" He gives me a look, something of surprise with a tinge of admiration. "You must've had an upsetting experience in the capital. But you needn't return there. Your future is here. Music is your home now."

"Then I'm destined to go from city to city conducting symphonies and overtures and concertos? That's it? Your plan? The crippled girl, a curiosity? Oh, look how she endures her fate!"

"That could be a great career for you." He cringes a second when I give him my reaction. "You could do it. I believe in you."

"Or am I supposed to return to a dusty town out west and teach kids how to play instruments? Only that? To the end of my days? Is that my fate?"

"It wouldn't be such an awful life, would it?" He takes a breath, backed into a corner. "I am truly sorry, dear Maggie, but you must remember: your fate, your destiny, is whatever *you* make of it. You might gain some assistance along the way, yes, and I'm happy to help, yet every step you take – indeed, every direction you go – is by your choice. It is your act alone."

I shake my head. "You sound like my mother."

He regards me, hoping for a smile, I'm sure, but deep in my gut I feel only wild horses charging through me. I can't find the words to respond to him. What is this destiny he's talking about?

"I only wish to be at your side," he dares speak using a low voice, as though he's fearful of my response. "Whatever you choose to do. Wherever you may go. If you will accept me."

"I accept most everyone," I say and force a little laugh. "Only you dare to accept me in return. It's a mystery why."

19

HOME

THE PERFORMANCE IS "STELLAR", "the triumph of determined rage met with heavenly bliss," writes Miss Benton. Her *Interesting People* report this week is full of praise, despite her reputation as a notoriously harsh critic. She never mentions my injury or a scandal other than Dad's heroics involving the governor years before. Her analysis of the concert, and my performance in particular, is more positive than most of her reviews, says Hal. He tells me her reports are regularly picked up by other city news agencies so I should be well-known in coming days. I'm pleased with the article she wrote and grab a few copies of the printed news-papers to take home to show everyone. I'll pack them in a trunk for safe-keeping.

The concert was a huge success, though I have little to compare it to. As for my effort, after five rehearsals, our performance of the *Adagietto* remains exceptionally ethereal, easily the crowd favorite. I wore the sleeveless black gown I'd bought just for the performance and it fit well for the exercise I put it through. Rather than make a fuss adjusting the stage in the middle of the symphony, they had all of us candidates use the wooden lectern. None complained.

I felt less confident this time with a packed concert hall than my first attempt with no audience. Still, I knew the orchestra could give it the emotion it deserved. I waved the baton as if I were dancing to soaring waves of angelic filigree. I have no idea how I looked! Like a fool, most likely, flitting along. We claimed the loudest applause – after an eternal instant in which you could hear a pin drop.

However, after everything is concluded, I do not get the assistant to the assistant conductor position. Chandra Park gets it, and well-deserved, I have to admit. She had a much more difficult movement to conduct than I had. She carried the orchestra like a true maestro. I'm pleased a woman was chosen. The male candidates were phony as paper *dollars*. I can go home with my head held high. I achieved something, no matter how minor.

"I can be happy teaching kids music," I say to myself and Jackie asks what I say. "Helping them to play instruments. Helping them enjoy music for themselves. It can be a happy life."

Jackie helps me pack. We gather all our new belongings, enough to require an extra footlocker to bear over to the railway terminal on a hire-carriage. One last trip through the city streets, admiring the tall buildings, the elegant architecture, happy people walking the clean streets. Jackie wants to return someday.

Hal assists us. He seems aware of our shifting relationship. I feel sorry for him, for how I've treated him. Not sure how justified I may have been in setting him straight about us. Maybe I'm letting him go because I know I would only be a burden on him.

So I'll sacrifice myself to save him.

My little laugh catches Jackie off-guard.

"Nothing," I reply to her inquiry.

Hal gives me a stare, perhaps believing I must be thinking about him, about us, as we arrive at the terminal.

We unload, and a porter puts our bags on the train.

It is the final kindness of the musician guild: tickets home.

Jackie pats the side of our train car, muttering: "Iron horse, iron horse, take us home."

Hal helps me stand, though I can do it myself. The porter hefts my wheel-chair into the women's car.

Hal holds me up, in a kind of loose embrace which I don't mind. I think I love him, despite his quirks, yet I know what is best for us, we two odd-balls. He toys with a smile, deciding his next move.

"Maggie, I wish to—"

But I cut off his farewell speech with a big kiss. He is flummoxed and nearly trips backwards into a matron and her young helpmate.

"Well, I dare say!" He's blushing as he recovers.

"It's nothing," I say. "Well, perhaps a thank you."

"A thanks only?" He smiles at me, like he thinks we still have a chance. "I remain ever at your service, my dear."

"I know, Hal.... I know. That's what I love about you." I give him a long look, memorizing his fine features, especially that whimsical mustache he takes pride in. "Someday you may return to Skinner Canyon. We should go riding horses there. Are you up for it?"

"But your infirmity. How...?"

"I intend to get back on that horse," I tell him. "You're welcome to get on, too."

+　+　+

What is this world coming to? I think of my childhood, growing up in the capital, with its tall buildings and spotless sidewalks. My school was strict yet always cheerful. We sang songs praising our nation, had parades, marching and waving flags. I thought I was having the best life ever, like being an adult was something other people did. I would never have to do what they did, not me.

After Dad died, however, Mom took me and my brothers west to a very different place and we had a lot to learn. Most of all was why there was a town like this out west and why anyone would want to go there rather than to the great cities of the north. Escape, mostly. Freedom. A chance to start over. Mom said we were starting a new life and we should forget the old one. The capital no longer existed.

I knew there had been a pandemic for about ten years in which half the population died, either from the deadly virus or other things resulting because of the virus: starvation, violence, accidents. Dad talked about it, repeated stories his mother told, had me read some notebooks Grandma's father wrote. Dad made a video of Grandma – I can still recall watching him play it back and forth as he edited it in his office at the station. "Grammy!" I'd exclaim and Dad shushed me. When we visited Grandma Isla, I was a baby and never could be still for the recordings. She'd laughed at me, called me "feisty" and saying I had "good lungs". Dad told me to be good granddaughter as

Grandma Isla sat outside her shack, telling stories of being born on a coastal island in the seventh year of the pandemic, how her young parents took her north and hid in the forest of a national park, how they met other survivor families there, how they thought the whole world had ended and planned how to start again, how they were harassed by marauders and militia. Later, Dad told me everything that was in his Grampa Sandy's notebooks. I couldn't believe half the things he wrote, not after we were taught in school that none of it ever happened—

I look out the windows of the train car and see the endless waves of tall grass, not even a husky buffalo to break up the monotonous yellow wash as we pass by. Jackie naps beside me. Her head rolls against my shoulder and I brush her hair. She got to visit the big city, after all, but she's happy to be heading home. I'm happy to see home again, too. I can't wait to pull that tuba onto my lap and play some tunes that have accumulated in my head.

Then the train slows, pulls up to the depot, and we get off with the porter's help. We have so many bundles and bags, more than we left with. I say they're well-earned. Down goes the wheel-chair and the porter holds it as I sit like an old lady. He rolls me away from the platform to be safe, parks me, returns to the train. Jackie stands with me and our baggage, gazing around for who will meet us for the ride to Skinner Canyon.

"Jackie!" shouts my nephew Jeb, running in zigzags through the passengers, waving his hand.

She sees him, her face brightens, and the two rush together like comets, arms wrapped tight and a big kiss for everyone to see.

"Well, don't that beat all?" says a grizzled old man who comes up behind me. I startle, then relax.

It's Ephraim Briggs who's come to collect us at the depot with a wagon large enough for us and our bags.

"Where's Frank?" I ask him.

"Oh, he got things to do," says Briggs. "Deputy things. Jeb was gonna pick y'all up but his pa didn't want him goin' alone. So I said I come get ya. Now Jeb here, he wanna come along, on account of him wantin' to see his gal soon as he can. Look it them two."

"Then we should hurry back," I say, glancing at the two young folks, standing arm in arm. "Before it gets dark."

Briggs lets out a long sigh, fights a grin.

"Oh, it'll be dark. That I know."

We ride over the chaparral country mostly in silence. We see a few tribals on horseback watching us from a fair distance as the sun paints the sky red. Jackie stands up in back and waves at them, gives some hand signals, and sits again.

Feeling too tired to talk about our trip, I'm glad Briggs doesn't ask questions. Jeb asks Jackie a few but she gives short answers in her usual way. He doesn't mind; he's smitten.

Miles down the road, rolling at a steady pace along the ragged edge of the canyon, Briggs' words continue to annoy me. I ask him what he meant by 'dark'.

"Did something happen?" I ask, but he doesn't look at me.

"Sumpin'," is all he says.

"You won't tell me?"

"Yer brother told me wait till he can talk to ya."

We roll into town at dusk, going down Main Street. I see some of the townsfolk stop to give a nod as we pass. A few men take off their hats as we pass.

"Why are they acting that way," I ask Briggs.

"They bein' polite, is all."

"Polite for what reason?"

"You'll see."

"See what? Tell me."

I almost make him stop the wagon right there but he insists we go on. Take us straight to the cabin, I command. Everything will be clear to us there. I fill with fear, thinking awful thoughts.

My brother James is standing there in his cassock, appearing to pray before the dark, burnt ruins of the cabin.

+   +   +

James wraps his arms around me as I stare at what remains of the cabin, a dark hulk with hardly any roof. He pats my back as I sob.

"But why?"

I can't look at the cabin yet I must. Our home for so many years, now gone. It's at that place where it's too damaged to ever repair but not completely swept away, so it just stands like a hollow monument to the people who lived in it.

"Now don't you worry," says James, keeping his hand firmly on my shoulder, the silver cross hanging on his necklace jabbing me, "those boys, bless them, they stayed strong. They knew what to do. They saved that cursèd tuba of yours. And that box of old notebooks you love so much. Mostly. They got smoke damage, I'm sure, but you can likely restore them."

I look up at him, feeling uncomfortable. "I don't care about them. What about the women? They're fine?"

"Frank should be the one," he says.

Things fall into place. "It's not just about a fire, is it?"

"What's done is done," he chants, and tries to hug me again.

"Are they all right?" I ask from within his arms. "How'd it start?"

James lets go of me. "Evil comes this way sometimes. We have to expect it. They weren't prepared for it."

"Where are they? Where's Eve? Faith? The boys?"

He looks over my shoulder at the blackened cabin, then scans the yard as the darkness completes its spread over us. I feel a storm piling up, ready to blow in.

"It's better if we let Frank do the explaining," says James. "He's put it together from what the boys said. Anything I can say would be second-hand information."

"It was an accident?" I ask, certain it must be, boys being boys, getting in trouble, a stray spark and...

"There's more," says Briggs. "Best Frank tell ya."

"Why can't you tell me? Are they all right?"

"Come on," calls Briggs, starting back to the wagon. "Y'all cain't stay out here tonight anyways."

So Briggs drives the wagon back into town, taking us straight to the Sheriff's office.

Frank steps out, expecting us. Wearing a stern face, he waves us inside. Jeb sits with Jackie on the side bench, holding her hand, as they watch me get myself up the steps. I walk by myself, using my cane, up those three steps, and into Frank's office, sit myself in the chair before his desk.

He moves papers to the side of the desktop, sets his hands there, clasped like he's about to pronounce a new law.

"You saw the cabin, right?" he says, staring at me.

"I saw it. Now tell me: what happened?"

He stands, shakes his head a few times, and regards me. With a loud breath to set his words, he comes around the desk and sits on the corner. He shifts his pistol in its holster.

"It was that Billy Kirk fellow," says Frank. "Remember him?"

That shakes me to my bones. "He came back?"

"Couldn't stay away, no matter the penalty he risked."

"Where's he now?" I ask, afraid to even look around. The cell was empty when I brought myself inside.

"You don't need to worry no more about him," says Frank.

"He's gone?"

"He's very gone. Dead, in fact."

I see a slight quiver in his lip. Then he clears his throat, adjusts his holster once more.

"And buried," he adds. "Going on a week now."

But I feel more worried, not less.

"And Eve? Faith?" I ask, feeling desperate.

"We'll get to them."

But I can't be settled. "Tell me, are they all right?"

He gives me a strained look. "Yes, good enough. For now."

"Every time I leave town something bad happens. Like Mom."

"No, this isn't like with Mom. That was pure accident. A terrible accident. This was determined, an act of revenge, clear as day."

"Revenge?" I ask, but suddenly I understand.

He glances at James, standing by the doorway. "They better stay at the inn tonight. We'll make other arrangements tomorrow."

James nods, steps out to take care of things.

"He came back?" I can't believe he would, given the punishment that would await him. I'm shaking like he's still alive, still in town, looking for me.

Frank resets himself. "Well, see, the best I can tell is he came on back here wanting to get his revenge. You know: for what you done to him. And what Eve done, too: shot him. Seems he set fire to the garden out back. Then Faith runs out to put the fire out, grabbing buckets and filling them at the well. Takes a while. That's when he shot her."

"Oh no!" Tears come to my eyes. "Is she all right?"

"Shot her once in the back, and when she turned around to look at him, another in the chest. And she fell right there."

"Oh my god!" I put my hands to my face. "Oh. My. God." Then I look up, tears blocking my view. "She's...dead?"

"Guess he thought she was you. Anyways, the boys fetched us to come help. We saw the fire in the fields, so people rushed over."

"Are the boys all right?" I ask between sobs.

"Last thing she did was call out for her sons to hide. Benny said he did, but when he heard more shots, he took Clemson and they run out, heading to town."

I gasp. "Where was Eve?"

"She was there," says Frank, pinching his lips.

"Was she hurt?"

"She'll be fine."

"Did she get shot, too?"

"That bastard tried to start a fire on your cabin next. Eve came out front and called him out, told him to stop or she's gonna shoot. She got the shotgun. But he wasn't afraid of her no more and shot at her. Got her in the shoulder as she tried to duck. But she shot back, got him square in the face. Made a real mess of him."

"She's all right?"

"So the cabin started getting flames going. We could see it from town so people hurried over. Tried to get it under control but it was too strong."

"Is she all right?"

"Doc says she should be fine. Got the bullet out. Maybe she gets some pain in that shoulder if she tries lifting too much."

"But Faith is...dead?"

His face freezes, then he glances out his office to Jeb and Jackie, sitting in the outer office, then over at the empty jail cell.

"I'm afraid she's gone," he says, staring at the metal bars. "Lost to us. She never had a chance. Sneaky bastard."

I weep louder. Despite her sad history, she took us in and cared for us. She was kind and gentle with us, even when we were playing music. I remembered her saying one night as we finished a bottle of something strong she liked to drink on special occasions, how she took that first babe of hers and Raymond, the idiot child, deformed and pitiful, out into the wilderness and left it. She got the blame but that night she told me it was Raymond who told her to do it, said he wouldn't stay with her if she didn't, said he didn't want a child like that having his name. But who was he? No better than a renegade. She obeyed him but he left for prison later anyway.

Frank is speaking and I'm lost in my memories.

"Don't you worry none," he says, leaning over to pat my arm as I sit in the chair. Straightening up, he says: "I can take those boys, raise them up. Vera's approved. Jeb and Joe are on their own now, working ranches, staying in bunkhouses, so it's only Jon now. We can take you in for a spell, too. Can't stay at the inn for too long."

I nod to his offer, his suggestion, then I meet his eyes.

"Where's Eve?"

The faintest of grins lays on his face and I feel hopeful.

"She's over at the doc's."

When Dr. Baker's wife, peeking through the curtains, lets me in, I find Mr. Briggs sitting by Eve's bed. I have to smile, the way they look at each other.

"I think I must be gettin' on forty now," says Eve, her voice weak yet sounding cheerful. "Ain't kept up on countin' them years an' they take so long to get over. So it's just a guess."

"That seems 'bout right by my count," says Briggs, looking crusty and mean even in his happier moments.

"That make Maggie going on thirty, I reckon," says Eve. "Jackie, she gonna be 'round twenty, so she's ready to get with that Jeb boy, I reckon. Be mighty happy ta see them two wedded 'fore I die."

"Y'ain't gonna die, Miss Eve," says Briggs in a firm voice.

I step into the room, see Eve flat on her back on the narrow bed, her arm in a sling above the covers, strap going around her shoulder and neck, Otherwise, she looks fine.

"Maggie!" she cries at the sight of me.

Briggs scoots his chair back out of the way.

I drop to my knees beside the bed. We try to maneuver ourselves into a hug, with her arm getting in the way and my hip complaining. We find a way to come together and it feels so good to hold her. Then we both seem to think the same thing at the same time and release.

"Faith," says Eve softly, "she's gone."

I wipe my tears. "Frank told me."

"She never got no chance to fight back."

"But she saved her boys."

"That's good. They gonna grow up big an' strong fer shore."

Briggs excuses himself, saying ladies need time to talk without a man around, and he pulls on his hat and steps out.

Eve tells me more, recounts the incident from the beginning, at the moment she heard the first gunshot. She didn't think it was any more than Faith shooing away coyotes. But the second shot got her attention and she went to look out back, saw Faith on the ground and a man at the edge of the garden, lit torch in his hand. The rows of tomatoes were going up in flames.

"I says damn them veggies, gotta see to my cousin," Eve says in a cloud of sorrow. "So I grab the shotgun, check on the boys, hiding under their bed. I says to them 'you best run to town an' get help' so they did."

"The boys are fine," I tell her, and repeat what Frank said.

"They brung lots of folks over but before they got there that man he come around the front with his torch, tryna get a fire going on the cabin. So I called him out, holdin' up that shotgun, but now he weren't afraid an' he shot at me with a pistol. I tried to get outta the way but he ding me." She nods toward her shoulder. "Looks like I ain't gotta do no work fer while. Doc says I gotta rest a spell."

"But you shot him," I say, more to myself.

"Shore did, an' ain't feel no regret of it. He deserve what he got an' he knowed it."

"But you went and shot him again, after he was down."

"That's right. Gotta be sure a varmint's dead completely."

"Frank said it was hard to identify him...the way his face was."

"Well, he weren't no fancy lad anyway, not like yer Doctor Hill."

She always has a way of summing things that's colorful. I love that about her. I stretch over to hug her again and we both let go a noise of complaint for our injuries.

"Guess ya don't know," says Eve, "but they buried Faith already. A week now. Doc said she was getting kinda fresh, had to put her in the ground. I wanted him to wait for y'all to get back. Least she ain't next to Raymond. She got her own plot, next to yer mama."

20

THE EDGE OF THE WORLD

EVERY TIME I GO AWAY from this place something bad happens. If I hadn't gone off on that fool's adventure to Kanza City, maybe Faith would still be alive. If I'd been here when that Billy arrived, I would've shot him straightaway before he ever got to Faith. It's my fault. Everything involving him is my fault.

I went all the way down to Amy June's funeral, out of respect, in Dad's place, then returned home to find Mom dead and buried.

But you went all the way to the capital, James reminds me, on a search for our family's precious items and no one died. Yes, but I did pick up a virus, one as evil as what they suffered during the great pandemic a century ago. The Billy Kirk virus: it looks innocent but it can be deadly. It keeps coming back.

Now he's gone, thankfully. I wish I could've been here to witness his cold body being dropped into a grave and covered. Then I'd know for sure. It's not marked, somewhere out the west side of town. Only the gravedigger knows the location. Yet not knowing for certain, he stays in my mind, haunting me like an angry ghost.

I sit at the edge of the canyon that names this place, not far from Skinner's old 4x4 vehicle, staring across to the opposite ragged rim, thinking my thoughts as the summer sun beats down on me despite me holding up Faith's parasol. The warm breeze tugs at the grasses, teases the wildflowers, blows dust past me. I hear the clicking din of locusts in nearby fields. I see a herd of cattle being driven along on the opposite rim, a few cowpokes whistling at them.

This is my home. I can't say if we were meant to be here. I'm just a small part of everybody who lives in this land, this nation, for the past hundred-plus years, connected by name and blood, and a lot of hardship and pain. I think of Grandma Isla, her parents, and their parents. I know the stories of their lives and people they knew, back to Fritz who brought the tuba over from another country and started us here on this side of an ocean I haven't ever seen.

That tuba remains, reminds me. How many mouths have blown into that mouthpiece? Fingers on those keys, moving the valves up and down. I've played it, learned a lot, consider myself capable yet not up to professional skill level. It would be better if I had been in Kanza City looking for a tuba position than as assistant conductor.

I laugh, kicking some dirt clods over the side of the canyon with my toes. Pulling off my boots, I dare the snakes to come for me. Ain't afraid of stompin'em into bits, as Eve would say.

The tuba is safe but it got some damage. Dents and scratches as the boys pulled it out of the cabin. Lots of dirt down the bell I had to flush out. Help from Mr. Block and a good amount of oil and it's not like new but serviceable – if I had any service to play for.

And the notebooks, stacked in a wooden crate? Not the best way to keep them but those boys knew what was precious to me. Not yet knowing their mama had died out back, they pulled out everything of value before Eve told them to run for help. Later, I told them they should've left the tuba and those notebooks, and they started crying, saying Faith told them to be sure to save those things for the people that aren't yet born, and those people's kin, too.

A mote of dust gets in my eye and it prompts a few tears.

"There you are," calls someone from behind me.

It's James, holding up his hand. He's dressed in regular western clothes, looking like a cowpoke himself. Plus the priest collar.

"You're far from home," he says, striding up to me, and he can't understand why I laugh. "Way out here, huh? Lonely place. Is this where you come to talk with God?"

I give a nod, then look up at him. He stands to block the sun for me. "It's a place. You can talk to anyone here. Especially the people that're gone now."

"I see."

"You want something?" I ask in a kindly way.

"I was looking for you, thought I'd find you at Frank's but he said you headed out this way. Thought you might want to talk."

"Talk about what?"

"Everything."

"That's a mighty lot to discuss. Do you have the time? Sunday morning's coming soon."

"How about we start with that notice you got? How do you feel?"

He means the letter I received a few days ago from the head of the School Council saying my services are no longer needed. 'Good news', the letter begins, then announces they have hired someone as the new teacher. Moreover, the new person has training in music, so I don't even get to stay to lead the band. They knew my cousin was shot dead and my home burned down, yet they still had to send that notice to me as quick as they could.

"Unfortunate timing," says James. "I suppose they wanted to let you know as soon as possible to give you time to make your plans. Other plans."

"What plans are those?" I snap at him.

He almost jumps back but collects himself. "What you're going to do now." He gazes across the canyon. "Vegetable garden is half gone. People will be relying on you to keep it going."

"People relying on me?" I have to laugh. "It was Faith that ran that operation. Eve helped. They had a couple other women helping, too. I only watched. And now...?"

"Or you could sell it, what there is. Someone would buy it, I'm sure. Then you could go somewhere else."

"Go somewhere else?" Now I'm mad. "Where would that be?"

"Anywhere you like," he says, turning shy and sounding like he hasn't thought through what he planned to say. "I mean, it seems as though you're meant for city life. I heard Jackie talking about Kanza City. She was mighty impressed. Seems like she wants to live there. Just saying. Maybe you do, too."

"I failed at that," I say with a rough sigh. "No, James, I'm meant to be here. Here with the snakes and coyotes and locust and the dust. This is where I'm meant to be. It's fitting."

We share a gaze over the canyon, feeling the wind brushing us.

"Well, none of us are *meant* to be here," he says, more confident. "We're here because of Mom. She brought us because of Dad. It was Faith that led Dad to believe it was a good place to come to and he insisted Mom take us here. Anything to get out of that city and its restrictions—"

"Kanza City isn't like that," I jump in. "Not yet."

"News reports say a lot of cities are adopting the policies of the capital, clamping down on rights and freedom. Soon it will come out here, like another kind of virus."

"Virus!"

"Not every edict from the capital can work out here."

We stay quiet for a while. The cattle on the opposite rim are long past but even out of sight I can hear them on the wind. Locust keep up their din.

"It's got some charm," says my brother, who we had to take out of the city, according to Mom, or else they would change him into a girl. He was counted as an extra son. That was one policy they were starting in the capital.

I look up at him. "I'm sorry. We're all grown up now, as they say. Adults. No longer children who need to be told what to do every day. We're here because we had to go *someplace*. I'm sorry for what you had to go through. You'll always be my dear brother."

"And you're my dear sister." He reaches down to help me stand. "I'm proud of you, Maggie, and what you've done. I'm only trying to help you. Whatever I can do...."

"Thanks." I give him a hug. He stares at my hip, then looks up. "It's much better. I can walk on my own if I go slow enough. Cane's better over uneven ground and up steps."

"That's good. Mended. Ready to go on."

"Go on, hmm?"

"It's the only direction we can go."

I give him a nod. "I'll write to Doctor Hill, see what news there is in Kanza City. Maybe there's a job I can do. Since I'm not any kind of gardener. I'll take Eve with me. She didn't get to see it."

"Don't be so set on that," he says, brushing his hands together. "That Briggs fellow, he's showing her a lot of attention. The two of them play songs. Well, he plays banjo and she sings made-up words. Kind of silly, you ask me, but if that makes her happy – and being happy helps her heal.... Well, just don't be disappointed if she wants to stay here. That's all I'm saying."

+   +   +

It doesn't seem strange when Frank gets up at dinner one evening and announces the date for a wedding to unite his son Jeb with his bride-to-be, Miss Jackrabbit. It makes a lot of sense now considering she's starting to show how much they've already been acting like husband and wife. I'm happy for them.

A few months have passed and the two young people have been together practically every day and night. Jackie remains my helper, though. She and Eve, mended and at home, along with two women they hired, tried to get the garden growing again but then winter hit. The greengrocer had to send for what they had in Cimarron and the prices were high. A man came to town to look over the garden, said he would buy it for 'pennies on the dollar'.

Meantime, people from Jackie's village set up a pointed tent for us, called it a 'teepee', so we had a place to live. It was comfortable and shut out the cold wind. The floor covering was soft so we went barefoot inside, leaving our boots out. They brought clothing in their native style for me and Eve to wear since most of our wardrobe had gotten damaged in the fire. Moccasins, too, just like Jackie wears. So Eve and I had a nice place to sleep – whenever she wasn't staying in town with Briggs.

I'm happy for someone I love to have a chance to be happy with someone else. I wish her the best nearly every day.

And me? I have to look in the hand mirror Vera gave me so I can 'keep up my appearances'. I know she means well. She is well-put and always looks lovely. But I've seldom done anything to affect my appearance, thinking nobody cared how I looked. It's enough to be a cripple and gain people's sympathy. Now I realize a few things that flew by me. I could've been pretty when I wanted to be, but I hardly wanted to be. Part of the reason I like cowpoke clothes: easy to wear and no fuss. Same with my hair style: fairly short and just combed out, long enough for a ponytail. And cosmetics are a frilly nuisance I best avoid. But the time's come for nature to wake me up from my sleepwalking.

"You're surely not getting any younger," Vera declares one day. "Best you learn how to trick Mother Nature."

Calling me a girl-next-door, I allow Vera to do her best: fixing my face, getting me into a lady's wardrobe, putting my hair into a pretty style, though I feel silly looking at the unnatural results in the long mirror. I'm embarrassed to go out and show myself in this strange costume.

Now that I'm worthy of being presented to the general public, and to eligible bachelors in particular, I dare send a message to Hal explaining about changes that have come to Skinner Canyon. With the fire, I lost the electric terminal for the music machine. The machine seems damaged and many of the disks melted. I lost papers I'd written my songs on, too. I ask him for a box of music paper with the staves printed on them so I can try to write them again or write new songs. I'm sure feeling the blues, I tell him.

But I don't hear from him. Not a message, anyway. A box of that music paper arrives. A note on it says 'courtesy of Dr. Hal D. Hill' – no charge to me; a gift for my service. That's fair. I did provide a service: I helped him feel important among his musical colleagues. I went through that conducting contest to please him.

Even so, that precious evening of exploration we shared stays in my head, always a pleasant memory. Now that I feel healed with hardly a tweak to my hip unless I take a wrong step, I find myself thinking about finding a *beau*. Yes, I said it: *beau*. Vera's word, as in: "I'm very proud Miss Jackie finds my son Jeb a worthy *beau*."

Eve laughs when I tell her – like it should be her looking for someone even though she's sweet on Briggs now and he's sweet on her: two older folks trading barbs and smooches. He's got to be going on seventy, but Eve fancies him anyway, as crude and rude as he is. I wrote a song about them I call "Old Souls Blues".

Forgetting about Hal's reply, I start copying over the songs from the fire-damaged paper, then write a couple songs that have gotten stuck in my head during the past month. I got a lot of ideas when I was in Kanza City, hearing music every day. My mind was churning out songs constantly. I continue playing the solo part great-great-grandmother Polly wrote for her tuba concerto, and I try to imagine the orchestra part in each passage when the tuba rests. Someday I will create the orchestra parts and I will play her *Concerto for Tuba* with some orchestra and everyone will praise Polly's music.

I believed Hal would send a message under separate cover from the box of staff paper, yet nothing comes. I know things slow down during the winter, so I think little of it. As winter blows through, I read over our old messages and my warmth for him is rekindled. He could be a good *beau*.

By spring, however, his message finally arrives, delayed as usual by snow covering the railway. I'm so excited I tear it open then stop myself. I want it to be special, so I do everything else I must do first, clearing my list of tasks, then make myself comfortable, and I read what he has to say.

> *Dear Maggie,*
>
> *First, do allow me to apologize for the delay in my reply to your heart-felt message. Life here has been hectic, with the music business in full gear and the Symphonia having a full range of concerts. I am more engaged than ever before! Even so, not to put off important news for more than reasonable verbiage, I should inform you of significant changes to my status. Despite* la douleur exquise, *my heart has taken on a mind of its own.*
>
> *Indeed, I scarcely could have predicted this alteration even a year ago. However, it seems as though I find myself engaged in a marital way to a player of the bassoon by the name of Gloria. This lovely lady sits in front of me among Symphonia musicians and we have taken notice of each other throughout the concert season.*

Suffice to say, we have made plans to marry in late spring. Mother approves of her and our plans, so arrangements are imminent. It is a miracle for such as I, odd fellow that I am. Don't you agree? I often think of you and all I have learned from you. I give full credit to you for teaching me how to woo a woman, what to say and do, and what I must avoid. I confess I have wondered about you from time to time, feeling regret at regular intervals. As we each go forward, I wish you the very best and pray there is no ill-will between us.

Please inform me of whatever you may require in pursuit of your music career and I shall comply forthwith and straightway.

Musically yours,

Hal D. Hill, Ph.D. (Music)

All my breath leaves my chest, and I hold my heart tight lest it leap right out and run away in shame. It is the worst news I could imagine receiving short of someone's death. Yet it is a kind of death. Tears fall from my eyes and I feel awful for letting them ruin my cosmetics. Yet I must go on, no need to tell anyone of this message.

I see there's a note on the back of the last page. What more could he say to break me apart?

P.S. – In answer to your inquiry, I can report two items. First, your concert reviews were seen by many across the major orchestra cities & I have heard interest expressed in having the 'western woman' come to conduct a concert. I can follow up with them. As to positions available, there is one in Cincinnati at present. I hope you do not mind that I took the liberty of offering your name. They will be in contact if they are interested; I pray they are interested in such a fine & dedicated musician as yourself. Meanwhile, I wish you all the best – as always.

"Well, that's something," I mutter, my voice strained.

Jackie, living with me in the teepee until the wedding day, asks what I mean as she pats her round belly.

"I sure have made a lot of mistakes in my life," I tell her, keeping my eyes on the letter. "Every time I try something, I fail. Oh, there are small victories. They do count, I suppose. Maybe I'm being petty. But the big ones? Life-changing ones? Nothing. All failures. Every time I try something big, I fail. Now I have nothing."

Jackie sits up slowly, crossing her legs and leaning back on her arms, letting her belly out. I watch her find a comfortable position.

"You don't got nothing," she says with a grin she must've picked up from my nephew. "You got me and baby. You will be grandmama – *ikón*. Lots to do for you. Take care of *zhin̄gáhin̄ga*."

"Baby," I translate, but I'm in no mood for another lesson. "Yes, that's something." I have to laugh: me being a grandmother without ever being a mother, but I love her anyway. "A lot more important, I suppose, than that news-paper fellow coming all the way out here to write a story about me and our 'band in the desert' – 'out west', like it's a whole 'nother country."

"Not band in desert. Not desert here. *Mozhón̄*."

"No, it's not. We say 'chaparral' for this kind of land."

"Ah," Jackie responds.

I shake my head. "I'm not even the music teacher now, so what could that fellow write about? Well, I haven't read it so I don't know. I don't care. I'm just a woman getting to the next stage of her life and not seeing anything ahead of me."

"You got gramma job for you," my daughter says. "Gonna need you. Gonna be very busy."

"You have Vera to help. She's had four. She knows about babies, knows everything about raising kids. Besides, she'll love tending to her new grandchild – her eldest son's first child. That's special."

Satisfied that I'll be able to face my future as a grandmother, I return to my songs. I like how they sound. Getting permission to use the piano in the school house after class time, some kids greet me as they are leaving. I set my papers on the piano and play out the notes I've written, change a few, add more. They're simple tunes, a lot more clever than serious. It isn't orchestra music.

Then one evening in the school house, after pecking out simple songs and the lamp starting to run low on oil, I get a melody in my head and play it. I add more notes, my fingers knowing what keys to touch. I hear the full orchestra in my head but only a few of those notes sound on the piano. I put them to paper anyway. I play more, write more. From the top. Again. A little more. Counterpoint here, second melody there. This is the bridge to the conclusion. *Da capo.* Rising emotion, straight to the final chords. Big, powerful, tuba-led chords that say everything I want to shout to the world!

As I head home to the warm teepee next to the cabin remnants, I realize the melody is like the tuba concerto Polly wrote. I've been playing it over and over and it got stuck in my head. But now I have the start of the orchestra parts!

That gives me some satisfaction. Maybe I'll be able to finish it. I can put it on the music stand and conduct it to the walls. At least that's something, I tell myself. A project to occupy me.

"Or ya kin do it fer yew," says Eve, always my pal. She's playing blues songs with Briggs, just for fun, but people toss coins in the box when they're sitting outside making their music. I offer them my blues songs to sing. "Skinner Canyon Blues" is a favorite, gets the most coins. It's likely because everyone here can relate to feeling Skinner Canyon blues.

On a not-so-blue day, I stand on my own to watch the Fourth of Seven parade go by, waving and clapping for the kids in the band. They sound great. They have good marching discipline. I'm pleased by their performance. I'm happy the new teacher has built on what I started. I don't feel any jealousy. I'm proud of the kids.

When people beside me recognize me, however, they step away. Because I can stand on my own, people think I was tricking them all this time, getting undeserved sympathy. Eve gets some of that, too, because of how Judge Taylor refused to bring any charges against her for shooting that Billy Kirk a second time.

"Clearly a case of self-defense," he ruled and didn't give her even one day in jail, saying that her staying two weeks in Doc's office was enough punishment. She got that bullet in her shoulder as evidence. Briggs was there every day to sit with her, keeping her spirits up. And now look at those two! Acting like foolish children.

Weeks after the parade, the message comes that I feared would arrive: an invitation to conduct the Cincinnati Symphony as a guest. Their regular director is away, on tour in the capital, so they need someone to fill in for one concert. They are impressed with my story, would like to give me a chance. The whole 'western woman' angle will draw in the curious. The program can be of my choice with one exception. It seems that Bart Tuttle is the tuba player there now. He suggests I bring my tuba so we can play a duet as part of the concert. Included in the message is some music. Bart's written what he titles *Sonata for Two Tubas and Orchestra* and includes my part.

I look over the music.

"Me?" I muse like Life is a big joke. "Play the tuba? In front of an audience of concert-goers? He must be crazy."

"Ya gotta go, him bein' crazy or not," Eve insists, not looking up. She's stitching up rips in Briggs' trousers from too much scooting on that wooden bench. "This's what y'always want, ain't it?" We turn to look over at the tuba sitting safely in its soft-side case. "Look it tha' poor thing," she says, "wantin' ya so much, wantin' ya ta hold it tight. Gotta make love to it. Waitin' fer ya ta give it a blow."

I break into laughter. Eve joins in. Jackie chuckles, too.

"Not even sure where Cincinnati is," I say humbly.

"We passed through there when we's goin' ta the capital," says Eve, "but you's nappin' when we stopped."

"I can't just go there. It's so far away. Besides, he.... I don't even know him. Bart Tuttle? Who is he?"

"He ain't askin' ta marry, just play a song with him."

"I haven't played that tuba before more than a room full of kids. And it's old, kind of beat up now."

"So get it fixed. Y'always like fixin' things, don'tcha?"

"I suppose. Mister Block's done about all he can with it."

"So take it to a better shop. They'll fix'er right up."

"There isn't another shop in Skinner Canyon. Not in Cimarron, either."

"How about in Kanza City?" Eve suggests, looking up from under her tilted head.

"Kanza City?" I question and Jackie echoes me.

"Yeah, I knows ya wanna go on back there, see that fella. Gettin' yer tuba fixed up's good excuse, don'tcha know?"

I haven't yet told her about Hal's new relationship.

"I wouldn't go there, not to Kanza City, not for *that*."

"It's on the way to that other city. What's it called? Citynati?"

"Cincinnati," I say, feeling she's setting me up. "It's up the Ohio River, on the way to the capital."

"We bin all the way to the capital, so Citynati cain't be so far ta go. So ya better go."

"That's silly. I can't just go way over there for some...some crazy concert invitation."

"Why cain'tcha? They invited ya, so y'either go or ya gotta write out a note sayin' yer excuse."

"Well, I do hate writing excuse notes...."

"Then on ya get, on to yer new desternation. Ya gonna be great, Mags. Ya just gotta believe in yourself. I believe in ya. We all do. I'm gonna miss ya, shore will, but I wantcha ta go an' be great."

I give her a stern look. Can she be so generous? My gut starts to rattle, already imagining a crowd waiting for me to play.

"If you're really sure about this, I'll go."

She keeps on with her stitching and I wait for a response.

"I said, I'll go.... Just to say I did it."

She doesn't look up. "I heard ya."

"Fine. Then I'll go. I'll play this sonata Bart composed, no matter how it sounds. Then I'll come back. I'll come home straightaway."

But Eve doesn't respond, like she knows my mind.

Annoyed by her silence, I say: "I'm going, then."

"I heard ya."

"Fine."

+   +   +

I give the old gray tuba a good polishing, oil the valves, and wash out the dust. I play through a selection of warm-up exercises. I play a few of Polly's songs. I regain my breath, crucial for a tuba to sound good. Have to fill it completely. I sit on the floor in the teepee, using a cushion, tuba in my lap, and it almost fits. I can feel Polly's fingers pressing my fingers down on the keys, sense her in my chest, hear her instructions in my head – even though I never knew her, yet I know she's with me.

Before she moved into Frank's house with Jeb after the wedding, Jackie would cheer me on, saying the baby could hear me and by his gentle kicks she knew he liked the songs. I never played too loud, of course, or else Little Bear might cause a fuss. Jeb and his parents called the boy by his official name in the register: Jacob. They were so proud, and never expressed the obvious: that Jacob looked more like Jackie than Jeb. Faith's son Benjamin joked it was good the baby looked like Jackie and got cross words back from Jeb. Even so, everyone loved Jake Little Bear, the newest Baumann.

Before I get on that express I give a little concert for my family, all together for once, under the autumn trees in the yard of Frank's house. There are my brothers who always look out for me; Frank's wife Vera and their children: Jeb and Joe, the twins, and Jon, and Frances; and my daughter Jackie and her baby, Jacob. Plus my sweet cousin Eve and her beau, Mr. Briggs. I play some old songs they've heard before and new ones they haven't. I play through the solo part of Bart's *Sonata*. Mixed reactions. They need to hear it with the orchestra, I remind them. Lastly, I play what I've been working on in secret: orchestration for Polly's tuba concerto. Again, they can't hear it right with only me playing. I hear the orchestra in my head as I play the solo part. They applaud, praise my playing.

"Mighty fine tootin'," says Briggs.

"Mighty fine," Eve echoes.

My nephew Jon asks if he can blow into the tuba. Vera cautions him about putting his mouth where other people have put theirs, a remnant from the pandemic era. I wipe off the mouthpiece and he gives it a strong blow but doesn't make any sound. I tutor him a few minutes and finally he blasts a note – a note that awakens Jacob, who starts crying. He managed to sleep through all my playing. We laugh, enjoying our family time.

Later, Eve takes me aside. "I knows Faith wantcha ta go. Maybe she ain't never act like it but she did wantcha ta go an' be happy.

She be right pleased ya get yer chance at last."

I hug her tight, until neither of us can breathe.

Then Frank takes me over to the depot, just the two of us on the wagon plus my tuba and bags. We don't talk. We know everything each of us would say. As my big brother, he's always watched out for me, but it's time for me to go on by myself. Time for me to stand up for myself.

He looks over at me as if hearing my thoughts.

"Sure gonna miss you round here," he says, facing forward as we approach the depot.

"It's only a short time," I remind him. "Then I'll be straightaway home again. I have to be a grandmother."

"And don't you go getting married," he says.

"Don't worry about that. I've learned my lesson."

He nods, says: "Mm-hmm."

+   +   +

I board the express for Kanza City, on my own for the first time since my injury. My hip feels fine; I no longer wait for it to hurt. I try to relax but I'm full of nervous energy. So I take out my music pages and look them over, make changes, correcting a few errors I notice: changing sharps to naturals in one section. Starting a new page I use the theme from the first page but this time I put it in the French horns. Then I add punctuation by trumpets and trombones.

Arriving in Kanza City, I pause a few days to take the tuba to the shop Hal previously recommended. There, my tuba gets the full treatment: flush, oiling, dent repairs, mend loose solders, straighten joints and braces, and give it a fresh polishing. It's the best the old instrument has looked since the pandemic, when Polly took it with her when she and her son left the city. It had a lot of abuse over the years, but now it's like new – or as close as it can be. I point to the embossed plaque on the tuba's bell, the manufacturer's information, including the date: *1940*.

"I know," says Jimmy, the technician. "It's a real antique."

"Nearly two hundred years," I say, proudly.

"That's a long time to be around."

"Back when it was made there was a war going on. That's what my great-grandfather wrote in his journal. Back in nineteen-forty he was supposed to be a tuba player in a military band but they made him fight instead. He got captured and put in a camp."

"That's too bad," says Jimmy. "Better to play that tuba, I think."

"I agree. The war finally ended and he got out of the camp, met a woman, and they had a family. He went back to his ruined country to get this tuba, safe in the old house although his whole family was lost. He brought it here and played in an orchestra. Later he became a music professor. The tuba was passed on to his niece. And so on. All the way down to...me."

"That's quite a story you got there."

"Well, it's been through a lot. In fact, for a few years when things were the worst during the pandemic, it was buried in the ground."

He screws his face up. "In the ground?"

"Yes, but...not intentionally." I have to think a moment. "It was desperate times. It was saved from the pandemic by my family. That niece was my great-great-grandmother. She played in an orchestra, and she was a music professor, too. But the great pandemic ruined everything, ended her career."

"Yep, that was a bad time for everyone."

"She was composing a tuba concerto when the pandemic came. But she never got to finish it. So maybe, just maybe, I can finish it. I have the tuba solo she wrote out, and I've worked out some of the orchestra parts." I grin like I hold a big secret inside. "Maybe it's not what she had in mind, exactly, but it will finally be complete."

"That's amazing. It still plays, and it plays well. It's a miracle," says Jimmy. "Like you've brought it back to life. The tuba, and your relative's music."

"Back to life?"

"Maybe it's fate...if you wish to believe that way. It could be that you're meant to keep the music going."

With a big grin, I pull the tuba into my arms and give it a few playful toots, then play a song Polly wrote. I try different registers, high and low. It sounds great! I run scales up and down, and Jimmy is impressed.

"You're actually pretty good," he says, not believing I could play it so well. He said he'd never seen a woman play a tuba.

"Well, I'm not planning to be any kind of tuba player," I say, "but I promised to play a piece with another tuba player. It's more a joke than real music. Teaching music to kids is what I'm good at.... About all I'm good for."

While Jimmy was busy working on the tuba, I went on errands. I put on my new khaki skirt, crisp white blouse, and a tan vest with silver buttons. Setting my hair in a ponytail, I let the cowgirl hat hang down my back. Knowing I might cross paths with Hal, I wanted to dress so that I looked fine.

It would be only a random quirk to find myself face to face with Hal. I didn't know his home address so I asked the driver of the hire-carriage to take me by the factory where musical instruments were made. I thought Hal's office might be there, yet I saw no one like him. We went over to the concert hall next, pausing to watch people entering and exiting yet I didn't see him.

I return to my modest lodging, the cheapest that looked safe, so I had to share a room with another woman traveling alone, in town for her father's funeral.

Then I pick up my tuba from the shop and board the train for the long ride on to Cincinnati.

21

THE GUEST

ROLLING HILLS DIVIDE crop fields and patches of forest, and the same scenery starts to make me drowsy as the train rolls along. So I lay out my music on the little table by my seat and go over the solo part for Bart's *Sonata* as I press my fingers against my belly. I'm pretending I'm holding the tuba and playing the notes, adjusting my breathing as though I'm actually playing. I must look strange to the other passengers. But the ticketmaster only asks what song I have printed out on the little table.

Later, stopping in the sad-looking city of Louis, a pair of stern ladies older than me come aboard and take the seat opposite me. We exchange pleasantries before deciding to stare at each other a while, feeling safe with our thoughts. They see the music pages spread out on the table and ask what it is. They've never seen such 'scientific scribbling'. One says she used to be a mathematics teacher.

"It's music," I say, feeling put off by their inquiry.

Haven't they seen printed music? How the decades have fallen down! They believe music is something heard, not written.

"Yes, but this is the *score*. It's the set of notations that tells the musicians what to play on their instruments, how to play the notes so you hear the music the way they want it to sound."

My quick definition doesn't impress them much, so they ask how I can know so much. I'm just a young woman, after all.

"I'm a music conductor," I say rather boldly. That feels good. "I'm on the way to Cincinnati to conduct their orchestra in a concert."

The women nearly gasp in shock, then stare at me like I've told a big lie. They ask what instrument I might play.

"I might play any instrument," I say snobbishly, "but my main instrument is the tuba."

They try to giggle at my ridiculous answer but cannot make it sound authentic.

"What a queer notion," says the older woman. "You – playing the tuba. Do they make anything like that these days?"

"It's in the luggage closet at the rear of this car," I assure them, turning to point. "I'll be playing it in the concert, as well."

The younger one, less dismayed, inquires about the music that's laid across the table. Feeling annoyed by them, I begin packing the paper away so they won't think I'm trying to commandeer the table.

"I'm playing this piece," I reply.

"Oh?" says the younger one, raising an eyebrow.

"Yes," I say, "with the orchestra. I've been invited."

"Invited, you say?" challenges the older one.

So I explain, against my will, about my music career. I came in third in the conducting competition in Kanza City. And I started a kids' band in a little town out west called Skinner Canyon. You may have heard of it, being in the news-papers a couple years before and perhaps still on streams if you have the right device. Now I've been invited as guest conductor for the Cincinnati Symphony.

I understand how ridiculous that sounds to ordinary people.

"Thus, I've gotten noticed in the world of music, which sadly isn't much these days. Few people picking up an instrument and learning to play. Fewer interested in hearing music performed live."

It's the music machines producing it now, and it isn't the best. Most is bland and imitative, mechanical and repetitive: as though the machines mix the best of previous music but without any sense of musicality. In the capital the music is ridiculously patriotic, only serving to rile up the people, make them want to march in lockstep.

"Actually, I also write music," I tell them. "A few songs, anyway. But I'm working on completing a *concerto* started by my great-great-grandmother. It's also for tuba."

"Concerto?" asks the older woman. "What, by God, is that?"

262

"It's a musical piece featuring a solo instrument, usually in three contrasting movements, with an orchestra, or in some cases a piano as accompaniment."

"A piano?" She laughs like I've told a fabulous joke. "I remember seeing one of those. Who has one of those old things anymore?"

I frown. "There's one in the school house in my town."

And that is why we agree to stare the rest of the way.

The train takes a southerly route, I hear someone remark up the aisle, but it's still too close to the northern border for comfort. We avoid land that Quebeckers occupy – pronounced *Kay-beckers* by the passenger. They've renamed the large city up there as Chicageaux – saying it's the original name. Fighting breaks out constantly, that passenger explains to the seatmate, but they've managed to conquer everything from their homeland in the north down to the southwest – all the way to Dubuque on the Mississippi River. But it's hardly more than a stream where we pass over it leaving Louis. Similar to how the tribals claimed back their land in the west.

Quebeckers never had that land originally, the passenger says. But the state is called 'Illinois' – pronouncing it *Ee-lee-nwah* – the seatmate responds using a Quebecker accent. No, it's *Ill-uh-noiz*, the first one insists. I recall Dad talking about it, seeing streams in the capital commenting on the 'northern war'. When our lady governor married the president, he already had a grown son who was general of the army fighting up there. They'd lost cities across the entire tier south of the Ontario Lake, over to Detroit, pronounced *Day-twah* in Quebecker style. Their conversation drones on.

I'm glad to live far from that nonsense! No good can come from new-formed nations fighting over each other's territory, even though it's about resources like places to grow food and have water, what they need to survive. I think of Dad when I was a child living in the capital. Dad railed about that, got punished for it. Mom said he was a nervous type like it was his fault. I get nervous, too. My stomach churns if I sense a fearsome thing coming at me.

This train trip and the reason for it fills me with nervousness, but I must overcome it. I must be strong. There isn't anything else I can do. I cannot return home a failure – not again.

We stop in Indian City, another dirty place filled with smoking factories and weathered hovels – at least what I can see around the crumbling station. It seems every city is trying to rebuild what was lost during the past century. But as I saw in the capital, not every build-back plan gives us something better.

Several passengers get off, including my two dour seatmates, and others get on. The seat opposite me thankfully remains empty as we continue on. Not many people can afford tickets, I understand. The Symphony has provided mine. I'm worth a ticket.

I spread out my music again, this time the pages of Polly's tuba concerto, and I go over it once more, hearing the notes in my head as my eyes move across the pages. My hand rises, starts to conduct without command. Passengers stare at me.

Then we are arriving in Cincinnati, which looks quite lovely as we slow through the outer precincts, full of parks and rows of neat residential blocks. I see children playing. We come into an elegant terminal with twin towers rising high, architecture resembling the old style although I think the building must be newly built.

I pack everything, bid farewell to the guard of the Women's Car, and step down to the platform using my cane. The satchel of music hangs heavy on my shoulder, its wide strap tight across my chest.

In a flash, I'm greeted by a delegation from the Symphony and several reporters from the local news-papers. They're looking for a 'western woman' so I pull my cowgirl hat up onto my head, adjust my ponytail, and click my boots. A porter pushes the cart up to us, bearing my travel bag and my tuba in its damaged soft-side case.

Lights continue to flash at me and I blink, turn away, but they want me to pose for photographs, holding up their breadloaf-sized boxes they call cameras – the latest gadget. First is the head of the Performing Arts Commission, Albert Stanley, a portly man with a big, toothy smile. His large hands prompt me into the right pose as I lean on my cane. Then a quintet of ladies from the orchestra, young and older, wishing to have documentation that they once stood with the famous Maggie Baumann on a railway platform. I have to grin. Can I be famous? I'm nobody. A school teacher, exiled from home. I smile anyway, since I've been invited.

Then the group is disturbed by the arrival of Bart Tuttle, who is flustered at having to rush to the station, throwing apologies as he comes to an unsteady halt before me. He's just as tall and broad as I remember him being but a little less bulky now. His bright red hair has grown out significantly, enough to comb it to each side of his head, parted in the middle as the new style. He doesn't know what to do so he awkwardly reaches out to hug me.

"Howdy," Bart exclaims, to the chagrin of the others. He regards them. "That's what they say out west." He regards me. "Isn't that right?"

"We usually don't say anything," I respond, unprepared. "I mean not unless it's important. You get a mouthful of dust if you speak too much." I chuckle to let them know I'm joking, but they don't seem to be convinced.

"Then I apologize," he says, catching another breath.

"That's quite all right." I'm just happy to see a familiar face.

The others gathered around us exchange information about our plans, but Bart isn't finished with me.

"Good journey?" Bart asks, ignoring the others.

"Yes, acceptable," I reply. "I once took the train all the way to the capital so this was easy."

Bart appears alarmed. He looks around for my wheel-chair, but I tell him I don't need it now. I suffered in that chair for three years. However, it's helpful to use a cane, especially for stairs. He's pleased at the development. I like that he worries about me that way.

"What's it been, like a year?" he asks with a curious grin.

"Yes, a little more than," I reply in a weary voice, "but feels like two, I think."

"Seems like only yesterday you were conducting in Kanza City."

I act demure. "Yesterday sure was a while ago."

"I really liked your performance," says Bart, looking earnest.

"Thank you. I was so nervous. I can't believe I did that."

Bart chuckles, his cheeks rosy. "You sure did, though."

"Shall we go?" asks Mr. Stanley, asserting leadership. "Lots to do today. No time for yesterdays. Let us focus on tomorrow."

The delegation moves with me, keeping me surrounded as if in a cage. Bart carries my tuba. He seems to appreciate the heft of it as he swings it up onto his shoulders, his arms through the straps. The others bring my travel bag. I hold on to my satchel full of music and continue to use the cane as we exit the station.

The throng of reporters follows us. Mr. Stanley says there will be a formal interview later, after I've rested. Same protocol as in Kanza City. I will likely be famous for ten minutes, long enough to read the article they'll write about me. More for the memories trunk at home. I'm not expecting much more from this visit than a couple pleasant moments I'll remember for a while, then soon forget. Have fun, I tell myself. Have anecdotes to share. Then I'll go back home to Skinner Canyon and continue my ordinary life.

+   +   +

Same questions, same answers. How did I get interested in music? It was in me all along. Why the tuba? It's the family instrument. Do you have future plans here? I've only been invited to conduct one concert and to play one piece, a work Mr. Tuttle has composed for us. That's all I expect. Maybe take a look at your river. Is there a boat to go across? (The new bridge is under construction, the old one destroyed during the war.) Then I'll return home. So what do you think of Cincinnati? It's a nice place, better than I expected; I mean, better than in the capital. I've only seen the railway station and a hotel. Today is the concert hall. I'll meet the orchestra.

I try to be polite, but mostly I'm tired from the trip. My room in the fine hotel they put me in is so quiet having nobody to talk to. I miss having Eve and Jackie around. I write a message for them on note paper provided in the room, putting on a bright face, and have the hotel staff send it. I lay out my outfits, one for each public event. I'll wear the same black gown from Kanza City for my conducting debut here. They want me to wear a more Western outfit, part of my reputation. Sorry I no longer have to use the wheel-chair. Bart helps them understand I'm not a circus trick; I'm a serious musician.

He actually turns out to be a nice fellow, kind and all about the business of music. We spend time in a rehearsal room going over his

Sonata. We get out our tubas and take a while admiring each other's instruments. He is amazed at the manufacturer's plaque on the bell of my tuba, the embossed *1940* freshly polished. I tell him the whole story, all the way from Old Fritz to Granny Polly to me, and he is further amazed. We switch mouthpieces and play each other's tuba a little, comparing notes. I enjoy that, meeting another tuba player, getting some tips, and talking about something we both love.

I have what he calls the easier part of our duet, knowing I would have less time to practice before the concert, but it's still a daunting task to find those high notes and to run through those long scales at the end of it. In fact, he assumes I will also, somehow, conduct the orchestra, too. Is that even possible? Piano players do it, he says.

"That's what I expected would be the case when I wrote it," says Bart. "I was thinking of you. I mean, that you would also conduct. It makes sense for you to take the second part."

Rather than debate the logic of his idea, I suggest we give it a try first. We need to hear it regardless. So we begin: just the two of us playing, like we are in a dance together: a true duet, only the two tubas playing before the orchestra comes in around us. It's rather clever. We play through it as though the orchestra is in the room with us, stopping only twice to check a passage. I see he has written instructions on the pages for me to turn and conduct the orchestra for a few measures, then return to playing the tuba part. At the end of the *Sonata* it's only the two tubas playing once more, with the orchestra faded out. One movement with contrasting sections.

I couldn't have imagined it from just playing my part alone.

He beams with shyness, thanks me.

"I'll start us off," says Bart. "You start the orchestra when I get to bar twenty-one. Then it's your turn from bar thirty. They'll follow us to bar sixty. That's where you can set aside your tuba and check on them. I'll play on. At bar eighty-four it's tricky so watch out."

He points to the section on my pages, finger marking here and here, where the orchestra fights with us.

"Yes, I see." And I gaze at this man, impressed. "I get it."

We practice together like old friends. Yet he remains cordial. We are two business people negotiating a contract.

Later, he comes with me when we meet Mr. Stanley to confirm the concert selections. We have one week of rehearsals.

"Generally, we like to begin with something lively," Mr. Stanley says, sitting at his desk with his floppy bowtie giving him a comical look, "such as an overture or a march, or perhaps a few movements from a popular suite."

"I thought of something easy," I offer, and list three I think I can conduct with minimal time to rehearse.

"That's fine. Any of those will do," says Mr. Stanley.

"I would second *William Tell*," Bart speaks up, sitting back of me so I have the stage.

"I've played that with my band so I'm familiar with it," I say.

"Then it's done. I'll have the librarian prepare the parts," says Mr. Stanley and he calls in a loud voice to his secretary in the outer office. He returns his attention to me, then shifts his eyes to Bart. "Then the duet. Your...two tuba tango!" He laughs.

"It's serious music," Bart insists.

"I like it. It *is* good music," I speak up because it's true, not only to support him. "I'm surprised he wrote such a piece but, now that we've practiced it, I really like it."

"Thank you, Miss Baumann," says Bart.

"Call me Maggie. We're colleagues, aren't we?"

"So the *Sonata for Two Tubas and Orchestra* – what an ungodly name." Chuckles. "That comes second. Big applause – we hope. Then intermission. We like to present a longer work for the second half, something like a symphony or extended suite of some kind. I like your suggestions – very efficient of you, Miss Maggie."

"Those are what I can conduct. I don't have a long list."

"How do you feel about the Beethoven then?"

"I put it on the list," I boast.

"Wonderful. Then we shall conclude with the Fifth Symphony. A good choice for our music-going crowd. They prefer the standards."

As we're leaving Mr. Stanley's office, Bart praises my choices.

"We played the Beethoven last year in Kanza City," he tells me. That symphony doesn't require a tuba so he can sit in the audience and 'scrutinize' my conducting. I laugh awkwardly at the idea, but he acts as though I'm charming.

"I promise to start the applause," says Bart.

I give him a smile. "I suppose I chose it *because* it doesn't require a tuba. I'm the only tuba player in Skinner Canyon. But I have to be the conductor."

"That makes sense. You are really talented," he says, blushing a bit, his cheeks turning as red as his hair. "I can't believe you live out west there, in that little cow town, keeping your talents to yourself. That's the reason you're so impressive."

"Impressive? I'm sure I'm not. Ask anyone in Skinner Canyon."

He asks more about the town that's been my home since I was eleven. I give him the brief history and he nods at each fact I share. He's being polite as I go on and on. I stop when I sense he's heard enough.

"It does sound interesting," he concludes. "Maybe I should go see it for myself. Never got to ride a horse."

"You should. I'll show you around. Show you the spot where that horse stepped on me." Then I completely freeze. I was enjoying our conversation, then I have to say something weird! "Other places are better. Our burned-down cabin is an attraction for tourists. The five saloons, obviously. You'd like the saloon gals, I'm sure. The inn with the notorious gossip guarding the front desk. The teepee we're living in." My mind is drifting away.

"You say 'we'...." He frowns. "You're married? I recall you having the name Kirk before."

"Oh, that was a big misunderstanding." Scenes flash through my head and I try to shoo them away. "It's been resolved. Finally. And now I return to my dad's family name: Baumann."

"So who is 'we' then? If I may ask...?"

I feel myself blush. "I suppose there's no 'we' any longer. I meant my daughter. She's adopted from a local tribe, the indigenous people that live nearby. After her grandfather died, she had no one, so I took her in. She's a lovely girl. Now she's grown up and married with a new baby. So I suppose the teepee's all mine when I return. No one has offered to build a new cabin for me."

"A teepee? Hmm...." He seems interested.

Then I tell him about my dear cousin Eve, how she's spent more time with Mr. Briggs in the weeks before I left for Cincinnati. I talk about how I miss her – miss both of them.

"I see." He ponders my information until I ask about his family.

He gives me a short account: the youngest of three sons, the only musician in the family. His mother is still alive but angry at the world, a little crazy. His father works himself to the bone each day in a factory – right up the hill from us. Ironworks. He drinks a lot as a result. One brother works there, too. The other brother joined the army, was sent to fight the Quebeckers. But Bart's childhood wasn't too abusive, I'm pleased to hear. That came mostly from classmates who teased him for his red hair, always calling him a clown.

I nod sympathetically at each point he makes.

"I don't miss my family, not at all," he says and his tone makes me feel pity for him. "Glad to immerse myself in the music business and tell them I'm just too busy to bother with them, even at Sunday dinners. I haven't gone there since I returned from Kanza City, to be honest. I haven't told them I play in the Symphony. They wouldn't care anyway."

He seems sad, so I tell him about Sunday dinners at my brother Frank's house. Vera always puts out a big spread. How my brother, James, works on Sundays. Bart laughs at my detailed descriptions.

"I sure would like to meet them," he says, and I realize I've gone too far. Nobody wants to hear about other people's families. I mean, especially if they haven't done anything remarkable. "No, really. I do want to meet them. They sound interesting."

"Interesting is probably the best word for them," I say.

He grins playfully. "Do you think they'll like me?"

I can't recall the walk but suddenly I find us in the hotel and it's time for dinner. He suggests we dine in the hotel's restaurant. I tell him how there are no restaurants for ordinary people in the capital. But my dad got a Special Pass that allowed him to go in restaurants and get real food, not the pre-packaged fare in boxes for workers, based on their nutritional needs.

Bart is surprised, intrigued. He asks me to describe the capital more and I give him the whole sad story of my dad and his heroism involving the governor. But I also add the reasons Mom took us out of the city and we went out west. I don't want to tell him about our humiliating experience arriving in the capital last time.

"Have you heard about the protests in the capital?" he asks right as I raise my fork to my mouth.

I chew, then reply: "No, what are they protesting?"

I'm sure I can guess: everything that a tyrannical society wants to force citizens to do to create their 'ideal society'.

"It's the musicians guild this time," he says. "City leaders want to close the concert hall, put musicians to work in other jobs. They say they have enough music as it is, what they can make on their machines. Even if it's no good, it's easy to make and cheap compared to paying a group of musicians."

"That's awful," I say, meaning it. "What can they do?"

"The latest effort is protest concerts. They play on and on, won't stop, let people listen. It's to gather support."

"I would support that!"

We talk more but I don't like getting angry over all the terrible news from the capital so I gently nudge us back to our own concert, the music we will rehearse, and plans for the next day.

That covers dinner time, plus dessert: a lemon crème pie. I can't finish mine so I offer it to Bart. He gladly finishes it for me.

Pausing in the lobby of the hotel after our dinner, I have to end our conversation for the evening. I thank him for a delightful day. I look forward to rehearsals. He can't wait. Awkwardly, he leans over and gives me a peck on the cheek, nervously bids me a good night.

+   +   +

Fitful sleep: giant horns blaring through storm clouds, angry angels swinging low on fiery wings, war drums pounding. I awaken in a hot sweat. What am I doing here?

I sit alone at the table in the hotel restaurant, the fried eggs and toast unfinished, staring across the room at the other guests eating in a pensive mood, perhaps fearing what is ahead. I study myself in the wide mirror running along the wall, seeing a stranger.

We stick ourselves in the present moment and survey everything behind us. How did that road manage to bring us here? We squint to see what lies ahead. How will the road go? In either direction we see how others have stuck themselves, claiming a span of years as their own personal history, their private era. This is my span of years, I guess as I push away my plate. This is my life.

Then I go to the concert hall to begin a new chapter.

"Hello, everyone. I'm Maggie. I'll be your conductor today."

A few of the musicians chuckle. At least the kids back home like the joke. It's necessary to calm myself.

I give a bow and step onto the podium. The score is already there on the stand, thanks to Carla, a woman near my age with fabulously curly blond hair who they've assigned as my assistant.

"Actually, I'll be here all week," I say next.

I raise my hands, baton in my right, and we begin.

The *William Tell Overture* by Mr. Rossini, the introduction to his opera, a piece sampling its various themes, is a crowd favorite, said Mr. Stanley, owing to the popularity of horse racing in the city. But I've read that the music is about a sheriff out west who rides a silver horse. I love how the overture opens with a cello solo backed by a quartet of cellos playing a sad chorale. That develops into a section which portrays a storm with trombones threatening. It doesn't last long: the sun comes out, takes us into the lovely next section where English horn and flutes trade bird calls in the forest. What people eagerly await is when the trumpets and horns come in to sound the alarm and we are off to the races. We gallop to the finish!

Our first play-through goes well and I'm pleased. After all, these are professional level musicians, not a band of kids. The music is a little different, considering that the band played a simplified version for the instruments we had. This is the original for full orchestra and sounds marvelous. I praise the orchestra, then we go back over a few places I want to check. We play those sections a couple times, then play it from the top again.

Then comes the hard part.

We take a short break as stage hands bring chairs onto the stage for the tuba duet. Bart didn't have a part in the Rossini overture so he comes on stage with his golden tuba, having a different design than mine. His leans to the left although he uses his right hand to move the rotary valves. My tuba leans to the right while I also use my right hand but on piston valves. The effect is that, sitting side by side at the front of the stage, turned enough so we can keep an eye on each other, we barely can see the audience by gazing over or around the side of our instruments. That's fine with me; I'd rather play without seeing the audience looking at me.

We discussed this awkward situation the previous evening. With the principal conductor, Maestro Xavier, out of town for the protests in the capital, it's left to me to conduct the orchestra, even for this piece in which I'm also a performer. When I'm not playing, I'll check on the orchestra, giving directions as best I can before returning to the tuba part. It can be done, Bart insists. They know what to do.

So we try it.

Bart starts the *Sonata* with the low G – the piece is in G minor – then rises quickly up a cascade of scales to embark on a dance tune in uneven time, reminding me of Polly's song "Sandy's Bride". As he plays, I conduct the orchestra from my chair, holding my tuba in my left arm and swinging my right hand. I feel no pain in my hip and that encourages me when I pull my tuba to my mouth and play the same low note like the first tuba, follow his lead through the scales until we are playing a lively duet, each line of notes balancing and countering the other, back and forth. It's a brilliant concept. Full of teasing, of touching then running away. I feel confident playing this part, love the fun of it.

But the piece includes an orchestra, so I turn when my part rests and lead the orchestra through the new theme, with strings soaring and woodwinds pecking out the original theme. This piece is a true sonata: the first section's theme repeating in the third section with a contrasting theme in the middle, a single-movement of about twelve minutes. In the final section, when the theme returns, I signal the orchestra to charge onward to the end as Bart and I blast away on our tubas, high notes crackling, and the lows roaring. It's good he let me have the easier part because he runs up and down those scales with the facility of a clarinet player. I only play quarter notes and quarter rests. He has a good ear for using the strings to heighten the dramatic effect. I like the timpani at the end.

I swing my tuba into my left arm to lead the applause when we finish. He blushes, says to me it's nothing, as the orchestra members cheer. We stand and take a humble bow. The look he gives me, part thanks and part something more – admiration? affection? – sends a shiver through me. Thankfully, I can hand off my tuba to Carla and retake the podium to work on a few of the orchestra sections before we take another break. Bart acts shy, making recommendations as the composer, and we practice those sections.

He thanks everyone and steps off stage with his tuba.

The Beethoven symphony is also familiar to me, and I've listened to it many times using the disk on the music machine. I playfully tried conducting along with the music I heard, reacting rather than leading. But I know the music so well I think I can do it.

The first movement's *da-da-da-dum* motif is well-known. Even the capital's official anthem uses it, calling it the 'hammer of fate' – like the strikes are warnings for us to obey whatever silly rules they push on us. But I don't hear it that way. The softer section in this movement reminds us of the more pleasant aspects of life: a quiet meadow, fresh breeze, the touch of a loved one's hand, birds singing, brooks babbling – then the hammer returns to send it all away. The strings and woodwinds insist it doesn't have to be that way, if we only fight back, fight for our right to a happy life! But in the end the hammer demands obedience.

I confess it's the second movement, beginning as a stately dance, that captures my heart. I slip into dreams listening to the delicate flute and oboe melodies coupled with the richness of the strings. I'm reminded of Old Fritz' homeland, what little I know from reading the big book of music. I can see people dancing in a formal fashion. Then a fanfare interrupts, reminds them of the hammer of fate. But a clarinet says *Wait a moment!* and sets the tone as cellos introduce a strident new theme that expands into a fine line of flute notes, repeating the three-plus-one motif again, toying with the hammer of fate as if saying: "Not today, hammer!" The fanfare returns, like the people are shouting back, but they get quiet, afraid. Woodwinds and strings take over, give us a hopeful theme, playful like woodland critters chasing each other. But the hammer returns, and we don't know what to do. Give in or fight? The simple beauty of the world, light notes calling us, urges us to play nicely. The horn calls, the brass section reminds us of our fate, but it is not what the strings give us, nor the dark flutes and clarinets, playing a martial tune as though off to war we must go. Yet this theme bursts with joy, with a grand glory that promises to sustain us – only to fall back into that country dance that reminds us of simpler days. They will return if we have patience, stay aware, ready to stand up to tyranny. That's what I think, but I keep it to myself.

We lean into the third movement, *Scherzo*, strong and muscular, a dance of hammers rising from Hell, swinging left and right as an army of horns blast away! Here is Fate! Listen to our hammers! *Da-da-da-dum* once more! We haven't forgotten about you rough rubes and ragged rogues! Obey! Submit! Bow down before us, for we know what's best. Then the basses present their counterargument, a beefy insistence on the rule of law, of human rights, hammers be damned! Woodwinds sing along, then join in the dance, shunning the devilish theme. But it gets quiet all of a sudden as we dare to look back over our shoulders, survey the skies, see dangers hiding at every turn. Something is coming. What can it be? Oh, what can it be?

It is Glorious God sweeping back the storm clouds, smiling down on us as the fourth movement begins! Trombones and trumpets ring true! Strings soar like angel wings, a mighty army of sky chariots charging into battle! We stand in awe, bow in humility, thankful, as the full orchestra dismantles the hammer and all its kin. Trombones signal our triumph! We've won! We shall never bow to the hammer of fate! The three notes is *our* motif, not theirs. It shouts our fate is ours! But – no, wait; is it really ours? ask the woodwinds cautiously. We've been tricked before. The brass section pronounces the truth of our desires! Horns assure us of our strength! A frenzied rush to our victory celebration propels the full orchestra forward, the trumpets leading the way! We collapse, ravaged by the final chords!

My shirt is soaked, my back tense, my hip not complaining at all. I take a big breath and face the orchestra, meet their eyes. Most are smiling back at me. We've done it.

I've done it!

Bart, posed at the edge of the stage, claps for me. A few others in the orchestra applaud. They've played this famous work countless times yet it's the first time for me with a full orchestra.

I take a bow, my face flushed.

"Bravo! Bravo!" shout a few orchestra members.

Maybe they don't expect much from me and I've done better than that low standard. Now, if only the actual concert can go as well as this rehearsal, I pray. Then my life will be complete.

22

A CAPITAL MOMENT

PERHAPS BECAUSE I PRAYED, actually spoke words to Mom and Dad, and anyone else able to hear me, the concert is a great success. So many people came to see this odd 'western woman' conduct their orchestra and even play her tuba – "as good as Maestro Xavier on his best evening," one reporter writes in the review. And Bart's tuba duet is singled out as a "special delight, unexpected and flawlessly presented." He's so happy we swing into a loose embrace, our tubas almost clinking, and as we part it just happens: his big, wet smack to my cheek.

As he describes the moment at the after-party, he draws back in feigned horror, apologizing again.

"And she still has the Beethoven to conduct," he exclaims while those around us chuckle appreciatively.

"It was a fabulous moment," I tell him, giving a pat to his chest. "I'm sure it's allowed in that situation. I didn't mind."

So he kisses my cheek again and, with an instant to consider it, I dare to kiss him: a peck on his lips. That does it: we are a couple in everyone's eyes. *Bravo!*

We stand together at the after-party, everyone speaking with us, congratulating us. A few outright ask whether we are in a romantic relationship, using the odd metaphor of being bitten by a 'love bug'. I can't imagine such an insect, although I've been bitten by a few other kinds in Skinner Canyon. They don't get my joke.

"She came for the tuba sonata," says Bart to save me.

But why else would I have traveled this far? And played the duet with him? It must mean something, they insist. Bart blushes at the suggestion. I have to fan myself to keep calm. The social rules are different in a city, I suppose. He looks as uncomfortable as me with the dreadful teasing. We fumble with excuses, defending each other, but manage to make it clear we are simply professional colleagues who share a love of music.

At least the food is good, but we are tired and must bow out.

He walks me to my hotel, carrying my tuba on his back while his stays in a locker in the concert hall. It's a pleasantly warm evening. Our hands bump a few times. A tune sings in my head, and I hum a bit of it. Otherwise, we stroll in silence save for a blurting of silly small talk about the starry evening – they turn the streetlamps low to save on the electric – or some trivia we recall from the concert.

In the lobby he pauses like a shy school boy, same as I saw with my nephew Jeb when courting Jackie. He shakes off my tuba, sets it gently on the floor, leaning against his leg.

I watch him handle my tuba, seeing how careful he is with it. He bears a gentle strength in his arms. I could carried the tuba myself, now that my hip seems nearly back to normal.

Our eyes meet and it feels strange, yet we don't look away. I'm an adult woman, free to do as I please in this new era of equality for everyone. It's a written policy.

He hesitates, not wanting to give up my tuba and have to leave. I feel he's conjuring important words he wants to say, so I wait, but he doesn't say them.

So I ask him to carry my tuba up to my room.

"Miss Baumann," calls a man at the front desk, "a message for you. Quite a few, actually. But I have one marked 'urgent' here."

I gather the dozen messages and sort through them, all notes of praise for the concert, and find the urgent one. It's from Maestro Xavier, sent from the capital. Curious, I open the envelope and read it as Bart comes up behind me, looking over my shoulder. I glance at him, giving him permission to see what I'm reading.

The maestro begs me to stay longer, to conduct the next concert on his behalf. He has scheduled three pieces which should not be too difficult for me: a short symphony by Mr. Mozart, the ballet suite by Mr. Copland which Mr. Stanley had mentioned, and Sarita Conn, a famous pianist, is visiting for the concerto by Mr. Rachmaninov. The reason for this request is that he and several other musicians who are involved in the protests in the capital have been arrested. They are being treated well and he assures us it is only an inconvenience and the matter will be sorted out shortly. They will be free soon, but he worries about the citizens of this city, wondering how they will go on without another concert to sustain them.

"I'm sure the music isn't their most serious problem," I say in response to Bart's shock. "Lots of problems there. I was there a few years ago to claim my dad's tuba. Fortunately it was in a display of antique curiosities, so it was saved. Even so...."

Bart is aghast, fearing the worst. He explains his special affinity for the maestro, how Maestro Xavier rescued him, brought him to Cincinnati after he lost the job in Kanza City to Leyland Keller, a tubist from the capital. Most orchestras have only one tuba player, two for a few larger works, compared to thirty violins divided into two sections.

He states vehemently that the maestro shouldn't have gone, that nothing good could come from his presence there, the way things are in the capital. They want to ban the only orchestra remaining and send the musicians out to do other jobs.

"We have to make a stand," I declare. "Whatever happens in the capital spreads to other cities eventually."

I remind him the maestro believes he will be freed very soon.

"He's only being kind – so we won't worry about him," says Bart. "However, I'm sure it really is a very serious matter."

Agreeing, I remind him of some incidents my dad experienced in the capital, reasons why Mom took us away. He knows about all of that but he will continue to worry.

"We have to do something," he insists.

"Easy," I say, patting his shoulder. "You must be a nervous type, like my dad. Every little thing sent him into a rage."

He forces a grin, then falls back into his worry-face. "Maybe."

"He's made his request. We must honor his wish. Then we hope for the best. Like my dad would say: think positively."

Patting his chest again, his hand catches mine, holds it.

"I can't help but worry. Without him, the orchestra could be shut down, the same as in the capital. We'll all be out of jobs. And I can't do anything else. Even here, there are those who say it's a waste of resources, nothing more than a frivolous indulgence. Maestro had to argue with the City Council to establish and fund this orchestra he would lead. He convinced them it was in their best interests, good for society, especially with everything we've gone through the past century. People would vote for them, he said."

"I agree. People want – they *need* – music in their lives. But they don't see it that way in the capital." I shake my head. "Productivity is foremost. Get society back on track, they say. No time for play, for music. It's a distraction, they say. Such twisted minds! It's an awful place. Every policy is a new version of insanity."

"Most likely, he's contacted other people in the orchestra. They'll have ideas of what to do."

His face shows concern, mind full of thoughts, so I give his hand a squeeze. He clasps my hand tighter and I never realized how small my hand is until it's enfolded in this man's thick paw. He is built for a tuba. Not like me: too delicate, with small lungs, can barely carry it on my back.

"We can address the matter in the morning." I let out a sigh, a signal, as my chest tightens. "Tonight, I'm so tired I want to take a hot bath and sleep a long time." I try to smile, pondering tomorrow morning. "Then I'll awaken and face a new day, whatever that may bring. Everything will make sense then, I'm sure."

"But we can't wait till tomorrow," he says, still agitated.

"Nothing's going to happen overnight," I say in a calm voice.

"But will you stay on?" He seems serious. "Like he asks you?"

"I can stay. If they want me to."

"You will?"

"Yes."

Confirming my decision seems to help him relax.

"I'm so happy you'll stay longer...." His voice fades as though he can't think of anything else to say. He gives me that innocent grin of his, child-like, like he's expecting a trip to the candy store.

Likewise, I don't know what to say, so naturally I say something stupid: "We can work on my great-grandmother's concerto."

Maybe it's not much of a secret – news-paper reports like to tell all – but I have nothing else to do in my life. I'm completely free. I could return to Skinner Canyon in the morning. On random days I'd go out to the canyon and gaze across to the tribal lands or go in the opposite direction and gaze across the chaparral and count grasses, maybe wave off a bison or two as the wind blows my hat half-way to Cimarron. I could spend the rest of my life that way. Nothing else I have to do. Nobody requiring a thing of me. I could play that tuba each day, making up songs, and be happy. I sure wouldn't have to think about the miserable capital.

"Maggie?" calls Bart, seeing me go down that fox burrow, lost in my thoughts. "You all right?"

I shake back to reality. "Yes, fine. Sorry. I was thinking...."

"About staying?" He's still concerned, which makes him dear to me. Maybe he wishes me to stay for his own reasons. That wouldn't be so bad. The world is full of reasons, some good and others not.

"We can talk upstairs," I say in decidedly unflirtatious tone, my voice low. I indicate he should take my tuba up to my room.

He hefts my tuba, safe in its soft-side case, onto his shoulders, arms through the straps, and I see my dad carrying it, his mother bearing it, her father wearing it like armor, his mother hugging it, playing it, going back to Old Fritz. I smile and Bart doesn't have a clue. He thinks it's about the music. It's actually about life.

We step into the lift box and go up four levels. I glance at Bart as he stares forward in silence, perhaps afraid to look at me too long. For a moment I have to wonder: Is it actually a truth that a young man in possession of a good tuba, must also want a wife? Or am I being silly? I hold back a giggle. I tell myself to stay professional: I have completed my task to the best of my ability and I'm now free to leave. Must not allow myself to be drawn into tawdry detours – like the mess in the capital.

"Thank you," I say, as we step out of the lift box. "You're sweet."

"Anything for you, ma'am." He *is* sweet.

We pause outside my door, a moment for decisions.

"Well," he says and adds a sigh. "I guess it's good night."

I open the door. "Come in. We can talk."

Once inside the room, various clothing laid out in a haphazard way such that I must apologize for the mess, he stands shyly by the open door after unloading the tuba onto the bed. I move about the room in total freedom, like it's my own space.

Yet I have a guest.

When I regard him, me in my less-than-fresh black formal dress that's cut too low in front while he suffers in that stiff tuxedo, the bow tie tight around his neck, I have to grin. I remark how he looks like a statue and he turns more red, apologizes.

"No, I mean you look handsome in your concert suit," I say.

Yet he remains stiff, awaiting orders. I'm sure he wants to stay but he's ready to run out, too.

I move the tuba to the lounging chair in the corner of the room.

"You can come on in," I tell him but he doesn't believe me. "And close that door. I don't want other guests to catch a peek of whatever we choose to do. It's nothing for them to be concerned with."

"Yes, ma'am." Now it's a playful tone, I'm glad to hear.

He closes the door, appreciating my humor. I hear the lock catch, which is something I hadn't thought of. Maybe he has an idea, too. We've only discussed music thus far.

"We need time to go over Polly's concerto, if you will have some spare time before I leave."

"But you said you'd stay...."

"Yes, but I expect I'll leave someday. Isn't that true?"

"Oh," he says, then tries to chuckle. "Yes. I suppose."

I see this roughly handsome man standing before me in a formal suit, an ideal display, looking like a guardian angel, a helpmate, a kindred spirit, a step-brother, a shy lover. He isn't dandy Hal, with his flirty ways, always so well-put-together, neat and fastidious; nor is he brusque like that clumsy rogue Billy Kirk, thank goodness. Bart is different. He's a serious musician like me. Also a tubist. He knows what I know. We share particular interests. We've enjoyed a delightful experience playing together as we rehearsed his *Sonata*.

He wrote it with me in his mind, he swears. The piece is a wonderful work, I must admit despite my initial doubts. It's a worthy addition to the tuba repertoire.

"I want to tell you how much I love your *Sonata*."

His face brightens. "I'm so happy you like it."

"I said I *love* it. It's very good." And I go on describing everything I love about it, soon sounding like a blabbering child. I think he gets the idea after a while so I fall silent.

He smiles in thanks, steps toward me. "I have other ideas."

"My great-grandmother would certainly appreciate it," I start in again, feeling my nerves misfiring. "She would love it. I think I told you she wrote songs, too. I've played them on my tuba, but they're just fun tunes – what she wrote when they were stuck on an island waiting out the pandemic. Songs to pass boring days. But she was working on a tuba concerto during the first lockdowns."

"Is that right?" he asks, drawing in. I realize then that I told him before, but he's all smiles.

"But it's not finished. They had to leave the city, trying to find a better place. A safe place."

"That's sad. Did they survive?"

"Yes and no." I run my tongue across my lips, unsure how much to tell, trying to recall what I told him already. "According to what her son wrote about their adventures, she did not survive."

"Aww, that's too bad. Sorry." His eyes show genuine sadness at the news, more than a century past now.

We gaze at each other and the room falls silent.

"I have the solo part," I say to break the quiet. "But I don't have the orchestra's part. I know she wrote it, but it was lost. I've tried to compose something of my own around the solo passages, using the same themes. It's only a guess. Not at all what she had in mind, I'm sure. I have the first movement finished. Even got parts printed."

"Then you have to add your name to the credits," he says, slight amusement in his voice.

"Is that allowed?" I ask, seriously. "It's her music."

"Can you show me?" He smiles but his voice shakes.

"It's in my bag."

I go to the windowseat where my music satchel rests. He follows, stands behind me, too close – yet I don't feel concern. If he embraced me from behind me, wrapping his strong arms around me, nuzzling his cheek against mine, that would be fine.

When I turn, sheets of music in my hand, he is right there. We brush awkwardly against each other. He apologizes for the closeness and steps back, fumbling for words. I hold the music pages against my chest, slightly crumpling them.

We exchange apologies – apologies for whatever needs it.

As I straighten the pages, smoothing them, I speak plainly.

"Bart," I say. "I really appreciate what you've done...done for me. This entire experience. It's been a truly wonderful experience being here this week. And with you. And the music. It's fabulous! A great experience. I've never met another tuba player. It's really been a...a great experience playing with you."

"That's a lot of experience," he says with a wry grin.

I laugh, blushing. "Yes, experiences. Life's all about having great experiences."

He finds amusement in my words. "I've enjoyed having you here, too. A wonderful experience for me, too. If you don't mind me saying, I'll miss you when you go home again."

I regard him, the two of us standing close together, raising my eyes to him as I think through my checklist of choices.

"Bart," I say once more, "I want to be straightforward with you – about us. I have some issues you should know about.... More than, say, my hip. If you intend for us to continue to get closer, I mean. It's only fair. Though if I'm mistaken, do forgive me. I'm sometimes too clever—"

"No, ma'am," he says, his voice brighter. "You're not mistaken. I do want us to get...closer...if you want to, I should say."

"Just like your *Sonata*. A duet...."

A big grin erupts across his face, full of innocence and honesty, like I've released him from all restrictions. I feel the downbeat.

"Like that." He turns sullen. "Heck, I haven't been with nearly anyone." His face beams as bright as his hair.

"Nearly?" I ask, bemused. I'm playing with him now, everything feeling just right. I can relax. The counterpoint works.

"Well," he says, looking to the side, thinking, "there was a time a girl kissed me, but it was more like a bet she had. I saw the girls pushing her to do it. See, nobody wants to kiss a tuba player." He looks down shyly. "They think it's going to be sloppy."

I have to grin. "Oh, you poor boy! How sad!"

"Well, that was a long time ago," he says, his chest inflating. "I'm not that boy any more. Not a poor boy, no ma'am. In fact, Maggie, I feel very rich with you being here. I couldn't be happier."

His smile is so sincere, my heart kicks me as hard as that horse.

"I'm happy, too." My voice sounds like someone else's.

"I like you being here. I mean in Cincinnati," he says, his voice stumbling. "Sorry, I mean.... You are so talented. I like how you took charge of the orchestra. I like how you played my *Sonata*. I like how you...how you look. Sorry. I like...well, everything, I guess."

I grasp his shoulders, stare deep into his eyes.

"I'm a tuba player," I say. "And I've never given a sloppy kiss."

He blinks, like a hopeful little boy wanting the candy. "Really?"

With a warm smile, I say: "Let me show you."

I press against him, take his face in my hands. We kiss, just like putting mouth to mouthpiece, settling in for a good toot. He tastes like tuba: metal and valve oil. I must taste like crème cake from the party. But the kiss isn't sloppy, not at all. It's an entire symphonic movement before our lips part.

+   +   +

In the morning we gather at the concert hall to discuss what to do about the situation. Mr. Stanley received the same message as me. He's pleased to offer me an extended contract. That's the least of our concerns, I tell him. What about Maestro Xavier?

"He can take care of himself, I'm sure," says Mr. Stanley. "They will have a lot of aggravation in dealing with the maestro. He can be very persuasive – if they will listen."

"I'm sure they have ways of persuasion we can't think of," I dare say, thinking of my dad.

Other members of the Board state their opinions about how best to handle the matter. A representative of the Musicians Guild in the meeting approves me staying on, conducting an additional concert, scheduled for the next month, paid at the standard rate for a guest conductor. Yes, I can stay another month, I confirm, because sadly I have nothing else scheduled. I make a dramatic show of checking in my datebook: no names, so I'm free.

Mr. Stanley retrieves his tablet, taps a few times and a fresh document appears on the screen. I try to read it over but I'm sure it is in order.

Thumbprint here, name written there, the manager directs.

"Anything I can do to help, I will."

I still would rather see the maestro return unharmed, even if he returns in time so I don't need to take the next concert.

"He believes so strongly, you see, he had to go. He had to join the protest," Mr. Stanley explains. "You should relax. It doesn't concern you. Please look to the next concert. Prepare for that."

"Of course," I respond, but I'm still worried.

"I'll tell you," Mr. Stanley goes on, "he asked for you by name, because of your performance in Kanza City. He was there. He saw you conduct and he was impressed. We agree – seeing how well you led the orchestra this week. You have a natural sense. As you said, you come from a musical family. You feel the music. Without formal training in a music school, too. Self-taught."

"I study like mad," I cut in. "Mad Maggie, that's me."

"It is amazing, nevertheless. A 'western woman' conducts a city orchestra. The maestro imagined you would perform something in western style, like the Copland *Rodeo* suite."

"But...isn't it scheduled for the next concert?" I ask.

"Pure coincidence, I assure you. But you chose the Beethoven. So we moved it back."

"I'm not such a 'western woman', as you suspect. I wouldn't want the truth to ruin your publicity but I was born in the capital."

His face goes white like I'm a liar and a thief.

"As a child. That wouldn't be an issue. People would forgive you. Many people have left the capital over the years as everything has become more intolerable there."

"True. I was barely eleven when my mother took me and my two brothers out of there as soon as she could. That was after my father died, you see. You've heard the story? He saved the governor. That's Roberta Chesterfield, who married President Wornall, then became the vice-president. It's old news."

"Yes, yes, we know the story. Part of your allure. You're actually more famous than you can imagine."

"Famous?" I have to laugh. "Me? Who am I? A school teacher from a small town out on the western fringe of the nation. Daughter of a notorious citizen of the capital? That's the story? And I started a children's band. All I know is from books, and listening to music on disks in a machine."

"And yet you *have* learned everything," he says.

"But I'm certainly not any kind of protester. I have my beliefs, to be sure, but I...."

"Perhaps that is what is needed," he says, giving me a stern look. "Perhaps you should go to the capital, too, and join the protest. Your reputation would march ahead of you. That will give them a pause. They never could do anything to you, you being the famous daughter of a capital hero. You could break the stalemate."

"But I'm not famous!" That was a bit too loud. "I mean, I'm just a small person."

"Even a small person can make a difference. People swat at flies, do they not? Can you be a fly? Annoyance can be very powerful."

"But how can I be conducting here and still go to the capital? It defeats the purpose of the maestro's request, doesn't it?"

"You have time, I think," he says. The others in the room confirm the schedule. "We send you to the capital right away. You show up and express your concerns, your desires. Give that speech you gave before about the value of music and music education, of live music in our world – like that. They will listen. You are very persuasive."

"Me? Persuasive?" I must've blushed. "I couldn't talk myself out of a wide-open prairie."

"Then you return here," says Mr. Stanley, ignoring my response, "perhaps with the maestro at your side. You'll bring him home, both of you as heroes."

"I certainly don't want to be a hero. Not like that."

"You do not believe in their cause?" he asks, narrowing his eyes.

"Their cause?"

"The governor's policy to end live music, to abandon musicians to menial jobs. They think music is only needed for patriotic purposes, and it can be made on machines. Otherwise, people waste too much time thinking of music, playing music. A great waste of resources, they claim – those dastardly government officials. They say music is a waste of valuable work time. Those musicians, the last generation to play, the last orchestra there, have the easy life of children, they say. Better to put them to work in real jobs."

"Like sweeping the streets?" I sneer.

Mr. Stanley nods. "Like sweeping streets, exactly."

A knock on the office door and Bart has arrived after rushing to his home and changing clothes. He looks like a farmer, dressed in a plaid shirt and blue trousers. Definitely not city style. He apologizes for being late, then he is told he needn't have come, not being on the Board. I wave off Mr. Stanley.

"She's my guest, though," Bart says, breathless. "I'm supposed to escort her around."

I thank him for his consideration as he takes a seat behind me.

We share a smile that means a lot – if anyone catches it! Poor fellow had to hurry home, had to put on his rumpled tuxedo again and go out on the streets in broad daylight, amused pedestrians wondering why he would wear such a formal outfit at noontide.

Bart knows I forgive him for that social *faux pas*.

"Looks like I'm going to the capital," I tell him after the meeting. "It seems there's no polite way for me to avoid it. But I'll return in time for rehearsals. It may be Maestro Xavier conducting the next concert instead of me."

"Should I go with you?" he asks, his voice hesitant.

Staff of the concert hall passing in the corridor slow to catch a glimpse of us. I'm still famous here, but I try to ignore them.

"To protect me?" I regard Bart. "They won't do anything to me."

"Because your father saved the governor?"

"That's right. I have a Special Pass from when I was a child."

"Laws may have changed since then. Since your last visit, too."

"Perhaps. But if I go, I'll just say what I have to say, then leave. That's all. Then come back here. I'm not going to rant about trivial things. No grand statements about the pandemic, nor the civil war. As Mister Stanley and the maestro have stated, my reputation does precede me. This crazy 'western woman' they're fascinated by. It's ridiculous, but maybe...just maybe they will listen to me."

"But I must go," he says, looking seriously at me. "I couldn't live with myself if anything bad happened."

"Anything bad? I'm just giving a speech." A thought pops into my head. "Hah! Maybe I'll take my tuba, play a few songs for them, just to demonstrate how lovely live music can be."

"No, I mean...." He looks serious. "I'm afraid for you."

"Oh, that's sweet," I say, then: "I love you, too."

He looks up, smiling like a holiday morning. "You do?"

Gazing into his eyes a moment, I realize I may have spoken too soon. Do I mean it? Could it be true? What is he thinking?

"Well, I suppose so." Then I must look away, embarrassed at the memories we made. "After last night, how could I not?"

His grin spreads from ear to ear and he wants to hug me, but we are in an awkward situation. Anyway, it's the thought we count.

Then he drops to a knee, looking up at me. He raises his hands as if offering me a gift but they're empty.

"Oh, no!" I cry out. Others in the corridor turn to look.

"Miss Maggie, will you...." He takes a breath. "Will you—"

"Wait!" I gasp. "Don't."

But he continues: "Will you marry me?"

I close my eyes tight, and run through a variety of scenarios, life in the future surrounded by a world of music, concerts every week, and us being known as the two tubists.

"Oh, dear." Although I promised my brother I wouldn't rush into a serious decision like last time, I cannot stop myself: "Why not?"

"Really?" he exclaims, too boyishly.

"Yes. I said so, didn't I?"

I welcome him into my arms as he rises. We embrace. People in the corridor clap for us. I raise my hand to wave them off.

"But you must come out to Skinner Canyon," I say when we part. "My brothers will want to get a look at you. One brother is a priest. He can say the words for us."

His smile is huge. "Thank you, Maggie. I'll get my bags packed. You won't regret it, I promise."

"There's nothing to regret." I sigh, seeing the list of my mistakes unfolding in my mind. "I make my own decisions."

With my arms around his strong frame and my head against his chest, my mind sneaks back to our evening like it was a dream. He was charming, endearing like a child making progress on learning a musical instrument. We fumbled around; we shared laughter at our awkwardness. He kept apologizing for being clumsy; I said he was sweet, that nothing was wrong. In the end I remembered the steps. We closed our eyes and fell into it like hungry puppies.

"I loved your *Sonata*," I said, barely able to breathe afterwards. "Very strong *finale*. I felt it. Especially the timpani at the end."

"I'm glad. I composed it for you. For us."

"You must compose more. Something long and hard, with a lot of action. I like *arpeggio*s. And more timpani, I think. Maybe chimes."

He didn't know whether to laugh or take me seriously. "I'll try."

"I know I heard chimes."

"Oh, that's the cathedral down the street. Morning prayers."

Yet they rang right as he reached his peak!

We hardly slept, each of us pretending to, then trying it again later, and once more when we awoke at dawn. We worked out the difficult passages until everything flowed smoothly, quite satisfying by the final beat with no more wrong notes.

I awaken at first light: facing a new day, a new life – with my skinny arm laying across his broad chest, the chaparral of red hair, his red whiskers brushing my cheek. I don't want to move.

After we prepare ourselves for a long day, we go hand in hand to the windowseat, sit together with the morning sun at our backs, to talk about our trip to the capital. His worry returns.

"Yes, I do want you to come with me," I tell him as I take his arm in mine, "but not to protect me. To please me."

His half-smile is amusing. "Please you? But I...we...."

"I'm pleased whenever you're with me. It's an easy job."

He frowns, as though he hopes I mean something else.

After breakfast in the hotel's restaurant, we take a hire-carriage to the terminal, not looking at the city passing by as much as gazing at each other. I can see down to the bottom of his soul. We go off to affect change in a dire situation, yet I radiate happiness so brightly the driver has to glance back at the glare. He must've seen couples previously who awakened in each other's arms in a hotel room and boarded his carriage still in the throes of love.

We get on the train bound for the capital, still too early.

Bart carries my tuba on his back, looking fit and strong. He asks why I'm bringing it to the capital. Am I planning to play it?

"I'm not leaving it in Cincinnati," I reply. "No telling what could happen to it there. No, it must be with me – always. I have to look after it...for my grandmother. And for *her* grandmother, too. I'm the granddaughter."

23

FINALÉ

WE ARRIVE IN THE CAPITAL as evening takes hold of the city, grinding everything into its darkness. Even miles out we fall under its spell: dingy skies and oily rain of the industrial zones, reminding me of my earlier trip here with Eve. I know there's no reason for it but my body shakes with nervous energy I'd rather put into making music. Like my Dad did, I sense approaching doom and can't ignore it. Bart notices my discomfort, asking repeatedly if I'm all right, but I wave off his concern. He tries holding my hand. When he starts to become annoying I tell him it's simply a certain time of the month and he doesn't know what I mean.

"Oh," he says after a few minutes.

The terminal has gathered more layers of grime since I last was here. No more the obsessive cleanliness a former governor insisted on. Now people have given up, it seems, too weary to bother, beaten down with weighty hopelessness. People blithely toss down trash at random and monitors don't call them to pick it up. We sidestep piles of rotting garbage and sleeping vagabonds as we make our way to the station's exit.

Bart wants to lead the way, to clear a safe path for me, but only I know which way to go so he lets me go ahead of him, apologizing. I tell him he's dear to me.

We halt at the raised hand of the entry officer, checking us for citizenship. I fear having to spend a few days in labor to gain entry, like my previous visit. I get out my Special Pass.

"This is expired," he says gruffly, then looks me over. "When you turned twenty. What're you now? Thirty?"

"But it was good a few years ago when I was here."

He checks his tablet for information. "Yes, but you were assigned a three-day job. They must've not told you it expired."

"But we have to enter. We have business in the city."

"And what's that?" He doesn't seem too agreeable.

"I'm a teacher," I say, acting proud, having planned my ruse on our trip here. "Out west. I've come to purchase new textbooks, the updated ones, to take back in time for the new semester."

The officer nods, glances at Bart. "And who's he?"

I give Bart a loving smile, patting his arm. "He's my husband, of course. I brought him to help carry everything."

"Carry things?" He studies the tuba case on Bart's back. "Looks to be full already."

"Oh, no," I say and add a chuckle. "That's a musical instrument. We plan to sell it to get credits for purchasing the textbooks."

"Nobody will buy that here. In fact, there's a big push on now to eliminate those things for good. No need for them."

I act shocked, like it's the first I've heard of the policy.

"We'd better hurry, darling," says Bart, playing his role. "Before the deal is off."

The officer gives us another look, tilts his head toward the gate.

"Don't act bad," he says, waving us on.

We pass through the gate and feel relief at not having to work. Decrepit people huddling on the other side extend their dirty hands, begging for tokens or food boxes, or anything we could donate. It's both sad and frightening. Bart has to push a few back, has to keep his arm around me to guide me through the crowd.

"This is the capital?" he asks with a thick air of judgment as we get on a filthy tram for the city center. He pulls out a cloth to wipe down the seats. We can barely stand the smell, with the windows up against the oily rain. "I had no idea. All the news we get states it's a lovely place. An ideal society. This isn't the model city I expected."

"It wasn't like this when I was a child," I explain. "Nor when I was here a few years ago."

The sky is dark above, what I can see between the tall buildings, once white stone now smudged with a black residue. I recall a better view as a child and tell Bart about it as we go through the city to the concert hall. We get off the tram in the middle of large government buildings, once a grand display of the nation's power, now just sad monuments to what once was.

"We must hurry," I call back as I pull him along.

We push through loitering crowds of desperate workers seeking extra labor or another food box, some crying out in pain, physical or spiritual, maybe both. I can't keep from lingering, looking, but then it's Bart pausing in amazement at the disgusting scene.

"Let's go," I call to Bart.

"I doubt there's any need to hurry," he responds loudly. "They'll play until they can't anymore."

But I grasp his hand, feel the tuba shift on his shoulder, and we go through the gauntlet together.

We know we've arrived at the right place because a line of police block a noisy crowd from entering the monstrosity of a building. The concert hall is used mostly for political rallies now, was when I was a child, but that's the issue: the right to have concerts. Back then Dad told me about how the last of the musicians played as best they could but none of them were replaced as they died. The government didn't want living music, didn't want to pay the musicians, said any music they might need could be made on machines. But that music wasn't any good.

Bart is shocked by the state of the place, the crowds, the police.

"It's a human right," I speak out, gazing at the ugly building, so dirty and left to crumble. No need for a concert hall if there won't be any further concerts. All the more reason to play on – play until you cannot lift your arms and cannot blow another note.

Bart leans in to hear me with the noise around us.

"They want the people to know what they'll be missing," I say.

I can hear music coming from the building, see the bank of doors propped open. Some people in the crowd holler for justice in various phrasings, but most of the three or four hundred people are content to stand and listen. It's the last concert they're allowed.

I glance at Bart; he knows what I'm thinking and follows me as I dive into the crowd, arms pushing my way through.

"Excuse me, sorry, pardon me," I say at each nudge and step.

Bart keeps close behind me, he and the tuba dividing the crowd which quickly fills in after us. We push our way to the front, several minutes of struggle, coming out right at the police line.

"It's already full," says the officer we confront. "It's at capacity, more than what's allowed in there."

"We have to go in." I beg, gesturing to Bart and my tuba on his back. "We are expected. It's important."

I can't tell if the police are sympathetic or not. Are they keeping musicians out? Or just the crowd? If the policy is against musicians, they might prevent us from entering. If they are only holding back the crowd, then we can talk our way in.

I smile my brightest smile at the officer.

"Please, sir. We are late to the concert. But they're expecting us. The next piece is our solo. We have to get inside and be ready when this...what is it? a symphony of some kind...ends."

"You're music people?" he asks, while his attention is diverted to a spot down the line where others in the crowd jostle to get through.

"Yes, from the Music College," I lie. I don't even know where it is in this city, only that Old Fritz taught there long ago.

I'm not sure if he waves us through or simply nods and looks the other way, but we step forward and nobody stops us. Bart follows, the tuba on his back letting the crowd see we're part of the protest, part of the endless concert playing inside.

Up the steps we go, the police line and the crowd below, slowing as we reach the top where the doors are wide open.

A few police stand there. They stare at us but seem content to let us go in without any effort to check us. Maybe they see the tuba case and no questions are needed. Maybe they are content to listen to the music – clearly it's a symphony now, boisterous with the brass and drums at the moment we step inside the foyer.

I've only been on one side of a concert, being the conductor, so seeing the orchestra on stage with all of its emotional fury strikes me, forces me to halt. The splendor of musicians playing in unity, everyone enjoying the *mélange* of sounds, the emotions, the absolute beauty of the spectacle! I'm in awe!

This is what I want: to be in this venerable temple of music. To worship the dancing soundwaves, bow before the vibrations running through me, overwhelming me. Oh, I pity those who cannot hear!

"Look!" shouts Bart. "It's Maestro Xavier!"

"What?" I exclaim. "Is it him? He's on stage?"

"Maestro Xavier!" cries Bart, staring ahead to the stage.

I only know the maestro from the framed portrait in the concert hall: him in tuxedo, posed with gray hair flowing and baton raised, like God commanding the forces of the universe.

"There he is," I cry out so Bart can hear me through the music.

The movement comes to its end, repeated chords signal, rousing the crowd to applause.

We were told the maestro was arrested with other musicians, so I'm surprised to see him on the stage leading the orchestra. My first thought is that maybe everything's been resolved and they're letting them perform again. I feel foolish coming all this way, fearing the worst, when everything now seems to be settled.

"Maestro Xavier!" we shout as the applause lessens.

In the split-second of silence that brackets our outcry, my voice rings through and the maestro spins around to face the crowd, takes a bow, then seems to look for who has shouted his name.

I wave my hands in the air, call him again: "Maestro Xavier!"

He puts his hand to his brow, scans the crowd, then points.

"I'm Maggie Baumann," I shout to him. "The western woman!"

He sees me, waves his arm for me to come forward. The hall is a riot, people packed wall to wall. I know it's supposed to hold about a thousand people but more than that number have squeezed in.

I take Bart's hand and pull him with me as the crowd parts to let us through at the maestro's urging. They start up fresh applause as though welcoming us.

We approach the stage, swim over to the right side to go up the steps. Then we hurry back across the stage to the podium, passing the guards facing the crowd with their short-barreled weapons, as though they're protecting the orchestra from the rowdy audience.

I am standing on the great stage of the concert hall in the capital with my tuba! The thrill is a drug and I breathe deeply – as my hip decides to twitch for the first time in a long while. Too much strain climbing all those steps, pushing through the crowd. I almost double over as muscles knot. I grimace but grab hold of the maestro's hand, shaking it.

He helps me to the podium.

"It's good of you to come," says the maestro, raising his voice so I can hear him over the crowd's roar. "I am surprised to see you here. I rather expected you would stay in Cincinnati as I requested. You have a concert to prepare, no?"

"This is more important," I reply. "Then I'll return."

"Then there is no need," he says with false disappointment. "Else we should exchange positions. I go to Cincinnati, you stay here."

The crowd is getting anxious, wants the next piece to start. Some shout: "More! More!"

The maestro waves to the crowd, urging patience.

Then he gets an idea, his face brightening, and he takes me by the hand to the front of the stage. He gestures an introduction.

The crowd quiets a little.

"This is my colleague," he calls out. "Maestro Maggie Baumann, what many have called the Western Woman. She is fully self-taught but knowledgeable and magnificent. A conductor, composer, tubist! You have heard of her triumphs, yes? Like everyone here on stage, she is a hero of the music world – whatever we have remaining! It is crucial that we remain. This is the reason for our endless concert. I want everyone to hear what real music is! Today should not be our final concert."

The crowd cheers and I wave at them in appreciation.

Maestro leans toward me, speaks into my ear: "The governor has granted us one final concert. Before we are executed for our crimes. Yes, our crimes! Not for the music we dare to play. No, we defied the governor's order. One final concert, he grants us. So we must play as long as we can. Five days, so far! We will go out with the best music we can perform! We will play as long as we can. Look at this stack of scores." He points to the tower of folios beside the podium, rising to his knee. "And there is more in the wing over there."

"Execution?" I shout back into his ear. "How can it be?"

"It is the deal I made, sorry to say. The governor is a cruel man. Not a music lover. However, is it not better to die after the concert of a lifetime than to crawl in the gutter with no music?"

He breaks from me, standing proudly before the audience.

"We are joined today by this wonderful musician! A famous tuba player. Music teacher. Conductor. She also composes songs."

I'm blushing, but I gain strength with a glance to Bart standing at the side of the stage, the tuba off his back and resting against his leg. I'm sure I must be as red now as his hair, but I face the crowd with Maestro Xavier's praise unsettling me. I give a curt bow.

"Please, will you conduct the next piece for us?" he asks and the crowd cheers. Maybe they don't actually know me, or have heard of me, but want to see what this 'western woman' from the edge of the wilderness can do on a stage with a full orchestra at her command.

I nod acceptance although my heart is racing, and the cheering turns to excited applause.

The maestro helps me onto the podium. He closes the open score on the music stand and drops it to the floor, then reaches down to grab another from the stack there and places it on the music stand.

I'm almost shaking. But gazing down at the new score he opens, I see it's the *William Tell* overture. My heart flutters joyfully!

"I know you played this last week, so I have faith you can do it again," says the maestro.

"Yes, sir." I take deep breaths. I *can* do this!

Closing my eyes for what feels like a full day, I open them and meet the desperate eyes of the orchestra members. I regard them, the last musicians of the capital, the finest musicians in the entire nation, yet doomed to quit and forget their musical skills, put away their instruments and take up brooms to clean the streets – or some other job, important perhaps, yet not the best use of their talents. I must help save them, or else finish with a grand flourish!

I raise my hands, scan the orchestra, and give the downbeat.

We play straight through the lively Rossini overture. Every note is perfect. They are professional musicians. They've trained years, practiced and rehearsed to be this perfect. I'm only the one who gets to lead them through this overture. I try to keep up, to let them feel I'm with them, leading them, without faltering at thoughts of not being trained like they've been, or practicing enough. Maybe there's something that runs through me, after all, something all the way from Old Fritz down through my great-great-grandmother Polly to me: some kind of thread, a certain ingrained talent, a strong line of something special. I don't know.

The crowd erupts in applause when we come to the end. It feels grand to be on the podium bringing forth such glorious music! I'm in a state of ecstasy. I must turn to address the audience.

"This!" I cry out, pointing behind me with the baton in my hand. "This is what we offer: music to bring love and joy, music so we can bear our lives, music that soothes us, inspires us, gives us what we need: companionship! Machines cannot do this. Poor imitations at best. You may get used to machine music but it can never be a good substitute for the actual experience of living musicians creating the miraculous soundscape that envelops us and enriches us like...like breathing fresh air and drinking clean water. As great a difference as comparing this dirty city to the beautiful countryside. Have you been to the countryside?"

I listen to the audience cheer, but I see a few stern faces among the crowd, mostly in the center of the main seating area. I look to the maestro, find him seated among the violins, instrument tucked under his chin.

"We must preserve this," I declare. "It's our culture, our heritage, our art! It's everything we are as humans, it's the pinnacle of our existence. What other creature has made a life with enough leisure to sit around wondering what else to do? To have the idea of putting sounds together in a pleasing fashion? To make a song that has no purpose other than to give us pleasure? And in hard times we need music more than ever. We crave a song that gets us by, that lifts us up, gives us reasons to go on. A song that reminds us of times past when life was better. We cannot stop before the phrase is complete, before the movement ends, before the *finale* comes. I ask you: What are we without music, real music, living music?"

The crowd cheers, but a few people shout out their responses – a pitiful counter view. I choose to ignore them.

"We are not here to work and be efficient, to be productive and count our profits! No, we are here to enjoy, to take pleasure in what we create. It is our purpose to create – to be creative, to give pieces of ourselves for the symphony of life we all share. Even if different styles of music do not move you, there is some kind which should. In my darker moments I write blues songs. I'm from the dusty town of Skinner Canyon. I wrote a song called 'Skinner Canyon Blues' about how hard life is out there. That song – making up that song – made my life better if only for a few days. So I made up more songs. You can, too. Who will make the 'Capital City Blues' – *you?*"

The crowd murmurs at my remarks, uncommitted.

I go to the next score on the stand, a one-movement piece for the strings and woodwinds, *Salvation in C Major* by Marjorie Easton, a woman not mentioned in the big book of music. I knew from school days she was from the capital, one of the rising woman composers before the pandemic took her. This solemn chorale, perhaps the final piece she wrote, is humbling. Sniffles and whimpers cut through the audience.

Next we perform Florence Price's *Symphony in E minor*, also not mentioned in the book of music, but it's the next score on the stack beside the podium. We receive polite applause yet a few cheers erupt from a group along the side of the auditorium. I wave to them.

Next on the stack of music scores is a march: *Capital Victory* by Lenny Garcia, which we play with gusto, excessive cymbals and all. The tubas and trombones have a rousing finish in this one.

Applause. No one is checking the huge clock on the wall.

I wipe my brow, feel wetness saturating my shirt, my back tight, hip complaining, yet I cannot give up. I must go on!

Before I give the downbeat of a longer work, a seven movement suite from *The Nether Lands*, an opera by Karina Becker-Jones, one more post-pandemic work, I simply must speak to the audience.

I step to the front of the stage, baton in hand.

"We all should be musicians. These here on the stage do it at the highest level of achievement. Not only for themselves and their own enjoyment but for all of us. Support them, praise them, and most of all enjoy what they share with us. Yet you, too, can play music. At your homes. On the streets. In the parks. Play that music!"

The crowd applauds. I let them, then wave them quiet.

"Music must be separate from politics," I shout, growing bold, "from arbitrary policies, and free of governmental edicts, and most of all it must be allowed to exist in every venue, in every city, across the land. Do not silence our colleagues. We need them – need *music* – as a crucial refuge from all that assails us, to balance our lives, the hard and the easy, as remedy to the stresses in life that inevitably come upon us when we least expect them. There is music – just the right song – to heal us from a bad day. To make sense of a bad life. Music is not just something extra to fritter away a few minutes of the day but, rather, a central aspect of what we are as humans. Music is at the core of our humanity! We are not robots laboring like machines. No, we are singers! We are instrumentalists! Musicians expressing thoughts and feelings through sound. We are musicians who *produce* – to use industry's nauseous term – something that is forever beautiful and a complete good!"

I know I've gone too far when I have to stop for a breath and see the crowd standing silent before me. Even Maestro Xavier refuses to speak up, eyeing the crowd. He's set down his violin and stands up, ready to come to the podium. Maybe I've said something illegal.

The crowd chatters anxiously, waiting to see what will happen.

I look to the side of the stage: Bart isn't smiling, maybe ready to run out or to come protect me.

Police stationed around the auditorium do not move but stand ready to act, waiting for a signal. Maybe everyone is afraid to show their approval of my rant, the things I've said. Maybe they disagree with me. Maybe I'm done, as much a criminal as the musicians.

A few of the guards, in official gray uniforms, move up the steps to the stage on each side. I can sense their orders. I've gone too far. It will be over in an instant, the same as for Dad. He died saving the governor; I will die saving music in the capital.

I step off the podium.

The cello players to my right, turn and look behind them at what

I'm seeing. The first stand pair get up, hold their cellos to block attack. I feel violinists on my left do the same, protecting my back. Maestro Xavier comes up to the podium, guarding me. The row of trombone players rise and set down their instruments, preparing to fight. A man at the rear bangs on the bass drum like the final heartbeat counting down.

The crowd roars for something, too loud and too jumbled for me to determine if they are for me and what I've said or against me.

A trumpet player blares an alarm. Another joins in.

In the middle of the main seating area, the auditorium packed wall to wall with concert-goers, a lone figure stands. Not only stands up as if to leave but climbs on top of the seat to be taller than the others around her. I see it's a woman, long blond hair draped over her shoulders. I stare hard but cannot identify her. Who would dare make a scene like this?

She unbuttons her long overcoat, slides it off herself and tosses it aside, revealing a simple sweater and slacks. She reaches up, pulls off her hair – a bundle of false hair! The man beside her takes the wig as though it's planned.

People gasp at the deception, but the woman, standing upon the seat, begins to slowly clap. Once, twice, more. The hall is silent but for her lone clapping. She claps louder and everyone seems to relax, maybe wondering if they should applaud as well.

I go to the front of the stage.

"Thank you," I call out to the woman standing half-way back in the auditorium.

"I agree," she shouts to me. "I agree with you."

Murmurs ripple through the audience, fearful whispers churning into a nervous din as the crowd realizes who she is.

The concertmaster tucks his violin under his arm, tells me she is Angela Reading, the governor's sister. I'd better give a bow.

So I bow, like I would at the end of any performance.

I invite the orchestra members to stand and give a bow. They show appreciation as usual for the audience and their enthusiasm for the concert. But the hall remains quiet, everyone afraid to speak and maybe risk retaliation by this woman and the staff around her who are also disguised as ordinary citizens.

"Maestro Baumann, you say much that needs to be said."

Her voice is strong. The hall is quiet enough that she need not raise her voice to be heard. I wait nervously.

"I agree with you." She glances around. "Furthermore, I wish for my brother to hear what you say, so I have sent a video of your stage time to him. He will hear your speeches."

The tell-tale buzz of a tablet connecting to the stream. She holds up the tablet, directing her gaze to its screen.

"This is a secure channel," a man's voice speaks from the tablet, sounding through the auditorium. "You shouldn't use it when you're in a public area."

"Shut up, Gary, and listen to me," she snarls. "As your big sister, you *should* listen to me. I'm here at the protest concert – just listen to the silence – we're in the twenty-fifth straight hour now, and I've just heard the most amazing performance of one of those overtures, led by that woman from out west everyone's been talking about, Maggie Baumann, as reported on the streams. You know: *her*."

"I'm not sure I know," comes the response.

"Her dad saved Governor Wornall from those who captured her."

"Oh. That one. Old news, isn't it?"

"Careful what you say, Gary. I have you on public view. We can all hear you. Everyone needs to hear this, so it's in the record."

"Hear what?" The governor doesn't sound happy.

"This concert you've granted them, the last concert before their execution, it's gone on for five days now – twenty-five hours that I've been here. They play and play on, always another piece of music to play, and the crowd here loves it. Then this 'western woman' comes on the stage, takes charge, and it's even more spectacular. I'm not sure if a guest conductor counts in your scheme but I, for one, have been moved. I get it. I understand now."

"You're daffy, Angie. Too much music has warped your mind," he says, and some in the crowd laugh, others grumble, but no one dares curse. "My orders will be carried out as stated. I granted them one final concert. When it ends, it ends. Then they will end. The matter is closed. It's done."

"Don't be an ass, Gary," says his sister. "This woman came all the way here. It's obviously important to her. She spoke to us after each piece she's conducted. Good words. Thoughtful words. Inspiring ideas. And I have to agree with her. So I think you should rescind your order and let the musicians play on. What I'm telling you is we *should* have an orchestra of living musicians. They play much better than anything machines can produce. And being here among them, hearing it newly made, grants me a truly special privilege, a unique experience not available at home sitting beside a music machine."

"As I said: you've become music-drunk," the governor responds.

"I remind you that we are on public view. I want you to speak the words now, little brother, to stop this ridiculous conceit of yours. Right now. I want you to cancel your stupid order. Say it."

"I won't say it, Angie. I'm the governor, not you."

"But I'm your big sister. You've always bowed to whatever I wish or have you forgotten so soon? Shall I share some stories with the public here and now? Some of your childhood quirks? Embarrassing incidents, like with a certain someone who I can name now for all to hear? Should I? Or will you take back a stupid directive to dismiss musicians from their jobs and ban living music forever."

"You wouldn't do that," he says with a snort.

"As you wish. I'd like to report an incident that happened over in Mount Ellis, about ten years ago, when someone we all know—"

"All right!" shouts the governor – Gary to family members.

"Very well," replies the sister. "Speak the words for all to hear!"

A moment of grumbling, then: "I rescind my order, whatever the number is, where I demand all musicians be assigned to other labor not involving music, and for the orchestra and any similar groups, to be dissolved and forever banned."

"And?

"And what?"

"The execution order."

"Yes," he says after a long pause. "I rescind the execution order for the leaders of the stupid protest."

"Thank you. Now they will have no fear of being executed when the concert ends."

"Done."

The grumbling we hear from the governor causes an amused din throughout the auditorium.

"Thank you, Gary. Have a good evening." And she ends the video stream. She hands the tablet to her assistant.

The audience erupts in applause and cheering.

After a minute Angela waves them to be quiet.

Focusing on me, she calls out: "You must play on. And from now have no fear, for you are welcome in the capital. All of you. I want regularly scheduled concerts. Please invite me."

"Thank you, Miss Reading," I call back, and add a sincere bow.

Maestro Xavier also claps for her, shouts: "We have the best seat for you – always!"

"Please, play on," she offers. "I want to hear more."

The woman claps again, a steady rhythm. A few people join her, then most of the crowd also applaud – up to the moment she climbs down from standing upon the seat.

"What shall we play?" I ask the audience before I realize that my voice is too weak to be heard over the settling of their applause.

I turn to Maestro Xavier whose face is wet with tears, overcome with joy at this new development. He rushes to me.

I see Bart at the side of the stage, so I wave him to join me.

He hesitates. Me? he seems to ask. I gesture harder.

"It is a miracle," Maestro Xavier cries. He clasps my hand, then turns to the crowd, gesturing towards me, an invitation for more. As we enjoy their applause, I lean over and tell him my plan.

He breaks from me, stands at the front of the stage.

"We have a special treat for you," he announces.

I wave again at Bart and he shuffles out from the curtains, over to the podium bearing my tuba in his arms. Stepping humbly to me, he stands uncomfortably before the cheering crowd.

I face the audience, and wave them to get quiet.

"My great-great-grandmother played this tuba," I announce in a proud voice, my hand gesturing to Bart. "This tuba right here, now so old – yet it sounds marvelous. Would you like to hear it?"

Many in the crowd shout their desire, others seem confused.

"She wrote music, too," I say to the crowd. "In fact, she started a concerto – a concerto for tuba – but she left it unfinished when they had to flee from the city as the pandemic got worse."

Moans from the audience. Nobody wants to be reminded of that dark time in our recent history nor hear stories about events they've been taught never happened.

I hold up my hand. "When in difficult times, we listen to music to comfort us, to lift our spirits. Some of us who can write music for the same reasons. I'm sure there's a lot of *pandemic blues* out there, perhaps locked away and forgotten."

Motioning to Bart, he zips open the shoddy, worn case and lifts out my somewhat shiny silver/gray tuba, sets it gently on the top of his shoe. We exchange smiles like we're already a married couple, knowing each other's thoughts.

I gesture to a staff member at the side of the stage for a chair.

"Difficult times," I say, "like the pandemic that happened so long ago – maybe not too long ago. Some of you are old enough to have lived through it, like my grandmother when she was a child. That's when we needed music to remind us of ourselves, who we are, how we need to take care of each other, members of the same family, the human family, and how we need to always, *always* seek beauty and joy. It doesn't matter what happened – something did, we know, and that changed everything. I look at this city, at the whole nation, at the northern border – and I cannot believe you want to condemn music and art and books just to be able to control everything down to the private thoughts we have in our heads and the corrupted air we breathe? Is that how we carry on? Is that how we survive?"

Angela Reading stands again but not upon her seat this time. She claps, raising her hands over her head in appreciation. Others join in the praise, likewise raising their clapping hands.

Giving a thankful bow, I return to the podium.

I tell the orchestra members what we're playing as a quartet of librarians move carefully among them, distributing sheets of music. Some are puzzled; they've never seen this piece before. It will be our first play-through, but I'm confident they can handle it. The difficult part is the tuba solo.

"Don't worry," I tell them with a big smile. "Let's do the best we can. We can fix anything in rehearsals."

They give a quick look over the first movement of *Concerto for Tuba* by Polly Baumann, the only movement with orchestra parts.

When I nod at Bart, sitting on the chair with my tuba cradled in his big arms, ready to play, I know I have finally arrived – at long last. I have arrived at the place I am meant to be.

24

HOME ON THE RANGE

FROM TIME TO TIME I STILL THINK of the Protest Concert in the capital and how everything changed after that. I'll read once in a while an article mentioning it, some giving credit to me for a lot of important things that resulted from people realizing what they had been missing. However, what I remember most is how Bart played my tuba there on that grand stage in that spectacular hall, made it sound like God was singing in the shower, as he commanded Polly's *Concerto* like he'd played it all his life.

When my son was a little boy, I used to tell him about his father, Bartholomew Tuttle, and what happened to him. He liked hearing the story and could feel its meaning. I tried to tell it the same way each time so he'd remember it. As he got older, however, he asked to hear it less and less. I accepted his wishes and didn't push it.

Then one day he comes to me and says: "Mother, can I go on the posse with Uncle Frank? He says I'm old enough now. They're going after the outlaw J. C. Wells. He's bad news, they say. So can I?"

I gaze at this young man. He's got his father's red hair though not as bright. Got his father's wide cheeks and strong body. Taller than me as he's pushing sixteen. Thinks he's already a grown man. Yet I still recall when he was a little boy sitting in the middle of the empty auditorium during rehearsals, so cute the way he waved his arms like me while I rehearsed the orchestra.

I trust my brother to look after him. He's Sheriff now. He'll have the boy hold back if they come upon any real danger.

So I give a nod, sorry to see him go, and hoping no harm befalls him. Especially the dangers he can't see coming. Like how his father got struck by that freight truck as the crowd flooded down the steps of the concert hall that night after the final piece, the final applause. The crowd of a few hundred pushed out into the street at the worst time. With my tuba on his back, he couldn't see the truck. We got separated in that joyful crowd. When he stopped and looked back to see where I stood, he was hit. Several people were killed there, but they couldn't determine if it was an accident or a deliberate act by a crazed person who hated music. The result was the same.

It was awful, certainly, yet it was years ago. I remember how I screamed, seeing it happen as if everything had been slowed to show the horrid details. I fought my way through the crowd to get to him, tears filling my eyes so I couldn't see. But I was too late.

I still think of Bart, red-haired tubist, my friend and colleague and, by a miracle, dad of Bart junior – though I call my son Little B or LB whenever I'm feeling affectionate. He hates those nicknames. I gradually started calling him Bart, just like his dad.

How time goes by! Every year is another movement in a suite of music, each with its own mood, its own tempo. You have to turn the page and play on.

The capital is cleaner now, industries taking measures to reduce pollution even at the cost of decreased productivity. And music sings through the streets every day. The local band is the place to be, with children learning to play instruments and sing. There are concerts from a variety of music groups. There is a music festival a few times a year. Even some businesses have started music groups for workers and they compete with the bands of other businesses. Having music throughout the city improves everyone's moods, and a lot gets done. Productivity is improved. In fact, people started to care more about everything, such as making their neighborhoods neat. Within a year or so, it seemed like a whole new city.

Being a celebrity, people were curious, found I'd composed songs. My blues tunes are often performed. "Skinner Canyon Blues" is a favorite. So is "Protest Blues" which I wrote in the days after the concert. Also "Lost Love Blues" and "Baby Blues" as I continued to compose. It became my passion.

Maestro Xavier returned to his position in Cincinnati, of course. I was sad to learn the conductor of the capital orchestra, Maestro Schaeffer died from injuries he suffered during his public arrest. He may have been old, but he shouldn't have been treated that roughly by the governor's police. At Angela's urging I was invited to lead the capital orchestra after him – what became the National Symphony to distinguish it from other orchestras and bands organized there. Principal Conductor Maggie Baumann! If Mom and Dad could see me! If Grandma Isla could see me!

Governor Reading himself handed the contract to me, with his sister looking on. Angela took up the violin, perhaps more symbolic than serious, wanting to join in. She tried studying it but she never attained enough proficiency to play in the orchestra. They tolerated her, despite wrong notes and off timing, but after a while she chose to leave on her own without anyone needing to say anything to her. Even so, she remained a champion of the music scene. Gary refused to participate, likely because he considered the protest concert to be a failure of his administration. He never interfered, thankfully, but he would slip in a disparaging remark whenever he gave a speech. I was pleased to see a new governor elected: Stanton West, an oboe player from the National Symphony.

After my appointment, I found a lovely housing unit near a park in one of the better sectors. I recalled admiring it as a child but not being allowed to play there because I wasn't a resident of the sector. I made suggestions to authorities and, with my gold stamp speaking loudly, the park was opened to all children. LB made a lot of friends there. Many of the kids were learning an instrument like LB was. The parents knew me, knew who I was, of course, and treated us well. Unfortunately, my schedule was too full to allow me to teach their children individually but I welcomed the chance to conduct a kid's band just for fun in the park each summer.

It was difficult living there, of course, as ugly as the city was, and despite the potential health problems there, I couldn't pass the opportunity. The city got better. I also had several chances to go to other cities for guest conducting, even to Kanza City where, after the concert, I had dinner with Hal and his wife, Gloria, his favorite bassoonist. My first visit she was fat with a baby due. Second visit, fat again, same reason. I introduced LB and Hal beamed his joy for me. They'd heard about the accident, offered sympathy.

I hated returning to the capital after visiting other cities. Every day in the capital, despite having a spacious unit filled with many mementoes, awards, artwork, and various pretty things, I always thought of Bart, what he would think of my life now, how he was missing this life I had. I missed the sight of that pudgy, red-haired tubist, who I knew only a brief time. Someone captured him playing the *Concerto* on stage and sent the image to the orchestra office. I had that image printed; it rests in peace framed on my nightstand. He would've liked to know he lived on in LB. Adoring this dear boy of ours, and focusing on music, saved me from gloom. Music got me through the weeks of discomfort when I accepted the fact that I'd be having a little tuba player in my life very soon.

As I feared, the stretching of my belly put pressure on my hip, which caused pain. It was terrible toward the end, but I endured it. Thankfully, doctors in the capital were kind as well as proficient. And there he was: a beautiful baby boy! A mop of red hair upon his head. Joy overwhelmed me, made me forget every anguish I'd gone through. He was a bundle of delight that made me so happy I had to sing – and I did; I made several songs, sang them to him. And the torturous pressure to my hip seemed to push everything into proper alignment; after the birth I felt no more discomfort in that area.

Taking off a couple months around the birth – I conducted the *Symphonic Dances* by Mr. Rachmaninov at eight months! – I hired a few guest conductors. Maestro Xavier came to conduct one of those concerts. I used the time to compose more music, both for orchestra and simple songs. My most 'impressive' work was a piece I call a symphonic overture, which I titled *A Western Journey*. The life of a city woman going west as told in music. Yes, I borrowed a bit too much from other music I'd heard over the years, reviewers pointed out, but nobody else complained. The same with my only symphony: three movements in E minor and featuring a long tuba solo to open the *finale*. I completed it during my fourth season and we performed it, with me conducting, in the fifth season with Catherine London, our new tubist. In the seventh season, I debuted a concerto for horn, which Hal came to the capital to perform with us.

I remained in the capital a number of years as their conductor. I got better at it, always studying, always practicing before meeting with the orchestra, with LB as my audience. We performed a wide range of music, including a lot written since the Protest Concert. People still talked about that event. They were inspired. They spell it with 'capital' letters: The Protest Concert. There are anniversary concerts to commemorate the day the music was saved. I composed a special 'patriotic' anthem for a second year's concert. Another piece of mine was played by another orchestra, a *divertimento*, nothing special.

During my time with the National Symphony, I also searched for music composed by women in past years and found many works that had been forgotten, never mentioned in the big book of music. So I copied out several scores to make them available. The printers said I had neat notation. We tried to perform one such work by a woman composer at each concert, plus a special concert of all women's music every year, pieces from Louise Farrenc, Elizabeth Maconchy, Emilie Mayer, Fanny Mendelsshon, Dora Pejačević, and Florence Price (a great inspiration to me; we played her *Piano Concerto* with pianist Katy-Lynn Jefferson on a special program with William Grant Still and Samuel Coleridge-Taylor); also Gloria Coates, Minna Keal, Amy Beach, Alice Mary Smith, Maria Herz, and others – all of them fine compositions although not every one became a favorite. I only want them to be heard, let people decide for themselves what they like.

We played newer women composers, too: Albright Jackson, D. C. Wong, Velvet Pinter, Alma Abbas, Mavis Lee Smith, Talia Henricks, Bridget Ahn, and others who started composing after the pandemic era came to an end. Being an orchestra, of course, most of what we played were symphonies, but a lot of their other music exists and is heard in recitals or played by small groups: for example, a string quartet or a soloist with piano accompaniment. In fact, three piano manufacturers opened for business in the capital and could hardly keep up with the orders.

I arranged several of my great-great-grandmother Polly's songs into a suite for orchestra I called *A Musical Life*. I rewrote a version for kids' band. Angela financed its publication.

I never finished orchestrating the second and third movements of Polly's *Concerto for Tuba*, lacking motivation after losing Bart. Then I had no time once I returned to my music duties. That first movement stands well on its own and is performed in other cities. The way Bart played the opening sixteenth-note trills with gusto, the three-octave sweeps at the beginning and two-octave *arpeggios* at the very end of the movement stay in my memory. I could only play them at half-speed. Then trumpets come in and dance with the tuba, a kind of fanfare, until woodwinds play their counter theme before the strings return to support the final flourishes of the tuba solo, right up to the booming final chords, drums and all. I've kept track of the performances, happy that Polly's music can be heard – along with tuba concertos by older composers. And yet I never did play any of them. I never picked up a tuba again.

My friend, Hal, offered to have a tuba made for me but I politely refused. It wouldn't be the same. I'd been entrusted with the family instrument, passed down through generations, and I failed. No new tuba could replace it. What was crushed in that accident stays with me: the flattened metal inside that soft-side case. It covered Bart's body like a shield. That should've been me bearing the tuba into the street that night. I managed to save the mouthpiece from the case's pocket and that hunk of metal sits in an honored place in my home; the rest of the metal was disposed of, perhaps melted down, reused as fine tea sets for old ladies. Or bullets for the Northern war.

LB wanted to play something, seeing me being a music person. I remembered my speech at the Protest Concert, how I'd ranted that everyone should have the chance to play music. I conceded and gave him Eve's old cornet. He got good at it and I loved hearing him play both written songs and what he happened to think up. I encouraged him to write down his songs. He did it for a while, but lost interest over the years. One that stays with me is "Bart's Blues" which never fails to bring a tear, about being stuck way out here in a dusty town. Now he spends time with Frank's grandkids.

We returned to Skinner Canyon eventually – once my poor arms started to get too tired to make it through a whole concert. My back, too. Besides, this old town is my home. I've told my son about life in the capital when I was a child and he agrees we're in the right place out west. I hired a tutor to teach him what he needed to learn apart from the school in the capital. It's better that way. He likes learning. He likes playing kick-ball with Kanza boys who live over the border nobody can see.

My brothers were surprised when I showed up with a boy at my side. I wrote a letter or two at the beginning, but then I got too busy and kept promising to update them. I guess not much news from the capital made its way out west, but they were both sad then happy for me once they heard the whole story. Our Maggie's finally come home was all that mattered to them. Her foolish life in the capital's come to an end, thank goodness. No worse for wear, they teased, except for bearing a child. But we won't talk about that. He's a fine-looking boy, and welcome home!

On the trip west we kept hearing news-reports about fighting in the north, how the brave Iowans had pushed the Quebeckers out of Dubuque, how the Illini militias were engaged in the war. I knew it wasn't going to get better, no matter how hard they fought. I could imagine how everything might become worse as centuries unfolded.

Of course when we returned the teepee had long been packed up and taken away. The old cabin was gone, too. In its place was a new house, large enough for the entire Willoughby family, including the eight kids. They bought the farm Faith had operated and now run it. They're kind folks. Gave us a basket of vegetables.

I introduced my young son to their young daughters, but all of them were too shy to speak.

"Hi, I'm LB," my son spoke at my prompting.

"This here's Andrea," said Mrs. Willoughby. "That one's Lucinda, but we call her Lulu."

"Pleased to meet you," LB responded timidly.

"He sure got some red hair," Mrs. Willoughby laughed.

"It's from his dad," I responded. "Makes it easy to pick him out of a crowd."

"I bet it does indeed," she said with a chuckle.

We took a room in town at first. I was happy to show off LB to Mrs. Beale's nosey daughter, Bonnie, who hadn't fallen very far at all from the tree. She liked to ask a lot of questions, eager to share the answers around town. I told everyone my son's dad was killed in an accident in the capital, but nobody would believe me. They heard that story before.

Then we moved in with Frank's family for several months while a new house was being built for us. I helped Vera with grandkids – nephews Joe and Jon had gotten married and had their kids while I was away. I loved meeting their wives. Joe's wife, Hilda, can play piano and Jon's wife, Georgia, has a lovely singing voice. We enjoyed many recital evenings. Meantime, LB had other kids to play with.

Jeb was doing ranch work, but he got in with a bad bunch, and started being mean to Jackie, so she left him. She took their son to her village for a while but when I returned she joined us in the new house. Her son, Jake, plays with LB. They're great friends. As Eve says, "It's good to have cousins around."

We all live together in the new house, paid for with the credits I earned from my conducting career and from composing and selling music. Hal handles the publishing. I get credits every month. I even composed a bassoon sonata for his wife. As of today, on my fiftieth birthday, I've written 50 songs and 15 orchestra works. I've started working on an opera about Grandma Isla when she was a baby and her parents' adventures during the pandemic. I title it *The Way of the Son* – just like her dad, Grampa Sandy, titled his notebooks. I might finish it before I die – who knows?

Eve fixed up her room like a big playhouse and loves to spoil the little grand-nephews ever since Mr. Briggs passed. He got older and one morning didn't awaken. But he put his banjo in a Will for Eve. She plucks on it nearly every day. She recalls Briggs' tunes. She and I also play blues tunes together. We sit up late making up songs. We always make dinner together, a new ritual, and sometimes at night I go to her room when she's feeling lonely, or she joins me in mine.

That's one thing about Skinner Canyon. Sometimes I feel lonely, being lost out here in this chaparral country far from any sign of civilization. It's as though the rest of the world no longer exists, just me and the grass and the wind, the snakes and coyotes, buffalo that couldn't care less, and a lone hawk crying out overhead (played by the oboe in my symphonic overture). But I can hear the music on the wind. I feel it run through me. It seldom stops. When I go out to the edge of the canyon and sit for a spell, gazing across at new houses built by the tribal folks over there, putting up their tall antennas to catch the streaming, I think about my family.

Sometimes Jackie comes out to sit with me, often bringing Jake who likes to tell me his latest escapades. She calls me Mama and he calls me Grandma although I'm actually his great-aunt. She'll play her guitar and I'll make up words to her songs. Jake plays a wooden flute he got from Jackie's village. We watch the sun going down, a palette of colors most evenings – until it's getting a bit too dark and we have to head home while we can see the path.

And that is my life.

I think back to my childhood in the capital, living with Mom and Dad, then us moving out here without my dad. I think about my life going back and forth, being a musician, a conductor, a composer. And I think of Bart. Both of them.

I am who I am because of them – and despite them, these people who've escorted me through my life, shared the years with me.

Although he isn't so little any more, I recall holding my little boy in my lap and telling him stories of my dad, my dad's mother, her parents and siblings, and those who lived before them. I count all the people I've heard about and read about, and I make sure Bart remembers their names, knows them and what they did. He is next in line, I tell him, the next Baumann as it's stated in the national register, and he can do as he pleases.

GENEALOGY

Grandma Hannah's Line:

Sandy Baumann = Hannah Whistler
Isla
Frank =   (& Sandy = Lorraine, Frank's wife's twin)
Cherie   Polly
Trey (drifter) =
Iris
Sven (drifter) =
Jenny
Ajamu (preacher) =
Ellie
Big Joe =
Raymond
Sandy (return) =
Allie
Fred (custodian) =
(stillborn)

Isla's Line:

LJ (Big Joe's son) = Isla
Amy June
Lionel Chesterfield =
Bobbie & Abe
(brothel guest) =
(Lily, died in infancy)
Ajamu =
(miscarriage)
Frank (after Isla returns to national park) =
Fritz (Frank Jr.)
Julio (marshes) =
LJ (return) =

LJ's Line:

<pre>
                    LJ = Isla
                      Amy June
                        = Lori*
                  (Calvin, died from snakebite)
                    Grace -- nurse at military hospital
                    Faith -- goes with Raymond out west
                    Hope -- sleeps around

Raymond (brother to Isla & LJ) = Lori*
                        Eve
</pre>

*Lori was Big Joe's wife then widow after the wars.

Fritz's Line:

<pre>
          Frank = Isla
             Fritz (Frank Jr.) = Sandra
                    Frank III = Vera
                        Jeb & Joe (twins)
                        Jon
                        Frances
                    James (priest)
                    Maggie = Bart
                        Bart Jr.
</pre>

Faith's Line:

<pre>
          Raymond = Faith
              (idiot daughter, left to die)
              Taylor =
                  Benjamin
              **Clem =
                  Clemson
</pre>

**shot and killed by Raymond after release from jail
while Faith was pregnant with Clemson.

ACKNOWLEDGMENTS

In writing a novel various influences come together in seemingly random fashion to initiate the story idea and propel the writing forward.

The *Flu Season* trilogy began with a deliberate thought-experiment based on the film *A Boy and His Dog* (1975), a sardonic adventure set in an odd post-apocalyptic landscape, based on Harlan Ellison's short story. I gave my novel the working title of "A Boy and his Mom and her tuba". However, I couldn't work on it as the SARS-CoV-2 ("covid-19") pandemic worsened. Only when the crisis was coming to an end, did I find a "way in" to start *The Book of Mom*.

I wanted to focus not on those initial days we all experienced, when everything was immediate and real, but further into the future, when the worst we experienced had gotten worse still, say, six years into the future. Book 2 *The Way of the Son* continues the story and we pass through another year of the post-pandemic experience. Everything is irrevocably broken and the only way forward is to rebuild from scratch.

In Book 3 *Dawn of the Daughters*, the rebuilding begins but our family isn't aware of it for a while. When they enter the new society, they find it being rebuilt in horrible fashion. Book 4, *The Book of Dad*, shows us the beginnings of a society heading toward something akin to Orwell's world in *1984*. Book 5 provides a final chapter in the family saga.

I always select music to help me create the appropriate emotive soundscape for my writing time. The aural support unlocks my muse. I found the ideal soundtrack in the following music: Jeop Beving (entire album *Henosis*; "For Steven"); Bibi Dupont; Westerns scored by Ennio Morricone; and the soundtrack to *The Music Man*. Also, of course, the musical works mentioned in the text (only a few are fictitious). I recommend the second movement of Shostakovich's *Piano Concerto 2* for the final chapter.

Special thanks goes forever to those who worked the front lines during the pandemic, some of whom lost their lives alongside their patients. Our gratitude is immeasurable.

SPECIAL NOTE

Women composers named in the final chapter – Louise Farrenc, Elizabeth Maconchy, Emilie Mayer, Fanny Mendelsshon, Dora Pejačević, Florence Price, Gloria Coates, Minna Keal, Amy Beach, Alice Mary Smith, and Maria Herz – are actual composers (along with William Grant Still and Samuel Coleridge-Taylor), worth a listen yet underappreciated. Those named in the subsequent paragraphs are fictitious, including Polly Baumann.

ABOUT THE AUTHOR

Stephen Swartz is the author of eighteen novels, including this current volume, as well as several short stories in anthologies and literary journals. He also published scholarly articles and a Ph.D. dissertation on the role of identity in student composition. He has taught English at several colleges and universities over a thirty-year career. While teaching English courses at Langston University in Oklahoma during the past decade, Swartz realized his ambition to publish his previously written novels. Thanks to the notoriety of the Amazon Breakthrough Novel Award competition, the first of them, *After Ilium*, was published – followed quickly by *The Dream Land* and *A Beautiful Chill*.

Prior to attending graduate school and earning an M.A. (English) and M.F.A. (Creative Writing), Swartz lived in Japan for five years where he taught English at the middle school and high school levels. His experiences there helped inspire him to write his novel *Aiko*. Swartz also taught summer courses at a university in Beijing, China in recent years. His wide travels and interest in cultures and languages has propelled his fiction into explorations of situations where the main character is often a stranger in a strange land and must find ways to adapt – much as he has done during a lifetime and career of various excursions.

He borrows from those experiences for the *Flu Season* trilogy and this sequel.